THE DEEPEST SECRETS OF A WOMAN'S HEART—AND HER ULTIMATE STRUGGLE FOR HAPPINESS

Rooted in the very real modern world, this intensely dramatic novel exposes the innermost emotions and dilemmas of a lovely woman torn between today's liberation and enduring taboos, between the brave front she shows the world and her hidden doubts, fears and guilts. Here every corner of a woman's life is laid bare—in everything a woman's novel should be.

"Probing, moving, sensitive and realistic—*Abilene Reporter*

"A satisfying love story about an up-to-the-minute subject"—*Publishers Weekly*

"An involved, emotion-packed and thoroughly entertaining saga"—*Anniston Star*

"Absorbing and appealing"—*Saturday Evening Post*

"The triumphant culmination of *The Heart Listens*"—*Booklist*

THE MIXED BLESSING

HELEN VAN SLYKE

POPULAR LIBRARY • NEW YORK

for HAROLD

THE MIXED BLESSING

Copyright © 1975 by Helen Van Slyke

All Rights Reserved

Published by Popular Library, a unit of CBS Publications,
the Consumer Publishing Division of CBS Inc.,
by arrangement with Doubleday and Company, Inc.

ISBN: 0-445-08491-X

PRINTED IN THE UNITED STATES OF AMERICA

16   15   14   13   12   11   10   9   8   7

Prologue

Sunlight. She loved it so. The sun was life, as love was life, strong, vital and sensual, the very essence of existence. Even with her eyes closed Toni felt it dancing seductively across her body. At moments it became a solid rush of warmth, like a stream of concentrated energy, giving of its strength, renewing her with its infinite light. Then the golden particles became individual fingers, playing on her skin like a lover's hands, searching, demanding, nudging her to responsiveness.

I am a child of the sun, Toni thought. All the peaceful moments, the joyous ones have been spent in its healing aura. Why did the poets, the lyricists equate the moon with romance? Starlight had its twinkling beauty, and utter darkness its sensuous cloak of mystery. But the moon was cold, empty, green-white with the pallor of death.

The thoughts were like extensions of the dream from which she slowly emerged. Lying under the sun she felt suspended, disembodied, a thing apart from herself. Half awake, she saw in her mind the innocent child she'd been, the loved and sheltered child secure in the fierce adoration of her parents. The image shifted slowly to the picture of a bewildered young woman, torn with guilts and confused by loyalties that stripped her of the most basic loyalty of all—that to herself.

As though she were watching a rerun of her life, she saw the years in which she searched for love, believing it within her grasp, only to see it torn from her by cruelty and rejection. Those were the moonlight years, Toni thought. The ones filled with cold fears and desolation, with losses more terrible than she thought she could bear.

But she had borne them, hiding the pain as best she could, groping her way back into the sunlight, finding it once again. And she had not been alone, neither in the icy depths of despair nor in the happy emergence into the light. There had been the people she loved, to soothe her with glorious moments of serenity and faith, to give her glimpses of ecstasy, to provide those smooth surfaces of joy that covered the pits of sorrow that lay like pockmarks on her soul.

Toni weighed the good and bad in her life like jewels against ugly stones. And the jewels generously tipped the balance in her favor.

She smiled.

Life was golden and good.

Like the sun.

Chapter 1

Charlene leaned across the front seat of the station wagon and opened tlhe door on the passenger side.

"Be a good girl," she said.

Seven-year-old Antoinette Jenkins gave her mother a quick kiss before she hopped out of the car and ran eagerly toward the grade school where her classmates were gathering. Halfway up the walk she turned and squinted into the sunshine of that bright morning. She waved happily at the smiling woman behind the wheel and then was swallowed up in the noisy, pushing, shoving mass of tiny humanity.

Antoinette loved school. But then, Antionette loved everything about her life: the beautiful young mother, the handsome, adoring father, the modest but comfortable Pasadena house the three of them shared. She loved the uncomplaining invalid Elizabeth, her maternal grandmother, who lived serenely with a friend-companion in the big, beautiful house far up the California coast. Antoinette adored animals, flowers, her second-grade teacher and her neighborhood playmates, especially Karen Golden, her very best friend, with whom she shared her toys and her secrets.

In every way, Toni was a delight. She was a slim, sturdy child. Her small-boned frame belied robust health and stamina. The big, dark-brown eyes revealed a surprising depth of compassion and understanding in one so young. Her features were delicate, her mouth almost always upturned in pleasure, and her black curly hair was cropped short in the crisp "Greek-god cut" of the late 1950s which fashion models affected and which came naturally to her. The skin was ivory-colored, almost the same shade, she and her mother secretly agreed, as the morning mug of milk into which Charlene surreptitiously slipped a spoonful of coffee. Surreptitiously because Toni loved the taste and Jim disapproved of caffeine for children, not matter how minute and innocuous the amount.

There was no better word for her disposition than joyous, no more apt description for her grace and movements than the one her grandmother had pronounced when Toni was five.

"If butterflies walked instead of flew," Elizabeth had observed, "they'd walk like Antoinette."

It was true. She danced through her early days, happily unaware of what most of the world considered at best a burden and at worst a curse. Toni had no idea that she was what the scientific world called a "mulatto," what her parents knew as a "mixed-marriage child" and what unfeeling strangers would ultimately call "nigger."

She knew, of course, that her father's skin was dark compared to her mother's fair complexion. But it meant nothing to her in those first years of innocence. Her own was somewhere between the two. She could have been of Latin extraction. For that matter, she was even lighter than many of her little friends whose skin was burned deep mahogany by the blistering California sun. It never occurred to her that she was "different." The all-white, upper-middle-class, somewhat conservative community in which she lived compassionately concealed the fact that they would have preferred, given a choice, that their neighborhood not be "integrated." Most of them were long-time residents, second-generation Pasadenians as Charlene was. Their parents had known Elizabeth when she lived in the same house now occupied by her daughter, her granddaughter and her son-in-law. They were kind people. And if they did not "socialize" to any degree with Jim and Charlene Jenkins, neither did they make them feel uncomfortable. Charlene was a charming young woman. And Jim was a gentle, well-educated man who provided a better-than-average living for his family through his good job as an aeronautical engineer. It was unfortunate, the neighbors told each other privately, that Charlene had chosen to marry a black man and have a child. Unfortunate? It was incomprehensible. Almost frightening. But being basically well-mannered people, they did not communicate this to their own children. And so it was not until she was seven that Antoinette had her first confrontation with a very special kind of cruelty.

It happened at recess on the day that she had cheerfully waved goodbye to her mother. As usual, the second-grade class was turned out into the sunshine for half an hour of mid-morning play. As always, the boys went off by themselves to organize games of baseball or mumblety-peg or whatever mysterious things seven-year-old males did in groups. The girls had their own games: hopscotch and tag and hide-and-seek. Toni, about to join a group of rope skippers, suddenly saw a face that was unfamiliar to her, a sullen-looking little girl sitting alone on the school steps. Toni tugged at Karen's sleeve and pointed at the small stranger.

"Who's that?"

Karen shook her head. "I don't know her name. She's new."

Toni frowned. "She looks lonesome. Let's go over and see if she wants to play with us."

Karen, always blissfully happy following Toni's lead, nodded. Cautiously they approached the silent figure, who did not even look up.

"Hi!" Toni said. No answer.

"My name's Toni Jenkins. And this is my friend Karen Golden. What's your name?"

The little girl hesitated and when she spoke there was no friendliness in her voice. "Nadine Thompson," she said finally. Then she raised her head. "What's it to you? Go 'way."

"Come on, Toni," Karen said. "Miss Nadine Stuck-up Thompson doesn't want to be friends."

Toni didn't move. She'd never met anyone who didn't want to be friends. Maybe, she thought, Nadine is sick.

"Do you feel bad, Nadine? Should I call Miss Hanson? If you have a stomach ache, she can fix it."

Nadine stood up. She was a big girl, bigger than Karen, much bigger than Toni.

"I don't have a stomach ache," she said. "I just hate it here. I hate this school. And I hate my father for bringing us here from New York. Now go away and leave me alone!"

Toni wouldn't be budged. "It must be awful to leave your friends, Nadine, but you'll like it here. The kids are nice. Really they are. Come on. Play with us."

Nadine's face became even uglier. "I don't play with colored kids. Back home we keep them where they belong, in Harlem. I know about you, Toni Jenkins. Your father's black. You're a nigger." She began to hop around a bewildered Toni. "Eeny meeny miney mo. Catch a nigger by the toe! If he hollers let him go! Eeny meeny miney mo!" Nadine was enjoying herself. "Eeny meeny miney mo. Toni's a nigger ain't that so?" Over and over she repeated the phrase, pleased with her own interpretation of the horrid rhyme.

Toni and Karen stood rooted to the ground. They had never heard of "niggers" or some place called Harlem. All they knew was that this new schoolmate was angry with Toni for some reason they could not understand. The words were strange but the tone was terrible. Karen began to cry. Toni stood dry-eyed, looking at Nadine as though she were some weird creature, frightening and ugly. A crowd had gathered now, drawn by Nadine's high-pitched chant. Some of the children looked at her curiously. Others watched Toni. Quite a few knew what the words meant, but with the cruelty of children, none stepped forward to silence Toni's tormentor.

It was Miss Hanson, calling them in from recess who discovered what was going on and quickly snatched Nadine away. Out of hearing of the others, she took Nadine by the shoulders and gave her a little shake.

"You bad child! What a naughty thing to do, Nadine!"

She was met by defiance. "Why was it bad? It's true, isn't it? Toni's father is a nigger."

Miss Hanson wanted to strike her.

"Where did you hear such a thing?"

"From my mother."

"And did your mother teach you to say cruel things to your schoolmates?"

Nadine stood her ground. "She doesn't want me to play with people like that. In New York I went to a private school. The black kids went to public schools." She wrinkled her nose as though she smelled something bad. "Like this one," she added.

Miss Hanson released her. "Please tell your mother

that I'd like to have a talk with her. I'll send home a note with you this afternoon."

Slowly, sorrowfully, Miss Hanson returned to the classroom. In the second row, Toni Jenkins sat unusually still. Beside her, Karen continued to smile. I'll talk to Mrs. Thompson, the teacher thought, and I'd better talk to Mrs. Jenkins as well. That will be even harder.

When she came home that afternoon, Toni headed straight for her room with barely more than a "Hi, Mommy" to Charlene, who was working in the garden. Charlene, trowel in hand, sat back on her heels and looked after the straight-backed little figure disappearing so quickly into the house. It was out of character for Antoinette to rush by her that way, as though she wanted to avoid conversation. Their pattern was always a hug and a kiss, an account of the school day, some companionable chatter about her classmates or her teacher or Karen. It occurred to Charlene that she and Toni approached each other on an unusually adult level. That came, Charlene supposed, of Toni being an only child who was used to, and felt at ease with, adults. It was also, Charlene speculated, because there was only twenty years' difference in their ages. She smiled to herself at the phrase "only twenty years." It still represented another generation with inherent problems of communication.

For a moment she considered following Toni to find out what was wrong. It was obvious that something had seriously upset her. But Charlene didn't move. Slowly, she went back to digging in the rose bed. Even at seven she has a right to privacy, her mother thought. Charlene was a great respecter of privacy. Being married to Jim had taught her how precious was the right to be one's own person, to consider and solve one's own problems without the interference, no matter how well meant, of others. As she carefully loosened the soil around the plants she reflected that all living things had to have room to breathe. She would not smother her daughter with concern. When Toni was ready to talk about whatever was on her mind, she would.

It was not until the three of them were at dinner that Charlene found out what it was all about. Toni had been silent during the meal but her mother, unobtrusively watching her, noticed that she ate well. Whatever was wrong was not physical.

During dessert Toni, looking down at her plate, suddenly said, "Daddy?"

"Yes, honey?"

"What's a nigger?"

Charlene gasped. "Antoinette!"

Jim gave her a little signal to be quiet. In a calm, measured voice he said, "A nigger is a vulgar way of referring to a Negro, a person with black skin." He waited.

"Are you a nig . . . a Negro, Daddy?"

"Yes, I am, Toni."

Charlene wanted to cry out, to ask what had happened today. She wanted more than this constrained exchange of slow-moving questions and answers. But Jim's eyes sent her a silent message to stay out of it. A few endless seconds passed while Toni considered this piece of information.

"Mommy's not a Negro, is she?"

"No," Jim said. "She belongs to the white race."

The adults could almost see the child's mind absorbing this new information, adding it up, bringing it back to herself.

"Then if I'm your child half of me is Negro," Toni said. For the first time she looked directly at her father.

13

Jim looked back, unflinchingly. The tone of his voice did not change.

"That's right, darling. Half of you is."

Charlene could contain herself no longer. "Toni, what's this all about? What happened today?"

The whole story of Nadine Thompson came pouring out, told not in terms of self-pity but in an amazingly orderly fashion.

"Karen cried, but I didn't" Toni said proudly. "And Miss Hanson is sending a note to Mrs. Thompson. She told me after school that she wanted to talk to you, too, Mommy." The child paused. "Is it bad to be like me? Is that why Miss Hanson's going to call you? Did I do something wrong?"

Charlene bit her lips to hold back the tears. She wanted to rush to her baby, to assure her that none of them had done anything wrong, to try to explain how people felt about mixed marriages and the product of them. But the words wouldn't come. She looked at Jim, begging for his help. Her husband rose from his seat at the table and as though Antoinette were a grown woman he pulled back her chair and said, "Let's all go in the living room and talk this over."

Seated beside her on the sofa, Jim took his child's hand and began to speak very matter-of-factly.

"Toni, you know there are different races, don't you? There are white people and black ones and yellow-skinned ones like Chinese and American Indians who are called redskins. You've read about them in school, haven't you?"

She nodded solemnly.

"Well," Jim said, "these people may look different on the outside but underneath they are all the same, all human beings with things about them that are good and things that are bad. They are born with their color.

14

There's nothing they can do about that. I was born black and your mother white, but that had nothing to do with the kind of people we turned out to be. It didn't affect our minds or manners or the way we look at things. It is simply something over which we had no control. Intelligent people, nice people, understand that. They judge us for the way we behave, accept or reject us for the things we contribute to the world. They don't care about the color of our skins any more than they'd care if we had big noses or ears that stuck out."

Toni frowned. "Then why did Nadine say mean things about you and me, Daddy?"

"Because, unfortunately, there are a great many people who must consider themselves superior to people who aren't like them. It's a kind of protection for them, honey. They need something to make them feel important and better than the next guy. They must have someone to look down on. It's called prejudice. That's a big word for such a little girl, but you've run up against it for the first time, so you'd best understand it. The Thompsons are prejudiced people and they've made the sad mistake of giving their little girl their same wrong values. They don't like black people. And it upsets them terribly when Negroes come into their lives. People like that are especially angry when a Negro man marries a nice white woman. And even more so when they have a beautiful child like you."

Jim put his arm around her and tilted her face upward toward his own.

"Look at me, Toni. Am I any different than the man you saw at breakfast?"

She shook her head.

"Is your mother any different? Are you? All you've heard today are some ugly, ignorant words spoken by a child who doesn't know any better. They don't change us in any way."

Toni thought about this for a moment. She didn't really understand all that her father was trying to say. Enough came through to make some of what had happened at school a little less mysterious and puzzling, but there were still unanswered questions.

"But, Daddy, if you and Mommy knew that people would be angry about you getting married and having me, why did you do it?"

Charlene answered. "Very simple, sweetheart. We loved and respected each other. We still do. We wanted a life together, with you. That's all there is to it. We know who and what we are, Toni. Nothing anyone says can change that."

"But, Mommy, everybody is *something*. You're white and Daddy's black. But if I'm half-and-half, what am *I*?"

Jim held her close. "You can be either. Or both. You can choose to be a black woman or a white one or a beautiful blend of the two. There's time for that choice, Toni. Right now you're just what you've always been: just one of the kids on the block, with a lot of friends, a couple of parents and a grandmother, all of whom love you a lot. We think you have a pretty good family." His voice became serious. "Don't hate Nadine, baby. Her mother and father have been very unfair to her. They've deprived her of the right to make up her own mind. She can't help the way she feels. Many people can't, even when they know they're hurting others."

Jim and Charlene exchanged glances. They were thinking of Charlene's estranged sister Ann in New York. Ann, who lived a tight, close-minded, superficial life. Ann who had turned away when her sister married a Negro. Ann who was raising her own three children the way the Thompsons were raising Nadine.

16

"Is Mrs. Thompson coming to apologize for Nadine?"

"Perhaps she is, Toni, dear," her mother said, "but at least you know she doesn't think you've done anything wrong."

"But then neither has Nadine," Antoinette said logically. "She was only saying what her mommy and daddy told her. Miss Hanson doesn't have to feel bad about *that*, does she?"

"No, but I'm sure she does all the same. Don't worry. We'll set it right." Charlene rose. "Past bedtime, Toni, dear. Let's go."

Antoinette put her sturdy little arms around her father's neck and kissed him.

"Good night, Daddy." She stroked his cheek and then, with some deep insight, she added, "I love your face."

His eyes were moist but his tone was bantering.

"That's funny," he said. "I love yours, too."

When Toni was in bed, Charlene came back into the living room. Jim was sitting motionlessly, staring into space.

"I was rotten at it," he said.

"You were wonderful."

"No, I should have explained it better. But she's so young. How could she understand?" He rose and began to pace the room. "Damn it, Charlene, maybe we waited too long. We should have prepared her sooner. Even before she went to school."

"Darling, she wouldn't have known what we were talking about. She can barely grasp the edges of it now. And you were so tender and sensible with her tonight."

He snorted. "Half truths. Evasions. 'Don't blame Nadine.' What a bunch of crap! Why didn't I tell her to blame the whole stinking world for their bigotry and us for thinking we could beat it? Why didn't I tell her that her own mother and father should bear the blame for having

17

a mulatto child? My God, Charley, this is only the beginning and I face it with milk-sop platitudes like 'You don't have to choose now!' She has to choose, all right. She'll have to choose all her life."

"Sweetheart, stop blaming yourself. And stop blaming me. I love you. I wanted your child. We both knew she'd have to come to grips with ignorance at some point. I'm grateful that she had seven solid years of security before the first brush with it. At least she's reached what some people call 'the age of reason.' "

His self-anger refused to go away.

"You don't know what it's like to be called 'nigger.' Jesus Christ, I could kill that lousy kid and her stupid family!"

Charlene didn't answer. It was true. She didn't know what it was to be black or to be called ugly names. But she knew what it was to be part of a mixed marriage. It was full of pain and loneliness. But it was also resplendent with love and pride and happiness. There had been nine glorious, miserable, defiant, sequestered, unregretted years of marriage to Jim Jenkins. She would do it all over again tomorrow.

Karen came by the next morning to walk to school with Toni. The little girls scuffled up the sidewalk, saying nothing at first, kicking idly at loose pebbles and blades of freshly cut grass from the lawns that bordered their way.

"Did you tell your folks what happened?" Karen finally asked. "About that awful Nadine?"

"Uh-huh."

"What'd they say?"

"Daddy explained to me that some people don't like Negroes and he's one and since I belong to him and Mommy that makes me half-and-half. He said I can decide which I want to be, later, when I've had time to think about it."

"Have you decided?"

Toni shook her head. "I don't think he meant I should make up my mind until I'm grown up." She frowned. "Do I seem any different to you now that you know, Karen? I don't *feel* any different."

"Don't be a dummy. You're not different."

"Yes, I am. I don't know how much, but I am. It's the way I was born and I can't help it. A lot of people think it's important. I'm glad you don't."

Karen kicked viciously at a broken tree limb. "Wait till I get my hands on that nasty Nadine Thompson! I'll fix her!"

"No. Daddy says we should feel sorry for her. Her parents aren't bringing her up right."

"Pooh! She's a big creep!" Karen made a face. "Yuk! I wish she'd stayed in New York!"

They fell silent for a few moments and then Karen spoke again. "I told my folks what happened, too."

Toni looked interested. "What'd they say?"

"What yours did, I guess. Except for one thing." Karen seemed upset. "They got awful nervous. And then they said the same kind of thing might happen to me one day and I shouldn't get mad either."

Toni's eyes widened. "Karen, are you half Negro?"

"No. Half Jewish. It's sort of the same, I guess. A lot of people don't like Jews either. Of course, it's not as bad as being black. That is, I mean, they can't really look at my father and tell. . . ." Her voice trailed off in confusion. "Gee whiz, Toni, I didn't mean anything about your father. I think he's swell."

"Did you know?" Toni asked. "About being half Jewish, I mean?"

"Nope. I'm still not sure what it means. Mom and Dad

19

just said that it was another kind of different. Being Negro is about your color, but Jewish just means where you go to church and we don't go to church anywhere."

"But why would people *care* where you went to church?"

"Heck, Toni, I don't know!"

Toni began to giggle. "Let's share. You be part Negro and I'll be part Jewish."

Karen shouted with laughter. "And that stuck-up Nadine Thompson will go crazy!"

Charlene spent much of the next day thinking about her husband's talk with Toni and mentally reviewing her own background, different from her child's but equally unorthodox. Her mother, Elizabeth, had survived a terrible marriage to Charlene's father, a "successful" man but a psychotic whom she'd finally left, taking her daughters and her son Quigly with her. There'd been the early days when they'd been actually hungry at times, when Elizabeth, with no training except to be a gracious wife and hostess, had managed to carve out a successful career as a journalist and then as a decorator. There'd been prosperity again, finally, and a second, happy marriage for Elizabeth, an all-too-brief marriage ending in the death of Tony Alexander, the wonderful man for whom Charlene's Toni was named.

Elizabeth had survived it all, had seen her older daughter turn into a priggish, scheming young woman who trapped an honorable Peter Richards into a stultifyingly conventional marriage. She had seen Quigly become dissolute and finally mad. She'd watched Charlene fall in love with Jim and marry him, had grieved when Ann turned her back on them all when that happened. It had been years since Ann Richards had been in touch with her mother or her sister. Ann's children must be quite grown-up by now, Charlene calculated. Peter Richards III would be eighteen, Joanne sixteen and Alan fourteen. Like everything else in her well-ordered life, Ann had planned three children, two years apart. She'd deigned to send birth notices to California. Apart from that, one telephone conversation, and a single tragic visit Charlene knew almost nothing of her sister.

In the beginning, Elizabeth had tried to reach Ann, to make her understand that her little sister's happiness was more important than the man-made rules by which Ann lived. Mrs. Peter Richards II would have no part of it. She was disgusted by Jim Jenkins who was black, ashamed that Charlene could marry such a man, outraged that Elizabeth would permit this disgraceful thing. In time, Elizabeth gave up, stopped writing unanswered letters and making refused telephone calls to New York.

Then when Elizabeth had given her New Year's party, Ann, Peter and their children had come from New York. It was the first time Charlene had seen her sister in years. There seemed to be hope of a reconciliation between the sisters, and between Ann and Elizabeth. But Tony's death and Elizabeth's subsequent stroke had put an end to that hope. Ann had removed herself, coldly, dispassionately, from her family. She would never forgive Charlene's marriage or Elizabeth's sanction of it. And there was something that lay deeper, as well. Ann had always been "Daddy's girl." She refused to see him for the unfaithful, deranged man he was. She had never really forgiven Elizabeth for taking them away from the father who'd called her his "little princess." She had hated Elizabeth most of her life with a blind resentment that had no relationship to reality. Charlene's marriage was a convenient excuse to cut herself off from her mother once and for all.

We're quite a family, Charlene thought ruefully. And yet we're lucky. The little nucleus that's left is blessed

21

with more love and understanding than most "normal" families know.

She gave thanks every day of her life for Jim Jenkins, the beautiful young man who'd loved her so much he'd been reluctant to marry her. It was she who'd insisted, she who, at eighteen, had known she was strong enough for whatever came her way. The marriage had troubled Elizabeth deeply. That was understandable; she did not want her child hurt. But she recognized the depth of love Charlene and Jim felt and gave them her blessing over the angry protests of her other daughter, the worries of her friends, even over the doubts and fears in her own heart. Seeing them together, Elizabeth had never regretted that decision. And when Antionette was born, Elizabeth rejoiced.

"Jim loves that baby so much it hurts your eyes," she'd said to Charlene.

It was true. Toni was a miracle to James Jenkins. Just as he found it miraculous that anyone as soft and desirable as Charlene had wanted to belong to a young black man from a poor family in Denver. He adored his wife and child, cherishing them with all the strength and devotion of which he was capable. He gave them a good life, emotionally, spiritually and monetarily. His only moments of unhappiness were when he allowed himself to think of what effect this mixed marriage had on Charlene and what might lie ahead for their child.

Until now his fears had had little basis in fact. They'd survived the raised eyebrows, the self-imposed separation from most of the community. But Jim had been deeply wounded by yesterday's event, by the cruelty to Toni. Charlene knew he took all the blame upon himself. He had always dreaded this inevitable moment when his child would be the innocent, helpless victim of his own desires. His own upbringing told him what to expect. His marriage had been opposed even more by his family than by Charlene's. His parents knew the awful odds against success in the mating of two races. They had begged Jim not do it, for his sake and Charlene's, had even appealed to Elizabeth. But nothing could stop the two young people so deeply and irrevocably in love.

And it had been right, Charlene told herself now. It had been right for nine years. And it would be right again, for all three of them.

Chapter 2

For the next few years, Charlene's optimism seemed well founded. Life for the Jenkinses returned to its peaceful pattern. Jim received steady promotions at the aircraft company and he and Charlene pursued their quiet, contented ways, seeing a few friends occasionally, driving up to visit an aging but still spirited Elizabeth and watching their daughter develop into an increasingly beautiful, intelligent and popular teenager.

Toni, at sixteen, showed none of the rebelliousness of the much publicized young in the decade of the sixties. If she had questions or anxieties about herself, they were not evident to her parents or her friends. She did not openly identify with black people. How could she? The boys she dated, the girls, including Karen, who were her close friends were the white, middle-class, unsung, unnewsworthy majority of the time. They were not "hippies" or drug addicts, not drop-outs or protesters. Yet they were well aware of living in a troubled world, thoughtful about a civil-rights act passed in 1964, distressed about race riots the next year right in their own "back yard," the ghetto of Watts. They were full of convictions about

Vietnam and the draft. But they were concerned, informed onlookers, not militant rebels. Their discussions about racial strife were sensible and serious, but there was no thought in the minds of boys who came to take Toni to the movies or girls who rang up for endless telephone chats that she was not "one of them."

Even when they came to the Jenkins' house and saw an unmistakably Negro father, Toni's friends seemed to take it as a matter of no importance.

But it would be ridiculous and false to say that there were not some in the Pasadena community who "looked down" on Toni and her parents, some women who glanced the other way when they met Charlene at the supermarket and some men who ignored Jim at the public golf course. It did not escape Toni that when Martin Luther King led the march on Washington there were classmates who whispered about her, identifying her with a portion of America she knew nothing about. The little slights hurt Jim most of all. For it was his people who rioted in the cities, and an unquenchable rage lay within him when the National Advisory Council on Civil Disorders warned that the country was moving toward two societies, black and white, separate and unequal. Privately, Jim felt guilt about opting for a "white world." Yet it had been good to him. And more importantly it had accepted his child. At least she would not have to know, as he had known, what it was like to be poor and black and hated.

He watched Toni carefully as she grew into womanhood. Determinedly, he talked to her about racial problems, never overtly relating the conversations to themselves, but encouraging her in the dream of all thoughtful people: to accept each person as she found him, judging him for himself alone, not for the color of his skin, the nature of his origin or the basis of his faith.

Toni did not know that he was indulging in an ideal. It

was natural for her to think this way. She cried as bitterly over the assassination of Martin Luther King as she did over the killing of Robert Kennedy. She thought of them as great men, colorful only in the fairness and inspiration they projected. She seldom thought of people as black or white, her own family least of all. She did not know about the letters Jim received from his sister Clara in Denver. Even Charlene was unaware of those strident messages from the woman who was active in the black people's movement. In them, Clara frequently demanded that Jim make Toni aware of what she was, that he do at least that much to "atone for deserting his own people." She called him an "Uncle Tom" who had betrayed his parents as well as his race.

Jim did not reply. There was a certain amount of justification in what Clara said, he supposed. Certainly Fred and Addie Jenkins had felt sorrow over their son's marriage. On a personal level, they knew the social hardships this union would produce for Jim and Charlene. But beyond their concern lay displeasure and disappointment in the boy they'd been so proud of. They were "old-fashioned" Negroes, expecting nothing for themselves but filled with hopes for their children, believing theirs would be a better world. They'd worked hard as housemaid and porter to send Jim through college. He was more than a credit to them when he got his aeronautical engineering degree; he was proof that a poor black boy could become a brilliant, successful black man. Though his parents were not militant about race, they were saddened that he had not married a girl of his own color, produced full-blooded children and raised them to follow in his own footsteps and improve the lot of the Negro in America.

They had seen their son only twice in nine years. Once when they came sedately to the wedding and again when Toni was born. Jim's sister came neither time. It was a strange parallel that both sisters so strongly protested the marriage, unknowingly united in reverse prejudice.

Charlene remembered the look on Addie Jenkin's face when she'd come into the hospital room after viewing the newborn Antoinette. Jim's mother had taken Charlene's hand and said quietly, "She's the color of ivory. Thank the good Lord for that."

Charlene had not understood. She didn't care what color her baby was as long as it was perfect. There was no way she could comprehend that Addie, having resigned herself to the marriage, was realistically glad that the child, destined to live in a pale-skinned world, was almost as light as her peers. Later, when Charlene questioned Jim about Addie's reaction, he shrugged it off, saying that to people of his mother's generation black was not beautiful.

"She knows dark skins are a handicap," he'd said. "She's glad that her first grandchild is such a glorious, indefinable color."

In childhood, Toni's only thoughts about her father's family were that she had never seen them. But for that matter there was much of her mother's family she'd never seen either. She knew she had an aunt and uncle and three cousins in New York. She knew, because Charlene had told her, that the sisters did not see eye to eye on many things. But she did not know that Ann felt soiled by Charlene's marriage. Just as she did not know that her father's family felt he had betrayed them.

In the beginning she asked questions about all her mysterious relatives. She was told factual things, names and ages and locations, but she could never form a mental picture of any of them. At first it was puzzling but in time, as she matured, she simply accepted the fact that her mother and father had reasons of their own for this separation from their families. She instinctively knew better than to probe for answers though she longed to know why and how these estrangements had taken place. Someday, Toni told herself, she'd find out why there was so little discussion of her parents' early lives. She'd liked to have heard about them as children. But even her beloved grandmother was gently evasive about the past. Elizabeth, always so open and free, seemed reluctant to talk to her granddaughter about this subject. And so Toni decided, with a wisdom beyond her years, that it was best, for now, to say nothing.

She did not know that she was living in a carefully constructed cocoon, a thin, fragile, protective web woven by the two who wished they could keep her forever confined within the limits of the community in which she'd been raised. She was safe there, they thought, with the young people she'd known all her life, with teachers who loved her cheerful, alert mind, with neighbors who, for the most part, were content to live and let live.

But Charlene and Jim knew that this idyllic state could not last. There would come a day when Toni, independent for all her gentleness, would raise her eyes to a world beyond this limited one. She would reach out for new people, new experiences. Essentially loyal and trusting, eager to help, she would be used by the weak and the dependent, wounded by the unscrupulous. Her parents saw in her the same vulnerability that had plagued and at the same time enriched the life of her grandmother. Like Elizabeth, Toni was strong and intensely sympathetic, seeing only the good in people, refusing to admit, until it was no longer possible to deny their selfish motives.

Charlene saw traces of this already. There was Karen, a prime example. Karen, a little too plump, a little too plain, a worshipful hanger-on since both girls were little more than babies. Toni wangled dates for Karen, got her invited to parties from which she might have been excluded, spent long, patient hours listening sympathetically to Karen's self-pitying complaints about her lack of good looks, her dearth of boy friends, even her imagined feeling of rejection because of her Jewish parent. Toni listened and sympathized and reassured, stoutly taking Karen's side even when the other kids called her dull and dopey. She saw Karen as a dear and put-upon friend. She did not realize that Karen was, in fact, jealous and demanding. She would have liked to have been Toni's only friend and she clung to her, taking up more than her share of Toni's time with her pitiful problems.

Charlene tried, tactfully, to warn her daughter about these selfish, monopolizing tactics. Not that Charlene disliked Karen. She did not even believe the girl knew what she was doing to Toni. She knew, however, that Toni was being used, and that it was not good for either her or Karen. They had a long talk about it one day, sitting in the garden. Toni, frowning with anxiety, had just told her mother that Karen didn't have a date for the Sophomore Prom and that she'd been crying, literally crying, on the telephone for the past half hour.

"It's awful, Mom," Toni said. "The dance is only two days away and nobody will go with her. I'm trying to think who she can get."

"Darling, Karen isn't your responsibility. It's not up to you to make sure she's constantly happy, much as you'd like her to be."

Toni looked surprised. "She's my best friend!"

"She's certainly your friend of longest standing," Charlene corrected, "and she's a good friend. But, Toni, she's not your *child*. Karen leans too heavily on you and you allow it. She makes *you* feel guilty when *she's* slighted. She brings you every problem and complaint. She expects you to devote your life to her."

29

Toni didn't answer for a moment. Then she said, "Isn't that what friends are for, Mother?"

"No. Not in the way Karen presumes on friendship. Friends are for sharing, Toni. There has to be a balance in such a relationship. If it's all one-sided, one giving and the other taking, it's not healthy. I know you're fond of Karen. So am I." Charlene smiled. "I'll never forget the way she stood up for you when you were both in second grade and that dreadful little Nadine what's-her-name was so hateful."

"That's exactly what I mean," Toni said. "Karen has always been my best friend. From the time we were seven."

"But perhaps you've forgotten, darling, that it was *you* who wanted to share Karen's Jewishness. It was *you* who tried to make friends with Nadine. Karen gives lip service, but Karen is a taker, even though I'm sure she doesn't really mean to be."

"What am I supposed to do, ignore her?"

There was a note of resentment in Toni's voice.

"Of course not. But you mustn't let her use you as a crutch. Karen can make her own way."

"But she *can't*. That's just the problem. She isn't popular and she's not very pretty."

"Is that your fault, Toni?"

"No. Of course not. But she needs me."

Charlene sighed. "But do *you* need *her*? To this smothering extent, I mean? Friends are precious and they deserve our loyalty, but friendship isn't meant to be a burden. No kind of love is. It's not wrong to also think of yourself, dear. Friendship is an exchange of affection, not a demand. We're not saints, any of us. We get bored and irritated, even with our families. We must each be free, Toni, to follow the self-interests that are important and healthy for *us*."

The young girl was silent. "I never thought of it that way," she said finally. "I just hate to see Karen hurt. I hate to see anybody hurt."

"How about yourself? You can hurt yourself with this kind of overconcern. One day you may discover that Karen or someone else will take your loyalty for granted. And you'll feel a very normal resentment. It's wonderful to care more about the feelings of others than you do about your own, but martyrdom provokes very little admiration and much less appreciation. You'll find out as you grow older that people have to handle their own problems, particularly when you discover that you have your hands full with your own."

"I still don't see what's wrong about trying to help. Isn't that the Golden Rule—'Do unto others'?"

"Darling, it's not the *doing,* it's the *degree.* Your father and I want you to help others. We want you to be considerate of other people's feelings. But we don't ever want to see help become a duty rather than a pleasure. Not for your friends. Not even for us. How can I explain it to you without making you think I want you to become a selfish, self-centered young woman? I want you to care, but I want you to care about yourself as well. You're very like your grandmother, you know. You both can carry a heavy load on shoulders that are much broader than they look. But you must not be too vulnerable, too wide open to disillusionment." Charlene smiled. "I'm not a very good example, but I made a selfish decision when I married your father, and I've never regretted it, even though I hurt some other people. I found out that, in a way, my defiance earned me a little respect. In some quarters, at least." She stood up and stretched in the sunshine. "I guess your dad and I haven't made you tough enough, sweetheart. We've been overprotective. A little of our own anxiety not to hurt, I suppose. Just remember everybody

31

eventually learns to survive on his own, Toni. Even my mother, generous and concerned as she is, ultimately learned that she had a right to lead her own life and other people had to fend for themselves sometimes."

"I like it when we talk," Toni said.

"So do I. Even when it gets a little heavy."

"Mom, I've been thinking about what I'd like to do after graduation. I know it's two years away but it isn't too early to start planning, is it?"

"Not a bit. But I hope the plan includes college."

"Well, I'm not sure. I mean, not exactly college. I've been talking to Laurel. I showed her some of the fashion sketches I've made. She thinks I have some talent. That I could be a designer maybe. Or an illustrator. I'd love that. And if it's okay with you and Dad, I'd like to apply to Parsons when I graduate from high school."

Charlene was stunned. She had not even known that Toni had talked to Laurel Lane, her mother's friend and companion. It had been so many years since Laurel had come to California that Charlene had nearly forgotten Laurel was once editor in chief of *Enchantress,* the high-fashion magazine in New York. Laurel, never married, was, always had been, "career-minded." It shouldn't have come as a surprise that she would encourage Toni to "make a name for herself."

Not that the idea displeased Charlene. She simply had not thought of it. If anything, she might have imagined Toni finishing college and perhaps teaching for a while before marriage. The girl loved children and would want her own. I've been thinking of her life in terms of my own, Charlene realized. A good marriage, a happy home, a cared-for existence. I might have known better. She has her father's intellect and her grandmother's drive.

She managed to hide her surprise and the slight feeling of dismay that followed. Parsons was a good fashion school but it was in New York. How could they let an eighteen-year-old girl go off alone to a city so far away? She knew no one there. There was Ann, of course, but that didn't count. Charlene had no desire even to see her estranged sister much less give her an opportunity to infect Toni with her warped views on life. Besides, it was highly unlikely that Ann Richards would so much as acknowledge her half-black niece.

There was a little hurt, too. A very human reaction to the fact that Toni had discussed her future with Laurel before she even mentioned it to Charlene. I'm being petty, Charlene told herself. It's perfectly natural that Toni and Laurel would talk about this area. I'm the mother, but I've never worked a day in my life.

Toni was waiting for her answer. Charlene managed to bring her attention back to the moment.

"Well, you are full of surprises!" she said. "I'm glad Laurel thinks you have talent, honey. She'd know if anyone would. She was one of the great fashion authorities of her day. As for Parsons, let's think about it. We'll have to talk to your father, of course. Anyway, we're not exactly up to the wire."

"No. But you do have to apply early."

"Of course."

Toni looked disappointed. "You don't like the idea, do you? And Dad won't like it either."

"That's not true, sweetheart. Good grief, Toni, just give me a moment to adjust, will you? I haven't said no. Neither has your father. We all have to talk out a lot of things." She felt a pang of sympathy for the crestfallen little face. "Darling, all we want for you is what you want. Have a little faith, okay?"

"Sure, Mom. Of course. I'm sorry. I should have talked to you about anything this important before I talked to Laurel."

33

How perceptive she is, Charlene thought. She knows I'm feeling left out, even a little jealous. Charlene reached out and hugged her child.

"Don't be such a silly," she said. "Laurel was the logical one to talk to. I just hadn't known you were thinking of a career! Not that there's anything wrong with that. Everybody has to decide where he wants to fit in."

A fleeting look of unhappiness crossed Toni's face, but she said nothing. Charlene had inadvertently touched a sore spot. That was precisely the trouble. Toni didn't know where she wanted to fit in. There were things she kept hidden from everyone, doubts and fears that she hugged to herself, uncertain and unresolved. Her heritage was one of those, though it was a problem never discussed and seemingly nonexistent. She remembered a long-ago conversation with her father. She could choose to be black or white, he'd said. In the years between she had seldom thought of it. But now she knew she was approaching the time when a choice had to be made. She could opt for a white world, a white marriage. It was the sensible, logical thing to do. But something within her made her hesitate. She didn't feel black any more than she looked it. But it was part of her, to embrace or deny.

Perhaps subconsciously, though she did not recognize such an obscure motivation, this was why she was gravitating toward some part of the fashion world. Like the theater, like all the arts, it seemed to draw no color lines. An avid reader of fashion magazines, she saw Negro models and black designers treated as people, accepted without question into the most elegant and intellectual circles. She did not know, at sixteen, that she yearned for her own identity, the kind she could not have if she stayed in Pasadena.

For though Jim and Charlene might choose to ignore it, or pretend to, Toni knew that none of the parents of the boys she dated would give their blessing to a marriage with her. They all liked Toni and welcomed her into their homes. But not into their families. She recognized this instinctively. If she was to find her place it would be where she could start fresh, where no one knew her as anything but Antoinette Jenkins. Only then could she make that free choice. Suddenly she had a need to stand alone, to concentrate on her own future.

"I'm going in to call Karen," she said.

"Figure out who'll take her to the prom?"

"No," Toni said firmly, "that's her problem. She'll have to work it out, the way the rest of us do."

Watching her go, Charlene felt guilty. Poor Karen, she thought. That friendship will never be quite the same. Nor, she suddenly realized, would Toni.

Chapter 3

Toni leaned back in the window seat of the jumbo jet and let her thoughts turn backward as the huge machine raced ahead, carrying her to a new life in New York.

Even now she could hardly believe that she was on her own, an enrolled student at Parsons, yet another of the young hopefuls who saw themselves as the Norells and Balenciagas of the future.

The parental resistance to the idea of an unusually sheltered eighteen-year-old girl going so far away to school had not been at all what Toni had expected. She had thought it would be her father who'd oppose the idea, fearful for his beloved daughter's safety in a big, anonymous and dangerous city. Instead, Jim had been in favor almost immediately. It was Charlene who had shown reluctance in the beginning and who had tried not to look tight-lipped and worried even at the airline gate.

Perhaps it was because Mother once lived in New York, Toni thought. Even though Charlene had been only thirteen when she and Elizabeth left the city, her memories of the vast, impersonal metropolis gave her a frame of reference that Jim, who'd never been east of

Denver, did not have. Still, it was uncharacteristic of Charlene to worry. She was the eternal optimist. In most cases it was Jim who was alert and wary, in a guarded, polite way, of strange people and alien situations. She had not understood his approval until almost the very last minute.

Toni closed her eyes and in the strange limbo of flight relived that last long conversation with her father, a conversation that had been so revealing and so painful for them both, but which finally accounted for Jim's unhesitating approval of her plans. It had taken place the day before she left. Only yesterday and yet it already seemed so far behind her.

"How'd you like to go over to the driving range and hit a bucket of balls with me?" he'd asked. "Might be the last one for a long time."

Toni had quickly agreed. She'd been playing golf with her father since she was fourteen, loved the game, loved being with this beautiful, muscular man who was all grace and easy elegance. She would miss him so. Miss them both. It was early September and she would see them again when she came home for Christmas, but it was their first separation and now that she was on the verge of it she was torn between her desire to go and the frightening prospect of life without them.

In the car he'd turned to her and said, "Toni, I really don't want to bang away at golf balls this morning. I wanted a chance to be alone with you. Without even your mother around." He started the engine. "Okay with you if we just drive around and talk?"

"Sure, Dad. Anything you want."

He'd begun to talk then. Slowly, carefully as though he wanted her to understand not only what he said but why he was saying it.

"Honey, we've never talked much about color in our

37

house. You know that. We've been lucky living here. People have accepted a family that in a lot of places would have been forced out of the neighborhood. I give most of the credit to your mother and Elizabeth, of course. They were already accepted. I'm not sure a black stranger would have been greeted with the same tolerance if he'd moved in cold."

She started to protest but he raised his hand to silence her.

"Let me talk, baby. I couldn't say the things I must in front of your mother. She's so loyal, so wonderful. She'd shout me down with her refusal to admit that I'm looked on as an outsider, an inferior. Oh, I know what you're dying to say," Jim went on. "Just what Charlene would say. That I have an important job, that I'm well thought of in my profession, that I'm smart and above any stereotype. I'm the world's most fortunate man to have a wife who loves me blindly. A woman who really believes that I am what she thinks I am; bigger than bigots, impervious to condescension and subtle slights. It's not true, Toni. My mind is a library." He tapped his head. "Up here is filed away every thinly veiled insult, every cleverly worded put-down to you or your mother or me. I've catalogued the people who wish we didn't exist. Not just *us* but *all* black people and all whites who marry blacks and all children who carry mixed blood in their veins. I've made my way in a white man's world, honey, and some of my own family despise me for it. Sometimes I despise myself. But I've chosen reality over emotions—even emotions that go back three hundred years.

"My people have names for men like me. Not nice names. I probably deserve them. According to their standards, I do. But I'm a person of some modest intellect, Toni. I can discern between hard reality and wishful thinking. And the hard reality is that it's going to be a

38

long, long time before my people get the justice we morally deserve. The wishful thinkers of my race won't face that fact. God, I admire them for trying to change it overnight! But both sides have so much to learn. It just won't happen in my lifetime, Toni. Maybe not in yours. For all I know, it will never *really* change."

She sat silent, her eyes on the handsome, troubled face. Inexperienced and protected as she was, she felt her father's anguish, realized the decisions he'd had to make, imagined his self-doubts and questioning.

Jim took a deep breath. "So what I want to say to you, darling, is a betrayal of everything I should stand for. But I'm going to say it nonetheless. When you get to New York, where no one knows you, don't tell them your father is a black man. There's no reason anyone should know you're part Negro. You don't look, act or sound like people's idea of one. Don't let some misguided sense of loyalty to me make your life hard. Be a white woman, Toni. 'Pass,' as my sister Clara would say. Remember I told you years ago that you had a right to choose? I'm telling you now which way to choose. Try to understand that you must be realistic. Promise me."

Toni groped for the right words to tell him how she loved him, how she understood what he was urging her to do and why, how many questions were in her own mind. But she couldn't give him that promise. She was very much a part of him but she was her mother's child, too, with her mother's strong sense of conviction and courage. Instead of giving him an answer, she tried to approach it another way.

"Dad, are you sorry you married Mother?"

"My God, no, Toni! That's not what this is all about! I told you. I'm the luckiest man in the world. For me, it's been wonderful, but for her it hasn't been easy sledding. She's had to put up with ostracism, with a much more

39

limited social life than she should have had, with a lot of whispering behind her back. All because of me. It took guts for a girl like your mother to marry a Negro, Toni. She didn't have to. She could have had anyone she wanted.

"But that's my point," Toni said. "She didn't want anyone else. She didn't care what the world thought. All that mattered was her love for you and yours for her. How could I possibly make all that you two have lived for pointless by pretending it was something different?"

"Toni, Toni." Jim shook his head. "You refuse to understand. You're as much white as black. You can be either. All I'm saying is, you needn't go through what your mother has."

"What if I fall in love the way she did?"

"No. You mustn't."

"Daddy, I can't control that."

"But you can. Don't you see? That's why I'm glad you're going away. People won't know anything about you. You'll eventually meet some nice man and marry him."

"Some nice white man?"

"Yes."

Toni was suddenly angry. "And who'll give me away at my 'nice white wedding'? Some stranger? Do you really want me to lie, to pretend you and Mom don't exist? Will I never be able to come home with the man I love?"

He was shaken. "Toni, I only want to see you safe. Even if it meant never meeting the man you marry. I want it that much, for you." He tried to make a joke. "Couldn't you tell a little white lie, for me?"

She began to cry and Jim put his arms around her.

"Come on now, darling, we're both getting carried away! Let's not get all worked up about weddings at this point. Hell, baby, your mother and I may not even be

40

around by the time you marry! All I want is your promise that for now, in your new life, to your new friends, you'll try making Jim Jenkins a faceless father."

She shook her head. "I can't promise that."

"Okay, sweetheart, but think about it. Give me that much, won't you?"

She nodded, heartsick at refusing him anything.

Remembering the scene now, Toni felt the tears rise again behind her closed eyelids. It seemed to her that she's cried so much in the last week before she left home. She'd wept when she said goodbye to Elizabeth and Laurel, though those were happy, excited tears. Both the elderly women had painted such a glowing picture of New York and the satisfaction she could expect to find there.

"I wish I still knew some people at *Enchantress*," Laurel said, "but it's been so long since I left. All my staff, my 'industrial debutantes,' are probably grandmothers themselves by now! No matter. You'll be meeting the new breed of fashion-magazine people and a lot of other exciting creatures as well. Oh, Toni, how I envy you! How wonderful to be young and talented and beautiful!"

Elizabeth had kissed her gently, her hands lightly cupping Toni's face.

"Antoinette, it's going to be a tremendous experience," she said. "I was much older than you when I first saw New York, but it's a memory that's stayed with me forever." Elizabeth looked over Toni's head at Laurel and Charlene, who stood nearby. Her steady gaze seemed to send them a warning to be quiet. "Darling, if you should run into any problem that needs to be quickly handled, here's the address and phone number of your Aunt Ann and Uncle Peter. We haven't been in touch in years, but Ann is still my child, still your mother's sister. I know she would not fail you in any emergency." Elizabeth looked at the two women. "I'm not suggesting that Antoinette seek

41

out her aunt, but I recall something about blood being thicker. Ann may not wish to be reminded of any of us, but I seriously doubt that she would not come to her niece's aid if she were needed."

The firm, sensible voice boded no nonsense from the other women. Nor did its tone encourage questions from Toni. But on the drive back to Pasadena, Charlene told her daughter the whole terrible story.

"Your grandmother has forgiven Ann," Charlene concluded. "I guess it's in the nature of women to forgive anything their children might do. But your aunt is not anyone I'd care to have you know, Toni. I don't hate her. I pity her. But I see no reason to stir up old resentments. Keep the address and phone number, darling. Grandmother's right. There should be someone in town you could call, God forbid, in case of emergency. I think Ann would respond. If she didn't, Peter would. He's a nice man. I always liked him. I had a terrible crush on him when I was a kid and he was courting my big sister." Charlene smiled. "Anyway, that's ancient history, but I don't think Peter's changed. Any more, unfortunately than I think Ann probably has. I'm afraid she's made that man's life a living hell, poor devil."

Toni was horrified by the full story of Ann. Her impulse was to tear up the paper her grandmother had given her. In fact, she took it out of her pocket, intent on doing so, but Charlene stopped her.

"No, keep it. I want you to. Ann's problem and mine belong to another world, another life. I don't know what she is today. I can't help feel that she's paid a terrible price all these years for the way she's behaved to us and the way she's probably tormented Peter."

"If he's such a nice man," Toni said reasonably, "why didn't Grandmother give me his office address instead of

42

their home? It sounds like he's the only one I could count on if I did need help in a hurry."

Charlene thought about that. "That would be the logical thing to do, I agree. But don't you see, Toni, that even now Elizabeth can't bear to admit that her daughter would fail you? She'd feel that it was wrong to bypass Ann, even though she knows in her heart what my sister is. In her head she's aware, but I suppose that emotionally Mother still has to pretend, even to us, that Ann isn't a tragic disappointment." A sudden thought struck Charlene. Not taking her eyes off the road, she said, "Look on the other side of that paper, Toni. Anything written there?"

Toni turned it over. There, in small clear letters, was the name, address and telephone number of Peter Richards' law firm.

Charlene began to laugh. "God bless her. She's unique. I confess now that I was as surprised as you that she'd totally put her faith in Ann. It was all a big face-saving act! What a woman! My darling mother, the romantic realist. I feel much better. I might have known that she'd use her head, the marvelous, proud, delicious fraud!"

The paper was in Toni's purse now as she sped toward New York. I'll never use either address, she thought. I'd rather die than ask for help from that terrible woman. And her husband can't be much if he puts up with her. I don't want any part of either of them. Not that they'd be any happier to see me.

She leaned back in her seat, thinking what a strange week it had been. There had been the long, confusing talk with her troubled father, the years-overdue disclosures about her mother's family, even an emotional scene with Karen, who had cried and said she knew she was going to hate U.C.L.A.

"I wish I could go to school in New York with you,"

43

Karen said. "You're my best friend, Toni. What am I going to do without you?"

For a moment Toni felt upset and even guilty, but she remembered Charlene's advice. If Karen was to remain a friend it had to be on Toni's terms as well as her own.

"You'll be fine," Toni had said firmly. "We can't be children forever, Karen. We have to go our own ways."

It hadn't been easy. Karen had looked stunned. But this was the time to cut all the cords that held her to the old life. Karen wouldn't die without her. Nobody would.

The cabin of the airplane was quiet now, lights dimmed on this night flight, most passengers asleep or trying to read under the tiny pinpoints of light that inadequately illuminated their seats. Toni was too restless to read, too excited to sleep. She spent the next hours gazing out the window into black nothingness, waiting for dawn and her first glimpse of New York. When at last it came, it was something of a letdown. She'd expected to see the Empire State Building and the dignified façade of the United Nations. Instead she saw, far below, rows of identical, boring surburban houses, and highways dotted with tiny cars crawling like bugs in the early hours of the morning. It had never occurred to her that planes from California did not fly straight up the island of Manhattan on their way to John F. Kennedy airport. She finally would see the New York of picture postcards from the window of a dirty yellow taxicab as it crossed the Triborough Bridge. It was less dramatic, perhaps, but no less awesome.

The cab careened down the East River Drive toward the hotel in the East Fifties where a room was reserved for Toni. There had been talk of her taking up residence in the Barbizon Hotel for Women, a place Jim considered eminently more suitable, but Toni had protested that its location in the Sixties was too far from the school. It was

Elizabeth who had finally talked Jim into letting Toni make the choice.

"Jim, dear," her grandmother had said, "I know what you're thinking. But hotels for young women aren't worth a damn as long as there are apartments for young men." She'd given him that irresistible smile. "Besides, we know our Antoinette, don't we?"

He'd grinned, feeling foolish. She was right, of course. If his daughter was going to stray, no impersonal "chaperoned hotel" would stop her. He was thinking like a Victorian. Toni wouldn't give herself to the first persuasive man who came along. She was much more sexually aware than his generation had been and God knows she was no prissy, uninformed child. The kids of her time were less hung-up about sex and Toni had, in the last couple of years, discussed the subject openly and without embarrassment with Charlene and him. Still, he was sure she had her own set of values, reserved for herself alone. A realistic man, he did not expect her to be a virgin bride as her mother had been. He only hoped that she would be certain of her feelings before she got deeply involved. It wasn't easy for a father, any father, to think of his daughter in bed with a man. But Toni was the same age Charlene had been when they had married.

They had discussed it, he and Charlene, when it was certain that Toni was going away. It was difficult for Jim to put his feelings into words, even to the woman who was closer to him than any other human being.

"I know this is a different world," he'd said. "Freer. Better in many ways. But kids can get in trouble. Even good kids like ours. I can't stand the thought of it, Charley, but I know she might meet somebody. . . ."

Charlene knew what he meant. "It's already been taken care of, darling," she said gently. "Toni and I went to see

45

Dr. Wilkinson two weeks ago. She has a prescription for the pill."

In spite of his efforts to be modern, Jim was shocked.

"My God! How can you be so matter-of-fact about it? What do you think Toni's going to New York for—to screw her head off?"

She hadn't been angry. He didn't want to face the fact that his baby was a woman.

"We had a good talk, Toni and I," Charlene said. "We haven't raised a promiscuous child, Jim, but she's human and sexually aware, like most girls of her age. I don't know that she'll want or need birth-control pills and neither does she. But we agreed that if she falls deeply in love with someone she probably will go to bed with him. Girls feel that way these days. And if she does, I want her protected against some unwanted and binding pregnancy." Charlene's voice broke. "Darling, if our daughter is to be free, then let's set her really free. We're not the watchdogs of her mind or her virginity any more. She has to handle both those things on her own. And I haven't the least doubt that she'll take pride in both and not waste either."

He pulled her to him. "You're so goddamned wonderful. How did you get so wise?"

"Living with a genius, what else?"

Inside, she had not been as calm as she's seemed. It had been traumatic, taking Toni to the gynecologist, almost as though she were urging her toward a careless attitude about sex. But the move was realistic, and realism was something Charlene understood. Wishful thinking was a luxury she'd long since reluctantly abandoned.

And so Toni took her first step toward her own identity fortified by a father so unselfish that he would disappear from her life if that would mean her happiness; calmly,

46

sensibly reassured by a mother who trusted and respected her yet who did not run away from the "new morality."

She caught a glimpse of herself in the taxi's rear-view mirror. Almost as though she were examining some other young woman, she appraised Antoinette Jenkins. She saw a slim, good figure, neither too rounded nor too flat, a delicately featured face, light tan in color, with only a little pink lipstick for accent. She saw thick, long, dark hair smoothed out by man-made straightening and worn classically simple, pulled back and caught with a scarf at the nape. She touched the hair. Did straightening it represent a symbolic withdrawal from the black part of her? Not necessarily. All the curly-haired white girls she knew had the same thing done. It was the fashion in 1969. She'd been doing it for two years now.

"Here we are, lady," the cab driver said. "That'll be twelve-fifty, including the bridge toll."

Tony paid him and added what she hoped was a proper tip. A bellboy came out and opened the door for her and for the first time she set foot on a New York sidewalk. It was still peaceful and quiet. Manhattan had not yet come to life. She stood for a moment looking east toward the river. Then she turned and faced west toward the world of luxury apartments and elegant stores, beautiful people and expensive restaurants. That way lay Fifth Avenue, a magic name with magic images. She'd heard about it all her life, and now she lived near it, just a few blocks from one of the most exciting thoroughfares in the world.

Like a child she hugged herself with happiness. And then, like a grown-up lady, straight-backed and poised, she followed the bellboy with her bags into the lobby of the small hotel.

Chapter 4

Twenty blocks uptown, another woman was up early. Ann Richards stood looking out the window of the big Fifth Avenue cooperative apartment. It had been one of those nights when she'd slept fitfully, alone as always in the king-sized bed, waking three or four times to light a cigarette and smoke it in the darkness. Each time she lit a cigarette in the night she told herself that it was a stupid thing to do. I might drop off to sleep and set the whole room, the whole apartment on fire. So what? Who'd care if I did? Peter undoubtedly would manage to escape from his own room if, indeed, he was spending the night there at all. And aside from her husband, there was no one else in the apartment. The children were all gone. Peter III, now twenty-nine, had married a year ago and already made her a grandmother. Joanne was a fashion editor of *Glamour* with a life and an apartment of her own. Even her "baby," Alan, named for Ann's father, was "batching it" in a brownstone with a twenty-five-year-old contemporary, another copywriter from the same advertising agency where he worked.

As for Peter Richards II, her marriage to him had long

since become a farce, a civilized agreement between two middle-aged people living under the same roof and signing a joint income-tax return. Ann's lip curled. Nothing would irritate her husband more than being thought of as "middle-aged." Peter was fifty-five but he didn't look his age. Nor, Ann thought bitterly, act it. Peter's "little affairs" with other women had started long ago. In the beginning she'd been outraged, had fought back, first with anger and then with all the feminine wiles she possessed. Nothing worked. Peter recognized her for what she was: a beautiful, clever woman with an inordinate amount of social ambition and no capacity for pity, much less love. She had trapped him into marriage when they were very young. He had known it early and regretted it always. He had stood by, putting a good face on things until the children were grown. He'd been discreet about his indiscretions, considerate enough not to embarrass his family publicly. But for the past three years, ever since Alan left home, Peter had made no effort to conceal either his double life or his antipathy for the selfish woman he'd married. There were many nights when he did not come home at all. And on those he did, he worked in his library and retired to his own room with scarcely more than a dozen words exchanged between them.

Looking down on Fifth Avenue where life slowly began to stir, Ann thought for the thousandth time that Peter had been grossly unfair to her. He hadn't *had* to marry her. It was his own upper-middle-class code that had demanded it when he found, in that quaint, old-fashioned phrase, that he'd "deflowered" a virgin. How different people were back in 1936! All right, she'd planned it that way, relying on the conscience of a well-brought-up young man like Peter Richards to make her "an honest woman." But she knew she'd be good for him. She came of a good background herself, she'd fitted in with his stuffy parents, she'd given him three beautiful children and entertained charmingly to further his career. She had never really been madly in love with him nor, she supposed, he with her. But for a while they'd been reasonably content. Peter had always been restless, but until the filthy business with Charlene he'd never expressed open disdain for his wife.

Charlene. Ann lit a cigarette. ("For God's sake, Ann, if you must smoke, don't smoke before breakfast!" Dr. McClean had said. "To hell with you, Doctor," she'd thought as she meekly agreed that one cigarette before breakfast was worse than ten after.) She inhaled deeply now and thought about her sister's monstrous behavior. It had been more than twenty years, believe it or not, since Elizabeth had called to tell her that Charlene was deeply in love with that Negro and planned to marry him.

Ann could still remember the actual nausea that swept over her as she heard her mother's calm, quiet voice. Ann knew that Charlene had been going out with Jim Jenkins and she'd written scathing letters to Elizabeth about it. She could recall some of them even now.

"Mother, you must know the popular conception about the virility of these black bucks," Ann had written. "No doubt Charlene knows it too, though she's only seventeen. If she's having an affair with this boy, you must break it up! It's indecent!"

Elizabeth had replied in anger.

"You are thirteen years older than your sister and it's been years since you've seen her. But I am amazed, horrified, Ann, that you would even suggest that Charlene's love for Jim is only sexual! If you could see them together, you would know that this is no reckless girl titillated by stupid stories of black male prowess! She is a beautiful person, your sister. And so is the boy she loves. Your suggestions make me quite ill. I'm terribly disappointed in you, Ann. I don't know where this romance is going to lead, but I assure you it *is* a romance and not the passionate experiment you suggest."

Ann had not replied. She was quite convinced that she had correctly diagnosed the attraction. It had to be the only possible explanation for Charlene's attraction to a Negro. Elizabeth was blind about Charlene. Always had been. She'd loved her late baby much more than she'd loved her first child. It was Daddy who loved me, Ann thought. I'll never forgive Mother for leaving him and depriving me of my father. There was a parallel in her own life. Peter Richards had his faults but he loved his children and they him. As long as she lived she would never let them be without him.

When the letter came, a year later, announcing that Charlene and Jim were to be married, Ann knew for certain that Charlene must be pregnant. Again she wrote to Elizabeth, trying to sound more concerned than outraged.

"I'm sure there can be only one possible reason why you would allow this marriage. If it is what I believe it must be, I'm more than willing to help. Send Charlene to New York. There are doctors here who perform safe abortions, and I'll see that it's taken care of. She *is* pregnant, of course, isn't she?"

"This time there was no letter in return. Just a telegram with one word: "No." Signed: "Mother."

No, what? Ann had wondered. No, she won't consent to an abortion? Or: No, Charlene isn't pregnant?

After that there was silence from the West Coast. The wedding invitation arrived and was thrown away unanswered. Ann told no one what was going on. She waited, instead, for a birth announcement. But it was two years before a calling card with the names Mr. and Mrs. James Jenkins arrived. Attached to it was a smaller card that said: "Antoinette Jenkins, August 9, 1951. Six pounds, four ounces."

Ann couldn't believe it. She was sure that Charlene must have had a baby more than a year before. Why else would she have married this man? But the evidence was there. Charlene was married more than a year before her pregnancy. The realization shook Ann. It simply was not possible that any decent white girl in her right mind would marry a Negro unless she was forced to. Those things happened only at the lowest level of society, to ignorant, immoral people. They didn't happen to the daughter of a man who'd once been a respected government official and a woman whose father had been a Harvard professor! Most of all, they did not happen to the sister of Ann Richards.

For the first time she told Peter the whole story. She had not even mentioned Charlene's "romance" or marriage before. She was too ashamed. But now she had to share her horror with someone and Peter was all she had. His response infuriated her almost as much as her sister's actions.

"Interesting," Peter had said calmly. "Charley always knew what she wanted, even when she was a little kid. More power to her. She must be terribly in love."

"Interesting!" Ann's voice was a scream. "Is that all you have to say? Do you realize what I'm telling you, Peter? We have a Negro for a brother-in-law and a mulatto for a niece!"

"I'm sure we'll survive."

She stared at him in disbelief. "Are you insane? Can you imagine what it would be like if this got out?"

"No," Peter said. "What would it be like?"

"We'd be ostracized, that's all! Our friends would think we were trash!"

"Correction. *Your* friends. Mine would think it was

52

none of their damned business or ours. An opinion, incidentally, with which I wholeheartedly agree."

Furiously Ann turned away from him, then wheeled around. "I believe you're *glad* this happened! You like nothing better than to see me humiliated! God knows, you've managed it often enough! Well, let me tell you one thing, Peter Richards, if you mention one word of this to anyone I'll kill you!"

He shrugged. "I don't gossip, Ann."

"What have you ever had to gossip *about?*"

Suddenly he was angry. "Nothing much. Just a woman who hates her own mother. A very proper lady who's insanely jealous of her own sister. A stifling, selfish, bigoted matriarch whose own children can't wait to move away from her."

She slapped him hard across the face.

"You!" she said. "How dare you? You with your dirty little affairs, your damned Westchester country club superiority! It's out in the open at last, isn't it? We hate each other. Good. I'm glad we know where we stand. Too bad the wonderful, noble Charlene was only a child when you and I met. Otherwise you could have married *her* since you admire her so much!" Ann was verging on hysteria. "And one more thing. My children are to know nothing of all this. As far as I'm concerned, I don't have a sister with no sense of rightness or a fatuous, unrealistic mother who's always been a ridiculous romantic!"

He had felt sorry for her. Even then, pity was all he had left. She had been so greedy, so demanding, so self-involved all these years. She had given him no tenderness. She had not led him gently into a good life, she had pushed him into what she wanted: a highly successful career, money for big apartments and private schools and trips to Europe. He hadn't needed it, hadn't wanted it. Her ravings about Charlene and Elizabeth had been irra-

53

tional but they held a great deal of truth. He admired Elizabeth more than anyone he knew. She'd endured so much and kept her serenity along with her strength of will. She was not bitter in spite of the betrayals of her life. And she had taught Charlene to be like her. Peter was sure of that. I wish Charley *had* been older, he thought. She had grown into a beautiful, gentle, loving woman.

Ann, he supposed, was like her father, who was dead before Peter Richards came into the picture. From what he'd heard later of Alan Whitman from men who had known him, he had been a brilliant man who failed, a frightened drunkard and a psychotic. Peter could imagine the idealized image Ann retained of the father who worshipped her, and how she sought unconsciously to vindicate him for his ineffectiveness as a husband, a parent and a man. She would be strong where he was weak, just as she would be conventional and defensive where Elizabeth was humane and vulnerable. Poor Ann, he'd thought then, eighteen years ago. She's made herself impossible to love.

She stood alone at her window now, steeped in secret self-pity. They had never understood her, none of them. They had all turned away from her. Peter to his own disgusting pursuits, the children to their own world. She saw them rarely, only when their consciences dictated "duty calls." She really had no family, not here or in California. And that was not her fault either. When Tony was killed (was if fifteen, sixteen years ago?) and Elizabeth had had a stroke, she had been too overcome to do anything. What had her sister expected?

She wanted no further contact with Charlene or Elizabeth. When Elizabeth did die, sometime in the future, she supposed Charlene would inform her. It wouldn't matter. For Ann, they hadn't lived for a long time. She wondered whether Charlene had had more babies to share that peculiar household with, what was her name, oh yes, "Antoinette." Even that was vulgar and overblown. Children should have simple, unpretentious names, reminiscent of other family members. She'd named her own that way: Peter for his father, Joanne for her mother-in-law, Alan for her own beloved father who was so misunderstood and badly used.

Ann did not connect "Antoinette" with "Tony," the name of Elizabeth's second husband. She simply reasoned that with a surname like Jenkins, Charlene had reached for something unusual. It might have been better, Ann thought nastily, to have called her Jemima. Jemima Jenkins. At least it would be euphonious. And fitting.

She rang for coffee. It took that slovenly girl forever to arrive with it and then she'd spilled it on the tray. Ann was too annoyed to reprimand her. It was hopeless trying to get help these days. Even colored girls were scarce and so uppity one hardly dared to correct them.

Damn them all, she thought, sipping the lukewarm liquid. Who needs them?

She wasn't sure whether she meant servants or families. Probably both.

Peter Richards slit open the neatly typed envelope marked "Personal." His secretary had long since learned not to open personal mail or to inquire about the "business affiliations" of women who called. He smiled. The disapproving Mrs. Myers would have been surprised to know that this letter carried the name and return address of his mother-in-law. For that matter, a letter from her came as a surprise to him, too, for different reasons.

He read Elizabeth's words carefully, remembering her vividly after all these years, trying to imagine her now, much older, an invalid in a wheelchair. He would bet that

55

only her legs didn't work. She was sixty-four but the spirit was still young, the mind lively and the humor delightfully apparent. Elizabeth would not be one for self-pity because of her handicap or querulous because of her advancing age. It was impossible to think of her as an old lady. She would never be old, Peter thought. Not if she reached ninety. He had not seen her since Tony's death when the stroke felled her but the words on the paper in front of him brought her back as clearly as though they'd met yesterday.

"Dear Peter," she wrote. "They do say that old age has few compensations, but one of them, I've found, is the license to meddle, acquired through the sheer right of survival. I try not to use it often, this 'meddler's license' of mine, but now and then, on a beautiful morning such as this one, I indulge myself. I am on my terrace, greedily soaking up a view that I pretend belongs only to me. My typewriter (infinitely more portable than I!) has been brought out and I'm glad I've not forgotten how to use it. Otherwise, you might mistakenly feel sorry for the somewhat spidery handwriting that's more revealing than all those damned candles they keep putting on my birthday cakes!

"But enough of this rambling. There's a very real purpose to this letter, the first one I've ever written to you. It is also, I think, the first favor I've ever asked of you. And if you find it impossible to grant, believe me, I shall understand.

"It is simply this: Charlene and Jim's daughter Antoinette has arrived in New York to study at the Parsons School of fashion design, and I am uneasy thinking of her there all alone, knowing no one in that big, wonderful but uncaring city. She is only eighteen, Peter. A very mature and sensitive eighteen, to be sure, but only eighteen nonetheless.

56

"No need to go into the family problems. You know Ann's attitude toward her sister's marriage and toward her sister's child. No need to tell you, either, how much I regret the estrangement for her sake as well as ours. But so be it. I accept her views even if I have difficulty understanding them and absolutely no ability to agree with them. There is no bitterness on this side of the world. A little sadness, of course. A flicker of wishful thinking, perhaps. But no real hope that at her age Ann will rethink her attitudes.

"You, Peter, may not share Ann's views. I am only guessing, of course. But it is an educated guess based on knowing you as you were, kind, honorable and loving. So I turn to you with a request. Over Charlene's silent but understandable doubts, I have given Antoinette your and Ann's address, (and your office one as well) just in case some emergency arises that needs handling before her parents can get there. I doubt that she will need it. Or, knowing a little of the story, that she would use it even if she did. But I'd feel more secure if *you* knew where *she* was. Perhaps, if you find it in your heart and do not consider it disloyal to Ann, you might give Antoinette a call one of these days. Just to see that she's all right. Just to let her know that someone is at hand if if she needs help. Just—and here's the real truth—to reassure a meddlesome grandmother that all is well.

"This is between us, needless to say. One of the impulses for which I've always been notorious. If, for any one of a hundred reasons, you think it wiser not to call, that will be easy for me to understand. To be honest, I don't know how such a call would be received by Antoinette. But my faith in her is total and her understanding is quite extraordinary in one so young. I think she would welcome a gesture of friendliness from you. I've spoken of

57

you often to her, always glowingly, and of her three older cousins whom she does not remember, of course. They must be wonderful children, Peter, for whatever my differences of opinion with Ann might be, I haven't a qualm about her ability to raise them properly nor about yours to love them deeply. Children indeed! They must be grown up, perhaps married by now. Where *have* the years gone?

"This letter, perhaps a foolish one, needs no answer, my dear. If it is a presumptuous one, I ask your forgiveness. It is not my intent to place you in an awkward position by asking you to say nothing to Ann, but I do ask that. She would be offended, I fear. Whereas you, my friend, will be understanding.

"My love to you, Peter. And my admiration.

"Elizabeth"

She enclosed a slip of paper with Antoinette Jenkins' address and the notation that even if she moved she could always be located through the school.

Peter read the letter again. It was so clearly Elizabeth. Concerned but not alarmed. Careful not to impose. Deftly giving him a way out if he chose not to make himself known to a child he'd seen only once, sixteen years ago. A girl irrationally resented by his wife. His mind lingered affectionately on Elizabeth. She knew nothing of his life with Ann, but she undoubtedly guessed a great deal. His mother-in-law saw through her daughter long before he did. It took me a few years to see Ann clearly, he thought, but Elizabeth has always known what an uncompassionate, selfish woman Mrs. Peter Richards really is. He had stayed married to her for more than thirty years. More than half of his life. In all the superficial things she was a perfect wife, including, as Elizabeth had said, the "proper" rearing of their children. He was grateful to her for that. They'd turned out well, all of them. But they didn't love Ann. They gave her the respect she demanded but not the depth of feeling she had not earned.

He thought often these days of asking for a divorce, as he had several times before. At fifty-five he had a right to enjoy whatever time was left. But Ann would continue to fight it. Even if he won, she'd ruin him financially. He wouldn't even mind that so much if there was someone he wanted to marry. But there wasn't. Just an endless procession of attractive, ego-building women who came and went in his life. To all intents and purposes he was as free as he needed to be. It was easier to drift.

Elizabeth would never understand such compromise, such a waste of lives. She'd always been a fighter, even against the most impossible odds. Ann had called her a "ridiculous romantic." Even after all these years he could hear the hysterical denunciation brought on by the birth of the child whom he was now being asked to meet.

I can't do it, Peter thought. I'd do anything for Elizabeth except this. It would only mean being snubbed by an eighteen-year-old, justly snubbed. Elizabeth must be wrong. If Antoinette knows her aunt's feelings, as she obviously does, how could she possibly suppose that her uncle by marriage did not share them? She'd despise me, and what's the point of putting either of us through that? If she's in trouble, Peter told himself, she'll call us. He hoped she'd be wise enough to use the office number if she needed help. God knows what kind of reception she'd get if she appealed to Ann. The idea made him uncomfortable. He'd probably never even know if Antoinette phoned the house.

Not very proud of himself, Peter put the letter in his desk drawer. He should answer it immediately, even though Elizabeth had considerately said that wasn't necessary. But what could he say? That he didn't believe his niece would welcome a call from him? He wasn't sure of that, any more than Elizabeth was. No, his reluctance was deeper. Something more like shame. He admitted to himself that he carried a burden of guilt for the severing of the relationship between the Richards family and Ann's own. He should have taken a stronger stand with his wife from the beginning, insisting that she accept her sister's husband and child and her mother's unselfish approval of them. Instead he'd done what was easier: resorted to sarcasm and then retreated. It was the way he faced every unpleasant situation with Ann. How could he account to this young girl for his spinelessness? How could she understand that he lived with a woman he detested, that he had fallen into a kind of hopeless lethargy about his life? At her age, it was all ahead, glowing and beautiful. She'd have nothing to compare his life with. He was certain that her own had been lived in an atmosphere of love and compatibility.

Repelled by his own weakness, he reached for the phone, and then drew back. Calling Antoinette was unthinkable. Intruding himself into her life after all these years of silence was insulting. She would feel scorn for a man who knuckled under to his wife's unconscionable behavior. But she did not really know her aunt. She could not understand or forgive as Elizabeth, with her years of wisdom, did. No. The one thing he would not do would be to see the contempt he felt for himself reflected in the face of this child.

The same self-hatred made it impossible for him to answer Elizabeth's letter. Her generous feeling about him was an unintended reproach and he did not know what to say in reply. I'll answer in a few days, he thought. I owe her that. I must give her reassurance that I'll do anything in my power to help her granddaughter if the need arises, even if I can't bring myself to seek out Antoinette. But I'll wait until I feel less emotional about it. I want to be able to write as easily and lovingly as she did. God, I wish I were half as much a man as Elizabeth is a woman!

Chapter 5

Any doubts Toni might have had about coming to Parsons, doubts that were tied up with anxiety about leaving home and a natural insecurity about her own talents, disappeared almost the first day she entered school. There was an attitude of seriousness overlaid with the irresistible attraction of young people dedicated to learning the trade of their choice. They shared, teachers and pupils alike, a common goal: a love of fashion and a respect for it and for all those who had made it not only a profession but a very special kind of art form.

All her life Toni had never had trouble making friends. She truly loved people and expected nothing but good from them. For the most part, they had always responded in kind. Nadine Thompson, so long ago, had been one of the rare exceptions. Except for Nadine and one or two others like her, Toni had enjoyed affection. It came bouncing back at her from all ages and both sexes, and it was as true in New York as it had been in Pasadena.

Admittedly the young people with whom she was thrown into contact were a great deal more sophisticated than those she'd left behind. They didn't *look* all that different in the international uniform of 1969, the jeans and shirts and sweaters of a sartorially unisex world. But they were much wiser in the ways of life, and most were older than Toni.

The girls were more openly relaxed about sex, the discussion of it as well as the performance. There was an easy acceptance of homosexuality, an area with which Toni had had almost no contact and which was pervasive in her new group. She did not recoil from it. Quite the contrary. She admired the freedom of these young men and women, most of whom she felt put her modest talents to shame. They were amusing companions, quick-witted and friendly to this newcomer in whom they sensed understanding and acceptance.

There were also a number of black students of both sexes and Toni felt an unexpected warmth toward them and something close to pride in the matter-of-fact way in which they were absorbed into the whole. They did not know, no one did, that she shared part of herself with them. In those few weeks there had been no reason to discuss race or religion. She wondered what she would have said had the question come up and was secretly glad that there'd been no need to openly "choose." Not yet, anyway. Not until she sorted out her own ambivalent feelings.

She made good progress in her work. Her sketching quickly improved and she spent many evenings in her hotel room working over her drawings and doing the endless research that was an important part of her training. She was not lonely and she had made two very special friends, Sarah Parkinson and Amy Greenberg, with whom she spent much of her free time. Sarah and Amy shared an apartment on Christopher Street in Greenwich Village with a model, Connie Heller. Connie worked on Seventh

Avenue and was "engaged" to a dress salesman. She'd soon be moving out to live with him.

"Are they getting married?" Toni asked. Her own question amused her. Only a few weeks ago she would have prefaced the query with "when." How quickly she'd become a part of this casual new world, this easy acceptance of sexual freedom, though she could not yet apply it to herself. The middle-class virtues so strongly but subtly ingrained did not disappear overnight. She wondered whether she would ever be able to live, unmarried, with a man and feel no guilt.

"Who knows?" Sarah said in answer to her spoken question. "If they find they can stand each other day and night, maybe they'll decide to make it legal. Meantime, Amy and I have some practical considerations, like one-third of a rent bill. To say nothing of Con Edison, Ma Bell and the friendly neighborhood wine merchant. All of which brings me to the point. How would you feel about moving into Christopher Street?"

There was only a second's hesitation on Toni's part. Sharing an apartment, standard practice among most of the students, would make her feel more as though she belonged. It would even reduce the considerable amount of money it cost Jim to keep her in New York, though he assured her that was no problem. Best of all, she really liked these two girls.

"I'd love it!" she said. "How soon may I come?"

"Well, Connie leaves next week. So anytime after that." Amy grinned. "Hey, I'm glad you want to. We'll really get to know each other now."

"There's one thing about me you should know before I move in," Toni said. She paused, thinking of her father's advice and recognizing in that instant that she couldn't follow it. "I'm half black. My father is a Negro."

Baldly. Just like that. No explanations of the kind of

man Jim Jenkins was. No cop-out about his intelligence or success or sensitivity. They—and whomever else she told in time to come—would have to take the fact straight and without apologies. She felt relief as she said it. It was more than being honest with them; it was being honest with herself.

Amy spoke first. "So what else is new?"

But, looking very serious, Sarah held up her hand. "Hold it," she said. "This could be a problem."

The others looked at her curiously. Toni felt the bitter taste of disappointment mingled with sadness. I've dipped my toe into the waters of reality and found them cold.

"What the hell are you talking about?" Amy said.

Sarah kept a straight face. "I'm only thinking of Mr. Gonzales, the super in our building. He moved his family all the way downtown to get away from those lousy minorities. Our friends won't mind, but José will pee in his Puerto Rican pants."

For a second Toni thought she was serious. But then Amy began to laugh and Sarah joined her. They broke up, looking at Toni's bewildered face.

"You dope," Amy said. "Jesus, Sarah, for a minute we both thought you were for real!"

Sarah was weak with laughter. "If you two could have seen your faces," she gasped. "Honest to God, Toni, did you really think you were telling us something important?"

Toni managed a smile. "I didn't know," she said quietly. "You see, I never really had to tell anybody before."

Suddenly her friends sobered.

"Look," Amy said, "you don't think it's anything to be ashamed of, do you? You're not hung up about it, are you? Because if you are, you're off base. This is 1969, kiddo. Lincoln's proclamation was effective a hundred and six years ago. We're all free and equal, even if the

65

news hasn't quite had time to reach the inner recesses of the bayou country."

"I know what's wrong," Sarah said. "She thought she was only going to have Thursday afternoon off and we wouldn't give her carfare."

It was as though some terrible weight had slipped from Toni's shoulders. Jim was wrong. Old-fashioned. Out of touch with the way people thought today. Today-people could make jokes about blackness. Just as they could kid about Jews and Poles and Italians and Puerto Ricans, unselfconsciously, even affectionately. She felt suddenly free and a little ridiculous, as thought she'd lived all these years with a problem that didn't exist.

That night, Toni called home and told her family she was moving into an apartment with two girls from school.

The Jenkinses responded with predictable questions.

"What girls?" Jim demanded.

"Nice ones, Daddy. Sarah Parkinson's twenty-one and Amy Greenberg's twenty-three. Sarah comes from somewhere in the South and Amy's family lives in the Bronx. They had a third roommate but she's moving out . . . to get married."

Her father was quiet for a moment. Then he said, "Do they know all about you, honey?"

Toni bristled. "Know what?" she said, understanding exactly what he meant. "I've told them about Mommy and you, if that's what you mean. And they were surprised that I thought it was important enough to mention." Her voice softened. "I'm sorry I couldn't do as you asked, Daddy. But I was right. People couldn't care less."

"One encounter does not a lifetime make," was all he said. "Your mother's on the extension."

Charlene seemed delighted with the news. She'd never liked the idea of Toni living alone in New York. It was too dangerous. "What's the apartment like, darling?"

Toni described it glowingly.

"Sounds wonderful," Charlene said. "But is the Village okay as a location? I mean, you read some pretty scary things about what goes on there."

"Mother! Christopher is a *nice* street! Not like Eighth Street with all the freaks and hookers."

In spite of herself Charlene was startled. Toni had been gone less than two months and already she sounded very worldly, spouting words like "hookers." She started to say just that and then curbed the impulse. What did they expect? That Toni would remain the innocent she'd been in Pasadena? Hadn't it been Charlene herself who had reluctantly but sensibly prepared her daughter for a new and different kind of world?

As though she read her mother's mind, Toni spoke softly into the phone. "Don't worry, Mom. I still have the prescription. Unfilled."

They chatted for a few more minutes and then hung up with their usual protestations of love and promises to keep in constant touch. Toni gave them the new address and phone number and said she would call again as soon as she was settled. Just before he put the receiver down, Jim asked one more question.

"You are still planning to come home for Christmas, aren't you?"

"Of course. Why on earth not?"

"No reason. I just wanted to make sure. I'll send you your ticket. We miss you, baby."

"I miss you, too. All of you. Not to worry now. Okay?"

"Okay," they said in unison.

When they hung up, Charlene and Jim looked at each other wordlessly.

"You don't like it, do you?" Charlene said.

"It's not that I don't like it. I'm glad she's made

67

friends. I wasn't any happier than you about her living all alone in New York."

"Then what is it, darling? You look so upset. I wish we knew a little more about Sarah and Amy, but Toni has always had a good instinct for people. I'm sure they're nice girls. Look at the way they accepted something that we all thought could be a problem."

"That's just the point," Jim said. "It was too easy. It's filled her with false confidence. She thinks everybody will react the way her new friends have."

"What makes you so sure they won't, Jim? Toni is a charming, attractive young woman. Why shouldn't the world accept her that way? Why shouldn't she expect it to?"

He shook his head. "She's eighteen years old and starry-eyed and drunk with success because she's finally admitted her blackness and two very advanced-thinking young women made nothing of it. That's no damned test, Charley! She hasn't even begun to find out what bastards people can be. She's taking one lucky break as a sign that no problem exists."

"I really don't understand you. Would you have preferred it if those girls had rejected her and broken her heart?"

"Maybe," he said, "I'd rather have her heart cracked now by her rommates than smashed later by somebody more important." He looked at his wife. "In case part of that conversation confused you tonight, Toni was telling me that she couldn't keep a promise I asked her to make. I asked her not to tell anyone, ever, that she had Negro blood."

"Jim! How could you? You know how Toni adores you!"

"Of course I know. That has nothing to do with it. It's

her future I'm concerned about. What's filial loyalty compared to her chances for a good, uncomplicated life?"

Charlene was sad and angry all at the same time. She took his head between her hands and said, "Darling, why are you so ashamed of your color? I'm not. Toni's not."

He buried his face between her breasts.

"It's not shame, Charley. It's cold, unemotional, brutal reality. Mixed, I guess, with a hell of a lot of guilt."

She held him tightly. "You're wrong, you know."

"Am I? God in heaven I hope so! I want to be wrong more than I've ever wanted anything in my life."

When she moved into Christopher Street, the apartment seemed a good deal less attractive than she remembered it from her previous visits. In the broad light of day it had a shoddy, uncared-for look. The furniture was cheap and showed evidence of many parties: indelible rings on wood surfaces left by too many unheeded, dripping glasses; cigarette burns in the slipcovers and on the surface of the ugly broadloom rug in the living room. The place was not even clean. A thin film of dust covered everything, and the windows, Toni guessed, could not have been washed since the girls moved in two years before.

She had only been there at night before, and then the room had always been full of people. She felt something close to dismay as she looked around her, comparing it to the spotlessness of her mother's house. But almost immediately she took herself to task for her "small-town values." These details of housekeeping were unimportant. What mattered was that she had joined the mainstream. No more the place-for-everything-and-everything-in-its-place school of thought.

Sarah, who had helped her move her clothes, watched closely as Toni surveyed the room.

"Crummy, huh?"

Toni overprotested. "Oh no! Not at all! It's a terrific apartment!"

"Amy and I are not what you'd call great house-keepers. I never had to do anything at home, so I can't get in the habit. And Amy is on a rebellion trip against her Bronx-Jewish mother, who, when she isn't making chicken soup, is scrubbing the same floor she scrubbed yesterday." Sarah laughed. "To each his own, sez I. Feel free to do your own thing, Toni. If you want to redecorate, be our guest."

"Don't be silly. Which is my room?"

Her bedroom was the smallest of the three. Like the rest of the apartment, it begged for the tender ministrations of a cleaning woman. Balls of dust rolled in the corners, and the dirty windows almost, but not quite, disguised a view of the brick wall of the apartment next door.

"Tell you the truth," Sarah said, "this was my pad before. Last one in gets the lousiest room. When Connie left I took hers. Amy and I thought you'd understand."

"Sure. Of course. It makes sense."

"Anyway, this one at least has its own john. Amy and I have to share the other one."

"It's fine, Sarah. Really it is. I'll get some curtains and a spread and things and it'll be perfect."

"Of course there's only a stall shower. If you want a tub you have to take it in the other loo."

Why is she sounding so defensive? Toni wondered. Are they sorry they asked me to move in? It wasn't like Sarah to sound so uptight about things. She probably thinks I'm a spoiled brat, Toni decided. Maybe I am, at that.

"I love it all, Sarah. You can't imagine how glad I am to get out of that old ladies' home! And I'm grateful to you and Amy for letting me share. Just tell me what my duties are and I'll follow orders."

70

"Duties?"

Toni felt stupid. "I thought maybe you had a rotating system. Like one week I cook and you and Amy clean up, and the next week . . ." Her voice trailed off. She grinned. "No system, right?"

"Right. No system. It's not Pasadena, pal. We have more interesting things to do than worry about who's in charge of the Brillo pad next Thursday."

"Sarah, don't you want me here?" Toni couldn't keep from asking. Her friend was acting so strangely, almost hostile. "You act like something's bothering you."

"I didn't think it showed."

Toni didn't answer.

"Look. I like you a lot. But I am a little nervous about you being here. I don't know whether it's your scene. Hell, I'm not even sure it's mine."

Toni said nothing.

"Amy's hell-bent on being a liberated woman." Sarah said. "I'm not against that, God knows. So am I. But she overdoes it. Like this place. Housework is slavery for women, so Amy refuses to do it and I can't handle it alone, so the joint's a pigpen. And the people she invites. Jesus! I don't care how people live, but I'm up to here with faggots and black-leather-jacket horny guys and dikes."

"Is Amy a lesbian?"

"Only if the mood strikes her. She swings all ways. It's her business, but let's face it, Toni, I'm not sure you're ready for this. Look, I'm not even sure that to Amy you're not some sort of liberation symbol, too. The 'token nigger,' I think it's called."

Toni was visibly shaken. "But I thought you two were such good friends. If you hate all this so much, why do you stay?"

"It's cheap and handy and I can tune out. I'm used to it, and don't think Amy's a terrible person, in spite of what I've said. She's mixed up. She should be with a shrink. I can handle it but I don't know whether a nice, naïve kid like you should be part of this number."

"I still don't understand," Toni said. "You thought it was such a good idea in the beginning. And as for Amy using me as the 'token nigger,' she didn't even know about that until after you two had made the offer."

"Touché. Right on both counts. I've had second thoughts. And as far as the black thing goes, Amy's playing it up big. Like she's proud of sharing her pad with a colored girl. More proof of how 'liberated' she is." Sarah turned away. "I don't mean to hurt you, Toni. I just thought you should know it all. You're still free to choose."

There it is again, Toni. Choose. Decide. Life isn't an endless compromise; it's constant, nagging choices. And nothing's really simple and clear-cut. It's never just a matter of things being black or white. In spite of her anxiety she smiled at her own unconscious choice of words.

"What's so funny?" Sarah asked.

"Nothing. Not a thing. I'm going to stay, Sarah. I appreciate all the warnings, but it's about time I found out about all kinds of people."

"Fine. As long as you know what you're doing. You can always pretend you're Margaret Mead studying the natives."

The little joke cleared the air.

"Come on, I'll help you unpack," Sarah said. "It'll probably work out. Amy's really okay and she does like you. She just gets carried away."

"You're nice, Sarah."

"Don't run *that* past the Gallup poll."

In spite of some awkward moments in the next few weeks, the apartment sharing worked out pretty well. Toni never quite adjusted to the sloppiness, but she kept her reactions to herself, settling for keeping her own room in immaculate order, decorating it attractively with pink-and-white toile bedspread and curtains, with new white lamps and a wicker desk with a chair pad covered in the same fabric. She used fashion prints on the walls and re-painted the small bathroom herself. In a rent-controlled building, one didn't ask for a new paint job. She spent a good deal of time in this room, for she was alone quite often in the evenings. Amy and Sarah went out on dates several nights week. Frequently, they offered to "fix up" Toni with a blind date, but she shied away from it. She had seen their dates, bearded, long-haired young men in dungarees. She had nothing against them. She just wasn't ready for this breed of unwashed, unkempt male whose vocabulary seemed to consist entirely of four-letter words.

It troubled her that she didn't fit in. She concluded that she must be a terrible prude, though she made every effort to disguise it. When the girls had parties, she joined, but she stayed as much as possible in the background, smiling warmly at everyone, trying to make conversation and feeling like an outsider. It was not that she disapproved. It was as though she was being asked to run before she learned to walk.

The worst times were when one of her roommates—usually Amy—decided to show off Toni's bedroom.

"Hey, come look at the nursery!" Amy would announce, and ten or twelve people would crowd into the doorway of her small bedroom, making jokes about the fairy-tale decor.

"How about that?" Amy would say. "*House & Garden's* coming up next week to take pictures. Going to do a story on 'The Life of a New York Fashion Student.'

We're planning to blindfold the editors on their way through the living room."

There was a lot of good-natured laughter, but Toni found herself blushing. Amy didn't mean to be cruel, she told herself. The others didn't either. Not even the big, bearded blond man who said, "You got a pea under that mattress, Princess?"

Amy had responded quickly. "No, when she's gotta pee she has her own john."

Toni thought it was all crude and childish but she said nothing. They were high on marijuana and she was stone sober. It made a difference. Maybe, Toni thought, I should try that. Maybe I could relax and feel part of all this determined hilarity. She tried it on one rare evening when just the three of them were at home. Gingerly puffing the cigarette, she felt no reaction whatsoever.

"Nothing happens," she said after a few puffs. "I don't feel any different."

"Then why bother?" Sarah asked.

"It takes practice," Amy insisted. "You're not even inhaling. Look. Like this." She took a few slow, deep drags.

Toni tried again with the same lack of result.

"I guess it's not my bag," she said finally, handing the cigarette back.

"What *is* your bag?" Amy had asked, not unkindly but with curiosity. "You're sensational-looking but you don't date, much less sleep around. You don't drink or smoke. You don't seem to identify with the troops who come here. I've never heard you say anything stronger than 'damn' or 'hell.' What's your hang-up, Toni? Jesus, you must come from some repressive background! What's got you in knots, the race thing?"

Sarah cut in. "For Christ's sake, Amy, leave her alone. Knock off the curbstone analysis! Does everybody in the world need to be like you?"

Amy laughed. "They not only don't *need* to, but God help 'em if they *are*."

"I'm sorry," Toni said. "Maybe I don't belong here. I don't want to be a downer."

"Hey, did you hear that, Sarah? There's hope! She's beginning to pick up the lingo!" Amy looked suddenly young and defenseless. "Toni, you do belong here. We need you a helluva lot more than you need us. I'd almost forgotten there were people like you. You are what is known as a good influence. I'm sorry I sounded off. Maybe I envy you. You're the most secure person I've ever known. You must have had a great bringing up. At least you don't have to act like a show-off and the village idiot the way I do. End of speech. Good night, all."

She disappeared abruptly into her room, leaving Sarah and Toni staring at each other.

"I've never heard Amy talk like that," Toni said.

"Neither have I, and I've known her a lot longer. She's not like us, Toni. I don't think she's used to people from a so-called 'better class.' "

"Tell me about your family, Sarah. You never have."

"Not much to tell. Mother died when I was seven. Father remarried her best friend, nice lady, two years later. I went to school in Baltimore, where we lived. Dad's a successful attorney. The family's kind of social, but I didn't want the finishing school and the deb party, so I wangled permission to come up here. I like it okay. Amy was my first friend at Parsons and we just kind of drifted into sharing the apartment. In my way I guess I'm as much of a rebel as she. Only I'm rebelling against too much upper-class snobbishness and she's fighting an overdose of second-generation Jewishness. In her way she's thumbing her nose at an even stricter set of rules than I am. But we're both disenchanted with our parents' world. That's

75

where you have it over us. You're not. Crazy, isn't it? Amy and I both come from so-called 'conventional' families and yours is much more offbeat. Yet you're the adjusted one and we're floundering."

"Don't you ever see any of your old friends?"

"Now and then," Sarah said. "And I do go out with one guy whose father is a friend of my dad's. I'm really hung up on him. You haven't met him yet because he doesn't dig this scene. Usually, I see him outside, but he's coming to the party here Saturday night, so you'll meet him. I think he just may be the first one of our friends you'll really take to. He's kind of like you, Toni, fun, but feet on the ground. By the way, we've been sleeping together for a year."

Toni knew better than to ask whether Sarah was going to marry him. She was sure that Sarah didn't know the answer herself.

Toni lay awake for a long while that night thinking about Sarah and Amy and herself. She had no feeling, as Sarah had once suggested, that Amy was sniggering behind her back or using her as evidence of broadmindedness. Amy was really kind and sensitive in spite of her brash behavior. It was Sarah who was frantic under that cool surface. She had sounded a little superior, a touch condescending tonight when she talked about their roommate, but Toni realized that both girls were less secure than she. Amy had unerringly put her finger on it when she said that their need for her was greater than hers for them.

The awareness did not fill her with any particular happiness. On the contrary, she felt depressed. Her friends were as lost as she. Perhaps more lost. Once again she had gravitated toward the weak, just as she had done with Karen.

76

"You're crazy," she told herself. "Either that or you're a smug, conceited fool."

Both accusations were unjust and untrue. She was simply a deceptively strong person, a magnet for those who only pretended to be made of steel.

Chapter 6

The party on Saturday night was to celebrate the beginning of the Christmas holidays, and Sarah and Amy had invited about forty people, most of them Parsons students. They had considerately asked Toni whether there was anyone special she'd like to have, but she smiled and shook her head. In almost four months she hadn't made any close friends except her roommates. She had been on a few dates with boys at school, despite Amy's accusations to the contrary, but she never saw them socially more than once.

Two of them had expected her to go to bed with them immediately and were angry when she declined. The other had been sweet, but had spent most of the evening telling her about the older man with whom he was madly in love.

And so, once again, she found herself among a noisy, hilarious roomful of people, most of whom she knew slightly from school or from previous parties. They really bore me, Toni thought. They're trying so hard to be everything they read in books and see in films, the highly vocal, angry generation of the late sixties, prattling of defecting before the Army gets them, damning the government and Vietnam, screaming about the liberation of blacks and females. And talking sex, sex, sex, like lewd children.

She felt more mature than any of them. What did they know about discrimination, most of them? Even less, Toni thought mirthlessly, than she. As for sex, they knew only the physical coupling. To them it was liberation, not love, defiance instead of tenderness.

I wish I could go into my room and shut the door, Toni thought, knowing she dared not and wondering why she couldn't. These people subscribed to "doing your own thing." If hers was retreating from a scene that wearied her, why in hell shouldn't she do it? My damned good manners, she answered herself. My bloody polite upbringing. You don't just walk out on a party of which you're supposed to be a co-hostess. It's not nice. Besides, she thought more practically, my room doesn't have a lock on the door. In ten minutes flat some couple would wander in looking for a place to be alone. There probably are a couple of people in there right now, for all I know. She had a mental picture of walking into her bedroom and saying courteously to a copulating pair, "I beg your pardon, but could you finish that someplace else?" The ridiculous thought brought a smile.

"It's about time," a pleasant male voice said.

Toni looked up, startled, into a face she'd never seen before. A nice face. Young. Handsome with obvious breeding. Clean-shaven. He was casually but expensively dressed. Clean fingernails and shined shoes. Toni took it all in in a glance.

"Time for what?"

"For a smile," he said. "I've been watching you for ten minutes while Sarah's been fussing with the clam glop or

79

whatever that terrible stuff is. You look like you're about to expire of boredom."

"Not at all," Toni lied. "I'm giving a third of the party."

"I know. Sarah told me about you. You're Toni. I'm Alan."

The name meant nothing. It was, after all, a very commonplace name, but this had to be the man Sarah was mad for. He fitted the description.

"You're Sarah's 'friend,' " Toni said.

"I guess you could put it that way."

"I'm glad to know you." Damn. She sounded like a little girl at dancing school. He *is* nice, Toni thought. I could relate to him. I think I could almost fall in love with him. Probably in a second he'll go looking for Sarah. But he didn't.

"Let's sit down over there and talk," he said. "I don't know about you, but I'm awfully tired of juggling a drink and a cigarette. Besides, at cocktail parties my feet always hurt."

"I thought only women's feet ever hurt."

"Wrong. Feet are feet. Keep them jammed together for long periods in one spot and they're outraged. They strike back. And you'd better believe the male body can strike harder than the female's. Including the feet."

They perched on the window ledge. "Better," he said. "More convenient, too. If things get worse we can always jump. A suicide pact. 'Beautiful young student joins copywriter in death leap.' The *Daily News* will love it."

"You're crazy," Toni laughed.

"Don't be obvious. If I were sane would I be here? Would I be a copywriter? Not on your life!"

"What would you be if you were sane?"

"A real writer. A good one. Books, not ads." He smiled. "Certainly not a lawyer like my dad and my brother. They like continuity. Dad's Peter Richards the Second. First son is the Third. Son's new baby is the Fourth. Monotonous, isn't it?"

A tiny bell rang in Toni's head. A small but insistent alarm. Richards. Alan. Peter the Second and the Third. Oh no. Please don't let it be.

"Are you a New Yorker?" she asked.

"Born and bred. You?"

"I'm from California. Pasadena." She waited for a reaction, but Alan just smiled.

"Must be nice. Some of my mother's family live there but I haven't seen them since I was a child." He lowered his head to hers, pretended to look very fierce and said in a stage whisper, "It's all very mysterious. Skeletons in the closet. We Never Mention Their Names. In capital letters."

Toni closed her eyes. She wasn't smiling.

"What's the matter, Toni? Feel sick?"

She shook her head. "Not really. Alan, could we go for a walk? Just for a few minutes?"

The unexpected suggestion took him by surprise. He hesitated, involuntarily glancing toward Sarah. Then he looked back at Toni. She really did look ill. She wasn't making a play for him.

"Stay right there. I'll be back in a minute. Where's your coat?"

"I'll get it while you explain to Sarah."

Explain what? he wondered as he threaded his way through the bodies toward Sarah. I don't have to explain anything.

"Hon, your little chum Toni is feeling sick. She needs some air, I think. I'm going to walk her around the block. Be back in a few minutes."

It was Sarah's turn to look startled. "Toni's sick? Where is she?"

"Getting her coat. She'll be okay. It's just this damned room. Between the fireplace and the smell of pot, it's enough to make anybody groggy." He kissed her lightly. "Don't look so suspicious. I don't have designs on her."

"I'll cut your heart out if you do."

"First you have to find it." He grinned. "But you already have, haven't you?"

Mollified, she smiled. "You're sure Toni's all right? Want me to come with you?"

"No need. My strong arm and the crisp smell of carbon monoxide will do the trick. See you shortly."

Toni was waiting for him at the door. He pulled on his own coat and took her downstairs. He lined her arm in his and they began to walk slowly in the cold night air. They turned east toward the more garish part of the Village, walking slowly, pretending not to notice the strung-out hippies in the doorways, the bums huddled in the basement areaways. They walked for perhaps five minutes before Toni spoke.

"Alan, I have a crazy idea about something."

"My specialty, crazy ideas. I even get paid for some of them."

"No, I'm serious."

"Okay. Be serious."

"I think we're cousins."

He stopped dead still in the middle of the sidewalk. "Say that again. You think we're *what?*"

"Is your mother's name Ann?"

"Yes."

"And you're the youngest of three?"

"What the hell are you, clairvoyant?"

"No, I'm one of the skeletons from your California closet. Your mother and mine are sisters."

They were passing an espresso coffeehouse. Alan turned toward it. "Look, I don't know what this is all about but I think we'll be a lot more comfortable talking in a warm place."

At a little table he ordered coffee and then sat back looking at her searchingly.

"Tell me about it, Toni."

"You don't really know, do you? Not anything. Doesn't the name Charlene mean anything? Or Jim Jenkins?"

He shook his head frowning a little. "Vaguely."

"They're my father and mother. Part of your estranged family. Your aunt and uncle, to be exact." She tried to sound less grim. "Which," she said, "according to my calculations makes us cousins."

Alan's face was a study in wonderment. "But *you* knew about *us*. Our names. How many we were. Why in hell don't any of us know about you?"

She searched for the right words. "I only learned the whole story recently myself. You see, when I was coming to New York my, that is, *our,* grandmother gave me your parents' address in case of emergency. It's 932 Fifth Avenue, right?"

Alan nodded.

"That was when my mother told me the story. She hasn't spoken to yours since Grandmother had her stroke. And they've not been in touch since. None of them."

Their coffee sat untouched in front of them. The dim little restaurant was crowded but they felt as though they were alone, gazing intently at each other like lovers across the small table with its checkered cloth. A slim candle cast a warm glow on Toni's creamy skin and emphasized the deep blue of Alan's puzzled eyes.

"I don't understand. What happened?"

The words came with difficulty. "Your mother didn't approve of my mother's marriage. You see, Alan, my father is the best human being I know. He is also a Negro."

He drew in a deep breath. "I remember. We were together only once. All of us. We were children. Tell me about them, Toni. Your mother and father. And our grandmother."

She described them sweetly. Charlene's calm contentment. Jim's successful career and his strong devotion. Elizabeth's courage and humor. Every word spoke of her love and admiration for the relatives Alan had seen only once.

There was no apology in her voice, only tenderness and pride. Something in him stirred. She was lovely and brave and guileless. He wanted to reach out to her, to hold her, to protect her forever. Instead, he kept his feelings in check, knowing at the same time that something extraordinary had happened to him.

"What about your father's family?" he asked finally.

"I've never seen them. Not that I remember. They came when I was born, but never since. All I know is what I've been told." She sketched in the bare facts she had about Fred and Addie Jenkins and Jim's sister Clara. "Dad's the one who's kept us apart, I think," Toni said slowly. "I know he's torn about his decision not to live in a black world. Maybe remorseful that he's turned away from his people. But if that's so, he did it for Mother and me." She paused. "Someday I want to meet my other grandparents. I think everyone should know his family, don't you?"

She waited, letting him absorb what he'd heard. Why did I tell him? What irresistible urge made me feel he had to know? She realized that her last question had sounded unintentionally accusatory.

"It's all right," she said soothingly. "I don't even know why I told you. You'd never have had to know. It just seemed very important to me, Alan. But don't worry. I'll never be in touch with your family. I'm not looking for their acceptance or even their acknowledgment. But I

84

suppose," she said forthrightly, "I wanted yours. Or maybe I just wanted you to know what we share."

In that brief, intimate moment Alan knew he was in love. Insanity! he thought. This girl is a total stranger and, worse, a blood relative. But none of that mattered to him.

"I wish you hadn't told me," he said. "Why did you, Toni?"

She looked puzzled.

"This is going to sound weird," Alan went on, "but there's something very special about you, something that attracted me right away. I had a feeling about you back there at that party, the damndest feeling that I wanted to become involved with you. If you hadn't told me, it might have become something important." He banged his fist on the table. "Goddamn it, why did you have to put the pieces together? I wish you hadn't. I wish neither of us knew."

She knew now why she'd had to tell him. Because she felt the same way. She spoke very calmly, very sadly.

"I wish in a way I hadn't either, Alan. But you can't fall in love with your first cousin, and if I hadn't realized who you are, I think that's what would have happened to us. And then someday it would have all come out, and we'd have been terribly hurt. Much more than we are right now when we barely know each other."

He took her hand. "Toni, do you believe in love at first sight?"

"Yes, I do."

"Then you can't believe all those old wives' tales about cousins. Hell, in the royal families of Europe it's been going on for hundreds of years! Cousins marry and produce very normal, one-headed children! I believe in love at first sight, too, Toni. And I'm damned if I'm not already in love with you! What difference does it make if our mothers are sisters? None of that outmoded garbage matters!"

She was trying to hang on to reality. "Oh, but it does matter, Alan! Not just the relationship. The background of it. Our families. My blood. Alan, I'm a mulatto."

"I wouldn't give a damn if you were a Ubangi!"

She shook her head. "It's all wrong. I can't see you again. I'm going home for Christmas and when I come back I'm going to find another place to live. Not just because of this, honestly. That apartment isn't right for me. Sarah and Amy are fine. But we don't think alike."

"You're lying. Look, Toni, if you think you're doing something to come between Sarah and me, forget it. There's nothing permanent about that relationship. She knows it and so do I. It's just been fun and games. You must let me see you. Please. Give us a chance. Get your own place when you come back, but let me see you."

"We can't, Alan. We just can't. I know we'd fall in love. I knew it the moment you spoke to me. And that mustn't happen. I'm sorry. May I go home, please?"

In silence they walked back to the apartment.

"Are you coming up?"

"No," he said. "Tell Sarah I'm bushed, will you? I'll call her tomorrow."

Toni nodded and turned toward the door. Alan caught at her hand.

"One more thing I want to know," he said. "Is this all Mother's doing, or does Dad share her feeling?"

"I don't know," Toni answered. "Does it matter?"

She ran quickly into the hall and closed the door behind her. She leaned weakly against the elevator and let the tears come. Why did it have to be this way? In that single moment of desperate unhappiness, she searched for a target for her misery and, irrationally, it was not Ann. Why did *they* do this to me? Toni thought. In that second, and for that second only, she hated Charlene and Jim Jenkins.

Alan waited until Monday to call his father. He'd spent a bad weekend, had not called Sarah as he'd promised, fearing Toni would answer, wanting to talk to her and yet knowing that if he heard that gentle voice he'd rush over to Christopher Street and upset her again with his importuning. He'd never felt this way about any girl. It was all so sudden, so coincidental and so very real. As thousands before him had, he wondered if people really did love each other on sight. And against all logic he knew they did. He was in love with Antoinette Jenkins and she with him.

He was determined to hear the whole story. He'd never get it from Ann, but Peter Richards had always leveled with his children. It was one of the things they loved about him.

From his cubicle at the agency he dialed his father's office and was put through directly. He came right to the point.

"Dad, I have a problem."

"Something wrong at the agency?"

"No sir. It's personal."

A girl, Peter thought immediately. Has Alan made somebody pregnant? Or, God forbid, was it his health?

"Personal like what?"

"Can't talk about it on the phone. Could you have lunch today, by any chance?"

Peter looked at his desk calendar. He had a one-o'clock date with an important client. To hell with it, he thought. my son comes first, especially when his voice has the kind of urgency I've never heard before.

"Sure. Where and when?"

"How about twelve-thirty in the dining room at the Regency? It's quiet there. You never see anybody you know."

"You've got a deal."

Alan was already at the table when he arrived in the ornate, hushed hotel dining room. He had a vodka martini on the rocks in front of him.

"Same for me," Peter told the waiter. Then he turned to his son. "All right, Alan. Let's have it."

He listened as the young man told him about Toni Jenkins, about the coincidence of their meeting and the revelations of Saturday night.

"Is it true, Dad?"

"Yes, it's true. We haven't seen Charlene or your grandmother Elizabeth since she became ill. Antoinette told you the truth." He thought guiltily of Elizabeth's undemanding letter still lying unanswered in his desk drawer. Several times he'd started to write to his mother-in-law and each time he'd torn up the letter. What could he say to her? Besides, if Elizabeth was the woman she'd always been she would have meant it when she said she expected no reply. She knew that if Toni needed help, Peter would give it. That was all she really cared about.

Or was it? Elizabeth certainly must grieve for the daughter she never saw, the grandchildren kept from her. Perhaps she had hoped that this reaching out to him would reunite her family before it was too late. She was getting on. Maybe she still held on to a faint hope that the years had softened Ann or that Peter could bring her around to facing the senselessness of the anger she still carried. If so, she was wrong on both counts. If anything, two decades had made Ann more self-righteous and unyielding than ever. And the husband she hated was the last one who could change her narrow views about anything.

Silently, Alan signaled the waiter to bring another drink. When it arrived, he leaned toward his father.

"*In vino veritas,* Pop. You don't go along with all this, do you? It's Mother. She's the one with the rigid ideas about right and wrong." He laughed harshly. "My God, if it wasn't so tragic it would be funny. Of all people to have a black brother-in-law, she's the least likely candidate!"

"Don't put all the blame on your mother, Alan. There are things you don't understand."

"Like what? What's to understand except that she's a selfish, uptight woman who cares more about what people think than she does about her own flesh and blood? What kind of person turns her back on her own sister because she marries out of the conventional mold? How could anyone carry bigotry that far? And what about her own mother? My grandmother in a wheelchair and Mother never says a word about it. What the hell kind of famliy is this?"

Peter had never seen his son so angry. He couldn't blame him. It was a disgusting story of prudery and prejudice. But Peter sensed that there was more than outrage about the injustice involved. Alan was too emotional about it for it to be simply a matter of a family difference. The girl, he thought. It must be the girl. Instead of answering Alan's questions, he quietly put one of his own.

"Tell me about Antoinette," he said.

"You're ducking the issue."

"I don't think so. What's she like?"

A look of longing came over Alan's face.

"She's like no girl I ever met. Beautiful, of course. But much more than that. She has a kind of dignity that's very private and still very warm. You know she could love deeply, Dad, but she's like waiting to give that love to somebody who'll cherish and protect it. You have the feeling that she's strong and dependable and vulnerable

89

all at the same time." Alan paused. "This is going to sound insane. I spent one hour with her and I'm in love with her. I don't think I'll ever love anyone else and I don't think Toni will either."

Peter listened carefully. He could believe every word. Yes, she'd be like that, this Antoinette. Alan could have been describing Elizabeth or Charlene. They were the same kind of women, secure in the happiness of giving, offering life and laughter to those they touched. They were hurt often, women like these, but their rewards outweighed and obliterated their pain. They were strong in the most womanly kind of way, endlessly loyal to those they loved, eternally understanding as Elizabeth had been in her letter to him.

He looked at his son, seeing the despair on that beautiful young face.

"You're sure she loves you?" Peter asked.

"Yes. But she says she won't see me again." Alan's face suddenly hardened. "I didn't ask you to come here and give advice to the lovelorn, Dad. That's my problem, not yours. I want to know why and how Mother did this terrible thing."

"Alan, I can't defend what your mother did, any more than I can defend myself for permitting it. I can tell you truthfully that I didn't even know about Charlene's marriage at first. Ann kept it secret. I had no idea about Jim Jenkins until Antoinette was born and your mother was so hysterical that she confided the whole thing to me and made me swear I'd never tell you children or anyone else. I'd long since given up fighting her. Just as I'm sure you know I've long since given up loving her. She's been a good mother and a faithful wife and I suppose I feel guilty about her and sorry for her and," he said slowly, "willing to go along with a lot of things I don't believe in, just to keep peace in the family.

"I always loved and admired Elizabeth. She had more guts and compassion than any woman I've ever known. Charlene was always kind of solemn and yet she had a pixie quality that was irresistible."

Alan nodded. "Toni has the same thing."

"But Ann was different. More beautiful. More self-centered. Much more clever. I fell in love with her, Alan. At least I thought I did. But after the first few years I knew it wasn't love. I was being very skillfully handled, very adroitly manipulated to give Ann everything she wanted, from money and position to three perfect kids.

"I used to feel bitter about it. I felt I'd been used. Long ago I asked your mother for a divorce. Several times, in fact. Not that there was anyone else I wanted to marry. Just that I wanted to be free. I even convinced myself that you children would be better off seeing one parent at a time instead of living in a house that only pretended to be a home. She wouldn't agree, of course. And I suppose in the long run it's just as well. I've made a life for myself, of sorts. And you and Peter and Joanne have grown up and gone your own way. I feel sorry for Ann now. She has no one."

"Sorry for her! My God, she's ruined your life! She's been a monster to her mother and sister! She's a shallow, despicable, self-centered woman!"

"Hold it!" Peter commanded. "If she's ruined my life it's because I was spineless enough to let her. As for her selfishness and her attitude toward Charlene, try to understand your mother's background, Alan. Her father was a brilliant, weak man who went to pot because he was afraid of competition, afraid of the world. He made Elizabeth's life a living hell with his drinking and his women and his sadism. But Ann never saw that. She idealized her father and never forgave her mother for taking her away from him. Elizabeth never told her the truth about him. She preferred Ann's hatred to Ann's disillusionment.

"Your mother grew up vowing never to be like her own. She would have security and a lifetime marriage and all the proper, materialistic things that Elizabeth never really cared about. Elizabeth's idea of happiness was giving. Ann's was getting everything she could. She hated the 'poor life' Elizabeth gave them after she left Alan Whitman. In me she saw escape into a world where people behaved conventionally. Where they didn't leave the grocery bills unpaid so that they could have flowers and candles on the table. Or dodge the butcher so they could use the money to take their kids to the ballet. That's what Elizabeth did. And that's what Ann has always hated her for; her refusal to conform, her unwillingness to be put into the stupid position of caring what 'they' say.

"Charlene's thirteen years younger than your mother. She doesn't even remember the father who spoiled Ann and called her his 'little princess.' Charley was brought up to care about the things Elizabeth cares about—people and beauty and love. Knowing this, does it surprise you that when Charlene fell in love she was color blind? Or, conversely, that Ann reacted as violently as she did? Jim Jenkins is a hell of a man. Elizabeth thinks so too. But Ann can't think that way, Alan. It's not her fault. She's cared about one thing all her life—being accepted by the right people, having the right clothes and the right address. And never, never being the center of gossip as her courageous, unconventional mother was."

Alan was silent for a moment.

"Dad, I've been thinking of going to Pasadena for Christmas. I'll tell the other kids about this. I know they'll feel the way I do. I'd like Elizabeth and Charlene and Jim to know that we don't agree with Mother."

Peter shook his head. "I don't think it's a good idea, Alan. The best thing is to leave it alone. You can't do now what I should have done twenty years ago."

"But I want to know them! We know *your* parents."

"I understand that, son. And, believe me, your family in Pasadena would welcome you with open arms. But you can't do that to your mother, Alan. Misguided and unfair as you judge her to be, your loyalty must be with her. You won't accomplish anything by going to California except to increase Ann's feeling of rejection. And maybe break Toni's heart."

Alan looked as though he was in actual physical pain. "Dad, how can you even speak of a loyalty in connection with a woman who doesn't know the meaning of it?"

"Oh, but she does," Peter said, "within the framework of her own reference. She truly believes she has always been loyal to her 'martyred' father. She's been loyal in her way to me and to you and your brother and sister. She's even, strangely enough, been loyal to the code she set up for herself. She believes she's moral and just. You and I may not agree with that. But it's how she sees life. Don't hurt her, Alan. Not on the basis of one chance meeting. Don't sit in judgment on her as she has on her own family. She hasn't much left except her convictions and her pride. Let's leave her with those, okay?"

His son didn't answer but Peter knew he had temporarily won, empty and tenuous as the victory might be.

As soon as he returned to his office, Peter again read the letter in his desk drawer. This time he answered it. He told Elizabeth what had happened.

"Perhaps Antoinette will tell you herself," he wrote. "Perhaps not. But you will know how to handle it, Elizabeth, if you find that we have unwittingly sent home to you a confused and unhappy child. Forgive us. God knows we didn't need to add this wound to all the others we've infliced. Give Charlene a kiss for me, even though you can't tell her where it's from."

Before he could change his mind he sealed and stamped the letter and walked out to drop it down the mail chute in the hall.

Chapter 7

Like Alan, Toni spent a bad Saturday night and Sunday.
Her young mind, usually so disciplined, seemed to have
lost control. One moment she told herself that "love at
first sight" was romantic nonsense. Love, she had always
been certain, came slowly, starting with external attraction
or a provocative personality, building with the actual
knowing of the person, pyramiding with days, weeks of
conversation, shared interests and finally actually physical
contact.

In the next moment she knew that all this need not be
so. Love could happen in an instant. She had fallen in
love with Alan Richards almost the moment he spoke to
her, had become convinced in the dimness of that little
coffeehouse that he was the only man she would love in
this deep, unforgettable way. They had barely touched.
Not even kissed. Yet she loved him as passionately as
though they had lain in each other's arms, whispering
secret words, caressing, exploring, filled with wonder and
fulfillment. She had never been loved by a man, but she
knew how it would be with Alan: gentle, tender, over-

whelming, reaching a peak of ecstasy that she could visualize without ever having experienced it.

She knew that he felt the same. In that brief, strange encounter he had barely hinted at his desire and yet in every look, every word, every helpless gesture she felt the completeness of his love. It was as though they had known each other forever, deeply, intimately. Without more than a linking of arms, a slight touch of hands, they had become lovers. They had taken each other completely. She knew how he would look, naked and beautiful, reaching out for her. She knew how eagerly she would hold out her arms for him.

Tormented, she sought solace in playing devil's advocate. Perhaps he didn't feel as she did. To Alan, seven years older, so much more worldly, the moments might have been nothing more than a temporary surge of excitement, perhaps spurred by the incredible discovery of their relationship that lent a kind of illicit glamor to the idea. Perhaps she was being a romantic fool, reading her longings as his.

But she knew she was not engaging in some young girl's fantasy. She knew, as surely as she knew her name, that Alan Richards was as much in love with her as she was with him. And it was hopeless for so many reasons. Cousins could and did marry. She knew that. But they were cautioned not to have children, who were not necessarily "two-headed monsters" but who were unusually susceptible to diseases such as diabetes and heart defects and other genetic disorders. She remembered learning about the results of "inbreeding" from her biology courses in high school, never dreaming that such clinical information would ever affect her. She could live without children if she could have Alan. But it would be unfair to deprive him of fatherhood.

And of course, there was more. He was not the kind of

man who would be troubled by his wife's mixed blood, but like herself he was the kind who would be troubled by the bitterness that his family—and hers—would feel if these two young people chose a life together. The "family feud" demanded loyalties from each of them, loyalties that Toni was not sure they were strong or selfish enough to ignore.

Tossing in her bed, Toni tried to be sensible. She was young. She would meet other men, just as Alan would meet other women. They would put this futile longing somewhere in the back of their minds and, perhaps, almost forget it. At least the longing and frustration would grow dimmer. That was the healing power of time. Eventually this would become only a sad but bearable regret. She would never stop loving him. That one magic hour would stay with her, just as the wondering of how it might have been would be an eternal question. But she had to accept the fact that she could not have him, never dared be near him again.

When she had told him impulsively that she would move out of the apartment, she realized she meant it. She could not bear to hear Sarah mention his name, to know every time she looked at her roommate that Sarah knew Alan as Toni never would. She was afraid even to risk being where he could so easily find her. She toyed with the idea of not coming back to New York after the Christmas holidays. Put a continent between them. Perhaps that was the best way. In the next breath she rejected that thought. Geography would solve nothing if Alan chose not to accept the finality of their parting. But he would accept it. That quiet turning away on Saturday night was proof that he already had. He would do that for her. He would not seek her out in New York in deference to her wishes. And she would steel herself not to run to him.

She would come back, find a new place to live and go on with her schooling. She could lose herself, for now, in that. She was doing extremely well at Parsons. Her instructors were full of praise for her inventiveness as well as her technique. She had an inherent sense of the exciting in fashion, mixed with the taste and technique that made her designs practical to manufacture as well as interesting enough to sell. She'd been assured that she was a more than competent artist, a skill that could take her far in the fashion world. And lately she'd found herself more interested in the execution of her drawings rather than in the creation of clothes. She had been giving some thought to becoming a commercial artist rather than a designer. On her "field trips" to the mad world of Seventh Avenue, she had not related well to the frantic atmosphere of the dress houses, the ugliness of the area, the heedless, pushing crowds on the street, the falsely smiling faces of the harried manufacturers and the harassed rudeness of the buyers who shoved their way into the tightly packed elevators in the three or four buildings that housed all the good fashion firms.

The thought of facing that fierce jungle every day did not fill her with pleasure. Perhaps she would use her training to work as an artist on a fashion magazine or in an ad agency or a Fifth Avenue store. It seemed frivolous to choose one's career because of location and she was making no decisions right now. But if I'm to live in New York, Toni thought, my inclination is to go to work in elegant surroundings rather than grubby ones. She would see when she came back next year.

. Right now she yearned to get home, to wallow in all the uncomplicated love that waited for her there.

School had closed on Friday and she'd hoped to leave on Monday, but she'd been unable to get an airplane reservation until the Tuesday-morning flight. Everything was jammed at this season and anyway she'd wanted to stay for the party Saturday night, and spend Sunday packing and visiting with her friends. She wished now that she'd flown out on Saturday morning, having never met a man called Alan Richards.

Her thoughts came back to him again. Somehow she'd get through the remaining time before her departure without showing this inner turmoil. She'd make up some excuse about moving out. She'd have to tell the girls before she left. Neither was going home for Christmas. Sarah couldn't stand the idea of what she called "all that organized Baltimore cheer" and Amy's family did not, of course, celebrate the season even if she'd been inclined to make one of her rare, reluctant visits to the Bronx. They'd be seeing lots of other girls over the holidays. Hopefully they'd find a replacement for Toni then.

On Sunday, both her roommates rose late and left almost immediately for prearranged but unannounced dates. Toni smiled to herself. She'd never learn. She'd had a vision, before Saturday night, of their sharing a quiet Sunday, cleaning up the mess of the party, chatting companionably, spending a relaxed day. She wondered why she'd assumed that. It was typical of Sarah and Amy not to mention their plans. Just as it was typical of them to rush out with no more than a glance at the overflowing ash trays, the dirty glasses and the souring "clam glop," as Alan had called it, festering in a dish surrounded by broken bits of potato chips.

"See you later," Amy said on her way out. "Don't worry about this mess, Toni. We'll do it together tomorrow."

All Sarah said was: "If Alan calls, tell him I'll call when I get back."

Even the mention of his name hurt. Toni nodded. In a way, she was glad they were going. It gave her more time to think of a good reason to give them for moving. She wouldn't have to tell them until tomorrow. As for Sarah's message, there'd be none. If the phone rang, Toni had no intention of answering it.

Methodically she began to clear up the remnants of the party, not because she felt any obligation to do so but because it was a kind of therapy. She washed and dried the dishes, ran the ancient vacuum over the frayed rug and pushed chairs and tables back in place. Anything to be busy. To not think. She could see Charlene in the garden at home, busy pruning and feeding her precious flowers, finding release in activity. They'd talked about it once.

"When I have a problem," Charlene had said, "I do anything but sit in a chair and brood. The only answer is physical activity. Your grandmother was the same before her stroke. I remember when things were really bad I'd suddenly find her painting a room or cooking some elaborate dish. I'm a terrible painter and not such a hot cook, so I dig."

It must run in the family, Toni thought. I'm cleaning as though my life depended on it, as though soapsuds could wash away my problems. When she finished cleaning, she packed. And then she went for a long walk. It was a bleak, gray day and at the foot of Fifth Avenue, Washington Square was almost deserted. She walked around it for miles, thinking of the early morning, only four months ago, when she'd looked toward Fifth Avenue and hugged herself with happiness. She thought with bitterness of "Aunt Ann," who lived on this same street. I'm in trouble now, Toni said silently to Elizabeth, but your daughter is the *last* person I could call. She passed several telephone booths on her way to and from the Square and was tempted to look in the phone book for Alan's name. Not to call him. Just to find out where he lived. She didn't even know that. Maybe he wasn't listed. Maybe he lived at home, right at the number that was on the slip of paper in her bureau drawer.

There's so much about him I don't know, Toni thought. So much I'll never know. She wept quietly as she walked, allowing the slow tears to run unchecked down her cold cheeks. A few passers-by looked curiously at the pretty young girl but no one stopped to ask if she was in trouble, if there was something they could do to help. They were used to the sight of forlorn youngsters wandering almost in a daze through Washington Square. A strung-out kid, they thought. Maybe on something. Maybe a runaway. In any case, none of their business.

Toward evening, Toni made her weary way back to Christopher Street. She called the airline to see whether she could get on a plane on Monday, but there were no cancellations. She could go on "standby," they said, and hope for last-minute "no-shows," but Toni let her Tuesday reservation stand. Anxious as she was to get away, she rejected the idea of going out to Kennedy, sitting for hours in the frenzied airport with no assurance that she'd get a seat on a Monday flight. Besides, it would necessitate calling home and announcing a possible change of plans. She wasn't ready to talk to her family yet. She knew she'd break down and bawl like a baby if she heard Jim or Charlene's voice right now.

She'd eaten nothing since breakfast but she wasn't hungry. Instead, she showered and got into bed, trying to concentrate on a book. She was exhausted. She'd slept hardly at all the night before. Long before the others came home she was asleep and dreaming. In her dreams Charlene told her that she was an adopted child. She woke smiling, only to face the reality of the morning.

Telling Amy and Sarah her decision to live elsewhere wasn't easy. Sarah was giving herself a manicure and

101

Amy was deep in the *Daily News* when Toni made her announcement.

"Listen, kids, I have something to tell you."

They looked up, unsuspecting.

"I've loved sharing the apartment," Toni said, "but I'm going to get a place of my own when I get back. You've been terrific these past couple of months. I really appreciate your taking me in, but I think I'll look for something a little farther uptown."

Why didn't they say something instead of just sitting there staring at her? She knew it was a lame excuse. No excuse at all, really. Still, they could say *something*.

Amy finally did. "How come? I thought we were doing great."

"We were," Toni said. "I mean, we *are*. It's just me. I'm like my Dad, I guess. I'm kind of a loner by nature." She was sounding less and less believable. No help for it. She plunged on. "I hope it doesn't give you a problem, moneywise. I'm willing to pay my share through January. By that time you should find someone to move in."

"I still don't get it," Amy persisted.

Sarah's voice cut in. "Leave it alone, Amy. It's a free country. If Toni wants to be by herself that's her business." She looked coldly at Toni. "Maybe she has a secret love life. Or expects to start one."

She knows, Toni thought. Somehow she knows. But that's impossible. Unless she talked to Alan yesterday. No, she's taking a wild guess. Sarah knew that Toni and Alan had disappeared for more than an hour on Saturday night, that Toni had gone directly to her room when she returned and that Alan hadn't come back to the party at all. She was just putting pieces together in the intuitive way of a jealous woman. How right she is. And also how wrong. Toni tried to keep her voice easy.

102

"It isn't that, unfortunately. It's just that I really think I should be on my own. Nothing personal. Honest."

Sarah raised a cynical eyebrow. It was Amy who was honestly distressed and understandably confused.

"I wish you'd change your mind, Toni. It seems silly."

Sarah rose and started for her room. "Maybe not so silly," she said, "if you suddenly get a yen for your roommate's boy friend. Tough luck, Toni, but you're right to split."

As the door closed, Amy looked at Toni.

"Did that mean what I think it did? Does Sarah think you've got a thing for Alan? Is that why you're leaving?"

"In a way. But it's much more complicated and less threatening than Sarah knows. Anyway, Amy, I don't want to talk about it, if you don't mind. It's better this way. Let's just leave it at that and all stay friends, okay?"

Amy shook her head. "I don't know what's going on around here, but if you've got something going with Alan Richards, then I say go to it! Sarah thinks he's hers, but she's dead wrong, Toni. She's okay to sleep with, but he'll never marry her."

"What makes you so sure?"

"Sarah's background's pretty good. Her credentials are okay, but she'd never be the girl Alan would pick for a wife. It's not just the sleeping around. Everybody does that. It's just that she doesn't have class. Real class, I mean. Like you. That's what Alan will go for when he marries. He's a helluva guy, but at heart he's damned conservative. Sarah chases him and that's the wrong tactic. He's cool. Likes his fun and games. But when it comes to settling down, he won't go the route with an all-out swinger like Sarah. He'll pick somebody he can idolize, somebody he has to chase." She paused. "I'm not sure what's in Sarah's mind or yours, but I can guess. She got jealous Saturday night because Alan paid so much attention to you. And you're cutting out because you don't want a messy situation. You're nuts, Toni. If you like Alan Richards, then fight for him and don't worry about Sarah." Amy smiled. "Of course, I can see how you'd feel easier about fighting without Sarah on the premises. Anyway, if you must go, I hope that's what's in your mind. You and Alan would be good for each other."

Toni hugged her. "You're a real friend, Amy."

"I'm a bloody 'Dear Abby' at heart, that's what I am. And if you tell anybody, I'll kill you." She grinned. "Well. So you're really going to go. What about your furniture and things? You bought an awful lot of stuff for your room. Will you let me know where to send it?"

"I don't want any of it. Keep it as my house gift. I'll probably take a one-room apartment and won't need bedroom stuff anyway."

She didn't say that she never wanted to be reminded in any way of Alan. Not that he'd ever even seen her room. But she'd dreamed of him there, cried for him, wished him into the narrow little virginal bed. She couldn't sleep in that apartment another night, she suddenly realized. Not with Sarah sensing even part of the truth.

"I'm all packed," Toni said. "I think I'll get on my way."

"That's crazy! Your plane doesn't leave until tomorrow." Amy stopped. "Oh, of course. Sarah."

"I'm not really upset with Sarah. I know she's suspicious and angry but I can understand that. I just think it'll be less awkward if I spend tonight in a hotel."

"You have Alan's phone number at the office?"

"No. I don't know where he works or lives. And I don't want to, Amy, dear. Thanks anyway. Someday I'll tell you the whole story. You've been great."

In half an hour she was on her way, leaving Amy with

a warm hug and promises to get together in January. Sarah did not even come out to say goodbye.

On Tuesday morning, Elizabeth slit open the official-looking airmail special-delivery letter from "Richards & Richards, Attorneys at Law." It had been four months since she'd written to Peter and she'd long since decided he was not going to answer. The silence did not surprise or disturb her. No answer was necessary or even expected. She had simply wanted him to know that his niece was in New York, and she couldn't trust Ann to tell him about Antoinette. She smiled as she mentioned her granddaughter's name to herself. She was the first one who had called the girl "Toni." It had been an irresistible impulse, even though there was only one Toni—or Tony—in Elizabeth's life: the long-dead second husband who had been so precious to her. Antoinette had been named for him by Charlene and Jim, who adored the man Elizabeth married midway in her life and who gave her a few years of the greatest happiness she'd ever known. Tony Alexander's death had been a cruel and unexpected blow. He was irreplaceable, as real and dear to her now as he had been in all his laughing, joyous, mortal body. Elizabeth did not hold with the nonsense of heaven as a place where one was reunited with those who'd gone before. Her religion, informal as it was, did not include visions of the two of them with wings, flying into each other's arms. No, Tony was a spark of energy, a flicker of light in the sky, a force that waited undiminished for her to join her spirit to his.

She turned back to the envelope. How her mind wandered these days! It was as clear as it had been at twenty. Clearer, perhaps. Wiser, God willing. And yet she allowed herself to drift off into these satisfying side thoughts right in the middle of doing something else. She was doing it now.

Carefully she withdrew the handwritten letter and read it with dismay. Incredible that in a city of millions Antoinette and Alan Richards should have met at all. And yet, as Elizabeth remembered, New York was nothing more than a series of small towns, its segments distinct and different, so that those in each were likely to run across one another. Antoinette was not likely to know a cab driver from the Bronx or a housewife in Brooklyn. But it was entirely possible that in the young "fashion segment" of Manhattan she would meet people in publishing and advertising and allied fields. And so she had. Worse, judging from Peter's letter it was more than a meeting; it was a collision. "I hope we have not sent home to you an unhappy and confused child," he'd written. There had been no mention of Ann. Elizabeth judged correctly that she knew nothing of this. Poor Antoinette, Elizabeth thought. Poor Alan. And then, instinctively, poor Ann, who does not even have her children's confidence.

She debated what to do and decided for the moment to do nothing. Antoinette would be home today. Perhaps, Elizabeth thought, clutching at a dim hope, the girl was not as deeply involved as the boy. One look at Antoinette's face would tell her. Elizabeth knew all too well what it was like to be hopelessly, futilely in love. She thought she would recognize the look more quickly than Charlene or Jim, who had the only person either of them had ever wanted. Elizabeth had once deeply desired a man she could not have, a married man who loved her well but who placed duty first. She knew what it was to want and be denied. And she prayed that this momentary passion of Antoinette and Alan's was simply that: a special moment of beauty to be set aside and remembered with tenderness, like an unforgettable, impossible dream.

106

Thank God they're so young, Elizabeth thought. Wounds heal quicker when there's a seemingly endless future. Or do they? Perhaps it was worse to contemplate all the years without the one you love. If only I were wiser, she wished. I've lived so long and learned so little.

Chapter 8

Elizabeth underrated Charlene's perceptiveness, especially where Toni was concerned. The eighteen-year-old who came off the plane was outwardly unchanged, a little more "Eastern-looking," perhaps, in her well-tailored New York outfit, but otherwise to all appearances the same young woman who'd left a few months before. Only her mother saw a subtle difference behind those big, dark eyes, a kind of unhappy bewilderment that had not come through in her letters and did not, even now, make itself evident to Jim. He was enchanted by her effervescence and cheerfulness, seeing what he wanted to see: a smiling, charming girl, glad to be home.

Charlene felt the pain, caught a swift glimpse of the surprised, wounded look that came over Toni's face when she thought no one was watching. New York has not been kind to her, Charlene thought sadly. Will she talk about it when we're alone? Whatever it is, will she talk about it at all?

Toni certainly had no intention of doing so on the drive to Pasadena. She chattered incessantly, almost compulsively, making Jim laugh with her stories of school and her amusing anecdotes of life in the big city. Charlene joined the laughter, uncomfortably aware that Toni was too flippant, too determinedly gay.

"I'll leave you two to catch up," Jim said as he carried Toni's bags into the little house. "I have to go back to the plant for a few hours."

"Today?" Toni sounded disappointed.

"Every day," Charlene answered. "Your father's working round the clock, even weekends. He's in charge of a big new design project. A superplane, the KJ-16. He's wildly excited about it, as you can see. Nothing less would keep him from declaring *this* a full holiday! Anyway, we'll see him later. He's promised to get home at a decent hour for a change. We're going to Grandmother's for dinner. She's chomping at the bit, waiting to see you."

There was no complaint in Charlene's voice but Toni sensed this had been a lonely time for her. Jim had his work, but with Toni gone Charlene's life had lost many of its pleasant demands. She took care of her house and garden, gave one day a week to the Art Museum and another to helping out at the hospital. She often drove up to see Elizabeth. But, Toni realized for the first time, Charlene had no close friends, no women like herself with whom to pass the empty hours. Bit by bit, the realization of little sacrifices Charlene had made for her marriage were coming through to her daughter. She was, even in this familiar atmosphere, something of an outcast, a bit of a "freak," a free spirit looked on suspiciously by "conventional" wives.

Toni unpacked and came to join her mother in the garden. She flopped into a chaise. It was a warm, beautiful day and Toni put her face gratefully up to the sun.

"I can't believe it's almost Christmas," she said. "Just a few hours ago I was freezing to death. They were even predicting snow when I left."

109

"What's New York like, Toni? Not the weather. I mean, what's it really like living there?"

"Different." Toni seemed to weigh her words. "It's another world. Exciting and stimulating and the only place to be, I guess, if you want a career. You're up against the best in New York, professionally speaking. Because that's where the best have to go."

"Do you feel strange there?"

"What do you mean, 'strange'?"

"I don't know," Charlene said. "I guess I mean do you feel out of place? Being on your own. Knowing nobody very well."

A pensive look crossed Toni's face.

"Yes, I guess I feel strange. Scared sometimes. Not physically scared, Mom, like of rapists or muggers. More afraid that I'm not ready to handle the whole thing."

"You mean school?"

"Partly. I'm not sure I have enough talent. Oh, I'm okay. But there are so many kids in that school who are good. Really good. Maybe I don't have what it takes for a successful career. And I'd hate being mediocre."

For a moment, Charlene felt a surge of hope and then shame at the selfishness of that emotion. Maybe Toni wasn't going back. Part of her mother wanted her to succeed in New York and part of her wanted Toni to stay home. Trying to sound offhand, she said, "But you're going back, of course."

"Yes. At least I guess so. I don't think I've given it a fair shake." She paused. "I'm not going to share the apartment any more, though. If it's okay with you and Dad, I'm going to get a place of my own. I told Amy and Sarah before I left."

Charlene digested this curious piece of news. In her letters, Toni had been amusing about the apartment and her roommates, making little jokes about the "informality" of her new life, admitting openly that she was really living in the middle of a strange new scene. "You'd faint if you saw the people who drop in here," Toni had written. "But they're interesting and bright, even though *I* think *they* think I'm left over from the Dark Ages! You know what I mean, Mom. The only 'pot' that turns me on is the one with your African violets! I guess I'm stuck with my nineteenth-century 'nice-girl syndrome.' But this is an education and it's *fun!*"

Apparently it had ceased to be fun. Or else something decisive had happened to make Toni change her mind about sharing the apartment. Maybe both.

"Why the sudden change? I thought your life was so exciting. Your letters sounded that way."

She could feel Toni withdraw. "It was exciting. But I think I'll be happier on my own."

"But won't you be lonely?"

"Maybe. But it's what I need to do."

For the first time, Charlene realized Toni was keeping secrets. The idea made her feel shut out, almost angry.

"Seems a very sudden decision."

"Not really. I'll feel more settled in a place of my own."

"You had that when you first went to New York and you couldn't wait to get out of it."

"That was a hotel," Toni said patiently. "I want an apartment that I can fix the way I like. And entertain anybody *I* want to see."

It was an unconscious giveaway. Charlene looked at her closely. "We've never tried to fool each other, Toni. You've met someone you want to be alone with. That's it, isn't it?"

"I only wish it were." Unexpectedly, Toni's eyes filled with tears. Her mother felt the anguish as though it were her own. She moved close to her child, touching her gently on the shoulder. "Don't cry, darling, please. Can you tell me about it? What's wrong?"

It was a relief to pour out the whole story of Alan. Hard as the telling was, it was a blessed, much needed release. Hearing the words aloud at least made it real, still an impossible fantasy but reduced now to the status of an unsurmountable problem. Small comfort, but comfort nonetheless. Toni was dry-eyed and in control when she finished. It was Charlene whose eyes were wet with pity.

"Sweetheart, I'm so sorry. You're paying for something that isn't your fault. We don't expect that of you, Toni. None of us. If you love Alan, forget who he is and what has gone on between his mother and us. It's your life, baby. Live it the way that's right for you."

"I can't, Mom. There are too many problems. Not just yours and Ann's. I'd never dare have children with Alan. I'd always feel I'd cheated him."

"Have you discussed that with him?"

"No," Toni admitted.

"Perhaps you should," Charlene said. "Perhaps he's quite right that you should really get to know each other before you decide this is a lost cause. Look, Toni, I can't say the idea of your falling in love with your cousin fills me with happiness. It's damned unfortunate. But it's happened. And if it's real, it's too important to run away from. I understand your wanting to move out, away from Sarah. Of course you should. But I'm surprised that you're afraid to see Alan again."

Toni looked up at the sky. "I'm not strong enough to see him. I know how it will turn out."

"But you're going back to New York. You're bound to run into him."

"Maybe not. It's a big town. Besides, I can't chuck everything and just hide here in my safe little nest. Maybe I'm not cut out to be a big success but I have to be sure of that, at least. I may have botched up my first love affair, if you can *call* it that, but I can't run away from the rest of my life."

Charlene nodded. "Yes, I can see that. Unfortunately I can't identify with your problem as I'd like to, Toni. You see, I was one of the lucky ones. There was only one man I ever wanted and I had the good fortune to get him. It must be sheer hell to be hopelessly in love. I'd give anything to help you, but I can't. Nobody can. This is a matter for your own conscience and your own common sense. I just want you to know that whatever you ultimately decide, you'll have your father's blessing and mine."

Toni looked alarmed. "You won't tell him any of this, will you, Mom? Promise. I don't want anybody to know. Not even Dad or Grandmother."

"It's your secret. I give you my word it will stop with me if that's the way you want it."

"I'm glad we could talk," Toni said. "It's such a relief to say it all out loud. I just hope I haven't hurt you or worried you too much. I'm going to come out of this okay, particularly now that I've finally told you. But don't let's discuss it again, do you mind? The best thing I can do is dwell on it as little as possible."

She's still such a child, Charlene thought. She really believes she can get over her first love just by willing it out of her mind. Poor baby. Poor Toni. She doesn't know she can't cut out this kind of deep feeling like a surgeon removing a useless appendix.

Involved in and excited as he was about his project, Jim Jenkins had a hard time keeping his mind on his work that day. It had been so good to see his daughter again, looking fit and happy. He worried too much about her. He knew that. Everyone said Toni was Charlene all over again, and in many ways she was. Jim could not

113

have asked for a better pattern for his child. She had her mother's sunny disposition, the same sincere liking of people. She also had Charlene's even temper and an enviable ability not to let little things become monumental problems.

But there was part of Jim in Toni, too, and it was the part that worried him. The girl had his acute sensitivity to situations, his inordinate need for privacy, his penchant for self-analysis, even some of the divided loyalties that plagued him. He tried to convince himself that these were not really such bad traits. Perhaps, in a way, they gave a greater dimension, acted as a balance that kept her from being unbearably nice. He smiled at the idea that imperfections could improve character. But they did. They made the owner more human, more accessible. God protect him from boring, selfless, wishy-washy "saints!" But Toni wasn't one of those. She had her faults but she was a blessing. A mixed blessing, Jim thought. In more ways than one.

He turned back to the maze of drawings and diagrams on the table in front of him. The KJ-16 was his other baby. He'd conceived the idea for this sleek new transport, sold it to management and was in full charge of its development. It was by far the most important thing he'd ever done and he was proud of its progress, proud of the recognition that had come his way because of it. Not only in terms of money, though he'd gotten a big increase. The reward was the admiration and approval of his fellow workers. "Genius Jim," the other engineers affectionately called him. And in the hangar he knew that the workmen spoke of the new aircraft as "Jenkins' Jumbo."

It was a good design and he would have been ridiculously immodest to deny it. It was not only beautiful to look at, it was quiet and easy to handle and economical to operate. For in the late sixties Jim Jenkins foresaw the need for aircraft that would utilize minimum fuel, accommodate maximum passengers and satisfy the needs of the environmentalists and the noise-abatement people.

In six months it would be ready for testing. His dream was to have that privilege himself but he knew he would not. He was a licensed pilot, but not a test pilot. The best he could hope for would be special permission to be a passenger on the first ride.

No matter. Even if he had to stand on the ground and watch this big silver bird being put through its paces in the sky, he'd feel a personal sense of achievement. Not that he'd done it alone, of course. Nothing this gigantic was possible without teamwork. And he'd had the best. The camaraderie that existed between him and those around him was the best, too. There was no self-consciousness about black and white, though he was the only Negro in an executive position. Even the mechanics felt free to tease him, knowing he'd understand that their wisecracks were compliments.

"What are we gonna christen her with, Jim? A slice of watermelon?"

"Yeah. And I'm spitting every goddamned black seed right in your eye if she isn't perfect!"

He could hardly wait to tell Toni all about it. Charlene had been filled in every step of the way and her eyes glowed with pride, though she pretended not to be surprised.

"I'd hardly expect any less from you," she'd said casually. "After all, you are *my* husband."

"Ergo I must be a genius, right?"

"Ergo exactly!"

They laughed and loved each other and felt that life had been very good to them in so many ways. Jim felt a thrill of anticipation at the thought of Toni's reaction. She'd be as proud of him as Charlene was. And it was

115

equally important. A man needed to be a hero to his child. His ego craved it. Particularly when the man never quite stopped feeling guilty about having sired her. It was stupid of him, he knew. Toni herself was the best justification of her own birth. And yet it was important to him to have some tangible thing to offer her, some accomplishment to atone for the disadvantages that were of his making. It was all mixed up with why this airplane meant so much to him. He wished it could be called the Antoinette instead of the KJ-16.

Amused by his own nonsense, he put his papers away, slipped on his jacket and left his office. It was four forty-five, more than two hours earlier than he normally left, and his departure caused some surprise as he sauntered out the door.

"Are you okay, Mr. Jenkins?" his secretary asked.

"Sure. Great. Why?"

She glanced at her watch. "It's so early. For you, I mean. Not quite five o'clock!"

He grinned. "Big day, Miss D. My kid got home from New York this morning. I decided to declare a holiday and quit at the hour personnel thinks *everybody* leaves."

"Have a nice evening."

"Thanks. You too."

Driving home on the freeway, he reflected that Toni's arrival was benefiting a lot of people. It had been weeks since his secretary got out of the office before six or seven at night. He'd bet she'd shut up shop five minutes after he left. And why not, poor girl? He'd been a slave driver for months. Simon Legree Jenkins, he thought. Now *there's* a switch. He whistled lightheartedly all the way to Pasadena.

Freshly showered and dressed, Toni joined her mother to await Jim's arrival.

"What time is Dad coming home?"

116

"He promised to be here by five-thirty." Charlene smiled. "I'm not sure I'll recognize him in daylight. As I told you, he leaves at the crack of dawn and usually doesn't get back until eight, sometimes even later. It's been going on since you left."

Toni frowned. "Mother?"

"Um-hum?"

"I've been so busy talking about myself I haven't even asked about you and Dad. Everything's okay, isn't it? I know you must be lonely, but there's nothing wrong between you, is there?"

"Of course not. My only 'rival' is a mechanical monster. Your father's dying to tell you all about it. Next to you, it's the greatest accomplishment of his life. I will admit, though, that I think he's working much too hard. He's under such pressure. Not that the company is pushing him. He's pushing himself. He has an idea that he has to prove more than the others. He's never admitted that, but I know he feels it."

"Because he's the only nonwhite engineer?"

"I suppose so. I guess he's like a woman executive who has to work longer hours, take less time off and struggle harder to prove that she's as good as any man. What a ridiculous sense of values we live under! And how awful that even the most intelligent people accept them."

"Maybe only intelligent people recognize them."

Charlene nodded. "Good point. But in that case I'd be easier in my mind if your father were a little less bright."

"You *are* worried about him, aren't you?"

"Yes, I am. He doesn't get enough rest. He works too hard and smokes too much and he's tight as a drum. He's only forty-one, Toni, but even so he can't take the physical punishment he could twenty years ago." She paused. "I can't even get him to take time off for a checkup. How does he look to you?"

"Just the same, Mom. Beautiful."

"Good. I'm glad to hear you say that. I'm sure all this fretting is just in my own mind. I'm probably sorry for myself, subconsciously angry that we have so little time together. He's a strong man, your father. I don't know why I'm being such an alarmist. It's just that if anything happened to him, Toni, I don't think I could stand it."

"Charlene Jenkins, is that you talking? I don't see a bit of change in your husband. I think you're right. You *are* having a case of the poor-little-me's. Anyway, this project can't last forever, can it?"

"No. Six more months."

"When it's over I think you two should take a second honeymoon. Hawaii. Some place like that."

"My, my!" Charlene said. "Aren't we the wise ones? Are you sure you haven't been taking a course in marriage counseling?" Her voice was affectionate. "Darling, I didn't mean to worry you. I know your father's well and happy. And it's wonderful to see a man take such pride in his work. It's just that I love him so much, Toni. The best thing I can wish for you is a marriage as perfect as mine."

Toni did not know that Jim had confessed to Charlene what he had asked of his daughter before she went off to school. Mother would be angry if she knew, Toni thought. No. She'd be sad. She'd think, as I first did, that Dad regretted the marriage, and that was the furthest thing from the truth. Still he did worry about it. Enough to urge his daughter not to make an unconventional liaison herself. What he asked of her was impossible. She couldn't imagine pretending to be anything but what she was, no matter what it cost. She felt terribly old. Older even than Charlene, who in spite of everything retained her young-girl ideals, her blissful conviction that nothing was more important than love.

"Mom, I know you first met Dad when you shared a

118

hospital room with his sister in Denver. But when did you know you were in love with him?" The question was impulsive, an involuntary extension of her own thoughts about Alan.

Charlene smiled. "I think I loved him the first minute I saw him. I *know* I did. Even though it was two years before we saw each other again, I loved him all the time. And I've never stopped."

Toni was surprised. "But you were only fourteen when you met."

"Yes. Too young to know what I really felt, but even then I knew he was special." She gave a little laugh. "After all, honey, Juliet was only fourteen when she was on that balcony."

"But that was a story!"

"Toni, darling, to paraphrase Shakespeare, life is a story. We only act out the roles assigned to us."

"Then you don't believe we control our destinies."

"I don't know," Charlene said. "I suppose I just believe one shouldn't argue with a good Scriptwriter."

Chapter 9

All through dinner Elizabeth watched her granddaughter and saw what Charlene had seen—Toni's conscious determination to cover up her unhappiness. She was too gay, too vivacious, to quick to respond with a quip to the simplest comment. Not that she hadn't always been a bubbly young girl, but that was a natural thing. Now she was acting, unaware that anyone but her mother recognized a performance.

Laurel was eager to hear about New York. Though she was many years removed from the fashion scene, her love of it endured and she was hungry for news of a world so different from this peaceful, slow-paced California scene. She asked a hundred questions. Toni described the changes in the city since Laurel's day: the great, anonymous glass buildings that had replaced the elegant apartments and hotels of Park Avenue; the proliferation of "far-out" fashion boutiques on Lexington and Third avenues; the demise of places like the Stork Club and the appearance of expensive new restaurants.

"Not that I have firsthand knowledge of *them*," Toni said. "I couldn't afford to tip the hat-check girl in places like La Grenouille and Côte Basque. But I read all about them in *Women's Wear* every day and see pictures, so I know they exist." She grinned. "And when I'm rich and famous I'll know exactly how to act in those places. Mme. Henriette won't admit ladies in pants at Côte Basque; Lafayette won't let you take a shopping bag or a package to your table or wear your sunglasses on top of your head! You have to sit upstairs at Orsini's, in the front room at La Grenouille and in the narrow part of La Caravelle. I'm all set. All I need is the money, or a friend with money."

"Maybe your mother and I will come to New York in the spring and the three of us will do a tour of those fancy spots," Jim said. "I assume they admit all races, colors and creeds."

Toni laughed. "Daddy, darling, they'd let in a green Martian with waving antennae as long as he had a pocketful of twenty-dollar bills."

"How's school?" Laurel asked.

"Fantastic! I had no idea of how much there is to know! But I have been thinking of switching schools. Maybe going to Pratt. I think commercial art is more my thing than fashion design." She told them about Seventh Avenue and her distaste for it. "Somehow I think I'd do better and be happier doing illustrations for a magazine or a retail store. Or maybe an advertising agency."

Elizabeth's pulse quickened. In Peter's letter he'd told her that Alan worked for an advertising agency. Coincidence? Subconscious, wishful thinking? Or did Antoinette plan to look for work in some place that would bring her near her cousin?

Toni was chattering on. "Anyway, that's in the future. Going to work, I mean. I need a lot more technical training before I can go job hunting."

"Maybe not too much more," Laurel said. "You have

121

an aptitude for art and perhaps you're right about switching fields. Designing is a tough field to crack and I'm sure there aren't too many good openings. Especially today when most clothes look like they've been run up on somebody's home sewing machine. From what I see in the magazines, only a handful of designers are still making elegant, quality clothes. Everything else looks like it came from the Army-Navy surplus store." She turned to Elizabeth. "It was different in our day, wasn't it? We had great American couture. Charley James. Hattie Carnegie. Valentina. Now *those* were clothes! Today it's pants and blue jeans and mini, midi, maxi. Fads and gimmicks and snythetics. Damn little room for creativity, if you ask me."

Elizabeth smiled. "That was another world, Laurel. Anyway, we're boring Jim with all this fashion chatter." She turned graciously to her son-in-law. "Have you told Antoinette about 'Jenkins' Jumbo'?"

He shook his head. "No chance yet. I thought I'd take her to the plant while she's here. Show her my big baby in work."

"Your father's saving that for a special treat," Charlene said. "You're going to be very proud of him, Toni."

"I always am." Again there was that faint look of unhappiness. Toni did not wish to remember the Saturday night she had stood in the apartment hallway and, for a split second, hated her parents. The reason for that fleeting moment of resentment came back. Alan. Where was he? What was he doing? Was he at his own family dinner table, pretending, as she was, that nothing had happened to change his life?

At that moment in New York, Alan was not at his own family dinner table. He'd not been near his parents' apartment in days. Although he had some exciting news to

122

pass on, news that he'd gotten only that morning, he did not choose to share it with anyone except his sister Joanne.

They were very close, he and Jo. Only two years apart, they understood each other well. It was not the same for either of them with Peter Richards III. Their older brother was a male version of their mother, with the same rigid, uncompromising standards, the same lack of tolerance for human imperfections, the same absence of humor. Ann loved him more than her two younger, irreverent rebels. Alan and Jo sensed this early, accepted it without visible scars and, with their father so little in evidence, had become comrades and confidants.

When Alan heard his good news, his first thought was to call his sister at the magazine.

"Free for a drink?" he asked.

"Lacking a call from Paul Newman, yes. Something special on your mind?"

"A couple of things."

"Good news or bad?"

"Both," Alan said.

She was already at the table when he rushed into the King Cole Bar at the St. Regis. Seeing her in profile, he stopped dead. Just for a second she reminded him of Toni. Not that there was any real resemblance. Joanne was fair-haired like her mother and she was older and infinitely more chic than the cousin she'd never heard of. But there was something in the dignified, proud way she held her head, something in the finely molded features that made him think of Toni. Maybe just a hint of family trait. Probably something both girls had inherited from their grandmother, the distant Elizabeth Alan's father had described with such admiration and affection.

Alan slid into the banquette beside his sister and kissed her quickly.

"For twenty-seven you're looking pretty good," he said.

"For twenty-five you look like hell," she answered. "What did you do, take a vow to give up sleeping?"

Alan frowned. He hadn't done much sleeping since Saturday night but he didn't know it showed.

"Bags under my baby-blues?"

"Satchels," she said. "Need one of my illegal French sleeping suppositories? They work great. No hangover." Joe smiled. "I wonder why the French insist that all medication is better shoved up the derriere? Did you know they even take a sore-throat remedy that way? Curious. Maybe the magazine should do an article about that. It must be very Freudian."

Alan looked at her lovingly. She was putting him at ease with this nonsense, sensing that he needed time to tell her his news. I must have sounded very uptight on the phone, he thought. Our ESP is working again. Somehow Jo knows that my bad news is even more important to me than my good.

He waited until their drinks were in front of them and then said, "Well, aren't you curious?"

Joanne took a sip of her martini. "Is Moshe Dayan Jewish? Which do I get first, the good news or the bad?"

"The good." He pulled a telegram out of his pocket. She read it aloud. "Congratulations. *Summer Romance* passed the Publishing Board with flying colors. You are now a Doubleday author. Best wishes. Tim Ashton." Jo's eyes widened with delight. "Alan! Your novel! They bought it!"

"Yep. Boy Wonder strikes again. It's just a fluke, having your first book accepted, but I'm pretty damned happy."

"Happy! *I'm* delirious! I can't believe it? Does the family know?"

"No. You're the first. Best friends first."

Jo's eyes unexpectedly filled with tears. She reached in her bag for a handkerchief. "Damn you. Look what you did to me. My mascara'll run right down my face." She dabbed carefully at her lashes, smiling at him. "It's great, Alan. I know it's what you've always wanted to do. When can I read it? When will it be published? Have you quit that boring job at the agency?"

"Whoa. Hold it! It won't be published till next fall but I'll let you read the galley proofs when they come through in a few months. As for quitting the agency, even *I'm* not that rash just yet. The advance is respectable but I can't live on it. Now if I sign for a *second* book, that'll be different. I'll tell 'em to take their sixty-second commercials and shove 'em into Sesame Street!" He paused. "By the way, I've decided to dedicate it to Dad. I'd planned on you being the recipient of that dubious honor but some things have happened in the last few days. I never really understood him until yesterday, Jo. Now I'd like to do something to make him happy. Even something as unimportant as this."

She waited. Then she said, "I think we're getting to the bad-news part."

Alan nodded. His face drawn and his voice trembling, he told her the whole story of Toni and their instant attraction, ending with his Monday lunch with his father. "I told Dad that I was going to tell you and Pete that I was thinking of flying to Pasadena to see them all. He thinks it's a bad idea. Jo, if you could have heard him! He took all the blame on himself, defending Mother, saying she was loyal to her own standards and that he was the one who should never have let this all happen. He's a real man. I never knew it before. He's had a rotten deal but he's stood by Mother and us, and he's still standing by. He takes it for granted that I won't do less."

Joanne could hardly grasp the whole story much less

125

realize the implications in that first telling. She was hearing about her western family, seeing a side of her parents that she had never seen before, watching her beloved brother caught up in a conflict that seemed to have no resolution. As her father had done, she said finally, "Tell me more about Toni. We were all so young. I barely remember her."

With Joanne he talked even more passionately about the girl he loved. Only another woman would understand the depths of his feeling, the certainty of his emotions. Peter had understood, had even accepted instant love between his son and his niece. But Jo felt the pain of it as though it was happening to her. How she loved this intelligent, handsome, decent brother of hers, and how well she knew him! She ached to comfort him and there was no way. Peter was right. Ann, for all her misguided beliefs, had done what she thought right, and to have her children turn against her would, indeed be stripping away the last vestiges of her self-confidence. Still, Alan's life mattered too. How much was one supposed to sacrifice for one's parents' blindness and stupidity? What was to be lost by Alan's going after Toni? Ann's pride? Peter's gentlemanly reluctance to see his wife "betrayed"? Weren't those trifles compared to the love that Alan and Toni had found?

"I think you should go to her," Jo said resolutely. "Damn all the old family feuds! What are we, Kentucky hillbillies? Dad's lived by some kind of antiquated code of honor all his life, but you don't have to. Mother isn't worth that, Alan. She really isn't."

He took her hand. "It isn't that easy, Jo. I reacted exactly the way you have. Give me that girl and to hell with everything else. But you don't know Toni. She's not as selfish as I. She made the decision that it couldn't be. And I have to respect that."

126

"Nonsense! One emotional renunciation and you take it as an irrevocable decision on her part? You don't know women. I'll bet she wishes you'd get your tail on a plane and come get her. I know in her place I'd be feeling that way."

"I don't know," Alan said. "I don't know what to do. I don't even know whether she's left for California yet."

"I'm telling you what to do: Go after her."

He shook his head. "I can't, Jo. I don't want to hurt her or her parents. They're to be considered, too. Imagine how Charlene must feel about us. How would *you* feel if your own sister refused to acknowledge your husband and your child? Toni adores her mother and father and she knows they've been ostracized by ours. Toni puts those things above her own desires. I know she does. She's that kind of a girl."

"But maybe her family wouldn't put their pride above Toni's happiness. Have you thought of that?"

"I've examined it from every angle, Jo. *I* can take the problems. The blood relationship. The Negro part. Even Mother's anger and Dad's disappointment. But I can't put Toni through torture. If she decides she can handle it, she'll let me know. I'm certain of that. She'll be back in New York after the holidays. I'm banking on the fact that she'll have talked it out with her family. She'll see it differently."

"Don't bank on it," Jo said sadly. "From what you've told me, I don't think she'll change her mind. If you don't move you won't hear from her after Christmas, Alan. If you don't take the initiative then you'd better try to forget it. I'm afraid that's what she'll do if you don't stop her."

"I can't stop her. She knows how I feel. The decision is hers."

"Oh, damn families!" Jo said. "Why don't they stay in the *Ladies' Home Journal* where they belong?"

He tried to lighten the gloom. "Don't be a fashion-magazine snob. It'll work out. She'll come back to me. I know she will."

"And if she doesn't?"

"Then I'll write lots of books and travel and get rich and famous."

"And marry somebody else whom you'll never love as much?"

He didn't answer.

"Alan, I simply cannot believe you're going to give up this easily!"

"I haven't given up," he corrected her. "I've only gone into a holding pattern."

Joanne sighed. He was either being ridiculous or heroic. She wasn't sure. In any case, he needed time to come to the right decision. So, she hoped, did that little cousin of hers who must be a terrific girl. In one hour she'd made an impression that would last a lifetime. Some people would find that an impossible idea.

"I wouldn't discuss this with our big brother, if I were you," Joanne said. "He'd think you were crazy."

"Right," Alan said. "Besides, he'd blab to Mother."

"I have a solution. Temporary but effective. Let's get roaring drunk."

Alan looked at her. "To celebrate or forget?"

Joanne shrugged. "Who cares? It works both ways."

He woke the next morning to the insistent ringing of the telephone. The bedside clock said ten past eleven. Jesus, Alan thought, I'm already an hour late for work! Then he remembered. It was Christmas Eve. The agency was closed for the long holiday. He pulled the covers over his head and tried to shut out the shrill demands of the phone but it wouldn't quit. Who the hell would call before noon on a holiday? Only one person. He picked up the receiver.

"Yes, Mother?"

She was startled. "How on earth did you know who it was?"

He propped himself up, still half asleep. "Intuition," he said. "Plus the fact that none of my friends get up this early on a nonworking day."

"They might if they didn't spend half the night in those disgusting singles bars, or whatever you call them. That's where you must have been. I called you until midnight."

He sighed. He was never ready for Ann's lectures, and this morning her moralizing was the last thing he needed.

"What's up?" he asked. Besides you, he added silently.

"I just wanted to make sure that you remembered you were due here at seven o'clock."

"Tonight?"

Ann did not hide her irritation. "Of course tonight! It's Christmas Eve. The whole family is going to be here." She gave a put-upon sigh. "Really, Alan, sometimes you can be so difficult! You know very well that we always have dinner and tree trimming. Your brother and Missy are bringing the baby. Even your father will be home."

He did not miss the heavy sarcasm in that last remark.

"If I'm alive I'll be there," Alan said.

"And just what is that supposed to mean?"

"It means, Mother, dear, that I have one hell of a hangover and if I survive the day I will appear as scheduled."

"There's obviously no point in talking to you this morning," Ann said. "We'll see you at seven. I suppose you *have* gotten around to shopping for gifts for your family?"

"Yes, ma'am." It was a lie. He hadn't bought the first present. Which meant that he'd have to struggle out into the overcrowded stores today. Joanne was right. Damn

129

families. Next year I'll get out of town for the holidays, Alan thought. Most of his friends did. They fled to the Islands or Mexico or somewhere. Any place to avoid the hypocritical, contrived "family reunions" with people who happened to be accidentally related and, for the most part, wouldn't have gotten together by choice on a bet. Except for Jo and his father, he wouldn't pick any of them for friends. That was the real test. If you weren't related to people like Ann and Peter III and his dumb little wife, you'd never even answer their phone calls much less go to dinner with them and bring presents. Even Sarah had guts enough not to knuckle under to convention and go to Baltimore for Christmas. He remembered her saying so sometime last night.

Last night. Vague recollections began coming back on a wave of nausea. He remembered only bits and pieces. He and Jo had gotten pretty drunk at the St. Regis. He thought they'd eaten somewhere, but he wasn't sure. He did recall that sometime after midnight he'd taken a taxi alone to Christopher Street and pounded on the door of 12-B. He'd been looking for Toni, hoping she hadn't left for California. Had he said so? He didn't know. He did know that he'd ended up in bed with Sarah. Drunk as he was, there'd been sex. Brutal, rough sex as though he was punishing her for his unhappiness. There was no pleasure for him but he remembered Sarah moaning in delight and whispering something about how glad she was that he'd come back. Sometime in the early morning he'd gotten into his clothes and stumbled back to his own apartment to collapse in an exhausted heap of self-disgust which was a hundred times worse this morning.

A gnawing fear suddenly attacked him. What if Toni had been in the apartment and he hadn't known it? Then relief. He remembered Amy saying that Toni had left for California that morning. There had been a lucid moment when he looked into the disgusted eyes of Amy Green-berg before she disappeared into her own room and Sar-ah had led him to the bed he'd occupied more than once before.

There was something else. Something that happened before he went to Sarah's room. He'd gone over and opened a door, the door Toni had gone into the night she got her coat to go walking with him. He knew he had stood in the doorway staring at an empty room. It was all pink and white and immaculately clean. A pretty room, in sharp contrast to the disarray of the rest of the apartment. He'd focused on it blearily before Sarah had pulled him away. He'd wanted to stay there. To sleep in that narrow little bed and feel even that much nearness to Toni. He must have mentioned her. Else why would Amy have told him she'd gone? He wondered what he'd said. Whatever it was, Sarah chose to overrule it with the best weapon she had: her voluptuous and expert body. He thought of that body now with shame and self-loathing. He hadn't wanted Sarah. He'd wanted forgetfulness and an object on which to vent his anger.

He got up painfully and went into the bathroom for an Alka-Seltzer. He tried to avoid the face that stared back at him from the mirror over the basin. How could he have behaved so disgustingly? He'd been a sadistic monster. "Making love" to Sarah—a euphemism for what he really felt—had been fair game in those days when he enjoyed her and knew that he gave as much pleasure as he got. But to use her, as he had, in an effort to blot out the face of another woman was revolting. Toni would despise him if she knew. Or would she? Would Toni, of all the people in the world, understand that it was his longing for her, his frustration at the things that kept them apart that had driven him to behave like an animal?

The phone rang again. It was Sarah.

"Just wanted to make sure you got home all right," she said. "You were pretty smashed."

"Sarah, I'm sorry. About everything." Such inadequate words. "I behaved like a pig. Please forgive me."

There was a second of silence on the other end of the wire. Then, with unusual dignity, Sarah said, "I understand, Alan. I've understood since Saturday night. I don't mind being second choice if that's all there is."

It made him feel more like a heel than ever. He'd have preferred, by far, to have been called any insulting name. He deserved them all. Sarah knew what he felt last night. And she loved him enough to forgive him, to want him, even knowing he wanted someone else. She was asking him to come back, to pick up where they'd left off before that fateful Saturday. And he couldn't. Realistically, he knew he'd make love to other women if Toni didn't come back to him. He was a young, healthy man. But never again to Sarah. He couldn't face her. Or, rather, he couldn't face the reminder of his behavior that was both masochistic and sadistic. He stood there holding the phone, not knowing what to say. He wasn't going to insult her further with lies, tell her he loved her and that things would be as they once were. She should hate him, not love him. His guilt was terrible.

"Alan? Are you still there?"

"Sarah, I don't know how to say it. You're a beautiful woman with a generous soul, but . . . ."

"But you don't love me and you're not coming back any more. That's it, isn't it?"

"I think too much of you to."

She laughed. Not bitterly but in a way that made him feel small and cowardly.

"Next thing you'll say is that I'm too good for you. That I deserve a better man."

"It's true. You do."

"Oh, Alan, spare me the clichés! You know where to find me when you want me, drunk or sober. Merry Christmas."

She hung up before he had a chance to reply. He started to dial the florist to send her flowers but put the phone down before he completed the call. That gesture was as phony as everything else he'd done in the last twelve hours.

Chapter 10

It was not until the day after Christmas that Elizabeth finally managed to be alone with her granddaughter. She had seen Toni the night the girl got home and they were all together on Christmas Day, but both those occasions were too full of family gaiety and excitement for the kind of serious, private conversation Elizabeth had in mind. Instead, after the gift exchange and the holiday meal, she formally invited Toni to drive out and spend the next day with her.

"Alone," she said pointedly. "My age, rank and serial number give me certain privileges of rudeness. Your mother is not invited and Laurel is to take herself off for the better part of the day. It wouldn't be a bad idea if she hopped into town and made sure our decorating business survived the office Christmas party!"

They laughed affectionately. Elizabeth never changed. There was always humor in her directness as there was now, but Toni pretended alarm.

"Sounds ominous. You have some deep, dark secret you want to share only with me, Grandmother?"

Unknowingly, she was close to the mark. Elizabeth

chose to look haughty. "When I tell my deep, dark secrets, child, and believe me I have plenty, it won't be to the likes of you. I'll put them in the pages of a juicy best seller."

"I'll bet you could write a book at that," Jim said. "After all, you were a newspaper writer once, weren't you?"

"I did a column, among other phases of my checkered career," Elizabeth answered. "But, dear Lord, that was the Ice Age! Charlene was just a baby and . . ." She hesitated. "And anyway there've already been too many books written about the thirties. Besides, I never really was a very good writer. My mind always went too fast for my fingers."

"Seems to me it still does," Laurel sniffed. "Even when she drags out that old portable typewriter to write a regal memo to the staff, you can hardly make it out for all the errors."

"Do you really do that, Mother?" Charlene asked. "Do you write regal memos?"

"Sometimes I send a note to the office," Elizabeth said, "but I'd hardly call it 'regal.' It always says 'I,' never 'We.' Anyway, I write very few memos these days. Laurel doesn't need any help running that company. It's never done better." She looked affectionately at her friend. "I don't know how she does it. Seeing to me and keeping the business going full tilt."

"On *your* reputation," Laurel said gently. "Yours and Tony's."

The mention of his name brought a sudden hush. I wish I had known him, Toni thought. That marvelous stepgrandfather for whom I was named. He must have made her so happy. She's happy now, just thinking of him.

Before Toni arrived next day, Elizabeth reread her correspondence with Peter. It was an old habit of hers, keep-

135

ing carbons of her letters, and she was pleased that the one she had written four months ago did not sound too heavy-handed and grim. She also read her son-in-law's much delayed reply. He had gone into great lengths about Antoinette's meeting with Alan, recounting nearly word for word what his son had said and what, reluctantly, Peter had revealed about his own life. He confessed finally that he'd been more than a little ambivalent about advising Alan to give up all thoughts of his cousin.

"It was a hard decision, Elizabeth," he wrote. "Harder on those kids than on me, but I can see no future for them. I don't know whether Alan will go along with my thoughts on the subject. Nor what Antoinette's reaction really is. I should have seen her when you first wrote, but I was too spineless. And by the time Alan met her, it was too late. What could she think of a man who hasn't had the strength to fight his wife's superficial values, and who now compounds the felony by urging his son to give up the girl he loves for reasons of 'honor'?

"Plead my case for me, Elizabeth, if you can find it in your heart. Make her understand that I've asked the impossible of Alan and if he accepts the burden it will be my fault, not something of his own choosing."

Elizabeth set the letters aside, awaiting Antoinette's arrival. I adore that child, she thought, just as I always adored Charlene. I could never feel the same way about Ann. How foolish to think that mothers and fathers must love their offspring equally. Merely delivering a child out of one's body is no guarantee that one has to really like it once it becomes a functioning person. Few parents could face that "shameful" fact. They clung hypocritically to the belief that each child must have the same amount of love, like an equal share of a financial inheritance. Psychiatrists' offices are full of children trying to rid themselves of guilt for not loving their parents as they think they're supposed to. I wonder how many parents have dared admit to a doctor that they really don't like the person to whom they've given birth?

A mischievous smile played around Elizabeth's mouth. What heretical thinking! How shocked most of the world would be if she wrote a magazine article expounding her plain, unvarnished beliefs about the "sanctity" of parenthood. Maybe she'd do it one of these days, just for the hell of it.

It was her own unusual ability to face her true feelings about her own daughters that would make her talk with Antoinette possible. She did not agree with Peter that these two should be apart because of family differences or admirable but foolish deference to their parents' pride. But it might be difficult to make Antoinette understand how vapid and ridiculous such sacrifice was. "Honor thy father and thy mother." Elizabeth saw it as an admonition to be kind; not as a commandment to love. Love could not be commanded. It had to come willingly, even to parents. She was sure the Lord had meant it that way. He hadn't told Moses to proclaim, "*Love* thy father and thy mother." There was a difference. Somehow she had to make that child see the fine distinction.

And furthermore, I must stop thinking of Antoinette as a child, Elizabeth thought. She's going on nineteen. Older than Charlene was when she married. Almost as old as Ann was when she set a trap and caught Peter Richards. She's a fully developed adult, with emotional needs and physical longings.

Elizabeth looked at the big, graceful tree beneath which lay buried the ashes of her beloved Tony. We had strength to defy the world and marry, she said to him. Even though you were much younger than I, my darling. Even though we were considered "unsuited" to each other. Our love was bigger than conventions and social ta-

137

boos, just as Charlene's was when she married Jim. Damn it, if Antoinette wants Alan Richards I'm going to try with all my strength to make her understand she's entitled.

She heard footsteps crossing the terrace behind her.

"Grandmother?" the voice said softly. "You awake?"

"Of course I'm awake. What do you think I am, some dotty old lady who nods off in the middle of the morning?" Elizabeth's words were severe but her eyes danced as Toni came around to the front of the wheelchair and flopped down on the stone floor, legs crossed, delicate arms and hands braced behind her. Toni looked at the view of mountains and great forests that faced the terrace.

"It's so beautiful here," she said. "I'd like to stay forever."

"This world is only for me," Elizabeth said. "Yours is somewhere out there, Antoinette. Your time for this kind of wonderful, boring serenity is a long way off."

"I know. But right now it seems so easy and uncomplicated to just sit here and look at all that peaceful grandeur."

They were silent for a long moment. Then, without preamble, Elizabeth said, "Let's talk about Alan."

Toni turned as sharply as though her grandmother had hit her with a stick.

"I know all about it," Elizabeth said. "At least I know as much as Alan's father does." She handed Toni the two letters. "Read these, darling."

She watched as Toni read the communications between her grandmother and her uncle, seeing a variety of expressions come and go: gratitude and warm amusement as she read what Elizabeth had written; sorrow and pain as she followed Peter's long account of his life with Ann, his lunch with Alan and his reluctant conclusion that the sooner the lovers tried to forget each other, the better.

138

There was no anger but pity as she read what Peter had written about Ann. Toni recognized resignation and defeat underscored with compassion for them all. When she finished she was close to tears.

"Grandmother, I'm so unhappy. I've tried to tell myself that people don't fall in love for a lifetime in an hour, but they do. I have. Alan has, too."

Elizabeth nodded. "Everything in this world has to happen at some instant. One minute you're healthy and the next you're out of business. Look at me. I was always strong as an ox, and then bang! Out of nowhere a stroke that will keep me sitting the rest of my life. I had no warning, Antoinette. Tragedy just struck. Love can do the same. You simply accept life. You can't rationalize it. Not the bad or the good."

"You make me ashamed to be whining about my problems when yours are so much greater."

"No," Elizabeth said. "Mine aren't greater. Of course I hate being so damned helpless! Sometimes I get so mad I could throw this wheelchair over the cliff!" She smiled. "But I never visualize myself *in* it. I love life. I want as much of it as I'm supposed to have. And, Antoinette, I've had so much. Two husbands, children, a career, even a lover. The problem you see now came late. There were years before when I lived. *Really* lived. It was tough sometimes and scary and there were moments when I felt helpless. But by God, it was all worth it because I wasn't afraid to try for what I knew was right for me. No matter what it cost."

"But you're extraordinary, Grandmother. You have such strength, such self-sufficiency. Look what you've gone through with Mother and Dad. And Ann. That awful estrangement. And losing Tony. I don't think I could have survived those things."

"People survive much more terrible things," Elizabeth

said. "Your parents are happy. In her own way, Ann has gotten what she wants. She doesn't owe me anything nor I her. As for Tony, I never feel as though I've lost him. He's with me always. But I would have lost him if I'd listened to other people. Because I'd never have had courage to marry him if I'd cared what 'they' said."

"You don't agree with Uncle Peter, do you?"

"I understand his position, but no, I don't agree. I don't think he or Ann or your own mother and father or I are qualified to decide what you and Alan do with your lives." She touched Toni's dark hair. "Think about it, love. Think of yourself. And Alan. Oh, I know all the things on your conscience. You wouldn't be you if you didn't worry about hurting other people. But what terrible harm will come if you and Alan see each other? Even if you decide to marry, which is, let's face it, a step you haven't really reached, what would be so terrible? Ann would be outraged but she's been outraged before. Charlene and Jim might feel betrayed, but they'd care much more that you were happy. Alan is your cousin. So what? Cousins often marry with no more than a few Mrs. Grundys raising their eyebrows."

Toni wanted so much to be persuaded but she didn't have her grandmother's years of wisdom and experience to fortify her. All the things Elizabeth said were true, but it wasn't as easy as Elizabeth made it sound. Toni's loyalties lay deep. Even if she found strength to overcome the things that Elizabeth dismissed as "not so terrible," would she reproach herself later? And there was the question of children. She couldn't deprive Alan. She said so to her grandmother.

"Nonsense! Who says that a man or a woman can only be complete with children? Of course if you feel that way, you could adopt. Or you could take a calculated risk and have your own. Doctors aren't gods, Antoinette. They

140

don't know for sure that the children of blood relatives always have defects." She recalled her early musings. "Anyway, children aren't a requisite for happy marriage. Two people can be wonderfully complete unto themselves. Do you feel you'll be 'unfullfilled' if you never give birth?"

"No. Not especially. I'd like to have kids, but I could give them up if I knew that Alan wouldn't care."

"And you don't know, do you? You have no idea how Alan feels about that. You're making assumptions all along the line, Antoinette. But you're doing something I like even less. You're quitting without a struggle. You're not even giving this thing a fighting chance. My God, child, shouldn't you even find out whether this is real?"

"That's what Alan said."

Elizabeth smiled. "I *knew* I liked that young man."

Toni began to pace the terrace. "Everything you say makes sense, Grandmother. But I'm afraid."

"Of what, Antoinette?"

"Of seeing him. I want to go to bed with him. And I know I'll want to marry him. And there are all these damned obstacles." She faced Elizabeth squarely. "He says he doesn't care, but how can I ask a man like that to marry a mulatto?"

"Well, now we're getting to the real core of the problem, aren't we? You think you're not good enough for him because half of you is black. All this other stuff is a convenient cover-up, isn't it?"

Toni didn't answer but her silence was a clear affirmative.

Elizabeth shook her head. "Antoinette, Antoinette," she said sadly. "I never thought I had a stupid granddaughter. Darling, where is your head? What you're considering a problem is the luckiest break you could ever have! Alan already knows you're a mixed-marriage child. It doesn't make a whit of difference to him. Will the same be true of some stranger you meet and tell? Or do you plan never to admit that you're half black?"

Elizabeth was testing her, daring her, baiting her with a heavy hand. It had taken a long time to get to the root of Toni's fears, but they were coming close. Elizabeth had known the day would come. She waited now for the answer.

"Daddy once tried to make me promise that I'd never tell." Toni's voice was almost a whisper. "He said it could be arranged so that any husband of mine would never have to meet my father. I don't think that's possible. But even if it were, I couldn't deny what I am. I'm not ashamed of it, Grandmother, no matter how I sound. But I don't want to see Alan hurt because his wife is half black. I don't want to see him suffer the way I've seen Dad suffer when he thinks someone's slighting Mother because she has a Negro husband.

"I always pretended not to notice. Like nothing was different with us. But I knew it was. Just little things. Things I never told anybody." She paused. "I have something terrible to confess to you, Grandmother. The night I met Alan was the only time in my life I ever felt I hated my parents. Not for being related to Alan. For making *me* what I am."

Elizabeth wanted to gather her in her arms and comfort her, but she made no gesture, showed no change of expression though her heart was heavy for this young girl she loved so much.

"That's a perfectly normal reaction, Antoinette," she said instead. "The only thing surprising to me is that you haven't felt it earlier and often. It's what Jim has always feared, what makes him so guilty that he'd rather disappear from your life than have you rejected. Don't punish yourself, sweetheart. In a way your parents *were* selfish to have you. But they wanted you so much. You've been everything a daughter could be. They'd want you to have Alan if they knew. Maybe they'd have more faith in him than you do."

Toni looked at her suspiciously. "You haven't told them anything of this, have you?"

"No," Elizabeth said humorously. "There are limits beyond which even I will not go."

Toni smiled. "Well, I told Mother about Alan. She was wonderful about it. But I don't want Dad to know. Not until I make up my mind what's right. It's my problem, Grandmother. My hang-ups. I'll have to sort them out and come to my own decision."

"I'm afraid you already have," Elizabeth said. "You're determined not to see Alan again, aren't you?"

"I don't think I can. I love him too much."

"You're dead wrong, Antoinette."

"Could be. You make a lot of sense, darling. So did Mother in her way. But you did say at the beginning that only Alan and I have the right to decide what to do with our lives."

"I did indeed. But if you remember, I also included Alan in that decision."

The subject was not mentioned again during that Christmas visit. There were no more talks with Elizabeth or Charlene and none of them mentioned the problem to Jim. Toni spent one happy morning at the plant with him, seeing his new airplane design, complimenting him on his brilliance. He was like a child with a new toy, glowing under her praise. He introduced her to everyone as "his daughter from New York." They were some who did not know him well and who were visibly surprised to find this light-skinned girl Jim Jenkins' child. One of the newer secretaries questioned Pat Day about it when Toni and Jim left the office.

"Where did your boss get a daughter like that? Who's Mr. Jenkins married to anyhow?"

"One of the finest ladies I've ever met," Pat said coldly. "Maybe you've heard of Mrs. Jenkins' mother. Her professional name is Elizabeth Quigly. She runs *the* interior-decorating business in Beverly Hills."

"You mean he has a *white* wife? A rich one? How'd he ever swing that?"

Pat managed to hide her anger. She adored Jim and was fiercely loyal to him and to Charlene, whom she'd met many times.

"I haven't the least idea what you're talking about," Pat said. "Mr. Jenkins would never have to 'swing anything.' He's a genius and maybe the most charming and thoughtful human being I've ever met."

"Sure," the girl said caustically, "but would you want your sister to marry one?"

Unaware of the buzz of speculation their appearance caused in some quarters, Jim and Toni did a tour of the huge factory, greeting, it seemed to Toni, hundreds of people who seemed to be genuinely fond of her father. She was bursting with pride and love for him. I could never hurt him, Toni thought. Nor Mother, either, no matter what she said. Her father's present happiness reinforced her decision about Alan. It would be too cruel, too worrisome to Jim and Charlene if she got herself into a mess with her own cousin. Even the wise Elizabeth was wrong. Time will take care of it, she told herself again. Gradually I'll forget. People always do. I must stop this wishful thinking. When I get back to New York I must make all new friends, meet someone, perhaps, who'll drive this romantic nonsense out of my mind. I owe it to everybody involved.

They lingered longest around the nearly complete KJ-16, Jim explaining some of the complexities of construc-

144

tion. The technical jargon was completely over her head, but Toni listened attentively, trying to look intelligent. Finally, she laughed.

"Dad, I haven't understood one thing you've said in the last five minutes. All I know is that it's breathtaking and I have the smartest father in the world. Are they going to let you fly your baby when she's ready?"

He grinned. "No way, honey. First of all, it's not a one-man plane. Takes a whole trained crew and I'm not checked out for anything bigger than a Cessna. I'll be content to be a passenger when she's ready. Maybe this is the magic carpet that will bring your mother and me to New York to see you. As far as I'm concerned, that's a good enough reason in itself for designing her!" He took both her hands and looked into her eyes. "You're happy, aren't you, Toni?"

"About the plane? You know I am!"

"I didn't mean just that. I want to be sure you're happy about going back to New York. You don't have to, you know. You could go on studying in Los Angeles."

She looked at him curiously. Had Charlene said anything to him? She was sure her mother wouldn't break her word.

"I really want to go back, Daddy. I miss all of you, but I think I'm in the right place at the right time. I'm pretty sure I want to go into commercial art. And the real opportunities for a career are in New York."

"Is that what you want? A career?" He hesitated. "What about a personal life, Toni? A home, a husband and family?"

She knew what was in his mind. He wanted to know if she'd met anyone in New York. But he wouldn't pry.

"So far I've not been swept off my feet by any dazzling offers of marriage," she said lightly. "If I am, I'll let you know."

145

"You promise that, don't you? That you'll let us know?"

"Darling, I'm not the quick-elopement type. You'll have plenty of warning." She smiled. "Hey, what's with you all of a sudden? Afraid you have an eighteen-year-old spinster on your hands?"

"Terrified." The old familiar grin came back. "Another couple of years and you'll be over the hill, old girl. Early marriages run in your family."

She wanted to change the subject quickly. It was almost as though Jim sensed something and it was hard to keep this secret from him. She turned back to the airplane.

"It's fantastic," she said again. "Dad, I'm so terribly proud of you. I think you must be the most brilliant man in your field."

He pretended not to notice the reluctance to discuss her future. Perhaps he was only imagining something.

"Let's get the hell out of here," he said, "before you completely turn my head."

Driving home, he forgot his momentary flash of fear. His Toni was in good shape. And this, he thought, was one of the happiest days of his life.

Chapter 11

January marked the beginning of a new decade and Toni optimistically took it as a sign of a whole new life. She came back to New York, to the same hotel, but she did not feel like the frightened girl who had approached it less than five months before. Being with the family again had reinforced her belief in herself and in sanity and decent, mature behavior.

She transferred to Pratt and knew immediately that she'd made the right choice. There was something satisfyingly disciplined in learning the techniques of illustration, of making a figure "come alive" on a page, of taking a "dumb dress" and, with a few deft strokes of the pen, giving it excitement and individuality in an imaginary ad or magazine editorial. And leaving Parsons also insured that she'd not have to see Sarah.

Once she had lunch with Amy, who told her that a new girl had taken her place in Christopher Street and that Toni needn't bother about paying through January as she'd offered. The holidays were pure crap, Amy said. They'd had a New Year's Eve party. Same faces, same dumb conversation.

"Alan Richards didn't come," Amy said, reading Toni's mind. "He doesn't see Sarah any more. He's only made one appearance since you left. The same day you left, in fact. He came roaring down to the apartment late that night, smashed to the gills." She watched Toni's face. "He spent a long time in the doorway of your room, just looking at it."

Outwardly, Toni did not react, but the mental picture turned her knees to water. She could see him there, trying to recapture her as she'd tried to visualize him with her.

"Did he stay long?" she asked casually.

Amy looked at her searchingly. "Long enough to get the anger out of his system. He wasn't Alan. He was some desperate other person trying to forget how miserable he was."

For a moment Toni felt sick, betrayed and jealous. She knew what Amy was telling her. Sarah was there to provide oblivion. I don't blame him, Toni thought sadly. He's human. He was striking out blindly. And he's never returned to Christopher Street.

"I heard Alan had a novel accepted," Amy was saying now. "A friend of mine who works at his publisher told me."

Toni's face lit up. "But how wonderful! When will it be out?"

"This fall. I guess he's pretty excited. Don't you think you should call and congratulate him?"

"No, Amy, I don't. You're hopelessly transparent, but you get A for effort."

"I still think you're a damned fool."

"You remind me of my grandmother."

"Of your *what*?"

Toni smiled. "Never mind, Amy, dear. It's not important."

"You're not upset that I told you about Alan coming to

the apartment? It was meaningless. Pure physical release. Even Sarah knows that, though she's willing to settle for it."

Every word was torture, but Toni took it in the well-intentioned way it was meant. Amy was trying to tell her that this infidelity only proved his love in a strange and yet understandable kind of way.

"Look, Amy," she said softly. "I love Alan and I believe he loves me. But there are things you don't know. Reasons I can't ever be with him. It's my decision. And since it is, I don't expect him to become a monk. I don't want to know about the other women who will come into his life, just as I'm sure he'd never want to hear about the men who someday may come into mine. I can't be the proverbial dog in the manger, not accepting him and yet not wanting him to make love to anyone else. I can imagine what was going through his mind the night he came to Christopher Street. He was, as you said, looking for forgetfulness."

"Not entirely," Amy said slowly. "He was really looking for you."

She deliberately avoided Amy after that. Not that she didn't like her or recognize the honest concern Amy felt. She didn't want to hear any more about Alan. The temptation was still too strong, the doubts too challenging. In spite of how convincing she tried to sound, she knew she would hate any woman who lay in Alan's arms, whatever his needs or motives.

She worked hard at school, and weekends she apartment-hunted, finally finding three rooms in a big building on First Avenue. She was lucky to get it. Apartments were scarce and overpriced. She hated to ask Jim for more money, but he agreed without hesitation, understanding her need for privacy, the excuse she gave him for moving. She felt guilty about being "subsidized" under false pretenses, but she loved the luxury of freedom in her own surroundings, light-years away from the memory-filled apartment on Christopher Street. She knew she was beginning to recover. Her pain at the thought of Alan slowly lessened and the sick feeling she used to have every time she went out on the street, fearful that she'd bump into him, gradually began to diminish.

Sensibly, she even began to wish she could meet someone she might feel attracted to. She went out a few times with young men from her new school, but it was the same old story. She could not bring herself to discover sex with boys who meant nothing to her and to whom she was no more than a pleasant evening's diversion.

She knew she must be hopelessly old-fashioned. But it wasn't prudery or fear that kept her from experimenting. It wasn't even the lingering wish for Alan. She responded healthily to the touch of a man. On the few occasions when she'd been hungrily kissed at her doorway, when the stranger pushed the hard evidence of desire against her, she had wanted to make love. But always she pulled back, apologetic and ashamed. She knew she seemed to be making a big deal of her virginity. She was not. She simply waited for the moment when she could yield it without thought. When, she told herself mirthlessly, she could stop being so damned cerebral about sex.

At the end of January, a businessman named Bryce Sumner came to Pratt with an unusual proposition. He was introduced to the class one morning by the instructor.

"Mr. Sumner owns an advertising agency," the teacher said, "and he has a plan that could give all of you some active experience in commercial work. But I'll let him explain it."

Bryce stood up and smiled at the attentive faces. He was an attractive man, expensively dressed, handsome in a strong, craggy kind of way and well spoken with a voice that had a slight trace of Southern origin. He's older, Toni thought idly, as she waited for him to begin. At least thirty, maybe thirty-two. Still, that was young to own your own agency. He must be bright. He seemed nice. Related and sure of himself.

"First of all," Bryce said, "let's get one thing straight. My agency is not J. Walter Thompson. It's small. So small in fact that it consists of me, an overworked secretary, an art director and a couple of copywriters. So don't think you're dealing with somebody who can set you up in a swell office and pay you fifty grand a year. On the other hand, our smallness might be an advantage. Because big agencies don't need free-lance work, and I do. Big agencies don't take chances on people with no experience. Nor do they play hunches as I'm doing by coming here. I admit that economy is one of the reasons for the thing I'm going to suggest. Frankly, I'm using you. But if it works out, you'll also be using me for the experience you need. You see, I have a kind of offbeat gut feeling about originality and an idea that maybe I can find it here."

Quickly, concisely, convincingly he put his idea to them.

"You all know about big fashion and textile companies who underwrite design competitions. Winners get cash prizes and a chance to show the outfits they've made in a big fashion show at some store or hotel. There's nothing wrong with that. Sometimes the students get jobs in the company or with the competition, but mostly the sponsors get a lot of publicity and take big ads in *Women's Wear* to prove how devoted they are to 'the furtherance of young talent.' They also get a lot of fresh designs practically for free. I'm not knocking it. It's good for everybody. Except it's usually a one-night stand and I like old-

151

fashioned, long-range commitments." He grinned. "Professionally speaking, of course."

He had them in the palm of his hand as he went on to explain his idea. One of his accounts was a medium-sized French perfume company doing a volume of a couple of million dollars a year, and the simple truth was that Bryce Sumner, Inc., hadn't been able to come up with a good new magazine campaign for the client.

"We've gone the whole route in presenting ideas," he said. "We've had the sexy perfume approach, half-naked models in deliberately out-of-focus photographs. We've tried showing the bottle on black velvet like it was the goddamn Star of India. We've tried the sincere, educational approach of all-type ads with long, boring accounts of how the stuff is made. Everything's a rehash of somebody else's stuff. We know it. And, worse, the client knows it.

"My own overworked little staff is going out of their tree. We've pulled in professional free-lancers and they've bombed worse than we have. It's a helluva tough job, selling perfume. You can't see it, feel it, touch it or smell it on the page of a magazine. You can't get a mental image of it on yourself the way you can when you look at an ad for a dress or a fur coat or even a new eye shadow. People who've been kicking around the perfume-advertising business for years have fallen into all the stereotypes I mentioned, plus a few others. And you know what? Women don't believe us any more."

He wasn't smiling now. "Well, stupid as it may sound, that's why I'm here. I know you're all illustrators in the making. You're not really admakers. You probably don't know a damned thing about creating perfume campaigns and maybe you couldn't care less. But you're young, presumably inventive and with it. You're where it's coming from tomorrow. Best of all, you don't have preconceived

152

ideas about anything. And frankly, I'd like to cash in on that."

His idea was compelling. He wasn't offering big prizes or even publicity for the student who came up with the best idea. He'd pay one winner $250 and promise the campaign would run, if accepted by the client. There'd be $100 for each additional ad. No glory, he emphasized, but a little steady cash, which he presumed most of them could use. And, of course, they were free to include this work in their presentations when they went out job hunting. Any questions?

Toni raised her hand.

"Mr. Sumner, we're artists. Not writers. What about copy for the ads?"

"Good point. Fortunately, not a serious problem. Your artwork, if it's right and strong, will make it a cinch for a good writer to find the direction." He smiled. "At least I hope to God it will. Thanks for clarifying that, Miss . . ."

"Jenkins. Toni Jenkins."

"Thank you, Miss Jenkins. I hope you'll take a whack at the idea. I hope all of you will."

She fully intended to. Not that she felt she had a chance of winning. But all the things Bryce Sumner had said were true. Perfume ads *were* dumb. Unbelievable. Almost insulting. Like you were going to put a dab of something between your breasts and turn a man into a raving maniac. By the time he got that close, Toni thought, you didn't need perfume.

She picked up one of the forms Mr. Sumner had left behind. She noticed that nearly everyone in the class did, increasing her certainty that she couldn't win. She'd had less than a month of training in commercial art. Her technique couldn't compare with that of most of the students who'd been at it for a couple of years. But it wasn't a finished ad that was wanted. It was an *idea* the man was af-

153

ter. He'd probably translate the visual suggestion into photography or have it rerendered by a professional artist. He was looking for an unorthodox approach. In which case she was as qualified as anyone in the class.

She read the rules carefully. Ideas had to be submitted by April 1. All became the exclusive property of Bryce Sumner, Inc. The money terms were repeated. The product was mentioned only as a "high-priced French perfume." The anonymity was probably wise. It would keep the contestants from taking their clues from previous company advertising or from trying to make the work competitive with similar fragrances. Bryce Sumner was a smart man. He was risking little and he could gain a lot.

She could hardly wait to get home and start thinking about it. She'd set up a drawing board in one corner of the bedroom and spent many of her evenings there, working on school projects. It was a different kind of room than the one she'd put together on Christopher Street. The little-girlishness was gone, though the femininity remained, in spite of the workmanlike drawing board. She'd bought twin beds and covered them in patchwork coverlets which she'd made herself. A cheap round table hid under a patchwork cloth that reached to the floor. She'd seen pictures of Gloria Vanderbilt Cooper's all-patchwork room and loved it. That left space only for a dresser painted white and a matching table, two-tiered to hold a small TV set and a radio. The windows had white matchstick blinds and every available inch near them had pots of greens, ferns and philodendrons and African violets. Flowers were her passion, as they were her mother's and her grandmother's. It was hard to grow things in New York, but she filled the apartment with every kind of plant, tended them carefully, talked to them softly because she believed they responded to concern just as they did to light and water.

It was an apartment that told a great deal about the young woman who lived there. It said that she was soft and sensitive and womanly. That she had a flair for making much out of little. That she loved living things, cared for a quiet yet warm atmosphere and that she had taste and an interest in fashion. She doted on candles, burned them even when she dined alone and spent a shocking share of the allowance Jim provided on candlesticks. Antique ones had become her hobby and she would have laughed if it had been suggested that there was something Freudian about her collection of tall, slim holders. It seemed to her that all her happiest evenings were bathed in candlelight. In her mother's house and her grandmother's they dined in this soft glow. And sometimes, in the evenings, she and Charlene and Jim would turn out all the lights and sit listening to music in the warm, gentle illumination. Toni, alone, often did the same. She would light the candles in the living room, turn on the record player and let her mind float in the comfort of small flickering flames and the sweet, symphonic sound of the classics. These were not sad, self-pitying times. They were very composed, almost self-indulgent private moments.

But the night after Bryce Sumner's appearance she did not linger in the living room. Instead, she took a long, luxurious bath, recklessly pouring in scented oil and lying back in the tub, examining her own feelings as induced by the heady aroma of perfume. What made a woman want to be sweet-scented, a woman like herself who had no man impatiently waiting in the next room? What was the urge to lavish one's body with some aphrodisiacal aroma when there was no male to excite? Surely, this must be the case with many women. Not everyone used scent to attract. It was also a narcissistic thing. Part of loving yourself. And if you did not love yourself, how could you hope that others would love you?

Languidly she explored that train of thought. Was it unattractively self-indulgent? Wildly conceited? Or was the love of fragrance just part of being a woman for the simple pleasure of being a woman? Just that and nothing more? Did it mirror the yearning to be desirable not just to a man but to oneself? Did the fact that you wore perfume make you feel more secure, like a becoming dress or a hair style that gave you confidence?

Who really cared whether a famous actress wore the perfume? Who gave a damn whether it cost fifty dollars an ounce? Was it important that a couturier lent his or her name to it? Maybe some of these things mattered. Many women did need the reassurance of imitation or the status of price or the security of a famous-name label. It all counted. But it wasn't the guts of what made women buy. If she could capture that, she'd have something for Bryce Sumner. *If*. No inspiration came screaming at her. No miraculous solution wafted up out of the water. Get out of this damned tub, Toni, she told herself, before you are as shriveled as a prune. You're not going to solve the problem tonight.

She dried herself carefully and then stood looking at her full-length image in the mirror on the back of the bathroom door. She saw a slight but womanly figure. The breasts were small but firm, the waist narrow, the thighs slim and the legs well shaped. It was a body to give a man. A sexy body, she thought without shame. A body I like, she told herself defiantly. With or *without* perfume.

Bryce Sumner figured he'd probably wasted an hour and blown two hundred and fifty dollars on this far-out idea of asking a bunch of students to come up with something usable for the perfume account. None of them had even seemed very interested except for that one youngster, Toni something. She was the only one who'd even asked a question. Screw it, Bryce thought. Even if I lose the account I'll still have enough other business to guarantee pulling down a damned good living. Fifty, maybe sixty thousand this year. Net. Not bad for a kid from Texas.

He was amused by his own understatement. Not bad? It was more than his father made in the first fifteen years of Bryce's life. That son of a bitch, Bryce thought. I hope he's dead. It had been seventeen years since he'd seen or heard of the ugly Texas "redneck" who was his father. As a child, Bryce had been the butt of his father's cruel jokes, just as Bryce's mother had been the object of his abuse and his insatiable sexual desires.

The youngest of eight, Bryce had grown up hating Hank Sumner for his shiftlessness, his ignorance and bigotry. The father had pretended to farm. Pretended because he made no real effort to cultivate the small patch of rural land on which he was a tenant farmer. If it yielded three or four thousand dollars a year, they were fortunate. Hank was too lazy and usually too drunk to worry about it. Somehow they survived. Bryce's older brothers and sisters got odd jobs, his mother managed to feed and clothe them after a fashion, battling every day against the poverty that made her an old woman at forty-five. Pregnant with a child every year, she accepted her lot silently. Only when Hank attacked Bryce, physically or verbally, did Hannah protest. Bryce was special to her, her youngest child and the only one for whom she had any real hope. At her urging, he walked miles to the nearest town to borrow books from the limited public library or to sit and listen to the local band concert, a deplorable musical offering which at that time Bryce found enthralling. Later, when he heard his first big-city symphony orchestra, he could still remember the pathetic oomp-pa-pa of that small group of earnest, unskilled music makers.

Somehow, his mother had battled Hank Sumner with enough determination to let Bryce get through grade school and even two years of high school. Her husband sneered at the things Bryce loved, the reading, the music, even his efforts to stay neat and clean. He could hear his father to this day, violent, terrifying.

"Goddamned fairy!" Hank would shout. "Look at him! Skinny as a girl! Full of airs! Who the hell does he think he is? Why don't he go to work like the rest of us? He ain't the only mouth around here that's gotta be fed!"

Hannah would try to quiet him, try to divert his attention from Bryce. She was afraid of this big, hate-filled man whom she'd married at sixteen. But she was more afraid of what he'd do to her youngest child. Bryce loved his mother and when she died he was dry-eyed at the funeral, silently enraged at the hypocritical display of public grief put on by the husband who had killed her with his ignorance and cruelty and lust.

Even as they lowered Hannah Sumner into her poor grave, Bryce knew that he was never going to see any of them again. Not the slovenly sluts who were his sisters, or the bullying brothers who were imitations of the father he despised. He would get as far away as he could from them all, from their shiftless ways, their smug, stupid scorn of "nigras" and "spics," Mexican "wetbacks." He would escape from their distrust of people like himself who aspired to something better than sloppy farmwork, mindless sex and a cheap bottle of booze on Saturday night.

The day after Hannah's funeral he put his few possessions into a canvas bag and hitchhiked to Dallas. He did not even leave a note. He simply left, knowing no one would care. If they felt anything at all about his departure, it would be relief.

Years later, in interviews with the advertising trade papers such as *Ad Age* and *Anny,* he glossed smoothly over his beginnings. He said merely that he'd been born on a farm in Texas, that his parents were dead and his brothers and sisters married. He admitted, charmingly, that he'd had only a high-school education, leaving the impression that he was a self-taught, inherently brilliant man.

He did not tell the interviewers that he'd gotten where he was to spite his father and please his mother, even though neither of them knew of his accomplishments. He did say that he'd begun his business career as a stock boy at Neiman Marcus, which was true. He'd finished high school at night, but his real schooling had come at the store. He learned by watching and listening and imitating. Blessed with inherent taste and discernment, he spent his small salary carefully on a few good clothes bought on sale or with the help of his employee discount. He learned to flatter the right people, carefully making seemingly naïve suggestions for which he knew they would take credit.

In a short time he began to be noticed. This was no ordinary shipping clerk. With remarkable speed he made his way to an assistant-buyership and then to a buyer's job, all the while letting it be known that while he loved retailing his real interest was in advertising and promotion. By the time he was twenty-two, the store made him promotion director, on the basis of several splendid, original and highly workable suggestions for store events and publicity. In this new job he became involved in the advertising tied in with promotions and began to make frequent trips to New York to work out plans with some of the suppliers and their advertising agencies. It was during one of those store-sponsored trips that he met and became

159

friends with a partner in a big agency. A job offer followed and he spent the next five years building up a faithful following of accounts, loving the excitement of Manhattan, enjoying to the fullest his job, his excellent salary and his nontaxable expense account.

In 1965, at the urging of some of his clients, he opened his own small agency, Bryce Sumner, Inc. Though the ethics of leaving an agency and taking some of its billing with you was, at best, a dubious practice, Bryce got away with it. He started his own shop with a million dollars' worth of business of which fifteen per cent was his share. After expenses and overhead, he was grossing about forty thousand. Five years later he had a five-million-dollar agency, still small compared to the big ones, but, without the fixed costs of expensive offices or a big staff, proportionately more profitable than most. Even after taxes he kept his fifty to sixty thousand a year. A bachelor could live well on that, even in New York.

He'd been too busy to marry. Or perhaps, unconsciously, too turned off by the example of his parents. To him, marriage represented misery, hostility, unbearable bondage. He recognized the flaws in this rationale. He was seeing marriage through the eyes of his long-suffering mother. *His* marriage would not be bondage, when and if he chose it. His wife would not know poverty or degradation at the hands of a thick-skinned brute who represented all the bitter, biased, narrow views of the poor and ignorant. Bryce knew that Hank Sumner's unspeakable crudeness and terrible bigotry toward "inferiors," be they blacks, foreigners or women, was his unconscious way of reaffirming his manhood. The knowledge did not spark forgiveness or pity in his son. Bryce proved *his* manhood by financial success and the recognition of his peers. And by the easy, considerate conquest of some of the most attractive women in New York.

There was, he thought, time for marriage. He was in no hurry. Remembering his own family, he cared little about children and was in no rush to be a father. Besides, he was only thirty-two. Hardly too old for parenthood even if he waited a few years. And wait he would until he found the right woman. Then he would give her faithful and considerate love, for he was capable of it. His life would be, emotionally, all that he dreamed of. Just as it was already materialistically successful even beyond his wildest imagination. And this was only the beginning.

Versed in "cocktail-party psychiatry," he was thankful that he had not become homosexual. His hatred for his father, his reverence for his mother could, by all the pat notions, easily have pushed him in that direction. He even dreamed of Hannah Sumner, and in his sleep could smell the odor of turnip greens and cheap laundry soap that always surrounded the drawn, exhausted, old-looking woman. Awake, he wished she'd lived to see the dawn of Women's Liberation. Not that she'd have understood it or been allowed to be part of it, but no one needed more the release from slavery imposed by a foul-mouthed, stupid and arrogant husband. Only when it came to Bryce did Hannah stand her ground. With every ounce of her frail body she fought for this one child whose potential she instinctively recognized.

I wish I were a religious man, Bryce thought. Then I could believe she knows how far I've come. Hannah Rawlings, an uneducated sixteen-year-old girl who'd married the bottom of the barrel, would be proud to see that out of the dregs had come at least a semblance of the "quality folk" she'd wistfully admired.

Chapter 12

By mid-February, Toni was fully settled in the apartment,
engrossed in her studies and fascinated by Sumner's project. She even began building a quiet social life that had
nothing to do with the past. The girl who lived in the
apartment next door introduced her to some of the other
young people living in the building. They were easy to
know and pleasantly uncomplicated to be with. She
shared dinner and went to neighborhood movies with
these "singles" of both sexes. It was as though she was in
a period of waiting, among friends who were restoring her
peace of mind and strengthening her for the next turning
point in her life.

She still thought about Alan, but with quiet resignation,
half believing now that she had read more into the meeting than was really there. Perhaps I'm finally growing up,
she told herself. Certainly I'm less frantic than I was even
six weeks ago.

The only thing she could not come to terms with was
public admission of her heritage. She had not told anyone
that she was a mulatto, the way she had once straightfor-
wardly announced it to Amy and Sarah. Not that her new

friends probably would care, any more than the others had. But, she thought defensively, there just isn't any easy way to drop such a startling fact into an everyday conversation. You didn't casually say, "Oh, by the way, my father's a Negro." There had to be a valid reason for it. With Amy and Sarah, she felt that sharing an apartment was such a reason. Now there seemed to be no way to break the news easily, naturally, without awkwardness. Yet even while she thought it, she knew that was a lie. There had been plenty of chances to disclose the fact. The new group often discussed racial issues. And she always kept still. She was afraid to think why. Did she imagine it would embarrass them or herself? Was this Jim's nature coming out in her, this inherent awareness of the slights suffered by minorities and the selfish unwillingness to risk them?

That's disgusting! Toni thought. What's happening to me? Maybe New York is getting to me in a bad way. And yet she honestly faced the fact that she did not want to be classified with the flamboyant, overtly ethnic young people she saw in the subways. She admired them for their obvious pride in their blackness. They were right. And yet she cringed inwardly when she saw people step out of their way as the Negro students poured out of the Trade School at Second Avenue and Fifty-seventh Street. She was instinctively outraged by the looks directed at these uninhibited young men and women in their Afro hairdos, tight jeans and nail-studded jackets. Affronted by the fear and rejection and distaste on white faces, she hated the whites for feeling that way. But she also hated the young blacks for their provocative attitude, a mixture of defiance and hostility.

Most of all, she hated herself for being glad that the whites did not look at her with contempt or the blacks with any sign of recognition. She faced the fact that she

163

couldn't identify with them. At home, in Pasadena, almost the only Negroes one saw were unobtrusive, quiet domestics, neatly dressed women on their way to or from work. Here, dark skins were everywhere, demanding their right to be recognized, to be counted, to be people, taunting, challenging her to accept her "blood brothers and sisters."

Try as she would to understand and sympathize, she drew back from admitting her "relationship" to them. She was different, displaced even as her father was. Yet Jim Jenkins had something in common with his race: his appearance. His daughter did not even have that.

The problem was always in the back of her mind. She was a hypocrite, she decided. She pronounced harsh, possibly unfair judgments on herself. She'd told Jim she would never deny being black, and all the while she secretly hoped she would never have to admit it.

She made an effort to put all this aside. She'd face it when it needed to be faced. Right now, whatever she was was of no importance to anyone. Instead, she spent much of her free time thinking about the project Bryce Sumner had presented to her class.

After struggling with it for a few weeks, she could understand the adman's problem. To differentiate between perfumes was an impossible task unless a woman actually smelled them. On paper, how could a distinction for one be established? They all came in beautiful bottles, all gave off compelling aromas, all were made in more or less the same way with more less the same ingredients. She toured the shops, looking at the staggering array of French perfumes, listening to the various representatives give almost identical spiels about the merits of their products. To listen to the saleswomen, every fragrance had the same rich, rare components, the same long-lasting qualities, the same sensuous appeal. She knew she had not discovered a startling truth. The magazine ads she pored over reflected the

164

admakers' awareness that there was damned little new to say about a liquid that cost fifty dollars an ounce. Which probably was why perfume ads said so little and depended so much on the imagination of the reading audience. Bryce Sumner must be crazy to think that some amateur could come up with a solution to a problem that baffled the most experienced experts in the field. Not crazy, Toni amended. More like desperate. With six weeks to go, Toni shared his desperation. So far she'd sketched and thrown away fifty ideas. They were all trite and unconvincing. Not even as good as what she saw in the magazines. She wanted so much to come up with a great idea, to win Sumner's contest. It was not just the money, though that would help. Toni was by nature a competitive person, always eager to prove herself. She wondered if this desire to achieve had something to do with her heritage. Did Elizabeth's success inspire her, or was success more important because of her background? Did she, like her father, have to try harder?

She speculated again, as she had with Charlene, whether Jim's enormous pride in the airplane he designed was more excessive than it would have been had he been a white engineer. Aware of it or not, he probably was trying to prove that color had nothing to do with ability. In a way, Toni had a subliminal need to do the same.

She was deep in these thoughts one Saturday morning as she circled the perfume area at Saks, so engrossed that she did not notice the man coming toward her from the men's department which adjoined it. He touched her sleeve and said, almost timidly, "Toni?" Startled, she looked up into the face of Alan Richards.

"Hi," he said. "Trying to buy something to make you even more beautiful?"

The sight and sound of him brought everything back. All the strengthening of resolve in the past two months

165

seemed to melt under that deep tender gaze, that voice that held her rooted to the spot in a mixture of joy and dismay. She tried to sound natural, as though she had just bumped into a casual old friend.

"Alan! What a surprise! How are you?"

"Not too bad. And you?"

"Fine. Just fine." Liar. She was shaking inside. Even her voice sounded to her own ear like someone else's, high-pitched and nervous. Desperately, she sought refuge in rapid-fire small talk. "Did you have a good Christmas? I hear you have a book coming out. Congratulations! You must be terribly pleased." She was making an utter ass of herself and he didn't help. He simply stood there, looking at her with that same imploring look he'd had at the front door of Christopher Street.

She glanced at the packages in his hands. "You look as though you're on a buying spree."

He seemed to have forgotten them. "Oh, these. I've just been picking up a few last-minute things to tide me over. I'm leaving at noon. The agency is sending me to Paris for a couple of weeks. We have some problems there that the local office can't seem to handle."

It was ridiculously mundane. They had not been in touch with each other for nearly two months. Not a word or a gesture on either side since that one, unforgettable meeting. Did he know that his father had written to Elizabeth? Was he waiting now for her to confess that she had told Charlene all about him? What had he been thinking since last they talked? Why hadn't he come after her as she secretly hoped he would? She knew she was not making sense. It was she who had sent him away and then run herself. He would have been waiting for some sign from her. And yet, Toni thought almost angrily, if he'd really cared he'd never have let it all slide the way he had. He was the man. She was feminine and perhaps old-fashioned

166

enough to believe that he should be the aggressor. I've been making it all up, she told herself. Alan doesn't really care about me. His actions have proved it. She tried to sound very composed and casual.

"Well, it's been nice seeing you again," she said. "Good luck in Paris. And good luck with the book. Maybe you'll send me an autographed copy."

"Maybe you'll tell me where to send it." His distress was real. "I haven't even known where to find you."

In spite of herself, her words came out resentfully. "That shouldn't have been too hard. Why didn't you try asking your family?"

She was being cruel, petty, wanting unreasonably to punish him for the sentence she'd pronounced.

"Don't, Toni," he said. "Don't try to be tough. Darling, it was you who sent me away. What could I do but wait for you to call me back? Don't you know that's the only thing I've wanted all these weeks—some hint that you'd changed your mind?"

His gentleness was a reproach. He did care. He was offering himself to her, only waiting for her decision.

"It's no good," she said. "Nothing's changed."

She made a motion to leave but he caught her hand. Don't, she silently pleaded. Don't touch me. I want you so much.

"You're wrong," Alan said. "Everything has changed in the last two minutes. I won't lie to you, Toni. I tried to convince myself that last December was nothing more than a chance encounter. When I heard nothing I told myself that I was an ass to think that people fell in love in an instant. I tried every way I could to put you out of my mind. But it hasn't worked. I love you."

It was exquisite irony. Each had been waiting for a signal from the other, each growing more sure that it was a one-sided love, an imaginary, romantic ideal. They were

167

wrong. And yet, Toni told herself, none of the barriers have magically disappeared. It's still impossible. She tried to remove her hand from his warm, desperate grasp.

"We have to forget it," she said. And then because nothing could have stopped her, she added very quietly, "I love you, too."

She wrenched away from him and was gone, pushing through the crowd of shoppers, heedlessly bumping into startled dowagers who blocked her path to the street. He did not see her wipe away the tears as she ran, but he felt them. They matched his own. Goddammit, no! It's too real, too meant to be. His father was wrong about his "duty." Toni was wrong. His only duty was toward her and himself. This "noble" self-sacrifice was stupid. From now on he'd not be passive. He'd find her and make her see where she belonged. The rest of them could all go to hell. His mother's foolish pride, the Jenkins' hurt feelings, even the blood relationship—all these things were gnats to be swatted away. He damned the fact that his plane left in less than two hours. But he'd not be gone long. The minute he returned from Paris he'd be his own man, and hers. They'll all understand when they realize that this is the only thing in the world we both want. And if they don't, we can't help that either.

Feeling suddenly at peace, he went home, finished packing and hailed a cab for the airport. He couldn't sell himself long-distance. He wouldn't even try. But he'd be back in a short time. He'd find her and hold her and refuse to listen to all the reasons why they couldn't be together forever. I'm going to marry Toni Jenkins, he told himself over and over. The wheels of the taxi answered him, yes you are, yes you are, yes you are.

Bryce Sumner's project forgotten, Toni half ran back to her apartment, her mind filled with nothing but the

168

memory of Alan's face, his touch, the sound of his voice. Why did we have to meet again? The longing was as intense as ever, more intense perhaps. She wondered whether he would write to her from Paris. Probably not. He didn't know where she lived. Information would give him her phone number but not her address and there'd be no time to track that down before his plane took off. Unless he called his father. Peter Richards knew where she lived. And then, with dismay, she realized that he didn't. Elizabeth's letter had given him her first New York address and Parsons. She could not be found at either any more.

She thought she must be going crazy. She knew she must not see Alan again and she was praying that she would. She wished she could believe Charlene and Elizabeth. She wanted more than anything to be convinced that she and Alan had a right to love each other selfishly, heedlessly. But all their wisdom and advice was based on the presumption that desire was stronger than conscience, and for Toni, at that moment, it still was not.

The phone rang. She dared not answer it, for fear it was Alan. She let it peal five times, eight, ten. And then it stopped. Listlessly, she went down to the lobby to pick up her mail, unheeded on her way into the building. Among the bills and advertisements was a letter from Elizabeth.

"Dearest Antoinette," she wrote. "I must apologize. I've not written since you were home for Christmas, but I keep up with your doings through your mother. I'm so happy that you have an apartment you love and that the new school is going well. I envy you both enterprises. There is nothing more exciting than seeing your own home take shape, and this is the first one of your very own, the first in which you've 'put down roots.' Darling, that's a lovely experience. In my mind I see you in your 'house.' I imagine it high in the sky, filled with winter sunlight and seasonless growing things and little touches that say to the world, 'Antoinette lives here.' Some people say that it's silly and superficial to care about inanimate objects, that possessions come to possess the possessor. I don't believe that. There are things I've treasured for more than sixty years. Some junk, to be sure. Some quite nice, even so-called 'valuable' things. To me, they *all* have value—in memories and happy recollections of where I bought them and when, or of the people who gave them to me. They are all quite animate to me, from my mother's china to the needlepoint pillows I made when I was waiting for *your* mother to arrive. You'll collect your own 'living objects' now and have some of ours later. But meanwhile, I'd like, selfishly, to be part of Antoinette's private world while I'm still around to know it. I'm sending you a tiny object that Tony and I loved. Nothing of great value. Just a little golden-washed painting of the view from our terrace. It was a gift to us on our first anniversary and we always said that even on cold, dark, rainy days we had the sunshine to look at, to remind us that brightness inevitably comes.

"As for the school, will you hate your grandmother for admitting that I can never quite see you as the great, strong, dedicated career woman? Not that I doubt your talent but I question whether this is your ultimate fulfillment. Oh, I know that in this new world where women are supposed to be beset with determination to be 'individuals,' monetary success and professional recognition are presumably 'badges of freedom.' I had them both, my dear. And they were fine. But they never could compare with the success I felt myself to be when I saw the happiness I could bring to the face of the man I loved. Perhaps this is the moment to lose yourself in your work, Antoinette, but I remember our talk at Christmas, and my

170

inescapable feeling is that you are too gentle for the demanding and ruthless competition of the so-called career world. I think you must decide, one day soon, where your priorities lie, whether with Alan or someone else. You will succeed at work, if that is what you truly want. But somehow I sense that you're talking yourself into a life style that is, for you, only a substitute. Perhaps I sound as though I haven't enough faith either in your ability or in your dedication. That's not true, and I don't mean to sound discouraging. Let's just say that I feel things under the surface of my skin. Probably comes from my New England background; I've long suspected that at least one Salem witch crept into the branches of our family tree!

"But enough philosophy, the aphrodisiac of the aged! Things here are fine. Your mother is well and so is Jim, though working, as you know, far too hard on his monstrous KJ-16. Charlene has at least convinced him to take Sundays off—a major accomplishment. Of course, wouldn't you know that even on that day he has to be involved with aviation? He's joined a private flying club in South Pasadena and we are torn between being glad that he has some recreation and nervousness every time he goes scooting around in those little planes that look to me like toys. I suppose that's what they are, toys. Hardly an original thought, but men *are* just big boys at heart, aren't they, God bless 'em. Maybe that's why they need us—the sympathetic sex. Jim loves it and is trying to talk Charlene into taking lessons. My crazy daughter says she just may! At least she'd get to spend some more time with him.

"Oh, Antoinette, doesn't it make your heart sing to see how they love each other? And isn't there (said she slyly) a not too subtle moral in the good life these two people have managed in spite of all the obstacles?

171

"I love you, darling, even though I'm a rambling, meddling old

                                    "Grandmother."

There was a P.S. "To prove to you the awful truth of these last few words, I've done another naughty thing. I've sent Peter Richards your *new* address and the name of the new school. He won't bother you. I just sleep better knowing someone in the same city knows where you are. So sue me!"

Toni smiled. Perhaps Elizabeth was a witch. Or more like a fairy godmother. Her warm, understanding letter could not have arrived at a more needed moment. It was comforting to know that in California, at least, all was serene.

Chapter 13

Bryce Sumner was surprised by the high caliber of work he received from the students. There were three very possible campaigns. Much better than the professional efforts he'd seen. It had in fact been a hard choice, an embarrassment of riches, but he finally selected a "pop art" treatment by some boy named Juan Martinez. It was a daring, unorthodox ad but an attention getter. He wondered whether the client would be courageous enough to buy it. In any case, he had two good standby campaigns if the perfumer was not of the Andy Warhol school of thought. Bryce was sure he could sell either of the inventive but less shocking alternatives submitted by Antoinette Jenkins and Maryanne Webster.

He came back to present Martinez with a check, congratulate the class and explain why the winner had been chosen.

"Juan's idea is far-out," he told the students, "but it's not far-out just for the sake of being far-out. What I mean is, anybody can make an ad that will get the magazine reader to stop and look. The easiest and most obvious way, for example, would be to put a good, four-letter

Anglo-Saxon word right in the middle of the page. In very big type. But getting attention is only one thing. Making the potential consumer want the product is something else. I think this campaign does that. In fact, there were several ads I could, in clear conscience, try to sell to my client. If Juan's campaign doesn't make it, I'll offer Miss Jenkins' or Miss Webster's. And painful though it would be, I'll see that they get first-prize money, too. Thanks very much for probably saving my neck. If I can return the favor in any way, let me know. As long as it isn't a job you want."

"I think this has been a very instructive project," the teacher said, "and I hope we'll find other businessmen with Mr. Sumner's faith in young talent. One more thing. If any of you would like to stick around, Mr. Sumner says he'll be happy to talk advertising with you. Congratulations, everybody!"

Toni was elated that she had come in second or third. She had been so unsure of her ability that it was almost as good as winning. After the others had straggled out, she summoned her courage and approached Bryce Sumner.

"Mr. Sumner, I'm Antoinette Jenkins."

Bryce extended his hand and shook hers warmly. "The lady who 'placed' in my horse race. That's a damned good campaign you did, Miss Jenkins, even if you came in second."

"I'm delighted to have come that close to the winner's circle," Toni said. "I really didn't expect to. But, Mr. Sumner, would you tell me why Juan's campaign was better? Not that I question your judgment, I just wondered why, professionally, you chose his over mine. I mean, I'd like to know how mine could have been improved."

Listening to her serious, eager-to-learn voice, Bryce suddenly realized what an extraordinarily striking young

174

woman she was. How old was she? Twenty? Twenty-one? A baby, certainly, but appealing.

"You interested in advertising as a career, Miss Jenkins?"

"I'm not sure. Up to now, I was just heading for fashion illustration but I really got involved in this project. It was fun to think it through, as well as to execute the idea. In fact, the planning was almost more interesting than doing the artwork."

"We call that 'devising a strategy.' That's really what I was after, you know. A fresh approach, not just the visual. Artists are a dime a dozen. Original thinkers cost at least a quarter."

She liked him, felt at ease with this suave "older man" with his quick, big-city mind and his contradictory slow Southern accent. Emboldened by the rapport, Toni said, "What's the going rate on common sense?"

Bryce raised an eyebrow. "Beg pardon?"

Toni hesitated. "I don't mean to sound like a sore loser, Mr. Sumner. Juan's entry is probably good advertising from a man's point of view, but I don't think it will sell a nickel's worth of perfume to a woman. Where do you draw the line between originality and understanding of the subject?"

He looked at her with new respect. "I take it you think *your* campaign would have more appeal to buyers."

Toni was uncomfortable but determined. "Yes, I do. Juan's work was very clever. Too clever to appeal to potential female buyers of perfume." She was very earnest. "Juan's tried to make perfume a "necessity' by associating it with everyday things like canned soup and Coca-Cola. That's not the way women think about perfume. Nothing at fifty dollars an ounce can be made into a necessity! It's got to do much more for a woman than just make her smell good."

175

"For instance?"

"It's got to make her love herself. That was the first idea I had and I kept coming back to it. Not love herself in a superficial, narcissistic way, but with confidence and pride in her body and her mind."

"You don't think the love-sex-get-a-man thing has been overdone in perfume advertising?"

"Yes, I do," Toni said. "But I'm not talking about that. I'm talking about feeling secure within oneself, knowing you're worth loving. Maybe 'liking yourself' would be a better phrase than 'loving yourself.' " She stopped abruptly. "I'm sorry. I have some nerve telling you about advertising."

"You're not telling me about advertising," Bryce answered, "you're educating me about women." He pulled Toni's entry out of the portfolio he'd brought. "Let me look at this again in light of our conversation. I've liked it right along, but maybe I haven't understood it." He studied it for a long moment. " 'Love yourself and be loved.' Not a bad line. And the way you've drawn the woman is good. She looks like she's found serenity through herself. Like any guy with an ounce of sense would find serenity *with* her."

Toni's heart began to pound.

"You could be right about the appeal," Bryce said, "but I still think Juan's idea is stronger advertising. It will stand out from the competition, the brand will be remembered among thirty or forty others advertised in the same issue of *Vogue* or *Harper's Bazaar*. That's the first step. The idea that the perfume can make you love yourself is something the demonstrator can say at the counter. Juan's approach should make women curious enough about Perfume X to get them there in the first place. And, practically, at Christmas men are the big buyers of perfume. He looked at Toni's disappointed face. "You still think I'm wrong, don't you?"

She didn't answer.

"I'm a commercial whore. A thickheaded hack. A male chauvinist. Right?"

Toni smiled. "No, of course not."

"But you're disappointed in me."

She looked up at him. "A little."

"Are you always so honest, Antoinette Jenkins?" He sounded suddenly very protective. "Don't you know honest guys finish last?"

"I thought the quote was 'nice guys.' "

Bryce laughed. "Okay. Nice guys. Nice women. Nice people. Don't look so crushed. Your ad may be the one the client buys, you know. Particularly if he discusses it, as he will, with his wife. If it runs I'll not only give you the prize money, I'll buy you the best dinner in town." He paused. "That is, if you're available for dinners."

The smile reappeared. "I'm available," she said.

He called her a week later. "I'm glad you're not one of those chic, unlisted ladies," he said. "You forgot to give me your phone number. What's your favorite restaurant?"

Toni couldn't believe her ears. "You mean I *won?*"

"Nope, you lost. I think the client's wife has been out of town."

"Then you don't owe me a dinner. It's nice of you to offer a consolation prize, but honestly it isn't necessary."

"I know that. Only perfume is necessary, remember? This is pure self-indulgence. I'd like to see you again."

"Thank you," she said directly. "I'd like to see you, too."

It turned out to be a glorious evening. They dined at Côte Basque and Bryce was enchanted by this unaffected, intelligent and hauntingly beautiful young girl.

"Wait until I write my parents about having dinner

here," Toni said. "I've only read about it in *Women's Wear*. It's beautiful, just the way I knew it would be."

"Tell me about your family," Bryce said.

She told him about the house in Pasadena, the happy childhood. "I was spoiled rotten, I guess. An only child with fatuous parents and a doting, marvelous grandmother who's still the greatest lady I've ever known." She described Charlene with unaffected, uncomplicated admiration. "And my father's an angel," she said. "He's just designed a fabulous new airplane. I'm so proud of him." She told Bryce that she loved New York and school and that she really had the best of all possible worlds. There were also two things she did not tell him: her father's color and her hopeless love for her cousin.

Bryce listened attentively. "Sounds like you've got it made," he said. "Only one thing missing. No man in your life?"

"No." She paused. "Not really."

Some romance went sour somewhere, Bryce thought. This is the only time I've seen her look sad. Whoever the guy was, he was a fool to let her get away.

Toni was grateful that he didn't pursue the question. Instead, she said, "I've been doing all the talking. Now tell about you."

He gave her, in turn, a slightly edited version of his life. The same one he gave to interviewers, skipping the sordid facts of his early life, concentrating on his work, being appealingly modest about his self-made success.

Toni smiled impishly. "Only one thing missing," she echoed. "No woman in your life?"

He grinned. "No, but I'm taking applications."

Two nights later they had dinner again, this time at La Grenouille, sitting properly in the front section. On both evenings Bryce was scrupulously well behaved. He left her in the lobby of her building with only a casual little

178

kiss on the cheek. Toni was both glad and sorry. She didn't want him to spoil everything by acting like a sex-mad adeolescent, but she was slightly puzzled that he'd not made so much as a verbal pass. She hoped he wasn't gay. It was a possibility. Thirty-two years old, highly eligible and still a bachelor. In the next moment she rejected the idea. She was hanging labels on people, the way everybody did in this town. It wasn't fair. Someone might have said the same thing about Alan, unmarried at twenty-five.

Alan. The thought of him lay in her like a stone. More than six weeks since he'd gone to Paris and he said he'd be away only a couple of weeks. For all she knew he had returned and made no effort to get in touch with her. Even if he was still away, by now he could have written, now that she knew his father had her address.

I am going to stop thinking about him, she told herself. This obsession simply must end. If he really loved her he would have been bombarding her with letters and calls form Paris. She could no longer make excuses that he was a sensitive, gentle person who was trying to respect her wishes. He knew she loved him. Wasn't he going to fight for her? Bryce Sumner would, she thought. He wouldn't quietly accept the decision. He would overrule her objections, brush aside her fears and take what he and she wanted.

Determinedly she turned her thoughts to Bryce. He was attractive. She liked him and she knew that with a little effort she could deepen his attraction to her. Most of all, maybe he could make her forget Alan. She had to begin to "think like a man," or better still, like a young woman of this day. It was time she had an affair and Bryce Sumner was the logical choice. An affair would require no soul searching about whether or not to discuss her parentage. It was a way to grow up, to experience life, to

179

realize, hopefully, that there was more than one man in the world who could occupy her waking and sleeping thoughts.

It was unlike her to think in this calculating, cold-blooded way, but she was driven to it by hurt and bewilderment and a desperate need for affection, even the temporary kind. Bryce would not be harmed. He would enjoy it. Alan would never know or, probably, care. It's time I behaved like a woman, not a romantic child, Toni thought. Even my mother recognizes the way things are today.

The next day she had the prescription filled at the drugstore and began taking the pill.

Toni was right. Bryce Sumner was attracted to her and he found it damned disquieting. He'd taken her out only twice, had given her no more than a chaste kiss on the cheek, and yet he found himself constantly thinking about her. Even at the office where he normally lost himself in his work, he'd suddenly remember little things. The delicate, creamy color of her skin. The way her eyes sparkled when he took her to restaurants she candidly said she'd only read about. Her naïveté was refreshing, disarming. There was a kind of innocence about her that Bryce thought no longer existed in a girl of Toni's age. Yet there was a hint of invitation that belied the chaste exterior.

You never knew about girls these days. He'd been a little disturbed when this one admitted she was not quite nineteen. She was even more of a baby than he'd supposed and he, fourteen years her senior, felt like a dirty old man. It was what had kept him from suggesting that they go to his place after they left La Grenouille. He'd taken her home early, determined at that moment not to see her again. What did he think he was doing, even giving a moment's consideration to starting an affair with this

180

child? He was used to experienced women, the kind who understood that his interest was purely physical and in all likelihood temporary. They knew what it was all about. Toni was a different breed. Not, he supposed, that he'd be her first lover. These were different times. By eighteen, most girls, especially those in New York, were no longer virgins. She must have had some experience. He was almost positive of it, now that he thought back to the answer she'd given when he'd asked if she had a man in her life. "Not really" was like saying "I did have, but he's gone."

And fourteen years wasn't really all that much difference, was it? What was he getting so uptight about? Hell, he was only thinking of sleeping with her, not marrying her.

Still, he let two weeks go by before he called her. She was genuinely glad to hear from him, and obviously delighted to accept his invitation to dinner. He made no explanation for his silence and she didn't ask for one. Chalk up another point for Toni, he thought. Most women would have been petulant about his neglect, or at the least inquisitive.

He did not take her to an elegant restaurant that night. On the contrary, he walked her four blocks down First Avenue to Billy's, a noisy, crowded steakhouse not conducive, with its unglamorous surroundings, to a romantic buildup. He wondered whether he was testing her; whether she'd seem as alluring across a cheap checkered tablecloth as she did in the expensive, flower-filled, quiet ambiance of La Grenouille. Or was he setting up roadblocks for himself; almost hoping that in this neighborhood bar she'd be just another young, pretty student, a girl who could not possibly hold any real attraction for him?

Whatever his hopes, they were dashed the moment he

saw her. "Dress casually," he'd said on the phone. "We'll just grab a bite in the neighborhood." She had cheerfully agreed and Bryce was disconcerted to find that, if anything, she looked even more appealing in the skinny shirt and pants she'd put on that April night. All through dinner he'd had a growing urge to undress her, to take her home and make love to her, to discover the beauty that he could imagine under the shirt that clung to her breasts and the tight pants that fit so carefully over the trim buttocks and outlined the aristocratic legs.

"I missed you," he said in a low voice when they were seated, knowing every word could be overheard by the adjoining tables if they chose to eavesdrop.

Toni seemed unaware of the neighboring diners.

"I missed you, too," she said.

"Aren't you curious about why I haven't called?"

Toni cocked her head slightly. "No. Not really. I just assumed you were busy."

"Didn't you think maybe I'd dropped you?" He was being deliberately cruel but she wouldn't play the game. Instead she laughed.

"Well, we haven't exactly reached dizzying heights, have we? I mean, if you had dropped me it wouldn't be much of a fall, would it?"

Her laughter was infectious and Bryce joined it.

"You have a point there," he said. "That loud noise you just heard was my ego deflating."

They talked easily through dinner. The crazy perfume client was on the fence again. They might just go to Toni's idea after all.

"So you see," Bryce said, as they were finishing their steaks, "maybe you'll really wind up winning."

"I already have," Toni said. "After all, I've gotten to know you. A little."

They suddenly understood each other.

182

"Let's get the hell out of here," Bryce said. "I make good coffee at my place."

Toni nodded solemnly.

Hours later she lay awake beside him in the big bed, feeling wonderful. Surprisingly not even guilty. All the desires so carefully held in check had been released almost at the moment he touched her. She had expected to be self-conscious, but it had all been tender and natural. They had not even mentioned coffee when Bryce opened the door to his apartment. Inside he had taken her in his arms and kissed her deeply, running his hands over her body and then, wordlessly, had led her to the bedroom.

All he'd said was, "The bath's there, if you want it."

She'd shaken her head. Instead, never taking her eyes off him, she'd begun to slowly take off her clothes until she stood naked before him. She had no idea that she was, with these erotic, deliberate movements, behaving as provocatively as a strip-tease artist. It had been less a desire to be seductive than an instinctive, honest way to declare herself.

They'd made love and rested and made love again. She knew that Bryce was talking softly to her but she did not hear the words. She felt only his hands and his body and her delicious awakening to sexual desire that matched his own.

Now she felt his fingers lightly touching her breast. He lay on his back with his eyes closed, but he was as wide awake as she. She covered his hand with her own.

"Darling Toni," he said. And then, almost reluctantly, "This was a first for you, wasn't it?"

She held his hand more tightly. "Yes. Was it so obvious? Was I a disappointment, Bryce?"

In response he pulled her to him, caressing her gently, covering her face and throat with kisses.

"The world should only be full of such disappointments," he said. Then he released her. "I'm only sorry I was first," he said. "A man doesn't like to think he's been a beautiful child's downfall."

"I'm no child."

"Obviously. Still you were a virgin. And, Toni, I can't let you think that this means . . ."

She covered his mouth with her hand. "I know what it means. That we are two people who've given each other enormous pleasure. I hope we will again. This was such happiness for me, Bryce. I hope it was for you. But I don't consider it a proposal."

"Give me time," he said perversely.

"No. No promises. No plans. You're not ready for that and neither am I."

"You're in love with somebody, aren't you?"

"It's too long a story. Maybe someday I'll tell you all about it. But it has nothing to do with us."

She couldn't say that in a way she had used him far more than he'd used her. He was the instrument to exorcise the obsession. And in a strange way it had worked. She did not, even now, fancy herself in love with Bryce. Love was reserved for Alan. But she could be a woman, could feel normal desires and, perhaps most importantly, not feel guilt in a moral sense, or betrayal in a childishly emotional one. Realism. That's what it's all about, Toni thought. That's what it has to be about if one is to survive.

Bryce got out of bed. "I guess I have to take you home, don't I? You wouldn't possibly consider trying my coffee at breakfast, I suppose."

She smiled up at him. "Another time, maybe."

They dressed silently. Why am I going home? Toni wondered. If I want to stay out all night I have no one to account to. Yes, you do, her mind answered. You have your own peculiar morality. Spending the night represented a commitment. Somehow, to her, going home kept the affair the purely physical thing she wanted it to be.

It was almost four o'clock in the morning when Bryce let her out of the cab.

"Tomorrow night?" he said. It was put as a question but meant as a statement.

"Yes," Toni said. "Tomorrow night."

To the interested few, an announcement of World War III could not have brought a more stunned reaction than the gossip-column item which appeared in the New York *Daily News* one morning early in May. Ann and Joanne Richards read it at their respective breakfast tables the day it appeared. Alan Richards found it enclosed in a letter from his sister which arrived later in Paris. And several days after that, Elizabeth was wordlessly handed the news by Laurel Lane, who came across it in a bundle of newspaper clippings forwarded by the service which sent all publicity mentions of Elizabeth Quigly to her office.

It was, for those who cared about such things, a juicy item written in the breezy, irreverent style for which its lady society reporter was justly famous:

"Nothing tilts the tiaras of Manhattan hostesses to an angrier angle than the defection of a once-dependable bachelor. (You *know* how hard it is to find extra men!) And right now les grande dames are *veddy* annoyed with Mad Avenue's most eligible of the eligibles who seems to be directing his personal ad campaign at an audience of one. Headwaiters in New York's best beaneries swear on a stack of Holy menus that Bryce Sumner is serious (*despite* his initials!) about beautiful young Pratt design student Antoinette Jenkins, whose decorator-grand-mamma Elizabeth Quigly poshes up the plushest pads

185

from Palm Springs to Pasadena. Could be. The billing and cooing goes on every night between the caviar and the crepes suzette. And Toni is coyly wearing a brand-new star sapphire on the third finger of her *right* hand. Isn't that just daaaarling?"

The flippant paragraph was built on more than idle speculation. Toni had seen Bryce every night for two weeks, and while there was no overt "billing and cooing," the mutual attraction was building rapidly. There'd been no talk of marriage, though, and the star sapphire had been Bryce's surprise for her a week after their first time in bed. Toni had been reluctant to accept it, not sure whether it had meaning or, even more distressing, whether it was a sop for his conscience. Bryce assured her it was neither.

"Call it an advance birthday present," he said. "It spoke to me when I was walking down Fifth Avenue. It looked like you."

"It's beautiful." She slipped the small, perfect ring on her finger. "I love it, Bryce. Thank you, but you really didn't have to do it."

"I don't have to do anything I don't want to do."

On upper Fifth Avenue, the realization of what she'd read dawned slowly on Ann Richards. Had the item not mentioned her mother, she might have missed it entirely. "Antoinette Jenkins" meant nothing, but the link with Elizabeth was unmistakable.

Paper in hand, she charged in Peter's bedroom. "Have you read Suzy's column this morning?"

Surprised by her appearance in his private domain, Peter shook his head. "I told you long ago I'm not interested in gossip."

"Not even when it concerns my family? Listen to this."

186

She read the item aloud. "How do you like that? Charlene's mulatto child is in New York!"

"I know."

Ann looked at him uncomprehendingly. "You *know!* What do you mean, you *know?*"

"Elizabeth wrote me. When Antoinette came here to school, she gave the girl our address in case she needed anything. She even suggested it would be kind of me to look her up, but you'll be pleased to know that I haven't."

His wife was stunned. "And you never told me?"

"What was the point of telling you? What would you have done, invited her to dinner?"

Ann's anger turned, as it always had, toward Elizabeth. "That indecent old woman! How dare she give our name to that girl?"

"Maybe," Peter said unemotionally, "she loved Antoinette and only wanted to make her feel a little more secure. When you're eighteen years old and far from home, it's good to know that there's someone to turn to in case of a crisis."

"And of course that someone would be *you,*" Ann snapped. "It wouldn't be her own daughter."

Peter smiled. "Elizabeth included you. Writing to me was only a back-up. A logical one, Annie."

"Don't call me Annie! You know how I hate that!"

"Sorry. Slip of the tongue. You used to think it was kind of cute."

"I used to think a lot of things." Her voice was bitter. "Until I found out how selfish and irresponsible people are. Well, to hell with Antoinette Jenkins and this Bryce Sumner, whoever or whatever he is. To hell with all of them. They don't affect my life one iota."

They would, Peter thought, if you knew that your youngest son was in love with Toni. No point in going

187

into that, God knows. Alan had not mentioned it since that one lunch. I hope I really convinced him of how disastrous it would be to pursue that infatuation. Probably, Peter comforted himself, he's long since over it. Apparently Toni is.

Ann threw the newspaper into his wastebasket. "Well, so much for that garbage," she said. "Will you be home for dinner?"

"No. Not tonight."

"What else is new?" Ann said.

In her apartment twenty blocks away, Joanne Richards read the story with a mixture of pity and relief. Pity for Alan in temporary exile. She remembered his last letter from Paris. It had still been full of Toni. Since the chance meeting weeks ago, he'd been more determined than ever to plead his case. To Joanne, his only confidante, he'd poured out his feelings.

"It's no good trying to write to her or even to call," Alan had written. "I have to do a selling job when I get home. I really love her, Jo, and I've got to make her believe that that single fact outweighs all the others. Damn it, why has this trip stretched out so long? I've been in touch with the home office practically every day, asking when the hell I'm going to be allowed to come home. It was supposed to be a couple of weeks and it's been more than two months! If it goes on much longer I'll quit. I keep thinking how wonderful Paris would be if Toni were here. It's so beautiful right now, just the way it's supposed to be in the spring. But it's the city of lovers, not businessmen. I keep having terrible nightmares that she'll meet somebody else. She's so beautiful. Every guy in New York must be after her."

Poor Alan, Joanne thought now. The nightmares have apparently come true. I've met the persuasive Bryce Sumner. If he's serious, Toni's a dead duck. And so is Alan. She felt sorry for her brother and yet there was almost a feeling of relief. If Toni got married he'd have to give up this poetic but impractical yearning for her. Despite Jo's encouragement during that pre-Christmas dinner, she felt now that it would be better if Alan's "love affair" ended. It was going nowhere. It couldn't.

She debated whether to be the one to break the news to him. Sooner or later he'd hear about it. Better from her, if she could find the right words.

Reluctantly she went to her typewriter. What would Alan do when he heard about Toni and Bryce? Quit and come rushing home? Try to convince himself that it was only one of those unfounded rumors on which gossip columns thrive? Or would he accept the resolution fatalistically but perhaps resent his sister as the bearer of bad tidings. Not the latter, Jo knew. He would not be angry with her for sending the clipping. Nor, she knew, would he accept without a struggle that he'd lost the only woman he'd ever loved.

Sighing, she tried to compose a tender but sensible letter to him. On the fourth attempt she gave up. Everything she wrote sounded pat and phony. At last she settled for a brief note:

"Allan, dear, I take no joy in sending you the enclosed, unconfirmed piece of bad news. If I can do anything—anything at all—you have but to ask.

"All my love,
"Jo"

She dropped the letter in the mailbox on her way to the office. Damn it, she thought, why did I put in that last sentence? Suppose he asks me to find Toni and talk to her? What in the world could I say? But he wouldn't ask. She knew that. If he sensed that letters and calls from him would not be enough he would know that a plea from

189

a stranger would be futile. She's my cousin, Joanne thought, and I'm worse than a stranger. I could have tried to find her and I haven't. How Toni Jenkins must hate the Richards family! And I don't blame her. In her shoes I'd feel the same.

When he got his sister's airmail letter, Alan's reaction was instinctive and immediate. He didn't blame Toni. She'd declared herself from the first. And there was every reason for her to misunderstand his silence, interpreting it as indifference rather than a plea so deep-felt it could only be spoken with his arms around her. He blamed himself. First for letting his father talk him out of following Toni to California. Then for trying to rationalize his own feelings. And finally for holding still for this overextended absence. He'd been a fool in all cases. He'd deluded himself that he had time, that this love was destined to be, that neither silence nor distance could come between them.

He took action immediately. At three o'clock Paris time, when he knew the New York office would be open, he called his bosses and said flatly either he came home or they could accept his resignation. They cajoled him into a compromise. Just one more week, they said, and things would be solid enough there for him to return. He wasn't going to blow his future for the sake of a week, was he? they asked. They knew it had been tough but he'd done a great job. Just finish up. One more week.

Hating himself (Oh, God, why wasn't that damned book published and another contract signed?), Alan agreed.

"But that's *it*," he said. "One week. No more stalling. I'm booking a return flight next Thursday, job or no job."

He hung up and sent a cable to Joanne. "Nothing you

can do. Up to me. Returning Thursday next. Love. Alan."

He considered cabling Toni at Pratt. In Paris he'd gotten her home telephone number from New York information but those idiots with their rules and regulations wouldn't give him the address. It was another reason he hadn't written. There was something offensively impersonal about writing a love letter in care of an institution. And what could he hope to accomplish now in a cable? "I've got to get home," he said aloud. "I've got to get to Toni."

Even as Alan prepared to fly home, Elizabeth was reading the clipping silently handed to her by Laurel. Her first thought was almost impersonally businesslike and strangely irrelevant. How on earth did they tie Antoinette back to me? Elizabeth wondered. Not that she minded. It was fascinating but unimportant how these reporters got their facts. Easy enough to do through the school, she realized. What mattered was what it all meant. Charlene had said nothing about Antoinette and a man called Bryce Sumner. Chances were Charlene had never heard of him. He must have come into Antoinette's life since Christmas. Elizabeth didn't like it. Her grandchild was not a devious girl. If this thing had progressed far enough to make the gossip columns there must be something to it. Something she was not ready to tell her family.

Elizabeth held the clipping in her hand, debating.

"What do you think?" she asked Laurel.

Her friend shrugged. "Could be a lot of smoke and no fire. You know how inaccurate those columns are."

Elizabeth nodded absently.

"You're wondering whether to tell Charlene," Laurel said. "Don't you think you ought to stay out of it? School closes next month. Toni will be coming home for at least part of the summer. If she's thinking of getting married it's *her* right to tell Charlene and Jim, isn't it?"

"I suppose so." She wondered what was going on in Antoinette's mind. Apparently she'd clung stubbornly to her decision not to give in to her love for Alan. What fools "nice women" are! Only the bitches take what they want with selfish disregard for anyone else. And come out the better for it. Or so it often seemed. If Antoinette were not such a caring girl she wouldn't worry about family reaction or whether the man she loved could cope with a mulatto wife and the prospect of a necessarily childless marriage. I wish she didn't have such scruples, Elizabeth thought. Even Charlene had been more defiant. But then, Elizabeth realized, in Charlene's case the roles were reversed; she did not carry black blood to a white man as Antoinette would have to do. Charlene had been prepared to accept the consequences of her marriage. She was not plagued by concern for any hurt she might cause her husband. It was the other way around. Jim had been the guilty one all these years, always wondering whether he had done the right thing in marrying a white woman and fathering a child. He was, despite his happiness, guilty to this day. Just as his daughter would be if she believed she would cause problems and pain. She'd sacrifice happiness rather than bring misery. She's such a fool, Elizabeth thought tenderly. And I love her so much.

She wondered about Bryce Sumner. Had Antoinette told him about Jim? One thing was sadly certain: she couldn't love him as she loved Alan, else she'd have the same reluctance about "burdening" him with a mulatto wife. Perhaps, Elizabeth thought hopefully, Bryce was a big enough man not to care about such things. Somewhere there had to be a man who was right for Antoinette. She hoped with all her heart that Sumner was that man.

192

Chapter 14

He was waiting on the street for her that warm May afternoon when she came out of school. She spotted him as
she came through the door, even before he picked her out
of the throng of students. When he saw her, his face took
on such a look of joy and anticipation that Toni, despite
all her reservations, ran to him and threw her arms
around him, forgetting all the sensible talks she'd had
with herself, forgetting Bryce, forgetting everything except
the unexpected happiness of seeing Alan.

They stood holding each other, oblivious of the time
and place and people. They didn't kiss or speak; they
simply clung to each other, letting all the doubts and
loneliness drain away in that moment of reunion. If time
can be said to stand still, it did for these two. Without a
word or a caress, they were making love to each other,
silently proclaiming vows that were as real as if they were
speaking them before a marriage altar.

I don't want it to ever end, Toni thought. I want us to
stand right here, in this spot, holding each other until the
end of our lives. I wish we could be frozen here in a per-
petual embrace with no need to talk or think or doubt. I

wish a magician could wave his wand and make us invisible, together and complete for all time. And then Alan's words shattered the fantasy.

"I knew it," he said, his mouth close to her ear. "I knew it would be all right. Toni, darling, I've been such a fool. We've wasted so much time."

In that instant, the bleak truth returned. There was no invisibility, no escape from their problems. Nothing had changed. Not their love for each other or the things that forbade that love.

Slowly, unwillingly she drew away from him, her eyes never leaving the serious face. She had no words; only desire mingled with the old terrible feeling of futility. The conflict showed in her expression and Alan read it there.

"No," he said. "Not this time. This time I'm not going to let you or anybody else talk me out of it. You're going to marry me. It can't be any other way."

She wanted to shut out everything but those words. She yearned to have no reservations, no fears. She begged God to let her be a different person. And God declined.

Still silent she let him lead her up the street, his arm around her, not casually as kids walked with their arms around each other, but protectively, almost fiercely possessive. She was dazed, miserable and happy all at once, moving like a sleepwalker to she didn't know where.

"Where are we going?" she finally asked.

"Wherever we can talk. Wherever we can make plans."

She felt faint. She stumbled and would have fallen if Alan hadn't been holding her tightly.

"Sweetheart, are you all right?"

"I think we'd better sit down," Toni said.

He helped her into a little restaurant-bar, deserted at this hour of the afternoon.

"Do you want a drink? Some brandy?"

"No. Just coffee." For the first time she smiled. Coffee,

she thought inanely, seems to be our elixir of love. They had fallen in love in a coffeehouse in the Village. And here they were having coffee again. It was quite a contrast to champagne with Bryce. But everything about Alan was a contrast to Bryce. She sipped the hot liquid slowly, drinking him in with every swallow, listening as he told her all that had been in his heart these past months, declaring again and again that nothing mattered but their rightness for each other. Words were his ammunition, as silence was her unwilling defense.

"None of the things that trouble you matter," he said over and over. "I don't care about kids. Or families. I care about you." It was like a refrain she wanted to believe. But words, even those spoken with such passion and honest conviction, did not change facts. They did not alter bloodlines or erase the past. Love did not conquer all; it merely complicated it. And yet they wanted each other. Did that count for nothing? Wasn't Alan ready and willing to take the risks and the outrage, just as Charlene had been? But Charlene and Jim weren't cousins, her mind told her. Perhaps they should not have had a baby, but they did not run the risk of genetically imperfect children as she and Alan would. She thought of the eternal guilt her father felt. Would she, could she, go through life wondering whether she'd done her mate an injustice as Jim felt he'd done his?

And then, too, there was Bryce. He was her lover. Alan would have to know that. Would it alter his feelings to know that she had gone so quickly and easily to another man? Would he understand that she'd done it in a conscious effort to forget him?

In this new, permissive world, her "loss of virtue" was the least important of the hurdles they faced. She almost knew what he would say when she told him. Still, she avoided his eyes when she spoke.

"Alan, I've been seeing someone else for the past few weeks."

"I know. Bryce Sumner."

Toni looked up, surprised.

"News travels fast, love," he said.

Of course. The gossip column. A girl at school had shown it to her and she and Bryce had laughed about it at dinner.

Alan was reading her mind again. "Yes, darling, I saw that item and it really lit a fire under me. It finally knocked some sense into my head. Sumner was the clincher that brought me home. You didn't really think I was going to hang around Paris while somebody stole my girl? I told the boss men, 'I come home or I quit.' Thank God for rumormongers! Remind us to subscribe to the *Daily News* for the next fifty or sixty years, will you?"

Suddenly she was laughing, joyously, freely. She had never felt so happy, so certain of her future. It was going to be all right. Nothing could stop them. Let the world disapprove. They had each other. For always.

For once, Peter Richards looked forward to dining at his own table. All the children were coming this evening, a welcome-home gathering for Alan after that long stay in Paris. Peter really cared for them, though in quite different ways. Joanne was the "new breed" of woman, thoroughly independent, self-supporting and seemingly unperturbed by the fact that at twenty-seven she was still unmarried. Her father was not sure he understood her values and, in reluctant recognition of a generation gap, preferred not to think of the sexual freedom to which she subscribed. But he loved her deeply and admired her sincerely for her honesty and bigness of spirit. She is not, he thought gratefully, anything like Ann. Or, for that matter, like me.

He could not feel the same easy affection for Peter III, his eldest and his law partner. Not that his son was unadmirable. He was a good attorney, a proper husband and father, a solid member of the community. But he was a bore, a pompous, dull fellow. "Ditto," as Ann persisted in calling her firstborn, was twenty-nine going on sixty-five. He'd married a girl as humorless and conventional as Ann. And they had produced a solemn baby who seemed already to know that he was Peter Richards IV. I love my son dutifully, Peter thought, almost ashamed of the fact. Young Pete did not inspire fierce devotion.

Alan was dearest to his father's heart. Peter admitted only to himself that it was Alan whom he felt closest to, the one he understood best, the person he'd like to be if he could be twenty-five again. He was a free soul, Alan. Yet he understood that sometimes a man had to make disciplined decisions that went against his own desires. Look at the way he'd accepted his father's advice about Toni Jenkins. It had almost broken Peter's heart to point out why Alan should not have his young cousin. But Alan had understood that some things go deeper than self-indulgence. It took guts to sacrifice so much for a mother you did not even respect. Perhaps, Peter thought with a twinge of remorse, he did it more for me than for Ann. In any case, Alan had told him a few days before he went to Paris that he'd not seen Toni again. And in the meantime she had met someone else. He hoped Alan was over his infatuation. He hoped Charlene and Elizabeth were happy about Toni's new romance. He wished he'd looked up that child. I'm like everybody else in this town, Peter thought. I didn't want to Get Involved.

He'd been late getting home from the office and they were all there when he hurried into the living room. He smiled an automatic greeting at Ann, kissed Joanne and his daughter-in-law, shook hands formally with Ditto as though they hadn't parted an hour earlier. Then he turned to Alan and impulsively gave him a big hug.

"You look great!" Peter said. "Good God, we thought you were about to become an expatriate!"

Alan smiled. He looked happy, happier than he had in a long while. "I was beginning to think so myself," he said, "and it may still come to that. The office would like me to go back for two or three years, to run the whole European operation. This morning I told them flatly no. But tonight I'm reconsidering." He paused. He hadn't intended to bring it up so early in the evening but the opening just seemed to happen. He might as well get it over with.

"The fact is," Alan continued, "I'm getting married and we've decided to live in Paris."

There was a stunned silence, broken at last by his mother.

"Married! To whom? Some girl you met in France?"

"No. To a girl named Antoinette Jenkins."

The people in the room were a study in disparate reactions. Joanne covered her face with her hands, not certain whether she was glad or sorry, knowing that the clipping she'd sent had brought Alan flying home to plead his case, apparently successfully. Peter, too, felt mixed emotions. Happiness for his son no matter what the consequences, yet dismay that his unexpected reversal would have terrible repercussions. He looked at Ann. She was staring at Alan in disbelief, her face drained of color, her mouth half open in horror.

Only Alan's brother and sister-in-law had no idea why the announcement was such a bombshell.

"What's going on here?" Ditto finally asked. "Who is Antoinette Jenkins?"

"A girl I love," Alan said. "A girl who's tried to convince me that we shouldn't marry because we would hurt

198

other people. Today I made her see how wrong it is for us to be apart. She's a wonderful girl, Pete, the only one I've ever wanted, the only one I could ever want. If there's a God, He knows we're doing right."

Ann rose from her chair, trembling. "Why don't you tell him all of it, Alan? Why don't you tell him that this 'wonderful girl' is your first cousin and a half nigger? Why don't you say that her mother, my own sister, is married to a black man? He doesn't remember them. None of you children do. I didn't want you to!" She began to laugh hysterically. "I can see that this doesn't come as a surprise to your father or your sister. They're probably laughing inside. They probably encouraged you." Ann was out of control now. "Go ahead, Alan, marry her and have half-breed children who'll be idiots! Go ruin your life and bring shame on your family! What do you care about anybody else? You disgust me!"

He went to her, pain in his eyes, reaching out his arms. Ann recoiled as though they were snakes.

"Please, Mother. Please try to understand. I know how you felt, how you still feel about Toni's parents and about your own mother. I tried to spare you. I really did. And Toni was even more determined than I. But it has to be. We don't want to hurt you. We don't want to hurt her family in California, either. But we need each other. Can't you understand that? We've fought it hard, both of us. We know all the problems. That's why today we decided to live in Paris for a few years, just to save you any embarrassment you might feel in having us around."

Ann looked past him at Peter. "You aren't going to do anything about this, are you? You're going to stand there and let your son disgrace us." Her voice had a strange, almost melancholy sound.

Peter tried helplessly to be reasonable. "Ann, dear,
199

Alan is a grown man. He's been making his decisions for a long while. They may not be the ones we always want, but they're his. Peter and Jo have decided how they want to live their own lives. Alan must have the same freedom." He realized she wasn't listening but he kept on talking. "It's not the worst thing that could happen, you know. Toni must be a fine girl. In a way she's part of you."

It was an unfortunate allusion. Ann seemed to snap out of her near-trance. She looked at him with hatred.

"You are beneath contempt," she said. "I loathe you." She looked around. "All of you. You've never given a damn for me or what *I* want. You're only concerned with yourselves. What do you offer? Duty calls and obligatory deference. Only Ditto has had any concern for me. Your father has made a fool of me in front of the world. Joanne lives in a way she knows I disapprove of." She turned to Alan. "And now you. You've done the one thing that you knew would destroy me. You and that little black slut. You deserve each other."

"Mother!" Alan's cry was full of anguish.

"Don't call me that ever again. I can't believe I gave birth to someone like you."

Peter opened his mouth to protest but Ann cut him off. "Excuse me," she said formally. "I'm going to my room."

They sat staring mutely at each other when she left, unable to believe what they'd seen and heard.

It was Joanne who finally moved. "If you don't mind," she said, "I think I'll go. I don't want dinner."

"Neither do I," Alan said sadly. "Dad, I'm sorry."

Peter nodded. "It'll be all right, son. Your mother hasn't been feeling too well. She'll come around when she gets over the shock and be sorry for what she said. All she really wants is your happiness, yours and Joanne's

200

and Peter's. She'll realize that. We'll talk tomorrow, okay?"

"Sure," Alan said. "We all understand." He felt sorry for Ann. But he felt even sorrier for his father.

Chapter 15

Toni's dinner with Bryce that night had been, in its own way, as unnerving as Alan's experience. Not that there had been Ann's kind of vicious accusations and outrage when Toni told her lover she was going to marry Alan Richards. But she was not prepared for the impassioned outburst with which Bryce received her news. Her ego expected him to be disappointed and upset by the idea of losing her. They had become more than physically close; a genuine affection and mutual respect, something closely akin to love, had grown between them though marriage still was not mentioned. The thought had crossed their minds, a prospect fleetingly, independently entertained by each. But Bryce was not yet sure he was ready to "settle down" and Toni had told herself that much as she liked him, she did not feel certain enough of her own feelings to make a lifetime decision. Besides, there was always the nagging wonder of how he would react when she told him about Jim. And, though she tried to deny it, she knew she was not really over her passion for Alan.

Now that Alan had reappeared, refusing to take no for an answer, she was glad she had no deep commitment to

Bryce. He might even be relieved to be let out of a relationship that was growing closer with every meeting.

She did not reckon with Bryce's deep infatuation nor, even more tellingly, with his pride.

She'd told Alan she would see Bryce that evening and break off the relationship.

"It *has* been one, Alan," she'd said. "I can't lie to you about that."

"I can't honestly say I don't wish it hadn't, darling," he'd answered, "but I'm hardly in a stone-throwing position myself. Whatever either of us has done in the past isn't what counts; it's what we'll do together in the future." He was tempted to tell her about that nightmare Christmas Eve. But how could he explain what he himself did not fully understand? He didn't know how to tell Toni about an agony that pleaded for mindless forgetfulness, that drove him to seek self-debasing release from his yearning for her. Alcohol and anguish, he thought. A lethal combination for a frustrated man.

Toni didn't tell him she knew about that night with Sarah. They both had run seeking solutions in someone else. Alan was ashamed to tell her about his search for "therapy" but she felt better for having told him about hers. From now on there would be no deceptions between them, ever. She would be faithful to him in marriage, as he'd be to her.

Happy, grateful, she'd been genuinely shocked by Bryce's protestations when she told him her decision. His vehemence had come as a surprise.

"No! Toni, you can't marry somebody else! I love you. I want you to marry me!"

He'd been almost as surprised as she by the words. He'd had no intention of proposing. Not now, at least. Maybe never. But it came out involuntarily, and with an almost impersonal amazement he realized he meant it. He

203

did love her. He did want to marry her. He wasn't going to lose her.

She sat looking at him quietly for a moment. "Bryce, dear, you don't really want that. You and I have never even discussed marriage. We agreed the first night that making love was no lifetime pledge for us. I care for you. Very much. I always will. I'm grateful to you. You've made me grow up. Thanks to you, I've become a woman, but I've always been in love with someone else, and though you made me almost forget that, it's still there. I wouldn't be the kind of wife you deserve, feeling the way I do about another man."

"I'll make you forget him. Toni, we can have a good life. I never wanted anyone the way I want you."

"I don't mean to hurt you, Bryce, but isn't it possible you only think you want to marry me because someone else does?"

"That's a low blow," he said. "And it's not true. Okay, maybe the realization did come a little faster because of the threat of losing you, but the idea was always there, Toni. I always knew that one day I'd marry you. I suppose I just took it for granted that we'd drift into it, that you felt we would, too. I wasn't in a rush and I didn't think you were. I'm not asking you to marry me just because there's someone else. I'm asking you because I love you."

"Thank you for that," she said. "I believe you. And maybe a week ago I'd have accepted with joy. But Alan has come back and now I know I can't give you what I'd almost begun to believe I could. Please try to understand, Bryce. You're wonderful in every way and I hope you wish me luck."

"Who is he? Who is the guy?"

"He's Alan Richards, a writer, and ... he's my cousin."

204

"Your cousin!"

"Yes. I know all the problems that presents, but there are others that it solves. Bryce, I've never told you everything about me. There are things about my family that Alan knows and accepts. My father . . ."

He interrupted her. "I don't give a damn about your father and your family problems. I don't care about all that. There are a few things in my background I don't discuss, secrets I'm not proud of either, but people don't get married to solve problems, Toni! That's a helluva reason for a choice!"

"You don't understand. Let me tell you. . . ."

"I don't want to hear it! I'm not interested. I couldn't care less whether your father is a rapist or a murderer or an embezzler. Richards 'knows and accepts'! Big deal! I accept *without* knowing. I want *you,* the woman, and to hell with whatever has to be 'accepted'! Toni, are you marrying this guy because you love him or because it's the easy thing to do? Because by God if it's only the latter I'll kill you!"

She had never seen him so excited.

"Believe me, Bryce, I'm marrying him because I love him. Oh, the rest of it makes life a little easier, perhaps, but it isn't the motivation. If I loved you that way, I'd insist on telling you everything Alan already knows. I feel that sure of your understanding."

He shook his head. "I hope you know what you're doing, Toni."

"I do, darling. I really do." She slipped the sapphire off her finger and handed it to him. "I have no right to keep this now."

Bryce brushed it away. "I don't want it." His voice was bitter. "It was only an early birthday present, remember? Or doesn't your fiancé want you to wear it?"

"Don't, Bryce. Alan isn't petty. And neither are you."

"Then keep the ring, Toni. It suits you."

She slipped it back onto her right hand. "Thank you. I love it. I'll treasure it, Bryce."

He took her home and left her in the lobby. He shook her hand almost formally.

"Goodbye, Toni. I hope your problems really are solved. And I do wish you luck."

"I wish it could have been us, Bryce."

He gave her a knowing look. "Cheap sentiment doesn't become you."

She reddened. "I didn't mean it to come out that way. I just meant I wish . . ."

"Never mind. I think we've said it all."

Watching him leave, Toni felt a strange sense of loss. Alan was all she wanted and yet Bryce was dear to her. At another time, under other circumstances, she thought, the story would have had a very different ending.

The telephone was ringing as she entered the apartment.

Alan had been calling ever since he left his parents' apartment. It was only ten o'clock when she answered and he knew that she was dining with Bryce to tell him about them, but his jealousy and anxiety increased every time he dialed and got no response. What if Sumner somehow talked her out of her decision? What if he made her once more doubt the rightness of what she was doing? Nonsense, Alan told himself. He just needed to hear her voice. It had been a bitch of an evening. When she picked up the phone his fears went away.

"How did it go, darling?" he asked.

"All right," Toni said. "He's a nice man, Alan. He wishes us well. What about you?"

"I wish I could say the same. Mother made a hell of fuss, but I expected that. Anyway, now they know. I told them it was our life. Period. Dad was great. So was

Joanne. It's okay, sweetheart. The worst is over. Pretty soon we'll be on our way to Paris. God, Toni, I can't wait!"

"Neither can I. I'm sorry it went badly. I know we expected it. But I just hoped . . ."

"Well, maybe I did, too, in a way. It would have been easier all around. But I didn't really look for miracles. When shall we call your family? Shall I come over now?"

She wanted to see him, to feel his arms around her, to be reassured once again that their happiness took priority. But each of them was emotionally exhausted.

"We both could use a night's sleep, darling," she said. "You, probably, even more than I. We'll call them tomorrow evening, all right?"

"You're still worried about their reaction."

"No, I'm not," she said honestly. "But I'd like to be calm and coherent when I tell them, even though I know it's going to be all right. Dad's the most fiercely protective of the two. He's the father-tiger figure!"

Alan laughed. "I'm going to love them, Toni."

"And they you, dearest. As I do. So very, very much."

She could hear him sigh. "I think I must be the luckiest man in the world. Good night, angel. Sweet dreams. I'll call you first thing in the morning."

She undressed slowly and climbed into bed. Before she turned out the light she looked at the sunshine-filled picture on the night table, the one Elizabeth had given her. She's right, Toni thought. The dawn always comes. I've been stupid to worry about my conscience, my imaginary disloyalty. People are going to be hurt. Some already have been. People Alan and I care about. But damn it, nobody's going to die of it! We deserve our happiness. We're not going into this lightly. We've earned it. It's too much to ask that we think only of other people. She fell asleep feeling justified and filled with anticipation.

He did not phone her first thing next morning. Instead, midway through her first class she was handed a note asking her to call an unfamiliar number. At the first break she hurried to a phone booth and dialed. A woman's voice answered.

"This is Toni Jenkins, did someone there call me?"

"Toni, this is Joanne. Joanne Richards. Alan's sister. He's right here. He wants to talk to you." She paused. "Before I put him on, though, do you mind if I say something to you? I haven't seen you since you were a tiny child, but I feel as though I know you through Alan. I know we're going to be good friends. I'm very happy that you're marrying my brother."

"Thank you." Toni was touched. "You don't know how much that means to me, Joanne. Will I see you soon?"

"As soon as possible. Wait a minute, here's Alan."

"Darling, I couldn't call you earlier. It's been quite a morning."

"Where are you?"

"At Lenox Hospital. In the waiting room. They brought Mother in early this morning." His voice sounded flat, weary.

"What is it? What happened?"

"Sleeping pills. She took a handful. Dad found her this morning when he looked in before breakfast. He . . . he knew she was upset last night, so he checked early. She'll be okay, but it's been pretty busy since about seven A.M."

Toni was speechless.

"Toni, it's okay. She was careful to take them only an hour or so before she knew Dad would find her. There was more than enough time to get the stomach pump. It was quite a grandstand play, complete with note consigning me to the lower level of hell."

208

Toni felt as though her knees were about to buckle. She held on to the side of the phone booth for support.

"Your mother tried to kill herself? Because of us?"

"I can't talk now. But believe me, she didn't *really* try. If she'd wanted it to work she'd have taken those pills when she went to bed; not at six o'clock this morning."

"How can you be sure? How do you know she wasn't awake all night, thinking about doing it?"

"Sweetheart, this is not the time or place. I'm in a phone booth. We'll discuss it tonight, all right? I'll pick you up about seven." He lowered his voice even more. "I love you," he said.

"Yes," Toni answered dully.

Real or not, Ann's attempted suicide accomplished what she wanted. Almost from the moment Toni heard the news, she knew the dream was over. She couldn't marry Alan. Woodenly she told him so that evening. He looked at her as though she had lost her mind.

"What in God's name are you saying?" he demanded. "You're not taken in by this act! I told you. She had no intention of dying! It was all planned to bring me into line! Don't you see, darling? You're playing right into her hands. You don't know Mother. She'd go to any lengths to frighten us. She's obsessed!"

"But we don't know for *sure* that she didn't mean it to work, do we? We're only speculating. And we don't know whether she'll try it again. Suppose next time it does work. Suppose you and I felt directly responsible for her death? How could we live with that?"

"You're being absurd!" He was almost shouting at her. "She won't try it again. I tell you, she never meant it the first time! It was a trick, Toni. She probably figured it would come out just the way you're trying to make it. She knew *I'd* see through her, but she gambled *you* wouldn't!

You don't know her. You can't even *imagine* someone doing such a thing! She counted on that. Look, if you don't believe me, come talk to my father. He'll tell you the same thing. When she sees it hasn't worked she'll never pull a stunt like this again. Sweetheart, you can't let an unbalanced woman ruin our lives!"

"She's not just any woman," Toni said sadly. "She's your mother. I never realized how much she hates me."

"But that's all part of her irrational outlook! My darling, don't *you* be irrational too!"

"I don't know what's rational, Alan. Maybe there's never been anything rational about our love for each other. I know I love you more than I love my own life. But not more than your mother's. As long as she lives we'd never have a truly peaceful moment. We'd always wonder whether this would happen again. And maybe next time it would be real. It would always be between us. She's made sure of that."

He was desperate. "How can I make you understand how wrong you are? Toni, trust me. I know this woman. I feel no more emotion about her than I feel for that ash tray." He gave the little dish a shove across the coffee table.

"That wasn't the way you sounded when you called this morning," Toni said. "You spoke differently in the beginning. I heard the fright in your voice until you began to cover it up."

"That's nonsense. Of course I was frightened at first. Bewildered. But it only took the sound of *your* voice to make me realize what it was all about. She's my mother. I can't ignore that. But I don't love her and she has no right to ruin my life. Yours as well. Toni, I can't live without you. I *won't* live without you."

"Wondering every day whether we'll get a call saying we've killed your mother?"

210

"Stop it! It won't be like that."

"Yes, it would," Toni said. "Even if it wasn't that way for you, it would be for me. I was willing to hurt, to defy, to take my own punishment if necessary. But, Alan, I'm not strong enough to risk this. Everything you say may be true. I know you believe it is. I want to believe it is, too, but I can't. I'm afraid, and fear would destroy us. What kind of life would we have with this cloud over our heads?"

He wanted to shake her, to pound some sense into her head. She hadn't lived around Ann, didn't know how angry at life this woman was. But Ann would never be angry enough to take her own life. She'd only try to rearrange others' lives the way she wanted. Toni could not comprehend such selfishness. She could not bring herself to believe that this was Ann's sly attempt to get her own way.

"It's your cloud, darling," he said quietly. "Your imaginary thunderbolt. Lightning that's never going to strike. But I can't make you see that, can I?"

At the door he kissed her gently. "I'm not giving up," Alan said. "Remember that. I won't press you because I know you need time to think it through. But even if you don't hear from me for a while you'll know that I want you. I'll wait, Toni. I'll wait years if I have to. I have no choice."

She slept badly and woke as the first rays of the summer sun began sneaking through the blinds. She could hear the yawning noises of the city, the trucks snorting up First Avenue, a few sleepy doormen whistling for cabs. She could feel the beginning of the humid, oppressive heat bearing down on the eight million bee-people who inhabited the hive called Manhattan. It took only a second to recall the horror of the day before. With all her heart she wished she was tough. Peculiarly, at that moment she thought of Sarah Parkinson. Sarah who also loved Alan. Sarah who would fight Ann for him, as Toni could not. Sarah who very likely still wanted him and maybe now would get him.

Toni lay on her back staring at the ceiling. There was a terrible finality about it all. She felt numb, vacant, scornful of her own weakness, and unable to change. Nothing mattered to her except the one thing she could not have. She was being a fool, an immature, cowardly fool. And there was no help for it.

I want to go home, Toni thought.

Within three days she was flying West. There'd been no problem getting rid of the apartment; the building always had a waiting list for sublets. School would close in another week anyway, so she was able to leave without missing an important part of the term. She didn't know whether she'd come back in the fall, but she put her furniture in storage. She could always send for it later. On impulse she called Bryce. It seemed only decent to let him know. After all, he'd been physically closer to her than anyone. She felt an obligation to say goodbye to a man who, for whatever reasons, had asked her to marry him. She reached him at the office the day before she left.

"I'm going back to California tomorrow," Toni said.

His voice was cool. He hadn't tried to get in touch since she'd told him about Alan. Not because he had no wish to. He had only fully realized his love for Toni after he knew he'd lost her, but then it was too late. He'd thought of her with longing, remembering the soft little body, the unexpected passion within it, the look and feel and smell of her skin. But she'd rejected him. He was damned if he'd let her see how much that hurt.

"To get ready for the wedding?"

Toni didn't answer immediately. Then she said, "The wedding's off. I'm just going home."

He felt a wave of happiness.

"Off? Or just postponed?"

"I'm not going to marry Alan," Toni said, trying to keep her voice steady. "I'm sorry, Bryce, but I don't want to say any more than that. I just called to say goodbye."

"Toni, wait! What about . . ." He wanted to say, "What about us?" but he changed it to "What about your plans? Are you coming back in the fall?"

"I don't know. At the moment I don't have any plans. I can't think straight right now."

What happened? Bryce wondered. Did that bastard back out? From the sound of her voice it was evident that she was miserable.

"I'd like to see you before you go," he said. "Would you let my buy you dinner tonight? Just dinner, I promise. Nothing more."

"No. Thanks, Bryce, but I think not. Take care of yourself. You've been very dear."

"Toni, at least let's keep in touch. Give me your address and phone number in Pasadena."

She hesitated and then gave it to him. "But don't use it, please," she said. "I'm confused enough. I need to get away from everything and everybody for a while. Maybe later I'll have things more in perspective."

He couldn't resist. "I love you. I still want to marry you. Will you think about it?"

Irony. First Alan begging her to think. Now Bryce. They both loved her and in a strange way she loved them both, though quite differently.

"I have so much thinking to do," Toni said. "But I don't want you to include me in your future plans."

"You can't really stop that, can you?" He was deadly serious. "I'm a sore loser. Don't write me off just yet."

If I had any sense, Toni thought as she hung up, I'd run to Bryce, just as I did once before. But it's different now. Before, it was merely an escape. It's not that easy any longer. I've tried that and it doesn't work for me.

There was one last thing to do, a foolish, schoolgirlish thing to do, but necessary to her. She had to write to Alan. Words spoken aloud or gone over and over inside one's head never had the same orderliness as those put on paper. I know now why people write love letters, she mused. It's a way of making emotion tangible, of lifting the terrible fog of confusion. Love letters are not meant so much for the one who receives them as for the one who writes them. It's a kind of purge, a need to put your feelings on a piece of paper and send them away. A strange kind of relief comes when all the things one silently says are set down for another to read. In a way, it's like shifting the burden of misery by making sure that all one feels is irrevocably there. Words spoken disappear. Written, they have dimension, no matter how pointless their size and shape.

Slowly she began to write. It was a sad, sweet, naïve letter that held back nothing, none of the longing, none of the love and none of the determination.

"You are everything to me," Toni wrote in the last paragraph, "and everything in me reaches out to you in an agony of longing. But though I would give my soul to be 'sensible'—to think only of a life with you, and greedily, heedlessly, ignore what might or might not happen—I would rather live with the memory of a perfect love than spend my days in fear of its ending in hatred.

"I am young and inexperienced and not very wise, my darling. I know only one thing. I will love you for as many years as there are. I rebel at this injustice. But I accept, as you must, this finality."

She reread it, debating whether or not to send it. Just

the writing of such a letter, overly sentimental as it was, somehow made her feel better. It was like tying everything into a neat, sad little package. And though the desolation did not disappear, the mere fact of pouring out her emotions without interruption let her draw the first deep breath she'd managed since Alan's call. Would he understand? Would he misinterpret her cry as an invitation to come after her? Or would he know, sensitive man that he was, how necessary it was for her to tell him clearly and for the last time what she felt and would always feel? He was a writer. She was not. But she spoke from the depths of unshakable conviction and the unassailable sincerity of love. She was young and bewildered and cringing with pain, and her words were truth, as bitter as only truth can be.

Chapter 16

Charlene had been surprised and vaguely suspicious when Toni phoned to say she was coming home earlier than planned. Not that Charlene wasn't delighted. She missed her daughter. Christmas seemed very long ago and it had brought a subdued and unhappy Toni. She had not repeated her conversation with her daughter to anyone. She'd promised not to tell Jim and she'd kept her word. Charlene suspected that Elizabeth knew the truth. Toni had returned from her "private visit" with her grandmother looking even more troubled and remote. But she did not volunteer what they talked about that day, nor had Elizabeth revealed anything since then.

If Jim noticed any difference in Toni during her visit he did not mention it. Apparently he didn't know anything was wrong, didn't suspect that his "two ladies" were keeping anything from him. He was simply delighted to have Toni home. That and his intense preoccupation with his work left him little time for speculation about a changed and suffering child. And after she left, he did not have long empty hours, as Charlene did, to worry about Toni's future.

On the surface, the girl seemed normal enough. Her letters home that spring were full of good spirits, but Charlene's anxieties wouldn't go away. I seem to have too many anxieties these days, she thought. She worried that Toni was unhappy. And she fretted about Jim's long hours, the strain he was under. She'd be so damned glad when that airplane was over and done with. Only another month before it was finished. Perhaps he'd relax then. Right now he took no time off, had no relaxation. In the last month he'd even stopped going to the Sunday Flying Club. In a way that was a relief and yet it was better for him than spending seven days a week locked in the office. She saw him so little. He was pushing himself beyond endurance. Sometimes she worried that'd he'd have a heart attack or collapse from exhaustion.

And, she faced it, she felt neglected. She knew it wasn't intentional, that it was even unavoidable. But she was feeling very sorry for herself. She seemed to be so thin-skinned these days. Like feeling hurt that Elizabeth hadn't told her about her talk with Toni. Or that Toni hadn't said whether or not she'd told her grandmother about Alan.

I must be starting pre-menopausal blues, Charlene told herself. It's early but possible. She made a mental note to call Dr. Wilkinson and have a checkup. She hadn't had one in more than a year. She hadn't even been near his office since the day she took Toni there early last fall.

That was another thing. In their talk at Christmas nothing had been said about a physical relationship with Alan. Toni had never referred to the prescription except in that one early message saying it was still unfilled. Was it now? Charlene guessed not. She would not have been surprised to learn that Toni had been to bed with her cousin, an event that would only compound her confusion and add to her guilt. Poor little thing, Charlene thought.

She must be overwhelmed with doubts and anxieties herself while I sit here behaving like some clucking hen. I must stop jumping to conclusions about everything. Why can't I be like Elizabeth, calm and logical and fatalistic?

She had a sudden desire to see her mother. For all her thirty-nine years, Charlene still felt like a secure child in Elizabeth's presence. She sustains people, her daughter thought. She's a bit of a mystic and yet she's so comfortingly down-to-earth. Charlene didn't know how much like Elizabeth she really was. She, too, had perception and common sense. And there was nothing she would not do for those she loved. But she did not realize the similarity. She knew only that she adored Elizabeth, appreciated her and remembered all that the extraordinary woman had accomplished for herself and her children against all odds. Ann would never admit what a solid basis for love and life her mother had given her. How sad that she'd turned her back on it, had missed so many good years of warmth and comfort and deep understanding. Ann. Charlene could see her as she used to be, as she probably still was—beautiful, vain and selfish. A hostile woman whose anger had deeply wounded them all, but whose self-inflicted wounds must surely be even harder to live with.

She didn't know what made her suddenly think of her sister. She seldom did. She could not know that even at that moment Ann was recuperating from an "accidental overdose" of sleeping pills. In her wildest dreams Charlene could not have imagined the melodramatic action that had changed the course of Toni's life. And yet something made Ann come into her mind while she was thinking of Elizabeth and Toni. The vision of the sister she'd not see in many years was so strong that Charlene felt frightened. She believed in ESP, had had more than one evidence of mental contact between people who were

218

far apart. But for her, it had always been with those who were dear to her. She always knew when Elizabeth was having a bad day. Invariably when she called, her mother had not been feeling well. It worked with Jim, too. Sometimes she knew, even before he came home, that he'd been struggling with a particularly knotty problem. She'd had this feeling about Toni lately. Today it was strong, and somehow tied in with Ann.

Feeling slightly ridiculous, she called Elizabeth, ostensibly to tell her about Toni's early arrival. Elizabeth sounded cheerful and well and delighted by the news. They chatted for a few minutes and then Charlene said, "Mother, this is going to sound odd, but have you by any chance had any word about Ann?"

Elizabeth was startled.

"No. What on earth makes you ask?"

"I told you it would sound silly. I don't know. Ever since Toni's call I've been thinking about Ann. Isn't that crazy? But it's such a strong feeling. Like she's trying to tell me something." Charlene laughed apologetically. "You must think I'm certifiable. *I* do."

Elizabeth didn't think it was crazy. Inexplicable, perhaps, but not crazy. There was enough of the "mystic" in her to accept the fact that Charlene was picking up vibrations from her talk with Toni. Perhaps that item about the Sumner chap was unfounded. Maybe Toni and Alan were together again and in trouble because of Ann. Elizabeth didn't know what to think. She only knew that it was time she and Charlene compared notes.

"Why don't you drive up this morning?" she said. "We haven't had a visit in a long time."

Charlene laughed. "You *do* think I'm crazy."

"No more than usual," Elizabeth said affectionately. "Seriously, I'd like to see you. Can you make it by one

219

o'clock? We'll have lunch, just the two of us. Laurel's at the office."

Elizabeth looked at her watch as she hung up. It was only ten o'clock. But it was 1 P.M., lunch hour, in New York. She'd wait till noon. Then she'd call Peter Richards.

When he came back to his office after lunch, Peter couldn't believe the note his secretary handed him.

"Only one message," she said. "From California. They asked you to call Operator six. There's an Elizabeth Quigly who wants to speak to you."

"You're sure you got the name right?"

The girl looked offended. "Of course. I always do."

Peter was almost amused by the oblique reference to the many women who called him. She probably thought this was still another of his extramarital affairs. Who cared what she thought? He had too many real troubles. His secretary's inferences were the least of them. There'd been the terrifying experience with Ann's "suicide attempt." Even though he knew it was a bluff, it was alarming. It made him finally face the fact that Ann was truly deranged. She had been teetering on the brink for a long while and Alan had unwittingly pushed her over the edge of reason with his unexpected announcement. Peter was sure that his wife was unbalanced, perhaps dangerously so. He was cold with the knowledge that something had to be done.

And no less worrisome was Alan himself. Peter had tried to talk to him again, this time to reverse his advice. His son's life must not be ruined by the evil machinations of a warped mind. Not even if that mind was his mother's. But Alan wouldn't listen. Or, as he explained to his father, Toni wouldn't. He clung to the belief that Toni would come to see things clearly, but in the meantime he was going back to Paris for a little while to take the job he'd been offered, the one he'd thought might be the answer for him and Toni. Peter had protested.

"You can't leave now. I was wrong. This girl belongs to you. You can't run the risk that she'll marry someone else. Remember Bryce Sumner. It almost happened once before. Alan, don't be an idealistic fool! Take what you want now. Life's too short."

"I know. But I have no choice. I'd like you to read this, Dad. I wouldn't show it to anyone else."

He'd handed Peter Toni's sad, hopeless letter. His father read it slowly, feeling a lump come into his throat. He handed it back and said, "You're going to lose her, Alan."

"I have to take that chance. But whatever happens, I'll never stop loving her."

He'd flown off to Paris without seeing his mother. When Peter told Ann that he'd gone, she only shrugged her shoulders.

"At least he's gone alone," she said.

"Is that all that matters to you?"

Ann leaned back on the pillows, pulling her lacy bed jacket around her.

"You have no comprehension, have you?" she said. "You really can't see what a sacrifice I made to save him."

There was no point in discussing it.

Jo had added her pleas to Peter's. "Our parents and Toni's have had their lives," she told her brother. "It's idiotic for you two to sacrifice yours!"

"I wish you could convince Toni of that."

"She's a child, Alan," Jo protested. "She's reacting to Mother's transparent ploy like a submissive kid."

He wished they'd leave him alone. They meant well. They were suffering with him. But he couldn't stay here

221

and make life hell for Toni with his endless arguments. She'll sort it out for herself, he reassured himself. She'll see that there's only one life for her. He was sure that going back to Paris was the best thing right now. Thank God he'd signed a contract for a new book. That and the job would keep him too busy to think. At least he knew to whom he'd dedicate his second novel.

Peter used his private wire to return the call to Elizabeth. The same soft, melodious voice he remembered came on the wire.

"Peter? How wonderful to hear you again."

"You, too, Elizabeth. How are you? How's Charlene?"

"We're all fine. And Ann? The children?"

He paused. Had she somehow heard about Ann? Had Toni arrived and told her the whole terrible thing? Not likely from the tone of her voice. And yet what was the reason for this out-of-the-blue call?

"Ann's all right now," he hedged.

"Now?" Elizabeth echoed. "What do you mean, 'now'? Has she been sick?"

So she didn't know. What, then, was the purpose of the call? Even over three thousand miles of telephone wire, Elizabeth seemed to be reading his mind.

"Something has happened to Ann, hasn't it?" Elizabeth's voice was calm but certain. "We knew it. That is, Charlene sensed it and so did I. We get hunches we can't account for. What's wrong?"

He told her everything. He could feel her pity for her daughter, for the ill-used grandchildren, even for Peter himself.

"It's incredible that you and Charlene had such vibrations," he concluded. "I was sure when you called that Toni had come home and told you about it. I feel so damned rotten about all this. So heartsick for those kids.

But there's nothing I can do about it. Nothing. I tried to talk to Alan. He's determined to let it ride for now. He's gone back to Paris, to give Toni the time he thinks she needs. I begged him not to go. Can you help? You and Charlene? Can you talk to Toni?"

"I don't know. We can talk. But how do you reshape a conscience?"

Peter sighed. "I wish I knew. If I did, I'd do something about mine."

Elizabeth knew he was referring to his own unhappy life with Ann. It must be hell for him and yet he couldn't bring himself to leave her. Especially now. As it had over Peter's, a terrible feeling swept across Elizabeth's mind. Ann must be mad, as her father had been. Only a madwoman would have gone to such lengths to preserve a semblance of "decency." Or what Ann thought of as decency. Elizabeth tried to sound optimistic.

"Maybe Alan's right," she said. "Maybe with time to digest all this, and her mother's help and whatever I can offer, Toni will get it in perspective. Alan *is* planning to stay in touch with her, isn't he?"

"Apparently not. As far as I know, he doesn't have Charlene's address. Of course I suppose he knows that he could always find Toni through me, but I don't think he even intends to write. He's convinced that when you don't know what to do, the best thing is to do noting."

"Send him her address, please," Elizabeth said. "And give me his in Paris. I don't know whether Toni has it."

They exchanged the information and promised to keep in touch. It was not much, but it was something. Before she hung up, Elizabeth had one last, troubled thing to say.

"You're sure Ann's all right, Peter? I know she doesn't care, but I love her. She's my child."

"She's all right, Elizabeth." He couldn't resist a cynical comment. "Probably better than any of us."

Charlene didn't know what to expect as she and Jim waited at the airport for Toni's plane. Feeling disloyal, she had broken her word. After hearing Elizabeth's report, Charlene had told Jim everything about Toni and Alan and Ann, being careful only to omit their daughter's deep worries about her heritage. She put the whole blame on the blood relationship. She didn't fool Jim for a minute. There were too many holes.

"Come on, darling," he'd said. "How stupid do you think I am? It's much more than a question of marriage between cousins."

Charlene had been silent.

"You'd make a lousy poker player, honey," he'd said. "You're absolutely unable to bluff. It's all too obvious why Ann stopped the marriage. She hates her black brother-in-law and her mulatto niece. And I don't think Toni's greatest worry is her fear that she'll cause Ann's death. That's a big part, I'm sure, but only part. If I know our daughter she's reluctant to saddle Alan with a wife who's half Negro." He'd become terribly agitated. "What's going to happen to her? Whom can she ever marry? God forgive me, what have I done to her?"

Charlene had tried to comfort him. "Let's wait until we hear the story from her, darling. There's so much none of us really know. Maybe when we get all the facts we can help her see that it's different than the way she's looking at it now."

He would have none of it. "How can it ever be different for her with any white man? And she couldn't relate to a black."

"Why not? I did."

224

Jim looked at her. "Is that what you want for Toni? The kind of life you've had?"

"I've had a wonderful life," Charlene said. "And don't you ever dare say I haven't." She took him in her arms. "I don't know whom Toni will marry. Maybe Alan. Maybe this Bryce Sumner Elizabeth heard she's been seeing. Or maybe she'll end up with some wonderful young man, black *or* white, who hasn't come into her life yet. All I know is that when she does marry it will be openly and honestly, with no secrets or doubts. She couldn't do it any other way."

"Not if I have anything to say about it." Jim's voice was grim.

She tried to tease him. "Who says you or I will have anything to say about it? Haven't you heard about the new freedom of the young? They marry *whom* they please, *when* they please, *if* they please." Charlene sobered. "We know what kind of young woman Toni is. We know what she can live with. And what she can't. We have to trust her, Jim. And offer as much help as she wants. Right now I suspect she doesn't need philosophy or interference. She needs security and love."

When Toni came off the plane, Charlene knew her maternal analysis had been right. This was not like the last time she came home, all false cheerfulness and play-acting. She looked drawn, almost ill, in spite of the smile she tried hard to conjure up for her parents.

Jim and Charlene hung back, waiting quietly for Toni to come to them. A current of understanding flowed between the three. Toni instinctively sensed that they both knew what she'd been through and that they did not condemn her or question her decision. She could feel their sorrow, the misery that was akin to her own. They asked nothing for themselves and everything for her. She felt

225

tears come to her eyes. She cried so much and so easily these days. But these were different tears, drops of relief and gratitude for their unspoken support. She didn't know how they knew, but it didn't matter. She was so tired. It was good to be home and safe at last.

Jim held her tightly. "It's been rough, baby, hasn't it?"

Toni nodded.

"You're going to have a summer of rest," Charlene said practically. "Lots of sleep and sunshine." And then, because she couldn't help it, Charlene said, "We all heal, Toni. We think we never will, but we do."

"I know, Mom. Thanks."

Jim was falsely hearty. "Well, now, how about getting home? Or do you find the ambiance of the Los Angeles Airport more attractive than the neat but not gaudy old homestead in Pasadena?"

Toni's eyes begged him not to pretend everything was normal. He felt awkward and gauche under that steady, tender gaze. There was no point in acting as though things were the same as they'd always been. His little girl had grown up. She was entitled to her sadness. It was indecent of him to make noises like a Rotarian.

"I'm sorry," Jim said. "It's no time for stupid jokes, is it? We know all about it. Let's go home, sweetheart. Let's go where you belong."

That evening an enormous box of anemones and roses was delivered to Toni. She was afraid to open the small sealed envelope. Alan, she thought. Oh God, am I never to have peace? Slowly she withdrew the card. A local florist had written a message signed "Bryce." Toni read it without expression. "Grenouille couldn't possibly miss these the way I miss you. Love." A few weeks earlier she would have been delighted by the thoughtfulness, touched

226

by the romantic implication. She and Bryce always had the same table at La Grenouille and on a ledge over their heads was massed a profusion of anemones and roses, the restaurant's "trademark." Toni never failed to comment on them, no matter how many times they dined there. Bryce had teased her about it. "You're repeating yourself," he'd said. "A sure sign of senility. And at such an early age!"

She fingered the delicate, expensive flowers, feeling nothing inside. She didn't want to be reminded of New York or Bryce or any part of the life she'd left behind. It wasn't going to be that easy. She was no longer innocent, neither spiritually nor physically, and Bryce Sumner was not going to let her forget it.

Charlene's eyes widened when she saw the extravagant gift.

"Good lord! My petunias will die of shame!"

Toni seemed indifferent. "They're from Bryce Sumner. A man I dated in New York."

"Oh?" Charlene's voice was casual. "He must have more money than brains. Imagine sending flowers to California! Like coals to Newcastle!"

"It's his style," Toni said. "He's in advertising."

"Well, they're beautiful in any case," Charlene said. "Want them in your room?"

"I don't care. Anywhere you like."

"Honey, they're *your* flowers." Then, sensing that their arrival disturbed Toni, she said, "Okay. I'll put them in the living room where we can all enjoy them. Bryce Sumner must be a very generous man."

Toni sounded almost cynical. "He knows how to run a good campaign."

Charlene made no reply. She'd only recently learned about Bryce Sumner from Elizabeth. Evidently there was

227

more than invented gossip here. Only someone deeply involved would send such an extravagant reminder of
himself on, Toni's first night home. The campaign was for
Toni, she realized. She wondered what had been between
them. Whatever it was, it must have ended when Alan
reappeared. Foolishly, a little surge of hope rose in
Charlene's breast. Maybe Bryce Sumner's "campaign"
was a good thing. Toni was only human. Any girl would
respond to the attentiveness of a man as seemingly devoted and as reputedly attractive as the sender of the
flowers.

Wearily, Toni knew exactly what Bryce intended to do.
He would bombard her with flowers and phone calls and
letters and gifts. She rejected the whole idea. If it were
not for Alan she might have been receptive to such attention. She had almost believed herself in love with Bryce
once. She had come to him hesitantly and selfishly and
found herself enjoying it. If she had not rediscovered her
real love she might have married Bryce. But now she did
not want him or any other man. She felt dead, incapable
of even a mild interest, much less a recaptured passion.
Under Charlene's noncommittal eyes she tore the florist's
card into little pieces. The action was more specific than
words.

Bryce ran true to form, just as Toni knew he would. As
the first weeks of summer passed, his attentions to her increased, only heightened by her indifference. Had she deliberately planned to intrigue him, she could not have
used more effective means. She didn't answer his letters or
acknowledge his flowers. She even made Charlene lie and
say that Toni was not home when Bryce phoned, and she
never returned the New York calls.

It was not that she didn't care about him. She had a

deeper need for an almost mindless existence, uncluttered by Bryce's desires as well as the shattering memories of Alan. Alan was out of her life. She had made up her mind to that. But there was not yet room for his replacement.

She kept very much to herself in those first weeks. She sat for hours in the garden, trying to read and eventually putting down the book to stare into space. The only people she saw in that period were her family. Charlene and Elizabeth were wise enough to keep quiet. They sensed that Toni was not ready to talk, not ready to plan beyond the moment. They did not give even the slightest indication that they recognized she was going through her own private kind of hell.

Jim was another story. He reluctantly promised Charlene that he would not get into any discussions with his daughter about the past or the future, but he thought it was a mistake.

"I defer to you and Elizabeth," he told Charlene, "but I don't think we're doing the right thing by leaving her alone with her problems. Talking it out would be good for her. My God, there's nothing worse than having all your unhappiness bottled up inside you! She should be yelling and screaming at the dirty deal she's gotten, not sitting there like some beautiful zombie!"

"It will come, darling," Charlene said. "Have patience. She's been under terrible pressure. She'll talk when she's ready."

"What about this Sumner? Do you think she'll marry him? Does he know about us?"

"I can't answer any of those questions," Charlene said. "Toni has barely mentioned him. Jim, dear, please try to relax. Everything will work itself out. I know you have so much on your mind these days, but you're too uptight, love. Toni's been hurt and that pains me as much as it

229

does you. But she's not the first girl or the last who's survived a broken love affair. She'll come out of it. We just have to wait." Charlene tried to divert him. "The only thing she's really excited about is the KJ-16. Only one more month, hallelujah! We *are* going to be allowed to watch the test flight, aren't we?"

"Yes. At least that much has been arranged." He sounded depressed.

Charlene looked at him curiously. "Sweetheart, what's wrong? I know you can't bear to see Toni unhappy, but you know she has to take her licks just like everybody else. We can't keep her hermetically sealed. She has to live fully to become a real person. Disillusionment is part of life, Jim. So is frustration. You can't let her temporary misery get to you this way. It's affecting your whole personality. It's even putting a damper on your enthusiasm for your work. I don't understand. Your career has been so remarkable, such a source of joy for you and pride for the rest of us. Right now you act as though it's unimportant. Toni's troubles have nothing to do with your success, your future, and yet I almost feel that you're tying them together."

"Maybe in a way I am," he said. "Listen to me, Charlene. Even you who are in the marrow of my bones don't know what soul searching has gone on inside of me for the last twenty years. I'm a Negro playing the white man's game. In my personal life and in my business. Do you think that's been easy for one single moment? Do you think it hasn't torn me up to rationalize the course I've followed?"

"Yes, I know," she said calmly. "Some of it, at any rate. But isn't it a little late for regrets?"

"I don't regret you," he said. "It's what I've done to Toni. If it wasn't for me, all this wouldn't have happened."

230

"Look at it another way," Charlene said. "If it wasn't for you, Toni wouldn't exist. Anyway," Charlene said, pursuing her advantage, "I'm damned if I can see why all this has made you so listless about your work."

"I don't know," Jim said. "It just makes me feel that I'm such a phony. I told Toni years ago that her heritage didn't matter—and look what it's done to her. I've told myself the same thing about my job that as long as I play by the establishment rules, it doesn't matter that I'm a black man. The only important color, I told myself, is green—as in money. To hell with black power, I said. Concentrate on acceptance power, status power, recognition power. Toni's problems have come to haunt me about my own." He paused. "I know that all sounds very mixed up. My principles and my symbols get all confused. I begin to doubt my own integrity. Am I an 'Uncle Tom' or am I simply seeing the world the way it really is? Have I put economic success and social acceptance above the goddamned awful reality of what I am and what I've tried to make my child forget she is?"

The outpouring, confused and complex, troubled Charlene. Much as she loved him, she could not get into his head. He was blaming himself for his own success, hating his blackness and at the same time despising himself for rejecting it. It was the kind of agony that no white person could truly understand. Recognizing that, she fell back on the familiar things.

"Darling, you're just tired," she said. "That's why you're so depressed. You've been working inhuman hours for months. It's catching up with you. And Toni's unhappiness has been the last straw. Nobody can think straight when he's as physically exhausted as you are. Hang in there, love. One more month will make all the difference. The airplane will be flying. Toni will be coming out of her despair. And life will be beautiful."

231

He tried to smile. "You promise?"

"Guarantee it. Have I ever steered you wrong?"

"I love you both so much, Charlene."

"I know, darling. Believe me, I know."

Chapter 17

As time passed, Charlene was relieved to see Toni slowly shake off her lethargy. She was still withdrawn, but she began to show faint stirrings, like one coming out of a trance. She talked to Bryce on the phone, and though she did not return from the conversations starry-eyed, at least her mother saw the beginning of reawakened interest, if not in Bryce, at least in life.

After that one despairing outburst, Jim, too, had almost reverted to his sweet, confident self. The last few days before the test flight of the KJ-16 were exciting. He was the author of a play about to open, nervous but eager for the curtain to go up.

When it did, they were all there. Charlene and Toni, Elizabeth and Laurel. A chauffeured car, generously sent by Jim's boss, brought the elegant invalid to the test site, and of them all Elizabeth seemed the gayest and youngest.

The huge, beautiful airplane went through its paces like an inspired bird, taking off smoothly, disappearing into the blue sky, returning flawlessly and gracefully to the strip.

At a celebration lunch hosted by the company president, toasts were drunk to Jim, his co-workers and the crew. Flowery tributes to the designer made his family glow with pride.

"We're all grateful to you, Jim," the president said. "The KJ-16 is the finest product McVane Aircraft has developed in fifty years. It's the kind of thing a man can be proud of all his life." Joesph Bleeker smiled. "I know. You're going to say it was a team effort. We recognize that. And we know that another part of the team deserves some recognition, too. Mrs. Jenkins, will you step forward?"

Surprised, Charlene approached the president.

"You've had to put up with his absences, his absorption and, I daresay, his evil temper all these months. We'd like you to accept a small token of our appreciation for the temporary loss of a husband."

He handed Charlene a small box. Inside was a replica of the KJ-16 in gold studded with diamonds.

"May I pin on the decoration for bravery, Mrs. Jenkins?"

Blushing, Charlene nodded. She caught Jim's eye as the president attached the jewel to her dress. She had never seen so much love and happiness on any man's face. There was applause, followed by quiet. They were waiting for her to speak. She was nervous and unprepared. For a moment she hesitated, looking at the audience, coming at last to Toni's shining, uplifted face.

"I don't quite know what to say," Charlene began. "This is your moment and Jim's and all the men and women who worked with him. I've already shared in the excitement he's felt all these months. I know what the sweetness of achievement means to him and to me and to our daughter, and what the fruit of all your labors means to the future of aviation." She paused and looked at her husband. "If I could multiply three hundred and sixty-five days by twenty years, I could tell you how many times I've felt honored to carry Jim's name. I'll wear this beautiful jewel with pride, not as a reward *I've* earned but as a tribute to him and to you for your support and understanding and faith. You've made us very happy. And I love you."

The assembled group, touched by the simple words, paid her the tribute of moving silence. Quietly the president turned to her husband. "Jim?"

Rising at his place, Jim said, in a low voice, "Charlene has said it. I'm a fortunate man. Thank you."

Only then was there thunderous applause, a standing ovation. Toni, rising with the rest, had tears in her eyes. She felt Elizabeth's hand raise up to touch her arm. The two women, generations apart in years and so close in spirit, shared a special kind of understanding.

When she was seated again, Toni turned to her grandmother. "I'm such a selfish fool," she said. "Do you think I'll ever love like that?"

"Of course," Elizabeth said. "Your time is coming. And it will be your own kind of love."

In that moment, Toni felt she'd found maturity. The naked, unashamed sentimentality of her mother, the quiet, graceful dignity of her father made her self-involvement petulant and childish in her own eyes.

She finally faced the purely romantic quality of her dreams. How boring I must be, she thought, moping over my hopeless love! And how patient everyone has been with me. She had a sense of release and awareness. She could reach out now for adult love, for serenity and protection. She could learn, at last, the pleasure of giving. For the first time in many months she felt truly at peace.

The next day Toni avidly read the newspaper reports of the completion of the KJ-16. Disappointed, she found

235

that the only photographs were of the president and the test pilot standing beside the new airplane. Her father was mentioned prominently in the story but though there'd been many pictures taken, none of Jim were published.

"It's a gyp!" she said. *"Your* picture should be in the paper, Dad! All that pilot did was fly what you spent years developing!"

Jim laughed. "Engineers aren't glamorous. It's like Hollywood, baby. You always know the faces of the film stars and the studio heads but you damned seldom see a picture of the guy who wrote the story."

"I don't care. It's not fair!"

"I don't care either," Jim said, "about having my picture in the paper. Anyway, who ever said life was fair?"

They were alone in the garden while Charlene fixed breakfast. Toni was quiet for a moment. Then she said, "Dad?"

He didn't look up from the sports page. "Um-hum?"

"Remember the talk we had before I went to New York the first time?"

He lowered the paper. "Vividly."

"Do you still feel the same? I mean, about my choosing not to say I'm part of you?"

"Yes, I still feel the same. What signs of social progress have you seen that might make me change my mind?"

"What about yesterday?" Toni asked. "Nobody admired you any the less because you're a Negro. Nobody looked down on Mother because she was so proud of being married to you."

"How can you be so sure? How do you know what was going on in some of those minds? Have you noticed your mother and me inundated with social invitations from the company brass? Have they asked me to join the country club they all belong to? Why do you really think my picture wasn't in the paper, Toni? Look, sweetheart, your

236

mother and I have learned to live with it, but being a black-and-white couple is rough. Why should you take that on yourself when you don't have to? Your mother couldn't avoid it when she fell in love with me. I couldn't hide what I am. But you can, Toni. And I still think you should."

"But, Dad, if I marry I can't keep the truth from my husband! I don't want to! It's dishonest and ugly!"

"Perhaps," he agreed. "I never said it was commendable. I said it was expedient." He looked at her intently. "Is that why you fell in love with Alan Richards? Because he knew about your family and loved you in spite of it?"

Toni was shocked. The idea had never crossed her mind. And yet it was possible, she reluctantly supposed, that not having to hide anything from Alan might have added to the desire for him. In the next instant she knew that had nothing to do with it. She hadn't been looking for the easy way out. On the contrary, she'd wanted to spare him.

"Dad, how do you feel about Alan and me?"

He considered his answer. "Mixed."

"But you and Mom haven't said anything. Feeling the way you do about Ann, aren't you afraid I'll marry her son?"

Jim frowned. "Your mother and I are never afraid of what you'll do. We think we know how your mind works, where your loyalties lie, what your conscience tells you. We trust you, sweetheart. All we want is for you to be happy. It's you who has to decide what obstacles are too much. It's your life, Toni. We chose ours. You have the same selfish privilege. I mean selfish in the best sense. Selfish the way we were. And whatever you do, we'll understand, just as your grandmother understood us."

Charlene appeared with breakfast. "You two look awfully serious," she said.

Jim answered. "We were talking about Alan Richards."

"Oh?"

Toni looked uncomfortable. "I'm sorry I haven't been able to talk about it before. I just couldn't, after what Ann did. Anyway, it's over. I guess you know that. I'd have married Alan if it hadn't been for his mother."

"Would you, Toni?" Charlene asked gently. "I'm not sure."

Toni didn't answer for a moment. Finally she said, "It's funny. When I came home I knew you both knew something but I wasn't sure how much. I thought Dad was comforting me about a busted love affair with Bryce Sumner. I figured you'd seen the gossip column somehow. And all the time you both knew it was Alan I was desperate about." She looked at her mother. "I'm glad you told him, Mom. It was wrong of me to ask you not to. You do understand. Dad, don't you?"

Jim nodded. "I know you didn't want to upset me. At the time you probably were right."

"I'd like to talk about Bryce," Toni said at last. "He wants to marry me. He says he's in love with me."

"Says?" Jim repeated.

"I only mean we didn't discuss marriage until he thought he was losing me to Alan. Then he proposed. Alan and I didn't have an affair but Bryce . . . well, Bryce and I did. Even though I loved Alan, I needed someone and Bryce was kind and gentle." She looked at them. "Are you disgusted with me, loving one man and going to another?"

Jim and Charlene exchanged glances.

"How could we be disgusted?" Charlene asked. "Look, darling, it's not easy for parents, no matter how 'liberal,' to hear that their child has been with a man to whom she isn't married. But we try to live by today's standards. You know that. After all," she said almost shyly, "we even sent you off prepared to fall in love."

Toni looked at her father. "Dad?"

"I'm not as intelligent and rational as your mother. I suppose fathers never are about their daughters. But, honey, your mother speaks for both of us. You're a grown woman with normal desires. That's quite different from being a promiscuous, immoral girl. I hate the idea that it happened. But it did and God knows we don't presume to sit in judgment on you, whatever you do."

She was determined to be hard on herself. "But it wasn't love, the way Mom meant. I went to bed with Bryce knowing I loved someone else. That's worse than the act itself."

"No," Charlene said, "it's pathetically human. You were trying to forget, and Bryce almost made that happen."

Their attitude was at once a reproach and a relief. She was incredibly lucky to have such young, modern-thinking parents, but in a way it made her feel worse. If they'd been outraged, perversely she would perhaps have been defiant and less guilty. It was like having a fight with someone who wouldn't fight back. She really wanted to be punished. Instead she was given understanding and a kind of sad but realistic acceptance.

"What do you feel about Bryce now?" Charlene asked.

"I like him. I think in a way I do love him. We'd have a good life. He's attractive in every way. He's bright and successful and, as you know, very thoughtful."

"But you're not sure you want to marry him," Charlene said.

"For God's sake," Jim interrupted, "what's all this talk about marriage anyway? Toni's not quite nineteen! She'll meet dozens of men in the next few years!"

His vehemence broke the somber mood. Charlene and Toni laughed.

"If you had your way," Charlene chided him, "she'd never marry. You'd like her to be your little girl forever." She shook her head. "Fathers!"

Jim grinned sheepishly. "Maybe you're right. Only a man knows how selfish other men can be."

"Or," Toni said, "how great, like you." She looked at them admiringly. "You're super-parents. I'm glad the air's cleared. I know it's going to be a good summer."

"The best," Jim said. "One to remember."

It was. After that frank talk a new easiness came over the household. Toni came out of her shell to return to the "California way of life." She swam and played tennis and even took flying lessons with Jim, who'd resumed the hobby he'd discarded during the final days of work on the KJ-16. For her nineteenth birthday, Elizabeth gave Toni a Lincoln convertible, calling it a "selfish present" in the hope it would make it easier for her granddaughter to come and see her more often.

"This way," Elizabeth said, "you won't have to confine yourself only to the days when your mother isn't using her car."

Toni was overcome by the expensive present.

"Grandmother, you shouldn't have! It's much too generous!"

"I get a kick out of being able to do things for people I love. For so many years I couldn't afford a five-dollar gift," Elizabeth said. "Money's lovely, and for the first time in my life I have a lot of it. At least what *I* consider a lot of it. And money's for enjoying. I always swore that if I ever stopped being poor, I'd get pleasure out of the fact. I've seen too many people become more and more miserly with age. Maybe they get frightened about their security, start hoarding in the hopes of insuring their independence in their last years. I don't know. I remember an old aunt of mine in Boston. We used to give her little presents, like handbags and nightgowns. She never used them. She squirreled them away, God knows why. And when she died they were still in their boxes, and nobody wanted them. It was sad." Elizabeth smiled. "Anyway, I enjoy what I have, in the limited way these damned legs allow me to. And part of my enjoyment is seeing you behind the wheel of a shiny new car. Particularly when it's pulling into my driveway!"

"You'll see it often," Toni promised, "when I'm home."

They were alone on Elizabeth's terrace. The elderly woman nodded. "Then you *are* going back to New York in a few weeks. I wondered." Then, deliberately, "Alan's living in Paris, did you know?"

Toni shook her head.

"I've kept in touch with Peter off and on," Elizabeth said. "Ever since that horror with Ann. Alan is only waiting for you to make some signal. Antoinette. He knows it has to come from you. Don't you want to reach him? I can tell you where."

"I can't, Grandmother. I don't say I'm over it. I'll never love anyone that way again. I can't help but believe that kind of thing happens only once. But somewhere sanity has to return, doesn't it?"

"Always," Elizabeth said. "At least for women like you and me."

Toni looked directly at her. "I haven't even told Mother and Dad yet, but I'm going to marry Bryce Sumner." She smiled impishly. "I'm sure you know all about *him,* too, you wicked lady."

"Not too much," Elizabeth admitted. "I saw the gossip column, and Charlene has mentioned a few things you've told her." She looked troubled. "I don't doubt that he's a fine man, but there are important things to consider. Your career, for one. Have you completely given up the idea of that? And, back to Alan, are you positive this isn't what in my day we called 'rebound'?"

"I can still have a career if I want it. Bryce wouldn't mind that. He's used to working women. But I'm not sure that's really for me. Not full time, anyway. I'd always have to do *something*. I mean, I couldn't just marry and stay home trying to kill time. But I don't have the drive I thought I did. I'm not interested in being a big business success. Not like Laurel was. Or you. I could be happy taking free-lance work when it suited me. Or trying my hand at some 'serious' painting." Toni laughed. "I guess I'm a throwback. Out of step with the times. But I feel a stronger urge toward marriage and children than toward great commercial accomplishment."

"Children?" Elizabeth frowned. "Does Bryce know your background? I don't mean to sound cruel, darling, but does Bryce know you father is a Negro?"

"Not yet. But I mean to tell him, of course. He's a very sophisticated man. The possibility of dark-skinned babies won't worry him, any more than it will me."

"You seem very certain of that."

"Why shouldn't I be? This is a different world, Grandmother. Particularly in the circles Bryce travels in."

Elizabeth was silent.

"You're like Dad," Toni said almost accusingly. "You don't think I should tell Bryce. That's ridiculous! It would be immoral to keep it from him even if I wanted to. And I don't want to! I wouldn't marry any man from whom I had to keep the truth. Not even if it were physically possible!"

"I suppose you're right," Elizabeth agreed. "It would be dishonest as well as impractical. Especially if you want children."

"Exactly. I *know* I'm right. Dad calls it 'expedient if not commendable.' You see it the same way. But I don't."

"And yet," Elizabeth said quietly, "you wouldn't let Alan have a mulatto wife or mixed-blood children. In your heart, Antoinette, you know it's a burden. You can do it to Bryce, but not to Alan. Doesn't that tell you something?"

Toni was stubborn. "No. It doesn't tell me anything. The situations are completely different. Bryce and I aren't cousins, for one thing. And for another, he doesn't have a mother who'd rather kill herself than have me for a daughter-in-law!"

"All right, love, don't get excited. But you still haven't answered my question. *Is* this rebound, Antoinette?"

She quieted down. "No. It's right for me."

Elizabeth seemed satisfied. "Then that's good enough for us all. Tell me more about Bryce."

Toni told her about their meeting, their affair, the unceasing long-range courtship. "I haven't said 'yes' to him yet, but he knows I will. And in deference to any lingering doubts, Grandmother, I'm going back to New York and spend more time with him before I finally do say 'yes.' Then we'll come back here and be married. In your house, if you'll let us. The way you and Tony were. I'd like to get off to the same great start."

"I'd like nothing better, dear, if that's what you want. We'll ask Bryce's family, of course."

Toni hesitated. "I don't think he has much family. His parents are dead. And his brothers and sisters are scattered all over Texas. I don't think they keep in touch much. But we'll see when the time comes."

"Texas? I thought Bryce was a New Yorker."

"Only by adoption. He got his start in Dallas."

Elizabeth said nothing. She had known Southerners. Many fancied themselves liberal, unprejudiced people.

Many were. But ingrained in some, through no fault of their own, was a different attitude about dark-skinned people. It had been bred into them for hundreds of years. Would this Southern man marry Antoinette when she told him about Jim? Perhaps he's different, Elizabeth thought. The new breed, the new generation. This is 1970, she reminded herself. Things aren't as they were when she was her granddaughter's age. She wondered idly if Jim knew Bryce's origin and how he would react when he found out.

"You are going to tell your mother and father what you've decided before you go back to New York?"

"Yes," Toni said.

Elizabeth tried to sound gay. "Maybe you ought to let the victim know first."

"I think he's already guessed," Toni said again, "but that's an answer I really want to give him face to face. We have dinner most of the time in this beautiful restaurant full of flowers and candlelight. That's where I want to get engaged, Grandmother. Not over some long-distance wire." She looked happy. "It's going to be all right. I know it is. Even Dad will change his mind about my 'confessing' when I tell him what a worldly man Bryce is. They'll like each other. In many ways they're very much alike: dependable, strong, bright and yet sentimental for all their rugged masculinity." Toni laughed. "And don't you dare give me that amateur-psychiatrist look that says I'm marrying a father figure! Bryce is fourteen years older than I, but believe me I don't think of him as another Daddy!"

There was a twinkle in Elizabeth's eye. "As you may have heard, I don't attach much importance to age differences, one way or another."

After Toni drove off, sounding the horn in a long, cheery blast, her grandmother sat for a long while think-

244

ing of her, trying to still the uneasiness she felt. In many ways Antoinette was old for her age, sensible and discerning. In others she was an idealistic, optimistic child.

The evening was warm but the aging woman in the wheelchair felt cold. In her heart, she sympathized with Jim's feeling that it was sensible for his daughter to walk away from her "burden." Unrealistic, probably impossible as that idea was, nothing was going to get it out of Jim Jenkins' head. Similarly, nothing was going to change the determined child who was so like him. It was an impasse, and Elizabeth could only pray that it would not bring tragedy.

She sent a silent message to Bryce Sumner: Don't ever hurt Antoinette. Don't feel differently when you find out about the girl you want to marry.

Chapter 18

Toni was right. The "victim" as Elizabeth wryly dubbed him, did know without being told that Toni had decided to marry him. She refused to say so when he called, but she was now gay and tender on the telephone, even making subtle references to the intimate moments they'd had together. He'd had two letters from her in the past two weeks. They were nothing like the letter she'd written Alan, but they were warm, sweet and full of subtle promise. She would return to New York in early September and stay in a hotel. He took that, correctly, as an encouraging sign. There was no mention of taking an apartment of her own. She planned to go back to school "at least for a while," another reference which he correctly interpreted as a temporary step. But perhaps most encouraging of all, in her second letter she said that she was wearing his ring again.

"I must confess," Toni wrote, "that I took it off before I left New York. But it's too beautiful to lie in a dresser drawer. I started wearing it again on my birthday (it *was* an early birthday present, remember?) and though there are some raised parental eyebrows, they see that I wear it on the third finger of my *right* hand. So, no comment!"

He'd smiled as he read the letter and immediately sent her a telegram.

"Switch to the left. Love, Bryce."

She'd wired back one word: "Patience. Love, Toni."

As her letter had pleased him, so his telegram amused and delighted her. The Saturday afternoon she received it, she decided it was an omen. That evening she told Charlene and Jim that she was going to marry Bryce Sumner, outlining her plans to them as she had to Elizabeth.

"I thought a Christmas wedding, if you agree," Toni said. "And I want to be married at home. Or at my second home, really, Grandmother's."

For an endless moment they were silent. They were not totally surprised, but Jim, in particular, had hoped against hope that he would not have to face the inevitable. He didn't know what he expected. He knew she'd marry one day, just as he knew that she'd insist on marrying at home with her parents at her side. He'd given up hope that she'd play the "sensible" game he'd urged on her. Bitterly he wished now that she had married Alan Richards, from whom there was no need to keep secrets.

Charlene knew his thoughts, just as Toni did. Very gently she said, "Darling, if this is the man you want, your father and I are happy for you." She could not bring herself to ask whether Bryce knew about Jim. Instead she said, "I do think, though, that it would be nice for us to meet Bryce before the wedding. We'd kind of like to get a look at our prospective son-in-law. Why don't you invite him to visit?"

"I thought about that, and then I decided it would be much more fun if you and Dad came to New York early in the fall. You could meet then. Dad's never been there and it would be a vacation for you to stay in a hotel and see some shows. You didn't take the holiday you promised after the KJ-16 was put to bed, and a New York trip would solve everything. Besides," she went on, "I'd like you to see Bryce in his element, in the place where we'll live. You know I wouldn't marry anyone you hadn't met and approved of! But I really would love to have us all together in New York."

Charlene looked at her husband. His face was wooden, unreadable.

"Jim, darling," she said, "what do you think? Maybe Toni has a good idea. I haven't been to New York since I was a child and, as she says, you've never seen it." She tried to make a joke. "If we went in October that would still give us plenty of time to forbid the marriage if we find this big, bad man isn't the Galahad we want for our princess!"

For the first and only time in her life, Toni heard her father sound hateful. "Our 'princess' doesn't give a damn what we think. She's hell-bent on flaunting her black father, whether it's here or in New York."

Toni was wide-eyed. "Daddy! How can you say that? I'm not flaunting anything. I'm proud of you and Mother. You know I couldn't do what you asked. Bryce isn't the kind of ignorant, narrow-minded person who has to be lied to! Besides, I've told you over and over again your way is an impossible, unworkable idea! If I did that I'd never dare have children. And even worse, I'd never see you again! That's what it comes down to. It's *crazy*! This whole obsession of yours is crazy! I never want to hear about it again. *Never*!" She was angry. "I'm sorry you're ashamed of being a Negro but I'm not ashamed of you or the half of me that comes from you! Can't you get that

248

through your head? Can't you understand that I'm not apologetic about *any* of it?"

Charlene was torn. Toni was right. If the man she married did not accept her for what she was, then he was not the man she should marry. And yet she knew the depths of Jim's feelings, the certainty he held that in this still uncivilized world anyone who could escape his blackness would be a fool not to. He'd been hurt too often to feel any other way. His was a different generation, and though he'd defied the color line himself he was not blind to the price of that defiance.

She looked from her angry child to her despairing husband, who was striking out in a way that only Charlene understood. She could not let this rift come between them and she saw no way of stopping it. Toni was unable to understand and Jim was incapable of showing her that his anger was really love. The futility was unbearable. How could she make them see the rightness of either side of an argument when both sides were true?

It was Jim who suddenly capitulated.

"I'm sorry, baby," he said. "I have no right to ask you to go against the things you believe in. Especially when they're proud, honorable things. My way is cowardly and demeaning." He smiled. "I'll see that your mother gets back to her beloved New York this fall with all the glamorous high living that goes with it. Bryce must be a helluva guy. We'll all come out okay, honey. Forgive me. I'm hung up, as you kids say, on some outmoded ideas. Maybe it took a shock like that speech you just made to get them out of my head. If Bryce loves you and you love him, what else counts? You're prepared to take each other for better or worse. You're your mother's kid, all right. Nothing scares you, does it?"

Toni ran to him and hugged him with all her strength.

249

"Oh, Daddy, thank you! I knew you'd see it my way."
She looked up at him and laughed. "Lord, I feel twenty
years younger!"

He patted her cheek. "Interesting idea. That means you
haven't been born yet."

"Yes, I have. *Reborn!* You just don't know what this
means to me. You're wonderful! I haven't stopped worrying since the day we first talked about this, almost a year
ago."

Charlene also felt as though a weight had been lifted
from her shoulders. She could even be lighthearted. "How
about me?" she asked. "Am I not just a little wonderful,
too?"

Toni answered her, teasing, "You? Oh, I don't know.
Maybe a little terrific. Slightly sensational. But how great
can you be? After all, what *are* you except the best
mother in the world? That's nothing to get hysterical
about."

In their bed that night Charlene put her head on her
husband's shoulder and he softly, thoughtfully caressed
her hair.

"You did mean it, didn't you?" Charlene asked. "You
are going to accept Toni the way she has to be."

"Darling, I've always accepted you and our daughter
the way both you headstrong women have to be."

"But you're not worried any more, are you? I'm sure
Bryce is a fine man. He must be if Toni loves him."

"No, I'm not worried, sweetheart. There's no point in
fighting my personal dragon. I saw that tonight. I'm content. Except for one thing."

"What's that?"

"I can't wait any longer to make love to you."

Her laugh was younger than Toni's as she took him
into her arms.

It was not late when Toni appeared for breakfast next morning but Jim had already left the house.

"Where's Dad?" she asked Charlene.

"Left half an hour ago for his Sunday bird-man act."

"So early? Damn! I wanted to go flying with him today. Why didn't you wake me?"

Charlene busied herself with the toast and coffee. "To tell you the truth, Toni I think he wanted us to have some time alone this morning. You know. Mother-and-daughter stuff. Woman to woman. That was a pretty emotional scene we had last night. He also needs time to adjust, and he says he does his best thinking ten thousand feet off the ground."

Toni looked troubled. "He's still terribly upset."

"No, I don't think so. I think he's accepted it. At least as far as it's gone."

"Have *you* accepted it, Mom?"

Charlene didn't answer. Instead, she poured a cup of coffee for Toni and one for herself. They sat facing each other at the kitchen table, looking more like friends than mother and child.

"You never age," Toni said irrelevantly. "I swear you're exactly the same as my first memory of you."

"Not so with me," Charlene said. "My first memory of you was something only about *this big,* all creamy-skinned and gorgeous, but yelling the house down." She smiled at the recollection. "Now that I think of it, *you* haven't changed much either, except for size."

"Still yelling the house down," Toni said.

"A bit. But at least you know now *why* you're yelling."

"You do think I'm right about Bryce, don't you?"

Charlene looked very serious. "Honest answer? I'm not sure, Toni. I haven't said this to anyone, not even your father, but a few things still trouble me. For one, you haven't known Bryce very long, even though you've

251

known him, shall we say, *well*. For another, you're very young, though I can't really quarrel with that. I was a year younger than you when I married. Mostly I'm worried that you're trying to make sure that you *have* to forget Alan. If so, that's not a good reason for marriage. Wedlock isn't an escape, Toni, it's a commitment, and the motivation should be anticipation, not forgetfulness."

"I can't marry Alan, Mother. You know that."

"Yes, I suppose I do, though I want you to know that the last thing you should worry about is my feeling or your father's about Ann. That has nothing to do with you and Alan. I also wouldn't want you to run from him for fear of burdening him with so-called social problems."

"Those were my reasons in the beginning," Toni said. "Plus the problem of our very close relationship. But I'd begun to see how relatively unimportant they were. They could be handled. I was ready to marry him until Ann made it impossible. I can live with most things, Mom. But not with that kind of fear."

Charlene nodded. "I can understand that. If Jim's mother had done such a drastic thing I'd probably have had the same reluctance. Your grandparents—your father's family—never approved of his choice, you know. Especially his mother. That may seem strange on the surface. Historically, every Negro is supposed to covet a white member of the opposite sex, but that's not the way it is with proud people like Addie Jenkins. I know she wished Jim would stay with his own, in every way. But she's a good person. She'd never have blackmailed him the way Ann did you." Charlene sighed. "It's been hard for Jim, cut off from his family because of me. He doesn't understand that he's suffered more than I. At least I had my own mother's backing and understanding when things got rough, as they did sometimes, in this frowned-on marriage."

252

Where was this leading? Toni wondered. What did it have to do with her and Bryce?

As though she had spoken the questions aloud, Charlene answered them. "I hope Bryce's family and friends will accept you, Toni," she said. "I want you to be very sure of that before you get into this. I don't agree with your father that you should hide what you are. Sooner or later it would come out, even if we somehow managed never to meet your husband. Bryce must be told immediately and you must not be surprised or crushed if it changes his feelings about you. I know that sounds hard, baby, and I don't think it will happen, but better now than later. You prepare him, darling, as soon as you get back to New York. And if he reacts as you believe, then your father and I will come East this fall. You'll have a couple of months to make sure that this is the man and the marriage you want. And if it is, I'm all for it. Your father will be, too, when he sees that his fears are groundless. Just be sure, Toni, that this is what you really want. That's all I ask. That and being honest with Bryce and with yourself."

"You know I'm going to be," Toni said. "It's what I've insisted on all along."

"I know. But I also know you always want to please your father. And this time pleasing him would be wrong. I must say it once more: Follow your conscience. No matter what happens, that's what you have to live with."

"Dad *hasn't* really accepted it, has he?"

"No. I'm afraid not. It's too soon. But he will, Toni. As soon as he's sure that you're wisely and freely loved. He *says* he's stopped fighting it, but I know he hasn't. Not yet. He doesn't want you to be part Negro to the world. He thinks it's too great a cross to bear. But he'll see it differently. Please believe that. Otherwise, you'll have no life of your own as long as he lives." Charlene looked at the kitchen clock. "Good grief, we've talked half the morning away! I've got to get cleaned up before your father gets home." She started clearing the dishes. Toni helped absently.

"Mother, did you and Dad talk a lot last night after we all went to bed? I mean, did you reassure him that Bryce won't give a damn when I tell him?"

"We didn't talk too much," Charlene said. "We didn't have to. Your father understands what you're going to do and he also understands how much you love him, even if you go against his wishes."

Charlene was in the shower when the telephone rang and Toni answered. A strange voice asked to speak to Mrs. Jenkins.

"She can't come to the phone right now," Toni said. "This is her daughter. May I take a message?"

The man hesitated. "This is the South Pasadena airfield, Miss Jenkins. There's been an accident."

Toni broke out in a cold sweat. "My father. He's hurt."

There was a pause. She could almost visualize the unknown caller trying to find courage to say the words she knew were coming. Don't let him say it, she prayed. But he did.

"He's . . . he's dead." The man sounded on the verge of tears, struggling to get hold of himself. "We don't know what happened. He was coming in for a landing. Everything looked perfect. And then it seemed like the plane went out of control. We tried to get to him but the flames were too much."

"My God," Toni said. "My God, my God."

"I don't know what to say," the stricken voice went on. "I . . . we're all devastated. Whatever we can do for you and your mother, please just tell me."

She felt as though she were going to faint but she hung

on grimly to the phone. She couldn't give way. She had to help Charlene. When she spoke, the steadiness of her voice surprised her.

"When did it happen?"

"Just a few minutes ago. About eleven o'clock. We have the . . . we have your father here. We didn't know what you wanted done."

Toni didn't know either. She'd had no experience with the grim details of death. Distantly she heard the shower running and her mother singing, as she always did, a little off key. The sound was more than she could bear. She began to cry, deep, wracking sobs of realization and horror. Finally she managed to say, "I'll call you back."

"Yes. Of course. I'm Paul Harrington, the airport manager. Here's the number. I'll wait for your instructions."

Mechanically she wrote it down and wordlessly replaced the receiver. Then she dried her eyes and went to knock on the bathroom door.

It was Laurel, of course, who took charge. Laurel who broke the news to Elizabeth after Toni's call. Efficient, organized, strong Laurel who arranged to have the unrecognizable remains of Jim Jenkins put into a sealed casket at the funeral parlor. In the next few hours while Charlene sat stunned and frozen, while Toni coped with newspaper reporters and endless calls from her father's friends and co-workers, while the world seemed unreal and out of focus, it was Laurel who made the sad, quiet arrangements.

Charlene seemed incapable of motion or sound. She sat in her bedroom, hers and Jim's, staring at the wall, refusing food or drink, holding tightly to Toni's hand whenever her daughter came near. She rallied only at the sight of Elizabeth, whose grief-wracked face was as tragic as Charlene's own. Charlene spoke then, for the first time.

255

"Mother, has anyone called Denver?"

"Yes," Elizabeth said. "I did. Addie and Fred and Clara are on the way."

Charlene sounded like a robot. "Are they all right?"

"As you'd expect," Elizabeth said. "As we all are."

For a moment Charlene came out of her trance-like state.

"I won't let them take him away," she said.

"They won't, darling."

Charlene looked frightened. "They'll want a big funeral. Back in Denver. I won't have it. Jim wouldn't want it. I want him under the tree in your garden. Next to Tony."

Elizabeth held her hand while Toni stood close by. "That's the way it will be. The way you and Jim want it." Elizabeth spoke softly. "Try to get a little rest, Charlene. The doctor's here. He's going to give you a sedative. You have a great deal to face in the next few days."

Charlene nodded obediently. Then she said, "Toni?"

The girl came nearer. "Yes, darling?"

"Be kind to your grandparents and your aunt when they arrive. Be strong for both of us. I don't seem to be able to."

"I will, Mother. Please try to rest now."

"We had him a long time, Toni. And it was all perfect, wasn't it?"

The unbearable lump in Toni's throat kept her from answering. Instead she kissed Charlene and stroked her hair.

"Your father used to do that," Charlene said.

Toni ran from the room. In the hallway she leaned against the wall. This time the tears came silently. She let them roll like a warm stream down her cheeks. After a long while she made herself stop crying. She had to get through this as best she could. There would be time later for overt, unchecked grief. Now there was too much to do for the peace of her mother and the memory of her father.

It was strange, but the sight of her father's family came as a shock to Toni. Instantly ashamed of it, her first thought was, "They're so black!" Addie Jenkins was the stereotype of the lower-class colored woman. She looked like all those kind-faced, plainly dressed domestics in Pasadena. They were *all* stereotypes, Toni realized painfully in those first moments. Her grandfather was unmistakably a simple, working man with a lined face and gnarled hands. And her Aunt Clara, the same age as Charlene, was a tall, strong, angry-looking woman with a proud carriage and a startling Afro hairdo, the kind of woman whose militancy and hatred of whites was as obvious as if she'd carried a sign proclaiming it.

Toni approached her grandmother as the trio came quietly into the house. "I'm Toni," she said simply. She wanted to add "Grandmother," but somehow the word wouldn't come. She couldn't call this unknown woman by the name that for nineteen years had belonged to Elizabeth. Addie did not attempt to kiss her or even touch her. She looked at Toni with dignity and sadness.

"This is Jim's father," Addie said. "And his sister Clara. Where is your mother, child?"

"Mother's resting. The doctor gave her a sedative. She asked me to take care of you. I'm sorry the house isn't big enough for you to stay with us, but my grandmother would like you to be with her if that's all right."

"We'll stay in a motel," Clara said briskly. "That is, if there's one that will take us."

"Hush that!" Addie said sharply. "We appreciate the offer but we'd rather be nearby. Your grandmother lives quite a distance, doesn't she?"

"Yes," Toni said, "but we've arranged transportation. I'm sure you'd be more comfortable. . . ."

"We prefer the motel," Clara said again. "Is there one you can suggest?"

Why is she so angry? Toni wondered. Surely if there's a moment when hostility has no place, this is it. But she kept her voice polite.

"There's a very nice motel just three blocks from here," Toni said. "I'll call and make reservations if you like."

"That would be kindly of you," Addie said. "And then please tell me where I go to see my son."

She must know, Toni thought. Elizabeth must have told her that there was nothing to see. Nothing but a simple, closed box. A box that, with its contents, would be reduced to a handful of ashes destined to rest forever under the arms of a great California tree.

"We'd like to be alone with him," Addie persisted. "Before the funeral. When has your mother planned the service?"

It was weird. The four of them were still standing in the little foyer. Elizabeth sat in the bedroom with Charlene, and Laurel was at that very moment making the arrangements for Jim's cremation the next day. Toni was alone with these strangers who weren't strangers at all. They were her father's family. Their grief must be as intense as her own and yet they stood here formally speaking of funerals and services. Helplessly, Toni looked at Fred Jenkins. Did he never speak? Did the women in his family do all the talking while he stood stolidly by?

"Why don't we go in the living room and sit down?" Toni said inanely. "You must be tired from your flight. Can I get you something to eat or drink?"

"Thank you, no," Addie replied. "We'd like to go right to the funeral parlor and then talk to the minister. By that time maybe we'll be able to see your mother. I hope she'll let us take our boy back to Denver, to the family plot. I realize the services should be here, where all his friends are, but we'd like him laid to rest in the place he grew up. I suppose that will be agreeable?"

Toni felt as though she was having a bad dream. They were all so contained in their sorrow, as though tragedy was an expected part of their lives. She would have understood it better if they had shrieked and cried and carried on. Stereotypes again, she told herself. You think all Negroes are Holy Rollers! Her grandparents had great restraint, great courage. Perhaps, she thought, they are more used to sadness, better equipped to face unfairness. Hadn't her father once said something like that? "Who ever said life was fair?" She could almost hear the beloved voice.

"There aren't to be services," Toni said softly. "Not formal ones. Dad didn't want it. He'll be cremated tomorrow and his ashes buried next to my stepgrandfather's. There'll be a simple memorial service in a few days."

She knew it all sounded very cold, very unfeeling, especially compared to Addie's use of phrases such as "laid to rest" and her obvious expectation of a full, "respectful" funeral. Her expression confirmed Toni's guess.

"No funeral? No decent Christian burial for my son?" Addie drew herself up. "I know you're not a religious family, but our James was brought up in the church. I'd like to feel that he's gone to God the right way."

"I'm sorry," Toni said lamely.

"Sorry isn't enough," Clara said. "I think we'd better talk to your mother."

"She's in no condition." Suddenly Toni was angry. "Her husband, my father was killed a few hours ago. He's gone. Isn't *that* enough?"

Addie put her hand on Toni's arm. "Child, aren't you forgetting that he was our son and brother, too? Have we nothing to say about it?"

Toni softened under the unexpected contact, but remembering Charlene's fears, she was adamant. "I'm sorry," she said again. "I truly am. But we know how he felt about this kind of thing. He and Mother agreed long ago that drawn-out periods of mourning are barbaric. Neither of them wanted that for the other." She wiped her eyes. "I know how you feel. Your hearts must be breaking, as ours are. But Dad's wishes come first. I know Mother will tell you the same thing as soon as she can."

Addie broke. "I want to see my baby," she moaned. "Let me see my baby."

Fred put his arm around her. For the first time he addressed himself to Toni. "Tell us where the funeral parlor is, please. We need to go there and pray."

She gave them the address. "By the time you get back I'm sure Mother will be awake. I know she's anxious to see you."

"I'm sure." Clara's voice was heavy with sarcasm.

Fred Jenkins looked at his daughter and at last Toni saw the firmness and strength that was so like her own father's.

"This is no time for that kind of talk, Clara," he said. "This is your brother's home and this is his daughter. We're all one family. And we're all mourning. No place for hate here." He turned to Toni. "We'll come back in a while to see your mother. But don't trouble yourself about the motel. Since there's no funeral, we won't be staying."

"But the memorial service," Toni said. "Surely you'll want to . . ."

"No. We'll say goodbye to Jim now." He looked very sad. "We said goodbye to him a long time ago. We'll stop

260

by before we leave and pay our respects to Charlene and Elizabeth. They're fine ladies." For a moment he was almost wistful. "We never held it against your mother, marryin' our boy. But it was your grandmother we really admired. You see, we know what it's like when the Lord asks you to put your child's wishes ahead of your own feelings."

Toni felt a sudden warmth for this soft-spoken man. He must have suffered, as his wife did, over Jim's decision to "go into the white world." She was glad they didn't know how he'd begged his daughter to obliterate her heritage.

"I'll ask someone to drive you," she said. "All Dad's friends have offered to help."

"No need, thank you. We rented a car at the airport. Clara will find the way."

They left quietly, a solemn trio off on a useless mission. There'd be nothing for them to see at the funeral home, but the parents would find some kind of strength and finality in the very act of going. Clara was another matter. Toni sensed the woman's anger, as though she blamed Jim's defection for his death, as though his snuffed-out life was retribution for a betrayal to his race. She tried to realize that this was her aunt. It was impossible to make the association.

She was so tired. It was only eight hours since she'd taken the phone call that seemed like a hideous dream, but she felt as though she had been living with this sorrow forever. She realized that she had not called Bryce, had not even thought of him since early that morning. For some reason she did not want to call him. In a disturbing, mysterious way he seemed linked to the events of the past two days. Perhaps I don't love him at all, Toni thought. If I did, I'd be begging for his comfort. If it had been Alan

261

. . . She shook off the thought. I'm not making sense, Toni told herself. Nothing makes sense. I can't even realize that my father is gone. I keep expecting him to walk through that door, full of excitement about his wonderful day.

Chapter 19

On Monday morning, Bryce read *The New York Times* over breakfast. He was not one to pore over the obituaries as so many people did. He was still too young for that. That was a habit that came later in life when the awareness of one's own mortality crept farther forward in the mind. But as he passed over the death notices of that day, a fairly prominent item caught his eye and riveted his attention to the page.

AVIATION OFFICIAL
KILLED IN CRASH

Bryce read on.

"James Jenkins, 43, well-known aeronautical engineer, died yesterday in the crash of a small private airplane which he was attempting to land at the airport in South Pasadena, California. The cause of the accident is still undetermined. Mr. Jenkins was widely acclaimed as the designer of the new KJ-16 airplane unveiled last month. Officials of the company expressed sorrow and called it a tragic loss to aviation. He is survived by his wife,

Charlene, his daughter, Antoinette, his parents, Mr. and Mrs. Fred Jenkins of Denver, and a sister, Clara Jenkins, also of that city. Interment private. A memorial service will be held later."

Automatically, Bryce reached for the telephone and then stopped. It was five-thirty in the morning in California. He'd have to wait another couple of hours before calling Toni. He read the item again. There could be no mistake. There might be more than one engineer named James Jenkins but none with a wife named Charlene and a daughter called Antoinette. Besides, Toni had written glowingly about the KJ-16 and Bryce had read accounts of the new airplane in the paper and in *Time*. He felt confusion mixed with sorrow for his beloved. Why hadn't Toni called him? He'd have flown out immediately to be with her. He was the man she was going to marry and she did not even share this tragedy with him. Impatiently, he waited for the clock to tick off two more hours. He thought of packing and leaving immediately for California, but something held him back. If Toni had wanted him there, she would have called yesterday. *Damn* time! It perversely flew when you wanted it to go slowly and dragged, as now, when you begged its passage.

Over her coffee, Ann Richards also read about Jim. She perused the obituaries faithfully every morning, even reading the fine-print listing of the "unimportant" people. The notice of Jim Jenkins' death was one of the first she saw and the impact was electrifying. So he was dead. The Negro who had played such an important role in her life even though they'd only once met. He had separated her from her mother and her sister, and his mulatto child had very nearly caused her to lose her own son. She felt no sorrow. It changed nothing. Death did not confer sainthood upon this unwanted brother-in-law or erase the humiliating things Elizabeth and Charlene had done.

This time it was Peter who came into her room, paper in hand, as, months before, she'd burst into his with the gossip column.

"Ann! Have you seen the paper? Jim Jenkins is dead!"

She looked at him coolly. "Yes, I know. I read it."

"What do you want to do?"

Ann seemed surprised by the question. "Do? Why should I do anything?"

Peter stared at her. "I don't believe this," he said. "Your own sister's husband and you don't even intend to acknowledge his death?"

"Why should I? I never even acknowledged his *life!* For God's sake, Peter, what would you have me to do? Fly out and effect a reconciliation? Call and pretend to be sorry? I won't even send flowers. I may be many things, but I'm not a hypocrite!"

There was no use arguing. She couldn't see herself. She really believed that there was nothing hypocritical about the superficial life she lived, the dream world of childhood she'd invented, the holier-than-thou attitude she'd adopted toward her own family. Peter turned away in disgust.

"I suppose you'll make some fawning gesture," Ann said. "If so, you can leave my name off the wreath."

He didn't answer. He didn't know what he was going to do. He only knew that he wasn't going to ignore Charlene and Elizabeth and Toni at the worst time of their lives.

The cable from his father reached Alan Richards later that evening. "Toni's father killed in plane crash Sunday. Stop. Thought you should know. Stop. Her address 922 Palmleaf Drive Pasadena. Stop. Call me at office. Stop. Dad."

Alan's hands shook as he read the message. He closed

his eyes and saw Toni's face as vividly as though she stood beside him in the Left Bank apartment on the Rue Faubert. He heard her voice speaking lovingly of the father now taken so suddenly and tragically from her. He imagined her at this moment, a slim little figure moving with bewilderment through the mechanics of a final farewell. She'd be strong. For all her gentleness she had strength. God knows she proved that where we were concerned, Alan thought.

Now that he knew where to reach her, he would call. It would be unthinkable that he should not try to speak some words of comfort, that she would have only silence from him at the time she most needed solace. Even his father must think that. Otherwise, why would he have included the California address? And yet there was the final line in the cable telling him to call Peter's office.

It was a little after 7 P.M. in Paris, 2 P.M. in New York. That made it eleven in the morning in Pasadena. He'd speak to his father first, get details and then call Toni.

Suddenly he remembered Danielle. He was due to pick her up for dinner in an hour and a half. He was in no mood to see her this evening. Quickly he dialed her apartment. The sultry voice answered immediately.

"Forgive me," Alan said, "but I have to beg off from dinner tonight. I've just had a cable from New York. There's been a death . . . in my family."

She was, as always, flatteringly concerned about him. In her charmingly accented English she said, "A death? Oh, Alain, I am so sorry. Not your mother or father, I hope!"

"No. My uncle in California." The word "uncle" sounded strange to him. He'd never thought of Jim Jenkins except as Toni's father. Danielle knew about Toni. From the moment they met, Alan had been candid about where his affections lay, and what Danielle could expect from any relationship she'd form with this young American.

"I'm deeply and, I'm afraid permanently, in love with a girl back home," he'd told her over their first dinner. "I find you very attractive and if we see each other I'm sure I'll want to make love to you. But I want you to know now, Danielle, that there can't be any real commitment for me." He'd smiled. "I sound a bit egotistical, don't I? As though I assume that you'd want a lifetime arrangement. I'm sorry. I just had to tell you that there is someone else. It's my damned-fool, middle-class morality creeping through. And you're too nice a girl to lie to."

She'd returned the smile. "I'm glad you told me. It's better to know where one stands at the very beginning. Perhaps we will go to bed together. No, not perhaps. Probably is the right word. But I will not be surprised if one day you go back to your American."

And so the affair had started, an eminently practical and satisfying arrangement for them both. Alan was young, vigorous and alone in a strange city. He had physical as well as emotional needs and Danielle quietly satisfied both on a mutually understood, temporary basis. She, too, was a young woman who needed love. Nor was she averse to the pleasantries that Alan provided. As a couture model at Dior, she had fashion prestige and very little salary. She supplemented her income between collections by posing for advertising photographs and it was on one of these assignments for his French client that she met Alan. She liked him enormously and she also liked the good meals he provided, the small gifts he gave her. Such things helped when one was trying to live on very little money in a city as expensive as Paris.

She was not so dramatic as to consider she was "selling herself." She became, as the weeks went by, genuinely devoted to him, as he did to her. They suited each other

267

well in bed, and they enjoyed the companionship that preceded and followed it. Danielle was gay and charming with a gift for laughter and a lightheartedness about sex. To her it was natural pleasure with someone as kind and gentle as Alan Richards.

For Alan, she was a godsend. He was not a promiscuous person. Neither cheap whores nor expensive call girls were his style. It was good to have someone he respected as well as enjoyed. If it were not for Toni, he thought, I might really fall in love with Danielle. He did not feel unfaithful when he made love to the French girl. Toni would not expect him to deny his natural needs. But, he thought ruefully, I can't accept the idea of *her* being with anyone else. I'm still hung up on the double standard. And I'm still waiting for the signal that Toni wants me. Perhaps she will now, he thought, as he stood, telephone in hand, breaking his dinner date with Danielle. Perhaps her father's death will make her see how short and tenuous life is, how wrong not to take every moment of happiness that comes your way. Some of that hopeful feeling was in his mind as he continued his phone conversation with Danielle.

"I may have to fly back to the States right away."

"Of course."

Not knowing why, he said, "I may never come back, Danielle."

There was a little silence. "I know, Alain. But we've always known you'd go someday, haven't we? I'll miss you, *chéri*."

He hung up, feeling confused. He loved Danielle but he was in love with Toni. Why did he feel such a pang about the idea of never seeing Danielle again? And what made him think that Toni had begun to see things differently? I must be crazy, he thought. I really wanted Danielle to beg me not to go. Or at least to say that she hoped I'd come back, that she'd stand by until I did. It's just that Danielle has been so patient, so understanding. I will miss her. But right now my thoughts should be only with Toni. I want to get to her as quickly as I can. I'd like to take the next flight to California and comfort my love. Even at that moment he wondered why he felt vaguely let down because Danielle had not offered to wait patiently for his return. The male ego, he thought mirthlessly. What arrogant, overblown creatures we are!

He reached Peter, who could tell him only sketchy details of the accident and the quick arrangements for interment.

"I talked to your grandmother at Charlene's house this morning," Peter said. "Toni's grief-stricken but all right, considering. They're all numb with shock."

"Are you going out there?"

"No. Not now. Elizabeth wants me to come later. Jenkins was the executor of her will. She has to draw a new one now and she wants Charlene and me to be co-executors. I'll probably go out in a week or so."

"Didn't you talk to Toni or her mother?"

"Couldn't. Charlene's not able to talk and, frankly, I didn't ask to speak to Toni. I didn't feel it was the moment to reintroduce myself on the phone."

Alan said what was in his mind. "Dad, I'm going to fly out there. I should be with Toni. I *want* to be with her."

There was such a long pause he thought they'd been disconnected, but then Peter said. "I don't think you should. When I talked to Elizabeth she told me that Saturday night Toni informed her family she was going to marry Bryce Sumner."

It was like being doused with ice water. Toni couldn't marry anyone else! In spite of her letter, he refused to believe she ever would. He'd honestly thought that separation was just buying time for her to get over Ann. He'd

269

been blindly overconfident and now he'd lost her. He tried to keep his voice calm.

"Is that irrevocable?"

"Alan, I'm only reporting secondhand news. But Elizabeth seemed quite positive. Son, you can't really be surprised. You knew when you left she couldn't live with the situation."

"Maybe I knew it logically," Alan said, "but until now I've never accepted it emotionally. Jim Jenkins is dead, and so are my chances with Toni, aren't they?"

"Yes," his father said quietly, "I think they are."

Alan grasped at one last straw. "Maybe this will make her think differently about things. Maybe her father's death will help her see that nothing matters except being with the person you love while there's still time. If I came home maybe I could convince her of that."

"You're a grown man, Alan. I can't advise you. But I know you don't want to add to her misery, especially now. Looking at it as objectively as I can, I don't think Toni will change her mind. I think with her decision to marry Sumner, she buried her impossible dream. It's time you did the same." He paused. "I'll keep you informed. And you call me here any time you want."

"All right, Dad. I will." There was awful defeat in his voice.

"One more thing," Peter said. "I love you, son."

"I love you, too."

Only after he hung up did he realize that in the whole long conversation, neither he, nor his father had mentioned Ann.

Alan left his apartment and walked slowly into the soft summer night. Paris was so beautiful. The buildings, newly cleaned and brilliantly illuminated, were majestic reminders that some things did last forever. He strolled along the Seine, seeing the sightseeing boat *Le Bateau*

270

Mouche glide by, filled with the summer tourists who dined as they made their way down the romantic river, past the Place de la Concorde, past the Louvre and Notre Dame. Toni, Toni, he thought. How I wish you were here to share it with me.

He walked for miles, trying to make himself believe that it was really over. He had to believe it. His father was right. It was an impossible, romantic fantasy that must be laid to rest. They were like Romeo and Juliet, victims of their families. Except that he and Toni were not united in death; they were condemned to live apart in hopeless longing.

He passed a telegraph office. One last gesture, he thought. He sent her a cable. He was a writer but he had no words and he stood for a long while trying to think what to say. Finally he wrote, "I grieve. I accept. I adore. Alan."

And then in a blind rush to forget, he turned toward Danielle's apartment.

At ten-thirty New York time that Monday morning, Bryce called Toni. The strain in her voice was unmistakable and her effort not to break down when she heard him made him at once sad and happy. He knew from the sound of her voice that his call was welcome and he brushed aside her apologies for the fact that he'd had to read the awful news in the paper.

"I'm so sorry, Bryce," she said. "I should have called you immediately. I meant to. But it's been a nightmare. I've been so worried about Mother. And people kept coming. My . . . my relatives from Denver. Everything going on at once."

"It's all right, darling," he said. "It's only that I felt you might need me. There's no man there to take care of things, is there?"

271

Toni was surprised. She hadn't even realized it, but it was true. They were now a family of women. Strong ones, thank God. Elizabeth had been a pillar of strength, moving about the house in her wheelchair, watching over Charlene, a calm and loving mother protecting her child. And Laurel had done everything, from arranging the blanket of carnations that covered Jim's simple casket to getting permission for the simple burial they would attend that afternoon.

"Do you want me to fly out?" Bryce was asking now. "I can get the noon flight and be there mid-day. Sweetheart, I want to be with you. My place *is* with you, isn't it?"

Even now he was pressing her for a commitment. She would not make it this way. She couldn't think of her own future at this moment.

"There's nothing anyone can do right now, Bryce, dear," she said. "Thank you. It's wonderful of you to offer, but I'd rather you didn't come. Mother's in no condition to meet anyone. Not even you. And I need time to collect myself."

"All right. I'll call you tonight. Toni, love, I'm so terribly, terribly sorry."

"I know you are. Everyone has been so kind. I guess I haven't quite realized it all yet. There's an unreal quality about everything. I can't take it all in. It's unbelievable." Her voice broke then. "It's so cruel, Bryce, so impossible to accept."

"Darling, please let me come. You're going to need someone when the shock wears off."

"No. It's a comfort to know you *can* be here in a few hours. That's best for now. That and knowing you care. I'm all right. I really am. I know the reaction will come but I can't let it come yet. Mother needs me too much. I have to hold up for her. I have to devote every ounce of

272

strength to that and try not to think about anyone or anything else."

He had to be content with that. "You'll call me? Any hour?"

"Yes. I promise. I must go now, Bryce."

"I love you, darling. Be brave."

The pat phrase, so well meant, struck her as ironic. Be brave. She had spent most of her life never knowing the need for bravery, but in the last year it seemed that she had been called on to be nothing else. She'd had to make the rending decision about Alan and now she faced the incomprehensible fact of her father's death and the unexpected collapse of a mother who had always been so strong, so calm and sensible. Charlene would be herself again, but now she was like a woman deprived of her own life. Their whole attention was focused on her——Elizabeth's and Laurel's and Toni's. They sheltered her in this ghastly period, carrying her through her grief. They spared her not only the necessary details but the emotional blows that rained down on them. Charlene did not know how bitter Jim's family felt about the arrangements for his burial. They had come back to the house on Sunday night and gone in to see the widow. She was half sedated, mercifully unaware of the grim set of their faces, able only to embrace Addie and Fred and hold out her hand to Clara, who took it almost reluctantly.

Little had been said. Charlene had seemed bewildered that they were leaving immediately, that they would not stay for the brief ceremony under the tree or the quiet memorial at Elizabeth's house on Friday. But she accepted their departure without question, only nodding quietly when Addie said, "There's nothing more any of us can do for him, Charlene. We all did the best we could when he belonged to us."

Fred had taken Charlene's hand in his rough one. "You made him happy. We thank you for that."

Charlene's eyes had filled with tears. She looked like a little girl lying alone in the big bed. "Thank you for letting me have him," she said. "I know what it meant to you."

Addie had turned away, a handkerchief to her face, and Fred led her out of the room. Clara stood rigidly by the bed. Oh God, Toni thought, don't let her say anything unkind. But Clara said only three words.

"Good luck, Charlene."

Charlene made no answer but she smiled weakly with an almost fatalistic comprehension.

Toni followed Clara out. In the living room, Elizabeth was speaking sympathetically to the parents, who showed their affection and respect for her in the dark mirrors of their eyes.

"He was my son, too," Elizabeth said. "There never was a finer man."

"He loved you," Fred answered. The three older people looked at each other, locked in a silent communication that crossed all the lines of color or wealth or background. Watching them, Toni understood the meaning of unquestioned acceptance. They were not separated by class or race or education. They were contemporaries and friends in a way the Jenkinses could never be friends with their son's wife or his daughter. She was so engrossed in her thoughts that she jumped when Clara touched her arm.

"Could we go in the room and talk a minute?" her aunt asked.

"Of course." Toni led her into the kitchen.

Clara leaned against the sink, her arms folded, her voice low but riveting.

"I loved my brother," she said, "but I didn't approve of

him. He ran away from a problem he could have helped. He took the easy way, the white man's way. He licked their boots instead of fighting them the way we black people have to. I loved him, but he was a coward. I'll never forgive him for that."

Toni's breath came quickly. "You're wrong," she said. "He never fawned over anyone. He earned every bit of success he had. And his color had nothing to do with it. He was a realist. He wanted a better world for his people but he knew it was a long way off. It worried him that he wasn't doing anything about it. He told me that himself. But he wasn't an angry, hostile man. He only wanted to live in peace and make a good life for his family."

"His *white* family," Clara said.

"Yes. Because he fell in love with a white woman."

"You don't understand anything. And I don't have time to explain to you how your father failed. It's too late for that now. He's dead. But you're alive and no matter how light you are, you're black. What are you going to do about it?"

Toni didn't answer.

"You're a bright girl," Clara went on. "You know exactly what I'm saying. You have a chance to make up for some of the things your father didn't do. Do you intend to?"

"I don't know what you mean," Toni said. "What is it you think I should do?"

"Declare yourself. Work for the race you're part of. Don't be a closet nigger." Clara started out of the room. "Think about it," she said. "Maybe that would be the best memorial to Jim Jenkins. Maybe in death his soul could find peace. I doubt that it ever did in life."

Toni wanted to call out to her in angry denial, to tell her that that was exactly what Jim didn't want, that he would have done anything to erase the blackness he believed would spoil his child's life. But no sound came from her. Instead, she suddenly felt physically ill. She dashed to her bathroom and was violently, wrenchingly sick, vomiting not venom but fear.

The more she pushed back the terrible certainty, the more presistent the thought became. Reluctantly and inexorably in the next few days Toni put together the jigsaw puzzle that formed a picture of her father's death. Triggered by the strange, brief conversation with Clara, Toni's mind began slowly to work toward the truth: Jim Jenkins had deliberately crashed the airplane.

At first she refused to believe her suspicions, unable to accept the horror. But the evidence was too strong to be ignored, the timing too pat to be coincidence. Her father was an expert pilot. There was no possible technical explanation for the fatal landing on a clear, cloudless morning, no signs in the charred remnants of the airplane of any mechanical failure. "Pilot error" they officially called it. But that was absurd. Even she, with only a few hours' flying time, could have landed that airplane under such ideal conditions.

Even more telling was the "timetable" that preceded that last Sunday. It had begun a year before with Jim's urging her to keep her heritage secret and it had ended with her announcement the night before that she was going to marry Bryce Sumner *after* she told him all about herself. She remembered the talk with Charlene on Sunday morning and her mother's attempts to reassure her that Jim would accept her decision. Thinking back, Toni recognized that even then she was suspicious of his change of heart. It had been too quick, too facile for a man who had offered never to see her again if she would only pretend he did not exist.

With mounting agony, Toni knew what had happened.

She could almost follow him step by step as he planned the only sure way to insure her secret; a way as devastating as it was macabre. He knew that as long as he was alive she would never deny him, even at the sacrifice of her own happiness. Dead, he could free her from the need to be loyal. He counted on her acceptance of an "accident." It was his way of releasing her without guilt. He believed she'd be left with no need for deception, with only a white mother and grandmother to present as "family" to her prospective husband. He saw his suicide as her emotional insurance, never dreaming it would have the opposite effect.

She faced fully the enormity of his act and the depths of love that inspired it. Why did you do it? she asked silently. I told you over and over that I was proud of you, that any man right for me would accept me fully for what I am. But you couldn't believe that, Daddy. You were afraid that the part of you that is me would be too great a cross to bear. You couldn't convince me to keep quiet while you lived. So you preferred to die.

She lay face down on her bed, the tears soaking into the counterpane. Perhaps if Clara had not called him a coward, Toni would have accepted his death as a grim quirk of fate, as the others had. But the defense of her father to his sister had set the wheels in motion, bringing her finally to this deadly certain conclusion. And believing it, she knew what she had to do. For his sake she had to deny her blackness, her heritage. Which meant denying motherhood as well. Anything else would make a mockery of his ultimate sacrifice. How wrong you are, Clara, she thought grimly. The memorial my father wants is for me to forget my Negro blood, not declare it.

The only thing she had to be thankful for was the certainty that Charlene accepted her loss as a crushing, unfathomable blow from God. Even Elizabeth probably had no idea of the truth. Mother must never know, Toni thought. It would destroy her.

She turned over and lay on her back, very still, one arm shielding her eyes from the bright light that filled the room. I'll do what you want, Daddy, she told him. If you thought it worth dying for, I can't let that be in vain.

I should have married Alan, she thought. Then my father would have had no need to hide in death. God, how I wish I could take back these last months! How much better to have lived with the threat of Ann's suicide than with the reality of my father's. But it's too late now. Now the idea of Alan is truly impossible. If Ann were to destroy herself in some mad desire for revenge, the burden of Toni's guilt would be even more unbearable. No matter how I hate her, I cannot risk the possibility of compounding the unhappiness I've already been responsible for.

She reached out for Alan's cable, which lay on her bedside table, and reread it for the hundredth time. One word from me would bring him here, she thought. And I can't. I must not.

She got up and washed her face. Since the first hours she'd cried only once, yesterday, at the brief and moving tribute to Jim. Toni had been surprised by the number of people who'd come to Elizabeth's house. Jim had few close personal friends but he had many associates and flying companions who liked and respected him. Dozens came from long distances to remember; from the airfield manager and the company president to her father's secretary, who wept forlornly in the corner of the living room. How grateful he would have been, Toni thought. And how richly he deserved their tribute. Until yesterday she'd willed herself to be strong for Charlene's sake, but as she heard the soft words spoken about her father she could no longer control her tears. They came fully but silently

278

as she sat with bowed head, holding her mother's hand, listening to her grandmother's gently modulated voice.

Elizabeth had asked to be the one to speak and Charlene had unhesitatingly agreed. Practically, they had no minister and wanted no stranger, and there was no one else close enough to Jim to know the goodness within him. There was another equally important reason why this was the right person to say what he meant to them. Years before, a young Jim Jenkins had performed the same labor of love for Tony Alexander, Elizabeth's beloved husband. Toni had often heard about that day. Jim had stood in this same room and talked about his stepfather-in-law, not in a maudlin, histrionic way, but simply, with deep emotion that was all the more touching for its lack of pretension.

"I'd like to do for Jim what he did for Tony," Elizabeth had said. "Next to you and Antoinette, I think I knew and loved him better than anyone else in the world."

On this quiet morning, Elizabeth sat very still in a high-backed chair in front of the windows that framed the mountains and trees beyond. The sunlight touched the white hair and the aging, still beautiful face that reflected sadness even while it maintained its remarkable composure. How strong and sure she is, Toni thought. How utterly enviable. The voice, low and calm, still with a hint of the Boston background which molded it, cradled them in the arms of her unshakable faith. There was a long pause, like a moment of silent prayer, and then Elizabeth's first words came almost savagely, shocking them into harsh reality.

"Jim Jenkins is dead. We know that we will never see him again as we knew him. We think of his death and ask why. Why a life taken so soon? Why so short a span? Why were we so suddenly deprived of the man we knew

279

and loved? Eternal questions without answers. An enigma without hope of enlightenment. We dwell on the futile subject of what might have been. And in the end we reduce Jim Jenkins to a series of statistics—the date of his birth, the time of his death, the year of his marriage, the moment of his fatherhood.

"Numbers. Facts. Empty and unworthy of us and of him." The voice moderated. The words became as soft as kisses.

"Jim Jenkins was not a set of statistics. He was not a sinner or a saint. Exceptional in many ways, quite ordinary in others, filled to overflowing with love, he was still human enough to rebel, to resent, to come close to the natural emotions of bewilderment and bitterness. He was tried and tested as few men are and he passed those tests in a way that was peculiarly his own, fighting the devils within and around him with the weapons he knew best— truth, reality, loyalty, understanding and love.

"He was a beautiful man. More beautiful than most. And for those of us nearest to him he made life beautiful to look upon. We were made less selfish by the depth of his unselfishness, strengthened by his strength, reminded of the heights the human spirit can reach when it cares more for others than for itself. He had humor and tenderness and a sensitivity that we were privileged to share. He gave of himself, yet he cherished and was proud of the things that were rightly only his and guarded them fiercely. His talent was given to him. His use of it was of his own making. He lacked vanity, yet he took pleasure in his accomplishments in the way any normal man or woman should.

"But was he a 'normal man' in what some think of as 'normalcy' in the conventional sense? Perhaps not. Unless you accept one historian's definition of normality as 'that quality which can be recognized by its absence in everyone.' Reluctantly, not with reluctance for himself but for his wife, he made a marriage that shocked. An 'un-normal' marriage by some standards, but a glorious marriage for the woman who shared it, the child who was born of it, the caring ones around him who knew what this sweet moment cost him in ruthless self-examination, and how worthy he found it.

"Jim Jenkins was without guile and without ego. He held his handsome head high but his pride was a rare and precious blend of modesty and graciousness. He was never self-conscious or self-serving. He could feel anger and disdain for ignorance, just as he could feel compassion and tenderness for the woefully misinformed.

"It is the living Jim who stays with me. He was my son and my friend. I ordered him, not mindlessly but with full respect for his blind spots and endless enjoyment of his wit and wisdom and gaiety. I see his life as the breathing example of the professional area in which he excelled. It was a patterned life, as mathematically precise as a beautiful equation. It soared like the airplanes he loved. It took off gracefully, performed flawlessly and was finished when the fuel that drove it was exhausted. His feet were the wheels on the runway, his head the nose thrusting upward into the sky, his brain the intricate mechanism that performed with superhuman skill. He lived swiftly, freely and with heart-stopping beauty. He never wore out. Jim Jenkins was not meant for the scrap heap of old age and useless existence.

"We mourn him. Charlene and Antoinette, dearer to him than fame or riches or power. His friends and co-workers. The gentle loving parents who created the superstructure on which this extraordinary man fashioned a human being to be remembered with respect.

"We miss his laughter. His kindness. His integrity. His love. We shall never stop missing those mortal things. We will weep, and our tears will make the grass grow greener over the symbolic patch of land that represents his final earthly place.

"But that is all it is. A symbol of our beloved. His energy, his goodness, his eternal spark of being is with us for all time. There are no dates for Jim Jenkins' life. No pages on the calendar can represent him. For a passing moment he beckoned to us. And he beckons still, a source of power, a star in the evening sky, a dot of sunshine, a ray of light rimming a floating dark cloud of sorrow in our hearts.

"We can endure our selfishness, our self-pity, those shameful reminders of our own mortality, when we accept that Jim, dead, is still very much alive. Words and actions and life as we know it stop when a man dies. But the essence of life never dies. It is infinite and eternal and sustaining.

"It is the ultimate, undeniable evidence of love."

Elizabeth closed her eyes. She had spoken from her heart. Unrehearsed, the depth of her feeling flowed forth for the man her daughter had chosen above all others, the son she now saw as a glowing spark that would stay near them always.

With a dignity matching her mother's, Charlene rose and embraced her. Quietly, wordlessly, the people who loved Jim Jenkins left the house.

Earlier, one of the engineers who'd worked with her father had asked Toni if he might tape Elizabeth's remarks.

"I thought you and your mother might like to have them," he said almost diffidently. "And perhaps Jim's parents, too, since I understand they can't be here."

Her first impulse had been to say no. They did not need a mechanical reproduction of her grandmother's declaration of love. It seemed somehow out of place, cold and clinical. But Addie would like it, Toni thought. She

282

admires Grandmother so much, and I'm sure she wishes she were here. So she'd agreed, with thanks for the man's thoughtfulness. And during the simple eloquent tribute, the only sound in the big room was the faint, almost indiscernible hum of the recorder. She heard it click off when Elizabeth stopped speaking. Like a period. The end. But it was not the end. Her grandmother's tender words were the beginning of their return to sanity. She had given them, once again, the comfort of her seemingly limitless strength, her unselfish devotion, and above all, the benefit of her very personal kind of belief in the hereafter which was one with the past and the present.

Mother will be able to go on now, Toni thought.

And so, in my own troubled way, will I.

Chapter 20

Slowly Charlene began to recover. No, recover is not the word. She felt she would never truly heal. But as the weeks passed she assumed some semblance of "normal" behavior. She cried only in private, in the room she'd shared with Jim. Sometimes in the night she stroked his pillow and tried to feel that he was near her just as Elizabeth felt that Tony was always at her side. She did not have Elizabeth's sustaining belief in the endurance of the spirit, but she drew strength from her mother's faith and from the poor consolation of trying to believe that perhaps Jim had been spared some long, torturous illness. Seeking to understand, she could not, but she made a great and determined effort to remember only the good of the past twenty years. That part was the least difficult. Almost everything had been good.

She wrote to Addie and sent her the tape of Elizabeth's tribute, feeling glad that she could face doing that. She and Toni did not play their own copy. The words were etched forever in their minds. She went back to her garden, finding solace in the feel of the deep, rich earth, and hope in the miracle of nature. And at last she was able to talk with Toni about the girl's own plans.

"School is going to reopen any minute," Charlene said. "Aren't you going back?"

"I'm not sure I want to, Mom."

Charlene frowned. "Toni, life can't stop because your father is gone. He'd be the last one to want that. If you think it's your *duty* to stay here with me, you're wrong. It's your duty to pick up and go on, just as I have to."

"I'd rather be here with you."

"No, darling. You may think that at the moment because you don't want me to be alone, but you don't really want to settle in here with me. You've been on your own. And once that's happened to a young person things can never go back to the way they were. You are the most precious thing in my life, Toni, but the only way I can show my gratitude is by letting you go." She tried to laugh. "Besides, you know what the psychologists say about mothers and grown daughters trying to share the same house. It just doesn't work."

"But you've never lived alone," Toni said. "Never in your whole life. You were with Grandmother right up until you married Dad."

"True. It will be a tough adjustment, but millions of women have made it. And most of them much older than I."

Toni sometimes forgot how young her mother was. Only thirty-nine. She still had so much life ahead of her. I hope she'll marry again, Toni thought, feeling no disloyalty. Dad would want her to.

"Why don't you go on with the plan you and your father and I discussed?" Charlene suggested. "Go back to school. Besides, there's Bryce. In a month or so I'll come East to visit you and meet him. Remember what Dad said? He promised we'd have a trip to New York with all the trimmings. I think he'd still like that to happen for me."

The words were like stabbing Toni in her heart. She did remember. But more correctly than Charlene. That last night he'd said, "I'll see that your mother gets back to her beloved New York." Not *we'll* get back. Even then he must have known what he was going to do.

"Mom, may I ask you a very, very personal question?"

"Sure."

"The night before he . . . died. Did you and Dad make love?"

Charlene looked at her curiously. "Yes. We did. Very joyously." She bit her lip. "I've thought of it often since then. He was so happy. I believe it was because he'd pretty well come to terms with himself about you. There was such relief and delight in both of us." Charlene swallowed hard. "It seems ironic that his life was taken just when he seemed to be approaching the best time of it." She looked searchingly at Toni. "What made you ask that?"

"I don't know," Toni lied. "I guess I was thinking of Bryce and whether I love him in *all* ways, the way you loved Dad. And I suppose I just wanted the comfort of knowing you two had been together that last night. I'm glad you were, Mom."

Charlene smiled. "I'm glad too, darling. I'm glad for so many days and nights. Believe me, Toni, I'm going to be all right. I'll miss you when you go but you must go back to Bryce. Find out if he is your life, the way Jim was mine."

The girl nodded. "All right. I'll tell him tonight when he calls. But you're sure you'll be okay? Maybe you should move in with Grandmother and Laurel for a little while."

286

Charlene shook her head. "No need. I love my mother but it would be wrong to live with her. *I* can't be a little girl again either, Toni, dear."

She left three days earlier than planned only because Elizabeth announced to her and Charlene that Peter Richards was coming to the Coast to help her draw up a new will. When her grandmother reported this Toni became agitated.

"Why him? Aren't there plenty of good lawyers right here in California?"

"Of course," Elizabeth said. "But I also want Peter to be co-executor of my estate with Charlene. I want to talk to him about what I want done."

"Your grandmother is right," Charlene said. "After all, he is the only close male relative in the family now."

How can Grandmother be so calm? Toni wondered. Not bad enough to talk about death and estates, things that Toni in her youthful way did not want to think about, but to make Ann's husband a part of the picture was even more distasteful.

"We've always been fond of Peter," Elizabeth said kindly. "He's a good man as well as a good lawyer. Don't look so upset, Antoinette. I have no intention of dying for years, but these things must be planned for. And I have complete faith that Peter Richards will protect all the people I want taken care of. Some stranger might not be of as much help to your mother. They've always liked each other. They still do, in spite of everything. We'll be glad to see Peter after all these years. He'll stay with me for a few days and I hope you'll get to know him. He's anxious to know you."

Toni couldn't restrain her bitterness. "If he's so anxious he could have looked me up in New York."

Elizabeth looked troubled. "Maybe he thought it was

287

more tactful to stay out of all that. For your sake and Alan's. And Ann's."

Toni fell silent. Alan *had* begged her to go with him to meet his father, to hear Peter's assurance that Ann's performance was only a well-planned act. She had refused. She'd been stubborn as well as frightened. Still, she didn't want to meet Alan's father now, didn't want contact with anyone who reminded her of the man in France whose cable she hadn't answered. She'd told Elizabeth about that cable and her grandmother had offered an address to which she might reply. Toni had refused it. She didn't dare. Just as she didn't dare look at a face that probably was an older version of his son's.

She said nothing more, but when she and Charlene got back to Pasadena, Toni offhandedly remarked that she thought she'd go back to New York on Tuesday instead of Friday.

"The weekend is such a hassle at the airport," she said. "It makes more sense to fly in on a quiet day."

Charlene didn't argue with this transparent excuse. "Whatever you think best," she said. And then, "Toni, don't hate your Uncle Peter for whatever has happened to me or to you. For that matter, don't hate anybody. I don't, any more. I almost did, years ago. My sister hurt me so badly that I thought I really despised her. But I've come to understand that she can't help being what she is. Peter has known it for a long time, I think, but there wasn't much he could do about it."

"Why couldn't he?" Toni demanded. "He must be a jellyfish to let that woman push him around."

"He may be misguided, but he's not weak. He's a very kind and honorable man. Qualities, I suspect, his son may have inherited."

She made Toni feel six inches tall.

"I'm sorry, Mom. But I'd still rather not meet him."

"That's your privilege, dear. Or your loss. I think you two might be great friends."

"Under other circumstances, maybe."

"Yes," Charlene agreed. "Under other circumstances."

Bryce was at Kennedy to meet her flight. Toni knew she'd be glad to see him, but she didn't realize *how* glad until she saw the tall, elegant figure eagerly scanning the faces of the deplaning passengers. He looked almost boyish until he spied her. Then his face took on the expression of a happy, hungry man. He swept her into his arms and kissed her expertly, oblivious to the amused stares of other people.

"Baby, you'll never know how happy I am to have you back! No more separations, Toni. Not ever again."

"No, Bryce, never again."

"Cross your heart and hope to die?"

Involuntarily, she winced.

"I'm sorry," he said. "That was tactless."

"No, it wasn't, darling. I can't go through life never expecting to hear the word again." She smiled. "It's just that I'd rather say 'cross your heart and hope to live.' That's how I feel. That I want very much to live."

In the car on the way to the city, Bryce asked, "How's your mother?"

"Remarkable. Really remarkable. I wish I had her courage."

He put his hand over hers. "It was rough, wasn't it? Why didn't you let me come, Toni?"

"There was nothing you could do, dear. I told you that." There was a little silence, and then Toni said, "Tell me what's been happening. How's the perfume campaign progressing?"

"None of the ads have run yet, but the sales force is enthusiastic. We showed the new ads at their meeting last month. They flipped out over them." He smiled. "But then, of course, they're *men*. All they know about perfume is how to sell it to stores. We'll have to wait and see what the lady customer does. Naturally, if the company has a good fall season I'm prepared to take all the credit because of the ads. If sales bomb I'll blame the product, the packaging, the distribution and the state of the economy."

She laughed. "You're impossible."

"Undoubtedly. But lovable." He glanced at her. "What the hell are we doing talking business after all these months? Let's get right to the point. When are you going to marry me?"

Toni didn't answer.

"The other thing *is* over, isn't it?"

"Yes. Completely."

"Then what are we waiting for?"

"Bryce, we really don't know each other."

"Like hell we don't!"

"You know what I mean. We've really spent very little time together." She hesitated. "There's an awful lot about me you don't know."

"And vice versa. But we'll have a lifetime to find out. I know I love you. I believe you love me. I can take care of you and I think we can make each other happy. What more could any two people want? Darling, we're free, white and I, at least, am over twenty-one. Let's stop playing games." He looked straight ahead. "You're still wearing that ring on the wrong hand. Are you giving me a message?"

He's so dear, Toni thought. And I do care for him. I really do. I'll give him everything. Except babies. Life's so short and so precarious. I don't want to waste any of it. This is what Dad wanted. Slowly she shifted the sapphire to her left hand and held it up for him to see.

"Got the message?" she asked.

Bryce almost ran the car off the road.

She insisted upon going to the hotel instead of moving into his apartment as he suggested.

"Until it's legal," Toni said, "the least I can do is have a legal address!"

"Okay. I won't push my luck. But how long?"

"Just a few weeks. I want to get Mother here for a visit before we're married and I can hardly ask her to share our bed at your place! She's broad-minded, but not *that* broad-minded." Toni felt suddenly relieved and secure. "You're going to love her, Bryce. She's terribly pretty and young and fun."

"Maybe I'll prefer her to her daughter."

"If you had any sense you would."

He pulled the car up in front of the hotel. "I love you, Antoinette," he said. "We're going to have a great life. You believe that, don't you?"

"With all my heart."

He smiled at her. "Tomorrow we're going to go and replace that sapphire with a diamond as big as the Ritz."

She shook her head. "No chance. I'm superstitious about this ring. It's the only one I want."

He leaned out the window of the car and yelled at the passing traffic. "Hey, everybody, I'm engaged to a crazy lady who doesn't want diamonds!"

Laughing, she pulled him back. "Stop that, you fool! You'll get us arrested!"

He took her in his arms. "I *want* to give you diamonds, darling. I want to give you everything. You're not getting

291

any big bargain, Toni, but there's nothing I won't do to make you happy. You deserve the best. You're the most beautiful, intelligent, honest woman I've ever known. You give me a lot to live up to and I'm damned well going to try."

She couldn't answer. Instead, she kissed him, thinking, God forgive me for being just the opposite. I'm a fraud and he must never know that. I'm starting our life with a lie. I never meant to. I probably don't even have to. But I can't take a chance. I'm the only one who knows how much my father wanted it that way.

She'd told no one except Elizabeth what she suspected. She'd been foolish to ask Charlene about her last night with Jim. She'd come precariously close to alerting her mother that something was seriously wrong. Charlene wasn't stupid by any means. The unusualness of Toni's question did not escape her, but she put it down to the girl's distraught state. It did not cross Charlene's mind that Toni was convinced her father's death was planned to "release" her. She would have been horrified and dis-believing.

Even Elizabeth, in whom Toni finally confided her awful conviction, was appalled.

"Your imagination is running away with you," she said. "I have no doubt in the world that your father would have given his life for you if there was some real pur-pose—like saving your own. But to imagine he deliber-ately removed himself so that you would never have to admit your Negro blood is as ridiculous as it is morbid! Antoinette, what has gotten into you? You knew your fa-ther better than that. He might have wished you to do as he asked. He might even have figured ways never to meet whomever you marry. But to kill himself? Impossible! Jim loved his life. More than that, he loved your mother too

292

much to sacrifice her life as well as his own. No, my dear, I'll never accept that premise and you must get it out of your mind. Otherwise, you'll always believe you have a debt to repay. In this matter of declaring what you are, you must follow your own convictions, not those of your father. What was true for him may not be true for you. And if you persist in imagining that he died for your sake you'll never know a truly untroubled moment."

Toni had wanted desperately to believe her. Elizabeth was very convincing. What she said made sense. But Toni clung to her sad theory. He *had* done it. He had thought of it as the only viable solution for her. She did not argue with her grandmother. No point in upsetting her further and no point, ever, in telling Charlene. So she lied to Elizabeth as she would later lie to Bryce—by silence.

She'd only said to her grandmother, "I know you won't ever mention this to anyone, will you?"

Elizabeth looked almost offended. "Have I ever betrayed any of your confidences, Antoinette? As for this one, I'd cut my tongue out before I'd let Charlene know what you suspect. My God, child, it would kill her to even consider such a possibility!"

But it was not a possibility, Toni knew; it was the terrible truth. And so when she agreed to marry Bryce she kept quiet for Jim's sake, praying that she was doing the right thing. There was no need for him to know she was a mulatto. It was unlikely that Charlene, when she met Bryce, would talk about Toni's father in terms of color. She didn't even think about it in relation to Jim. She would dwell on his goodness, his brilliance, his devotion, but not his race. She had long since stopped seeing him as anything but her beloved husband, Toni's devoted, adoring father.

The only other people who might unwittingly give away

her secret were Toni's former classmates at Parsons. She made up her mind not to have any contact with them. She also decided not to go back to Pratt. It was pointless. She'd be married in a couple of months. She'd not even tell Amy she was back in town, not give her and Bryce a chance to meet. Amy really was the only one who might let something slip. Amy and the Richardses. But there was small chance that Bryce would ever meet any of Toni's "New York family."

Reluctantly she accepted the knowledge that she would be forever on a tightrope, never, as Elizabeth had said, knowing a truly untroubled moment. It would be so much easier to tell Bryce the truth instead of living with this eternal watchfulness. She was sure that it wouldn't matter to him. But was she really so sure? Bryce came from Texas. Perhaps, despite his New York orientation, he still held some inbred disdain for blacks. But even if that were so, even if he turned away from marrying a mulatto, Toni could bear that more easily than she could live with the knowledge that she had allowed her father to die for no purpose.

She convinced herself she had to risk it, even knowing, among other things, that she dared not have children. She and Bryce had not discussed that. She wondered how he felt about a family. A little pang of regret went through her. She'd like to have had children but it was too dangerous. Who knew what genetic forces might play tricks on her in the form of a dark-skinned baby?

You've made your choice, she told herself. Or, rather, it's been made for you. And it's the right one.

While Toni engaged in her introspection as she mechanically went about settling into her hotel room, Bryce drove home in a state of euphoria. It was true that his first proposal had been made somewhat as the result of the idea that he was losing Toni to another man. But as the weeks went by, separation increased his desire and confirmed his conviction that he was truly in love. He wished he'd insisted on her coming to the apartment tonight. When she stepped off the airplane, he knew that he wanted her more than he'd ever wanted anyone or anything in his life. But he'd wait another day. He smiled. Toni was the final triumph. The poor kid of the ignorant sharecropper had come a long way. His mother would have been happy. As for his father, Bryce only wished that that evil, stupid man could know what his "sissy son" had accomplished. He'd like to have rubbed his father's ugly face in Bryce Sumner's success as a prosperous businessman, a well-off cosmopolite and now the future husband of a beautiful young woman from a fine family. He didn't know whether the old man was dead or alive, and he didn't care. Unlike Toni, who believed she owed Jim Jenkins a debt, Bryce knew he owed his father nothing but contempt. He seldom thought of Hank Sumner, but at this moment, after so many years, it was as though he could hear the loud, drunken voice ranting against the "snotty rich folks" he hated and envied and the "spics and nigras" he despised. A shudder ran through Bryce. Thank God I escaped. All the others were probably just like him. All the brothers and sisters he had put out of his life forever. He had buried every one of them the day they buried his mother.

He'd never tell Toni any of it. She was marrying a different image. Not a bigoted, brutal redneck's son; a self-made sophisticate who'd left all that horror behind him. As an adolescent he'd sometimes fantasized that his mother had had an affair with an elegant gentleman passing through their part of the country, and that he was the offspring of that brief encounter. Even then he knew why he was indulging in wishful thinking: He did not want to be any part of Hank Sumner. But not even his vivid imagination could picture his cowed, overworked mother involved in an illicit affair, even if she'd had the chance. No, he was Hank's son all right. But for almost twenty years he'd thought of his father as dead. Much more dead and far less grieved for than Jim Jenkins.

Chapter 21

Peter Richards braced himself for an outburst when he told Ann that he was flying to California to revise Elizabeth's will, and he was right. She behaved so badly that he wished he'd not told her where he'd be for the next few days. But that couldn't be done. He couldn't simply disappear on a mysterious "business trip," leaving no word where he could be reached. What if something happened to one of the children or to Ann herself?

He'd thought she'd be scornful, sarcastic, but she was much more. She was infuriated beyond reason, even to the point of picking up a priceless porcelain vase and smashing it violently against the living-room wall. He'd never seen her behave so irrationally. It was understandable that she'd be angry about his persistent affection for Elizabeth; that she'd feel "betrayed" because he insisted upon staying in touch with the mother she hated. But her performance was more than anger and frustration. It was uncontrolled fury, the wild, incoherent raving of a madwoman.

It was not the first time that Peter had felt deeply troubled about Ann's mental state. Her vindictiveness, her cruelty were beyond the limits of a balanced mind. The suicide attempt, faked though he knew it to be, left Peter with the conviction that only a deranged woman would cunningly plan a performance designed to destroy her son's happiness without seriously jeopardizing her own life.

There had been other things lately, too, less overt and dramatic but equally revealing. Ann had become obsessed with the idea that her own daughter was no better than a common whore.

At first, Peter had tried to talk her out of such a ridiculous notion. He couldn't believe what he was hearing.

"You know Joanne better than that!" he'd said. "Ann, what are you saying? This is your own daughter you're talking about!"

Ann had narrowed her eyes. "I know what she does. She has all kinds of men in that apartment every night. Almost twenty-eight years old and not married. Why? Because no decent man would have her."

"I never heard such garbage," Peter said. "She's a lovely, successful woman. You should be proud of her instead of making such ludicrous accusations. My God, you must be insane!"

"Don't you dare say that to me, you, you alley cat! She's just like you. Sex-crazy. You probably encourage her, just as you encouraged Alan to take up with that black bitch! Ditto is the only one worth anything in this family. He's like me. Like my father."

Peter had left the room without another word but only last week he'd called Ann's doctor and asked him about her condition. He'd been told that organically she was in perfect health but, the doctor hesitated, he could understand why Mr. Richards was concerned about her.

"She's in menopause," he said, "and for some reason she refuses to take the hormones I've prescribed. Says she

298

doesn't need them, doesn't believe in them. I've tried to talk with her, but frankly I can't get through. I'm no psychiatrist, but I can see her trouble is much more than the nervous, sometimes erratic behavior of some women at her time of life. She really needs help, Mr. Richards, and I hope you can persuade her to get it."

Peter had tried, very cautiously, to suggest to Ann that therapy might do her good. His proposal had only brought about another tirade in which she accused him of prying into her life by having "underhanded conversations" with her doctor.

"He had no right to tell you anything!" Ann said. "He is violating the doctor-patient relationship of confidentiality. I'll never go back to that quack again!"

"Ann, I'm your husband! It's his duty to tell me anything that might affect your well-being!"

She'd sneered. "You're not my husband. You're just the man who shares this apartment. You're against me, the way they all are. I know everybody talks about me, don't think I don't! My suddenly concerned husband! To tell with all of you, including those women in California, those two virtuous, mealy-mouthed widows!"

Against this background, Peter feared, a week later, to tell her about the trip and yet he had no choice. She had raged and screamed, accusing him of making sure that she and her children would be left out of Elizabeth's will, just to spite her. She had even gone so far as to say that she knew he was going out there to see Charlene, probably to make love to her.

This was the last straw. Peter's indignation was stronger than his concern for this sick woman.

"Stop that!" he commanded. "I know what you think of me. I know I deserve some of your hatred. But don't say things like that about your sister! Do you hear me, Ann? Never speak that way about Charlene again!"

299

She was silent in the face of his towering fury. She had never seen the normally quiet, contained Peter in such a fit of rage. For a moment she thought he was going to strike her, and she cowered away from him like a frightened dog.

With effort, he got himself under control. "I don't intend to discuss your ugly accusations with you," he said. "I am going to California and I'll be gone about three days. You have your mother's address. You can reach me there if you need anything." Suddenly he felt sorry for her. "Wouldn't you like me to arrange for someone to sleep in the apartment while I'm gone? I'm sure we could get a woman to stay for a few days so you wouldn't be all alone."

His softness dispelled the momentary fear she'd felt.

"What kind of woman? Some strong-armed practical nurse to watch me and see that I don't really kill myself this time? Since when have I needed a keeper, Peter? I've been alone for years."

It was hopeless. Without even saying goodbye he packed a bag and left for Los Angeles. To his surprise Charlene was waiting for him at the airport. He recognized her immediately. She reminded him very much of Elizabeth, more in expression than in physical features. There was the same warm smile, the same hint of mirth even in eyes that were still shadowed by loss. She knew him too, and waved as he came through the gate.

She kissed him lightly on the cheek.

"It was good of you to come, Peter. Mother's very grateful and so am I." Then, after a pause, "How are Ann and the children?"

"Everybody's okay," he said, "all things considered."

Charlene did not pursue it. She could imagine how angry Ann must be by this "defection" of her husband. The knowledge lay heavily between them, just as the awareness of their children's love hung in the air like an unspoken reproach.

"You look wonderful," she said instead. "How do you do it?"

"Charley, I'm fifty-six years old and slightly paunchy in spite of the best efforts of the New York Athletic Club. I'm not that snappy young man you may remember. But you, you've blossomed with maturity. And good God, you're not even forty yet. So young to be . . ." His voice trailed off.

"A widow? Yes, I suppose that's young. But I had twenty years of total happiness, Peter. That's more than most people celebrating their golden anniversaries can say."

She was driving expertly up the coast road to Elizabeth's. He looked at the delicate profile, understanding better than ever before how Alan must have felt about this woman's child.

"I'm sorry about our kids," he said. "I guess you know it all."

"Yes. Toni told me everything. She's going to marry someone else, I think. I'm not really sure I know why. I know she loves Alan. Too much, I suppose, to marry him." She glanced briefly at her brother-in-law. "We tried to tell her that nothing mattered but their happiness. She couldn't accept that. After what happened, she was afraid."

Peter sighed heavily. "Do you approve of Bryce Sumner?"

"I haven't met him yet, but I trust Toni's instincts. I'm coming to New York this fall to meet my prospective son-in-law." For a fraction of a second her voice faltered. "We'd planned the trip the night before the accident. Jim was going to see New York for the first time."

"Charlene, I can't begin to tell you how terrible I feel about Jim. I wish I'd known him better."

"Me, too. You'd have understood why I loved him so."

"I understand even without that. I always trusted *your* instincts. Yours and Elizabeth's. How is she?"

Relieved to be on easier ground, she told him how strong and well Elizabeth was, despite her handicap. She even managed to inject some humor into little anecdotes about her mother in recent years, and she told him about Tony Alexander and how the memory of him and the belief that the core of him still lived comforted and sustained the woman who'd lost him.

"He was the only man she ever truly loved," Charlene said. "My father wasn't worthy of what she had to offer. I can say that with no feeing of disloyalty. I suppose he tried. He couldn't help being what he was. I hardly remember him, so it's less difficult for me than it must be for Ann to face the fact that he was more than weak. He was paranoid, Peter. Insane. Did you know that?"

"Yes. I heard all about it. From people who knew him. Not from Ann. She still thinks he was the greatest man who ever lived."

"I guessed as much. I've often thought that all her anger toward Mother and me was really much more mixed up with our early lives than it was with my marriage."

He didn't answer. There was so much to say and most of it impossible to put into words. How Ann has fouled up all our lives, he thought. If she'd seen things rationally, everything would be different today.

Deliberately, he turned the conversation to safer subjects. He hadn't been in California in years and found it much changed. He was eager to see Charlene's house, once Elizabeth's, and to see again the place where Elizabeth now lived. He asked with interest about them both, about Elizabeth's business and Laurel, whom he'd met

302

years before. They chatted easily the rest of the way, comfortable in each other's company, pleased to find that they were still fond of each other. Charlene was so relaxed that as they neared Elizabeth's she laughed and said, mischievously, "You know I was crushed when you married Ann. I hoped you'd wait for me."

He didn't return her laughter. His voice was very serious as he answered. "You were the most charming child I ever knew. And now you're the most charming woman."

"Wrong," Charlene said. "You're about to be reunited with the holder of that title!"

The next few days were the most pleasant Peter had spent in years. In spite of the seriousness of the assignment which had brought him to California, there was no grimness in his talks with Elizabeth about the things she wanted done after her death. It struck Peter, as it had many times before, that there was something incongruous about the fact that the closer people came to the end of their lives, the more calmly and unemotionally they could discuss dying. He would have thought it would be just the other way around; that the nearer the specter came, the more reluctant one would be to think about it. It did not work that way with most people, he'd found. And it certainly did not work that way with Elizabeth.

They spent the first evening quietly with Charlene and Laurel, catching up on the past, not avoiding the subject of Ann but feeling a certain constraint as her name came into the conversation. Peter did not reveal his anxiety about his wife. He would tell Elizabeth about that privately, later. Instead, they reminisced and joked about the past. Elizabeth was especially eager to know all about her grandchildren and Peter gave a proud account of them.

"I'm very lucky," he said. "They're all good human beings. All quite different, of course. Peter is very serious and settled; Joanne is lovely. Fiercely independent and

303

ambitious but a soft, sweet woman. And Alan"—he hesitated, feeling self-conscious for the first time—"well, you know a little bit about my youngest. He's the dreamer, the idealist and, I won't deny it, the one I feel closest to. He's had a novel accepted and that's what he wants to do—be a writer. I think he has the sensitivity for it."

They let it go at that.

Charlene stayed over at her mother's insistence.

"It's too late for you to drive home alone," Elizabeth said. "Besides, Peter's going to be here only a few days. You stay, too. You can chauffeur him around after we finish our business tomorrow."

Charlene shrugged her shoulders. "Aye, aye, sir!" She turned, smiling, to Peter. "I don't disobey orders from this one. Not that they're unwelcome commands. I look forward to giving you the grand tour. I'd like you to see my house, modest as it is, and a few other things including our new 'culture center.' Besides, it means I won't have to cook for a few days!"

It was more than that. She put up a front for everyone, including Toni, but she really hated being alone in her house. Peter's visit was a good chance to escape from the big empty bed at home, the rooms that still smelled warmly of Jim and Toni, the solitary dinners that were the worst part of the day.

Elizabeth bore Peter off early next morning to the little study and was locked in with him for hours.

"Charlene knows what I want as far as 'arrangements' are concerned," she said. "The same for me as for Tony and Jim. You can write it all down in legalese. No 'viewing' of me in some funeral director's idea of an old lady's made-up face! Quick cremation. Burial under the tree. A service like Jim's and Tony's later, if Charlene wants it. So much for all the trappings. Or, hopefully, lack of them."

He was surprised by the extent of her estate. The house, very valuable, was to go to Laurel for her lifetime, and then to Charlene. The decorating business was Charlene's to keep or sell as she chose, and Laurel was to have a guaranteed income from the business if it continued or a fifty per cent share of the sale price if it did not. The interest and dividends on her stocks, investments, savings and her insurance were to be Charlene's. They would provide for her comfortably. At Charlene's death, the estate was to be divided equally among Elizabeth's four grandchildren.

As she talked, Peter made notes.

"I know it's not wise to designate specific objects in a will," Elizabeth said. "So I've made up a little list to be kept separately. There are a few people I'd like to have something personal, provided they don't pre-decease me." She handed him a typed memorandum. He glanced at it. All but two of the names were unfamiliar. Probably long-time employees, he correctly guessed. The only names he recognized were his and Ann's. To Peter she had left Tony's large and valuable collection of books. To Ann, a framed letter of praise and affection written to Ann's father and signed, with a flourish, "Franklin Delano Roosevelt."

Peter looked up, surprised. Elizabeth smiled at him. "You must have many questions, Peter. Maybe you think it's unfair, my leaving Ann out, except for the letter?"

"No," he said frankly. "I don't think you owe Ann anything. I think you're being very generous providing for her children. We'll put in the necessary disclaimer, though, so that she can't contest this. Anyway, Elizabeth, you know that Ann will be well taken care of. I've seen to that."

She nodded. "I don't believe in being stupid about things like this. Jim left very little. Charlene needs the in-

305

come for herself and she may even need it for Antointte. Who knows what's going to happen to that child?"

"You've thought it through very carefully and sensibly," Peter agreed. "Any charitable bequests?"

"Nothing specific. I count on Charlene to do the same as I've always done in that area. Or contribute to things she might prefer." Elizabeth paused. "Are you curious about the small personal things for you and Ann?"

"I can understand the letter from FDR. I assume that was about all her father left."

"Exactly. And it will mean a great deal to her, I think. 'Concrete evidence' of what a great and famous man Alan Whitman was." There was a trace of irony in her voice. "I made the money myself. Or, rather, I made some of it and Tony and I built up the rest. It comes to a good bit, doesn't it?"

"At a quick guess, I'd say well over a million dollars."

Elizabeth laughed. "Isn't it ridiculous that a young woman who walked out on her husband not knowing where the next meal for her children was coming from should have ended up with all that money? I've never had a head for money, Peter. Neither did Tony, really. It just came. Like it was meant to do somebody some good. It has. And it will. You do think I'm being fair, don't you?"

He smiled. "Eminently. More than fair. After all, you haven't seen my children in years."

"But they're part of you and Ann and therefore part of me. They may not need their inheritance but they're as entitled as Charlene's child. They haven't done anything to wound me or the people I love."

"They've ignored you," he said reluctantly. "As I have. Even though they're not to blame. They had forgotten this part of the family until a few months ago. And then Alan wanted to come here to plead with Toni and see you

306

and Charlene and Jim. I talked him out of it. I wish to God I hadn't."

"Regrets don't change anything, Peter. You did what you thought was right for everybody concerned. Maybe it *was* right. Time will be the judge of that. I don't know if I'll be around when we get the answer, but I hope I am. I'd like to know how those kids' lives are going to turn out." Her voice was warm and light. "I've always had an insatiable curiosity about everything. Tony taught me so much about living and dying. Mostly to be interested in both. He had such an alive mind, Peter, and such an open one. Like yours. That's why I want you to have his books. I think you're the only man, maybe the only person I know whose life could be changed by the philosophy Tony discovered."

He looked at her curiously. What was she trying to tell him?

Elizabeth sensed his confusion. "There's wisdom in those old books," she said. "Old religions, ancient truths. Someday you may have the need for them. They may show you that sometimes what seems to be mystery is the only reality. That man-made rules and requirements are transient. You might even want to share them with Alan."

He wondered if she was possibly getting senile. None of this made sense, but that, he knew, was not because Elizabeth was meandering in her mind; she was being deliberately obtuse. He, in turn, could only be patient and wait for understanding.

After three days he reluctantly prepared to return to New York, promising to have the will drawn up quickly and returned to Elizabeth for her signature.

"Not that I think there's any hurry," he said affectionately. "You're like your daughter, getting younger and more beautiful by the day."

Elizabeth couldn't resist. "My daughter *Charlene,* I

presume you mean." Instantly, she was ashamed. The hurt in his face was overlaid by an expression of worry. Her flippancy was unbecoming. "I'm sorry, my dear," she said. "I shouldn't have said that. It was unkind and unfair."

"But not untrue," Peter said. Then, in a rush, he blurted out all that haunted him. He told her his fears for Ann's mental state, the agony of suspicion in which she lived, the rejection of help in which she persisted. "God knows, I haven't been the perfect husband," he said. "She has plenty to be bitter about, but it's gone beyond bitterness. She's alienated everyone. She has no friends, no love. Even her children have turned away from her, except Ditto, who's too insensitive to see her as anything but a mother. Everyone else recognizes the person she's become, angry and vicious and ugly. She's getting to look like an old woman, Elizabeth, and she's only in her early fifties. The hatred she feels for everyone is showing on her face as well as in her actions. It's terrifying and pathetic. Sometimes she doesn't leave the apartment for weeks. And she's begun to drink heavily. Physically she's still strong, but mentally she's lost all perspective.

"I don't know what to do about her," Peter went on. "I can't leave her and I can't stand the thought of spending the rest of my life with her. I've tried to give her everything she wants, materially, but it hasn't made her happy. Somehow I've failed her, I suppose. Not only by being less than faithful. I'm just not the man she thought she was marrying."

And she's not the woman, Elizabeth added silently. She felt so sorry for him, so sorry for them both, and so inadequate. She remembered feeling much the same way about Ann's father, thinking she had married the perfect man, watching him slowly disintegrate, standing by helplessly unable to make him see that he was destroying himself and everything he cared about. Alan Whitman had punished himself for his own lack of character, just as Ann, like Quigly before her, was now also unconsciously hell-bent on self-destruction. But Peter couldn't leave her as Elizabeth had finally left Alan. For all his anguish, Peter had not yet reached that point of self-preservation. Elizabeth had, at least, felt free of guilt. She had done everything she could, had been faithful, had left finally only because she could not let three children grow up in an atmosphere of evil. She'd run for her life—and theirs. But Peter had no such justification for leaving Ann. He'd broken his marriage vows and was guilty about it. He'd let a wrong union go on for more than thirty years and now, when Ann had no future to look forward to, no one who wanted her, he could not walk out on her. He probably persisted in the thought that what she had become was the result of her disappointment in him, even though he knew what a selfish, cold woman she was.

He was trying to smile now, apologetic, a little ashamed.

"Forgive me," Peter said, "I had no right to burden you with all this. There's nothing you can do about it. We'll have to work it out somehow, Ann and I. I must convince her to get help. How, I don't know. But there has to be a way."

"Peter, I'd do anything in the world for you and my daughter," Elizabeth said. "I'd even bring her out here to stay a while with me if I thought that would help, but I know it wouldn't. And of course she wouldn't come anyway. She hates me as much as she hates everyone else. Maybe more. Undoubtedly more, because she blames me for everything, whether she realizes it or not. I've always been the symbol of everything she detests, the ogre who deprived her of her father, the madwoman who persisted in thinking that there was more to life than a split-level house and a two-car garage. We've never understood each

309

other. I'm as much at fault as she. I expected her to have my values. I didn't let her know that I felt she was entitled to hers, even if I didn't agree with them."

"Don't!" Peter said. "Don't blame yourself, Elizabeth. There's enough guilt in me for both of us, and mine's real. You offered Ann everything you could and she spat on you for it. You mustn't reproach yourself. My god, I wouldn't have told you about her if I'd thought you'd feel remorse!"

"It's not remorse, it's sadness. She's still my child. I can't like her as a person but I can ache for her as a mother who bleeds for what was literally once a part of her."

"I know," he said. "I detest what she's become, but I remember what I once thought she was." He rose from his chair on the terrace, where they'd been having their private talk. "Goodbye for now, dear. May I come back soon?"

"Whenever and as often as you like. You're the only son I have left, and I cherish you."

He kissed her gently and left quickly. Charlene was in the car waiting to drive him to the airport. He did not tell her the things he'd confided to Elizabeth, but as they pulled up to the TWA area he said, "I'm afraid I burdened Elizabeth with a lot of my problems, Charley. It was selfish of me, but I just had to talk to someone who'd understand. Tell her for me that if she wants to discuss them with you, she has my permission, will you?"

Charlene nodded. "Goodbye, Peter. Come back soon."

"I hope to. I wish I didn't have to leave at all. Will you let me know when you're coming to New York to see Toni?"

She hesitated. "Maybe."

"Please do. I know what you're thinking, that you'd be

sneaking around behind Ann's back. But it really isn't that way, Charlene. We're family, you and I. Much more so than you and your sister. I don't want to lose touch with you and Elizabeth again. Ann won't know and it won't hurt her."

"We won't lose touch, Peter. I promise. But as for New York, I'm not sure. It's not only Ann. There's Toni to consider."

He had to be content with that.

Chapter 22

It was strange, Charlene thought, to be returning to the city she'd not seen in more than twenty years. But despite the physical changes, there was a reassuring sense of familiarity about New York that kept her from feeling alien and lost. She spent the lovely October days browsing through the antique shops on Madison Avenue, going again to the Metropolitan Museum and being introduced to the new splendor of Lincoln Center. She missed Jim constantly and thought how enthralled he would have been by this man-made masterpiece which, despite all its flaws, was still the most exciting city in the world.

Toni was busy with free-lance art jobs and she was presumably happy. Meeting Bryce, Charlene saw why. He was a strong, protective man. He obviously adored Toni and just as obviously responded with genuine liking to her mother. And yet there was something Charlene could not quite define, something that intuitively made her doubt that this was the right man for Toni. She wondered how much of the charm was acquired veneer, how much came from careful cultivation of the sophisticated image Bryce wanted to project. She chided herself for her uneasiness.

Perhaps she was comparing him to an unknown Alan, a young man who must be very like his father. She was being silly, she told herself. Bryce was a good man. He must be, to care so little for the facts of Toni's background.

"You do like Bryce, don't you?" Toni put the question to Charlene a week after she arrived. They were preparing for bed in Toni's hotel room.

"Yes. Very much. For one thing, he's more gentle than I expected." She laughed. "I think I've seen too many movies about advertising tycoons. I was afraid he'd smoke big cigars and brag about his clients."

"Mom!"

"I'm only teasing, you idiot." She sobered. "What about you, love? Sure you want to marry Bryce?"

"Quite sure."

"What about Alan?"

"What about him?"

"Is he really out of your mind for good, Toni?"

"He'll never really be out of my mind," Toni said. "Let's just say he's gone but not forgotten. 'The saddest words of tongue or pen . . .' That's the way I feel about Alan. I have to live for what *is*, Mother, not what might have been. I love Bryce. Not the way I loved Alan, but enough to be happily married to him. I'm really very lucky. He's everything a woman could want in a husband. I'm sure you can see that, even after knowing him only a week."

"Yes, I can, darling. And I'm happy for you. So, when will it be? Still want the Christmas wedding at your grandmother's?"

There was an almost imperceptible pause before Toni answered. "I don't think so, Mom. In fact, Bryce and I thought we'd be married quietly next week while you're here. He doesn't want to wait till Christmas and neither

313

do I. The hotel is expensive and even though I'm earning some money it's still a drain on your income, which isn't what it was. Besides, I don't want a big wedding. It's too soon after Dad."

Charlene was astonished. Perhaps what she was hearing was the truth, but only part of it. She said the first thing that came into her head.

"Toni, your grandmother will be so disappointed!"

"I know. I feel bad about that, but Bryce and I will come to see her later. We want to do this quickly and quietly, Mom. And having you here is the perfect opportunity. This is Bryce's busiest season and he really can't spare the time for a big do in California. We probably won't even take a wedding trip until later. You do understand, don't you?"

"No," Charlene said, "I don't. California isn't Outer Mongolia. You could both fly out over a weekend and have a quiet family wedding. As for a couple of months' postponement, that much additional hotel expense certainly isn't going to break me. I don't see the reason for the rush. . . ." She suddenly looked questioningly at Toni.

"Unless I'm pregnant? No, darling, this is no shotgun scene. I'm not going to have a baby, In fact, we've agreed that we're never going to have a baby."

Charlene looked at her levelly. "Toni, what are you *not* telling me? None of this makes any sense. Not the quick, anonymous wedding here. Not this sudden declaration that you won't have children. Something's wrong. You're holding back. We've always been honest with each other. I don't think you're being honest now."

Toni tried to be convincing. "Yes, I am. It's exactly the way I've told you."

"No. I'm sorry, but I don't believe you. You wouldn't suddenly change everything you've wanted, for no reason. You always wanted a nice wedding at your grandmother's. You've always wanted children. I know you said you'd give them up because of the blood relationship with Alan. I understood that. But I don't understand it with Bryce." She paused and then said slowly, "Yes, I do understand it. You haven't told Bryce about your father, have you? You don't want him to know, ever. That's why you won't come home. There is too much evidence of Jim there. Memories. And conversations with people who knew him well. People who might casually mention that he was black."

Toni refused to look at her.

"I see," Charlene went on sadly. "And you can't risk having a baby because you don't know what color it will be. Darling, how can you do this to Bryce? How can you do it to yourself and to your father's memory?"

Toni's lips tightened. "I don't see it that way," she said. "Have you forgotten, Mother, that Dad begged me never to tell anyone that I'm a mulatto?"

"He was wrong, Toni. He meant well, but he had a blind spot about that. Yes, he'd have liked to see you marry a white man. No question about that. He knew how hard it is to be black. Or for white and black to be married. But I don't believe if it had come to a real case he would have wanted you to deceive someone who loved you. In fact, I *know* he wouldn't, and so do you. You told us about Bryce the night before your father died, and Jim accepted it. He understood you well, Toni. He knew you couldn't play that kind of game."

The girl's voice quivered. "Did he? Did he accept it?"

"You know he did," Charlene repeated. "Toni, darling, don't betray all that your father saw in you. All that I see now. Your loyalty, your sense of rightness, your courage. Don't try to be what you could never be—a secretive, lying woman."

Unjust blame added to guilt made Toni oblivious to the

315

consequences of the words she would almost shout at her mother.

"Don't you see that I *have* to do this? Can't you understand that I'm doing it for Dad? He *couldn't* accept my telling Bryce about him and myself! No matter what he said to you that last night, I know he was desperate!"

Charlene stared at her. "What in God's name are you trying to say?"

Toni was almost hysterical. "Mother, I know he didn't die accidentally. He died for me. He crashed that plane because it was the only way he could make sure I'd never have to introduce him to Bryce!"

Horrified, she clapped her hand over her mouth. God forgive me! What have I done! Charlene's bewilderment and pain were more than Toni could bear. She threw herself, sobbing, onto the bed, unable to look at her mother.

It seemed hours before Charlene spoke, though only seconds had passed. Her voice was low and throbbing with grief.

"Look at me, Toni," she said.

Reluctantly, Toni sat up.

"You can't believe what you just said. Tell me you don't believe that."

The time for secrets from Charlene was past. Even though she was in an agony of remorse, Toni could not lie.

"I do believe it, Mother. I think he loved me so much he had to do it. God knows what courage it took to leave you, whom he loved more than anything. And God knows what he must have suffered, convinced that his existence threatened my happiness. Don't you see? It was the bravest, most wonderful sacrifice in the world. Could I erase it now by revealing the secret he died to protect?"

Charlene sat silent. Toni, slightly more composed, went on.

316

"Even *you* were afraid that Bryce might feel differently about me if he knew. You took the opposite view from Dad. You begged me to tell him. But you warned me that he might back off if he knew. Dad was *sure* he would." She put her arms around her mother. "Oh, darling, forgive me! I never meant to tell you. My God, I'd rather be unmarried all my life and have Dad alive! But he saw this as the solution for me. Maybe a way of repaying some kind of debt he felt. He left me the heritage of his blood, but he also left me the burden of this responsibility."

Charlene was numb. Then, like Elizabeth, she said, "Why are you so sure it wasn't an accident? Why do you accept this? You have no proof."

"I don't need proof. I know it in my heart."

It was Charlene's turn to cry. Her tears heightened Toni's remorse. Why had she told her? How could she have been so reckless? She'd promised herself and Elizabeth that Charlene would never know what Toni suspected, what even Elizabeth did not believe, and in one heedless moment Toni had plunged Charlene into a grief deeper than any she'd ever known. Terrible as it was, the widow had had to face the inevitable of an accident. To think that Jim's death was suicide was far, far worse. She'll never forgive me, Toni thought. She won't be able to. In a way I killed her husband. Is it her punishment I want?

But Charlene, like her own mother, would not accept the horror of what Toni believed. After a moment, she seemed to pull herself together.

"You're wrong, Toni," she said. "Jim didn't do that." There was a half smile on her lips. "You see, he was a very intelligent man. He'd have realized that even if he wasn't around, someday, somehow the truth would come out. He'd have recognized how pointless such a sacrifice would be. No, your father didn't kill himself, darling. I

317

knew him better than that. I'm afraid you're rationalizing your own desires."

Toni didn't answer. Let her believe that, she prayed. Thank you, God, for not punishing me any more.

"But," Charlene continued, "if, based on your conversations with Jim, you think this is what he would have wanted, what *you* want, then I'll go along with it. I don't think it's right, and it won't work, but it's your decision. Bryce will never hear from me or from your grandmother that Jim Jenkins was a Negro. I'm sorry you're determined to live a lie, Toni. Sorry your reasons for it are wrong. I'd hoped you'd have children. Selfishly, I've always wanted to be a grandmother, but it's your future, sweetheart, and you must do it your way. Keep your secret if you feel you must. But do you feel right depriving Bryce of children? Doesn't he want them?"

"He says he doesn't care one way or the other. He only wants me." She laughed harshly. "We've come full circle, haven't we? I was willing to sacrifice motherhood if I could have had Alan. Now Bryce will give up fatherhood if he can have me."

"It would seem to me," Charlene said softly, "that neither is the ideal answer. Tell him, Toni. Please. If he loves you so much it won't matter to him. You'll be able to have an honest life. And a family. You can work it out the way your father and I did."

"I'm sorry, Mother. I can't."

They were married the next week at City Hall with Charlene and a long-time friend of Bryce's as the witnesses. Bryce couldn't understand why Toni didn't even want the notice of their marriage sent out to *The New York Times*.

"You're ashamed of me," he teased. "You're not even

sending out announcements. What are we going to do, pretend to live in sin?"

He and Toni and Charlene were dining quietly together the night before the wedding. Charlene would leave for California the next afternoon.

"Darling, all that announcement nonsense is square," Toni said lightly. "It's really boring. People you haven't heard from in years—and never want to hear from— come popping out of the woodwork when they get that news. The people we care about, we'll tell."

Bryce had looked helplessly at Charlene. "My child bride," he'd said. "I'm not sure she doesn't think *getting married* is square!"

Toni laughed. "No, I think getting married is lovely. Especially to you."

Charlene made no comment. She knew why Toni didn't want announcements of any kind. Someone who knew about her might read the paper. One of those girls she'd roomed with, perhaps, the ones who took her "confession" so lightly. Or maybe she feared some kind of repercussion from the Richards family.

Feeling strangely awkward about it, Charlene had called Peter the day before and told him she was in town. He was disappointed when she said she'd been in New York for nearly two weeks and was leaving in two days.

"I thought you were going to let me know," he said.

"Peter, dear, I intended to, but it's all been rather hectic. Toni's getting married tomorrow, to Bryce Sumner. We've had a million things to do, even though they're just going to slip down to City Hall very quietly."

"I see. I'm sure you're happy about it."

"I like Bryce very much." That, at least, wasn't a lie.

"Look, Charlene, can't we at least have a drink? Or lunch? I'd like to see you while you're here."

She hesitated and then agreed to meet him for lunch

319

that afternoon. He suggested the Regency dining room, wondering as he did whether there was something symbolic about choosing the same place he and Alan had had their talks, and deciding that he was being ridiculous. It was simply one of the quietest places in town. On the way he stopped and bought a copy of Alan's novel, which had been published only a few days before. He didn't know whether Charlene or Toni had seen it. He was enormously proud, seeing it in the windows of bookstores, with his son's name displayed prominently on the cover.

He gave *Summer Romance* to Charlene when they were seated at the table. She hadn't seen it and she was delighted with the dedication: "For my father, with admiration and love." She turned it over and studied the photograph on the back of the dust jacket.

"So that's Alan. He looks like you, Peter. In fact, he looks exactly as you did the day I first met you."

"I was his age then."

"So you were! It's hard to believe it was so long ago." She continued to study the face of her nephew. "How is he?"

"From his letters I'd say he's okay. He's living in Paris and working on another book. There's a movie deal pending for this first one. If it comes through he'll quit the advertising agency and devote full time to writing."

"Does he plan to live there permanently?"

"What's permanent?" Peter said. "I'm sure he'll stay a while. For many reasons. Especially when he hears that Toni has married. Immodest of me as it may be to say it, I think Alan has behaved like a gentleman about all this. He's tried to be considerate of Toni, a damned sight more self-sacrificing than I could be if I loved anybody as much as he loves her. Of course, there are those who'd say he's been a fool. I lean a little in that direction sometimes, too. But on the whole, I'm proud of him, Charley. He realized

320

how tortured Toni was, and he wouldn't make things harder for her, no matter how wrong he thought she was. I only hope she's made the right choice now."

"So do I." Charlene looked troubled. "We've all done him and Toni a great disservice, Peter. Some of us deliberately, like Ann. Others indulgently, I suppose, like me. I should have tried harder to make Toni see how groundless her fears were. In all directions." She could not tell him Toni's theory about her father's death. She could tell no one, ever. Charlene did not share Toni's belief, but she regretfully knew that if the girl had accepted Alan, who knew all about her, she would not now be tormented by this imagined obligation to the dead. She would have recognized Jim's death for what Charlene would always believe it was, a tragic accident.

Too late now, Charlene thought. Too late for all of them. Unwilling, but feeling obliged to ask, she said, "How's Ann?"

Peter toyed with his food. "Did you ever talk to Elizabeth about that?"

"Yes. You told me I could. Mother's worried about her. And about you."

"Ann's getting worse by the day. And I'm no closer to finding a solution. She's become a recluse. She eats—and drinks—alone in her room. Refuses to see Joanne because she's developed a crazy idea that our daughter is a 'loose woman.' She won't even see Ditto and his family, convinced even they are 'against her.' As for me," Peter said, "forget it. The very sight of me sends her into a screaming rage."

Charlene was horrified. "She can't live like that, Peter! And neither can you."

"Easy to say. What do I do, have her committed? She's certifiable, but I can't bring myself to do it."

321

"You may have to." Charlene's voice was sad. "She may harm herself or someone else. Dear Lord, is there no end to the ironies in this world? Ann's father fixation, her determination to deify him, has brought her to the same mental state he was in at the end of his life. The drinking, the paranoia—those were the things that destroyed his marriage and eventually himself. And now the same thing is happening to the child who adored him just as it happened to Quigly."

She did not say that Ann's plight filled her with fear for Toni. Not that the girl would go this route. But in a strange parallel, Toni, too, was structuring her life on the memory of a dead father. She wished with all her heart that Toni would not marry Bryce Sumner under this cloud. Someday awareness that she'd obeyed an unreal "command" would come to her. Just as, perhaps, awareness had come too late to Ann.

Charlene tried hard to lighten the atmosphere, seeking safe ground in small talk about Elizabeth.

"She's hoping you'll come back to visit soon," Charlene said. "You did her a world of good, Peter."

"She did more for me. But I don't know when I'll get back. I dare not leave town even for a day. Give her my love, Charley. By the way, what does she think of Toni's marriage?"

"I spoke to her last night. She's disappointed that the wedding won't be in California and furious with those 'damned, dead legs,' as she calls them, that keep her from coming here. But otherwise, she's great. Except, of course, for her concern about you and Ann."

"Tell her we'll be all right." He smiled. "Everything will be. And wish Toni much happiness for me, will you? I hope one day I'll get to meet her. If she's anything like her mother, I'll love her on sight."

Charlene found herself unexpectedly blushing. "She's a much better person than I. I was selfish."

"But *you* found happiness," Peter said quietly.

In Paris, Alan read his father's letter with a kind of numb acceptance. He wasn't really surprised that Toni had married. He'd had enough warnings. The night he cabled he'd known there was no use fighting any longer. Still he'd waited for some answer. None came. Not that he'd expected it, but he couldn't seem to let go of his dream while there was any vestige of hope that Toni would change her mind. He tried to hate his mother, the real cause of it all. For a while he did hate her, passionately. But lately the news of her that came from Peter and Joanne had turned the hatred to a kind of remote pity. He thought of going home to share some of the burden that fell mostly on his father. But what could he do if he went back? Ann undoubtedly wouldn't see him. If she was so far gone that she even rejected her beloved Ditto, she'd certainly refuse to see the son who she believed had wanted to humiliate her.

Still, he wrote to Peter and offered to come if he could help.

"Maybe I'll need you more later," Peter had answered. "There's nothing you can do here now."

Alan knew what was implicit in that brief comment. Peter was fighting off the idea that Ann was insane, refusing to think that she might have to be put into an institution, but Alan knew this was always in the back of his mind. That was when he would need his son's moral support.

Meanwhile, Alan could not help but be pleased by the acceptance of his book. The reviews had been excellent. Even *The New York Times* had called it "a sensitive, deftly constructed story" and said that Alan Richards showed promise as one of the important new writers "in

323

the vast and normally dreary wasteland of modern fiction."

While his agent worked on a movie deal, Alan signed a contract for his next novel. Not surprisingly it was the tender, touching story of a beautiful young mulatto. Like Toni in her long-ago farewell letter to him, Alan was compelled to put into thinly disguised fiction his understanding of the mixed-marriage child beset by conflicting feelings about her origin and searching endlessly for her place in a racially divided world. He called it *Limbo*. *His editor in New York, having no idea how biographical it was, loved the book despite his "commercial reservations."*

"It won't sell worth a damn in some parts of the South," the editor had written. "And it'll bomb in the Bible Belt. But who cares? Most book buying is done in metropolitan areas. Besides, it's a subject that everybody thinks more and more about these days. Scares hell out of some whites and is anathema to militant blacks. But intelligent people will be curious and maybe even sympathetic. Go to it, Al. It's going to be a fine book. Hard to handle in writing, but I know you can pull it off."

It *was* hard to handle. Not only because the subject matter was delicate but because it was so personal to him. He sweated over it, wanting it to be good for the sake of his own career, but even more importantly wanting it to be a tribute to Toni. It was all he had to give her.

Chapter 23

In early January, Alan flew back to New York, took an apartment and tried to pick up the pieces of his life. He was glad to be home and it was a good thing for his father's sake as well that he'd decided to return. Ann was growing progressively worse and Peter's concern was sincere and evident. The handsome, buoyant man looked years older and emotionally exhausted. He said very little about his wife's condition to anyone, but the strain of it clearly showed. He seemed to have no interest in life. He was home every evening, an unwanted, watchful nurse. He came routinely back from the office, had a lonely dinner and read or looked at television, always with his senses alert to any sign of trouble. What Ann had always wanted she now had: a faithful husband. Even the women who had diverted him and bolstered the ego Ann destroyed were gone from his life. And the one who had raged for that no longer knew or cared.

The day after his return, Joanne told Alan the whole story of what was happening.

"Mother's mind is deteriorating fast," she said, "but she refuses psychiatric help. Dad forced her to accept the idea that a 'companion' should be in the apartment all day. She's a practical nurse, of course, and in her lucid moments Mother knows that and is furious about it. But somebody has to watch her. Dad takes over 'guard duty' at night. He's there in the apartment, even though she stays in her own room and barely speaks to him. Once in a while she gets actually violent. It's hell on earth for both of them. And the worst part is, it could go on for years."

"Do you and Pete see her?"

"We go up and have dinner with Dad regularly. Sometimes she'll see Pete for a few minutes, but never me. She's gotten it into her head that I'm a 'loose woman,' to use her expression. When I come, she won't let me in her room."

"Do you think she'll see me?"

"I have no idea," Joanne said. "I don't know what she remembers. About you and Toni, I mean. But at least you can spend some time with Dad. He needs us, Alan. He's suffering the tortures of the damned."

"I saw him in the office," Alan said. "He looks terrible. My God, Jo, what are we going to do about this?"

"I'm not sure there's anything we *can* do except wait it out. He won't put her in a sanitarium, which is where she belongs. We've begged him to, the doctors and I. It would be the best thing for her, as well as for him. At least there she'd get some sort of treatment. Maybe there'd even be a chance she'd recover. But Dad can't see it that way. I think he blames himself for what has happened to her. He's full of all kinds of self-torment because he knows he never really loved her and he's half convinced, I think, that the unfaithfulness she drove him to has been responsible for her breakdown. It's nonsense, of course, but there he is with his lousy life and his ridiculous guilt. Maybe you can help, Alan. Maybe you can get some sense into his head. He always loved you best of all."

326

"Don't be silly! He never played favorites."

"Sure he did. But that's okay. I don't think Pete knows it and I don't mind that Dad always felt closest to you. I know he loves Pete and me, but our big brother has always been a stuffy moralist and I've been too damned independent for my own good. You've always been able to touch him, Alan. Maybe you can now. Look at the way he stood up for you when you were determined to marry Toni."

Alan's face took on the faraway look it always did when Toni's name was mentioned.

"What do you hear of her?"

"Not too much," Jo said. "There wasn't even a formal announcement of her marriage. Dad told me about it. The only thing I ever hear is through him. He keeps in touch with Charlene and Elizabeth and I suppose they tell him how Toni is getting along." She hesitated. "I gather she's quite happy with Bryce Sumner."

"I'm glad." He managed to smile. "I never had much use for dogs in the manger."

The next day he called his father and invited himself for dinner. Peter was delighted, but then he said, carefully, "I don't know whether your mother will be well enough to join us, Alan."

"I understand, Dad. I had a long talk with Jo."

Peter seemed relieved. "Then you know all about it. The way things are, I mean. She may refuse to see you, Son. Don't be upset. She hardly sees anybody any more."

"I'm coming to see *you*. We have a lot to catch up on."

They made up for it that evening. When Alan arrived, Peter went in to Ann to tell her that her son was there. Even in the living room, Alan could hear her voice raised in anger. Snatches of her tirade were distinguishable. Words like "ungrateful" and "heartless." And terrible phrases like "nigger lover." She remembers, Alan thought

327

wryly. My God, how she remembers! He felt sorry for her, but dispassionately sorry, the way he would feel for any deranged human being. He could not hypocritically pretend to love her, even though she was his mother. She'd been cold and hateful too long, not only to him but to his father and to her mother and sister and her sister's husband and child. Had she been a wonderful woman who'd suffered a mental collapse he would have grieved, would have overlooked the irrational ravings, the demented behavior. But it was too late for personal sorrow. He could pity her only as some remote stranger.

Peter came back looking beaten and helpless.

"I'm sorry, Alan. It's one of her bad days. She can't see you. Maybe next time."

His father's playacting was more pathetic than his mother's real sickness. Alan ached for him. He didn't mention what he'd overheard. He went along with the game, at least for the moment.

"It's okay, Dad. I'll be around for a while. How about making us a drink?"

"Good idea," Peter said. "We could both use one."

They talked far into the night, quietly, companionably, avoiding the subject of Ann. Alan told his father about Danielle, the whole story, voicing his relief that it had not been anything more serious than an affair.

"I was reaching for something and I think I was lucky that I couldn't get it," Alan said. "In her own way she's a nice woman, but not the one I want to marry."

Peter nodded. "There's still only one for you, isn't there?"

For a moment, Alan didn't answer. "It's stupid, but I still can't get her out of my mind. Jo says she's fine and happy."

"I gather so. I correspond with the West Coast fairly regularly. Elizabeth consults me about her affairs and usually gives me news of Toni. Once in a while I have a note from Charlene. She's holding up very well, by the way. Jim Jenkins' death was a terrible blow. They loved each other deeply." There was a wistful note in Peter's voice. "In spite of some big handicaps, they had the kind of marriage people dream about and seldom find."

He had opened the door for Alan's soft-spoken question. "Dad, what are you going to do about this situation? You can't live like this."

Peter's words were almost an echo of Joanne's. "I don't think there's much I can do about it except wait it out. Your mother won't be 'put away,' as she calls it, and even though I could sign her into a private sanitarium I can't bring myself to do that."

"I know that would be a horrible thing to have to do," Alan said, "but maybe it's what you *must* do. Perhaps she'd have a chance that way. She has none like this. She'll only get worse with no professional help." He deliberately hardened his voice. "What are you waiting for—a miraculous recovery or the merciful release of death?"

"Alan!"

"Dad, I love you. I know you don't want her to die, but you know she's not going to get well this way. Why are you punishing yourself? You're still a healthy, vigorous man. And God knows, you're an intelligent one. What good is it doing either of you to waste away under this half life? Where's that compassionate but analytical mind I've always admired? The hair shirt doesn't become you!"

Peter had bowed his head during this outburst. Now he looked up and a tear ran slowly down each side of his cheeks. Alan was filled with remorse. He'd never seen his father cry and now this strong man was crumbling before his eyes. I shouldn't have said those things, Alan thought. I was wrong to try to shock him into reality. But Peter was not angry. He understood that real worry for him lay behind his son's ruthless words.

"She's given me more than thirty years of her life," Peter said. "I haven't tried very hard to make them happy for her. Oh, I know. She hasn't earned happiness. She's been cold and selfish and bitter. But maybe I was responsible for making her that way. Maybe if I'd cared more I could have made her understand a lot of things. About us. About her family. Even about herself. But I walked away, Alan. I didn't even try to make her see reason when she was capable of recognizing it. I can't leave her now when she's helpless. Maybe this is how I have to pay my dues for all the years when I was too impatient and self-engrossed to find out whether I could change her simply by loving her."

Alan felt helpless. Jo was right. Peter did believe this was retribution. He no longer remembered that Ann had been a scheming young woman long before he married her, that no power on earth could have transformed her from the willful, selfish child she'd always been into an understanding, giving woman. Peter saw only a wife and mother grown increasingly hard and unyielding because he had failed her. A woman whose mind had been warped by lack of love . . . love she neither worked for nor deserved. In his own mind, Alan put it into the bluntest possible words: Peter Richards actually believed that he had driven his wife insane. She'll destroy him, Alan thought. Or, rather, he'll destroy himself. Even now he could not grasp this change in his father. Peter had always been so sensible, so strong, so realistic about everything. My God, what guilt does to people! Even—or perhaps especially—guilt they don't deserve.

It was hopeless to try to make Peter see the truth, but something would have to be done before it was too late for both his parents. He wondered whom he could talk to.

330

His brother and sister were as helpless as he. So, apparently, were the doctors. There was no one Alan knew who even remotely cared about Ann Richards and her despairing husband. No one, he thought suddenly, except a wise and forgiving woman who loved them both. The next night he called his grandmother in California.

When Laurel handed her the phone that evening Elizabeth could not believe that the Alan Richards who was on the wire was her grandson. Her first thought was that it was some weird coincidence. Some salesman, perhaps, with the same name. In the next instant, cold fear struck. If this was Ann's Alan, then something terrible must have happened to his mother or father. Maybe to both. Her hands were trembling as she took the receiver from Laurel.

"It's Alan Richards," he repeated. "Ann's son." Then quickly, anticipating her reaction, he said, "It's all right. Nothing's happened. I'm calling because, well, I just don't know where else to turn for advice."

Elizabeth relaxed a little. It was all very odd, this call from a young man she'd not seen since he was a little boy. Something was troubling him, but it was not a disaster call as she'd feared in those first surprising seconds. When she spoke her voice was kind and calm.

"Alan," she said. "How wonderful. How incredibly wonderful!"

She could almost feel him relaxing, too. The pleasant young voice became less tentative. "This must be the last thing in the world you expected—a call from me."

Elizabeth gave a little laugh. "Well, you did give me a start for a moment, but I'm so happy to be talking to you! Isn't this a curious way for us to be reintroduced after all these years? But I'm so pleased. And also very curious."

She sounds just as I imagined her, Alan thought.

Warm, receptive and honest. How many women in the world could be so unflustered by a call from a grandson with whom they'd not exchanged a word in years? No wonder Toni adores her and Dad thinks she's so extraordinary. And no wonder, he thought sadly, that Mother has always resented her.

"I don't quite know how to put this," Alan said. "I honestly called on impulse. Out of desperation, I suppose. I don't know how much you know about Mother's mental state or what it's doing to Dad. I've just been home a few days from Europe. I had idea what was going on until I saw my father last night. Mother is in terrible shape and Dad is blaming himself and I don't know where to look for answers. I don't even know what I'm asking you now, for that matter. I just had to talk to someone. To try to help somehow. Maybe I called because I've always thought of you as special. I've loved everything I've ever heard about you . . . may I say 'Grandmother'?"

"Of course, dear. That's what I am. Your grandmother." Elizabeth tried to sort out the almost incoherent outburst. Peter had more than hinted that Ann was unstable. That terrible fake suicide attempt was evidence of her twisted mind. But recently Peter had said little about Ann. Apparently she was much worse. Elizabeth realized that her grandson was really frightened.

"How bad is she, Alan?"

"Physically sound, but mentally incompetent. She should be somewhere where she could get care, but she won't go voluntarily and Dad can't bring himself to do it. He blames himself, Grandmother. And it's not his fault. Truly."

Elizabeth groped for words. Never mind what Ann had done, she was still her child and the idea of her madness filled Elizabeth with unbearable sorrow. And there was Peter to think of in all this. Peter whom she loved, who had been so badly used and who now was blaming himself for what, Elizabeth suddenly realized, she'd always known was inevitable. And this nice boy. This young man who loved Toni and whom Toni had hopelessly loved. He, too, was caught in the agony and turning to her for help she did not know how to give. She tried to think of some way to come to his rescue, to offer at least reassurance and hope.

"I don't know why I'm calling," Alan said again. "I've just realized what a thoughtless thing I'm doing to you, telling you this awful news about your daughter. I'm sorry. I've been terribly selfish and inconsiderate. I'm an insensitive clod. Grandmother? Are you all right?"

"Yes, I'm all right, Alan. I'm trying to think what to do. I know Ann won't let me come near her. And I'd be the last person she'd listen to even if I forced my way in. All I can do is try to reach your father. We're very close, he and I. Perhaps now that I know how serious things are I can convince him to do the right thing for all of you." She paused and then, almost as though she were thinking aloud, she said, "It's difficult for me to travel. I haven't left the house in many years ... except when Jim died. I'll have to get Peter out here on some pretense about my will. Yes, that's the only possible way. I must speak to him face to face." Her voice became firm and decisive. "I'll call him tomorrow and ask him to fly out. I imagine, if we accomplish nothing more, it will do him good to get away for a few days."

"I don't know how to thank you," Alan said.

"My dear, there's nothing to thank me for. This may be completely futile, but I'm vain enough to think that if Peter will listen to anyone he may listen to me."

"Yes. That's why I called. I know how much he respects you. I feel you're his only hope."

"I have my daughter to think of too," Elizabeth said quietly. "That's still a big part of it."

333

Alan was silent. She could still love Ann. After all the hurt, all the disappointment, she still cared.

"Don't mention this call to your father," Elizabeth was saying now. "I'm going to play dumb about why I want to see him. But, Alan, when he tells you he's coming I'd like you to do something for me."

"Of course. Anything."

"Tell him you'd like to come, too."

He was surprised. "Do you think I can help?"

"Maybe. I know you can't hurt."

"I'd like to come, Grandmother. I've always wanted to know you better."

Elizabeth's laugh was almost girlish. "Funny. That's a big part of my motive, too."

It had been surprisingly easy to arrange. Peter was glad for a legitimate excuse to leave even briefly and arranged round-the-clock care for Ann. And when he told Alan his plans it seemed very natural that Alan should ask to accompany him.

"I'm at loose ends right now," Alan said casually. "The *Limbo* manuscript is finished and I'm waiting for the film deal to be nailed down for *Summer Romance*. Besides I'd like to see California again and to tell you the truth I'd like to see my grandmother. What do you think, Dad? Okay if I tag along? I can't remember when you and I have had a vacation together. Not since I was a kid. And even then, never just the two of us."

"I never was much of a father to you, was I, Alan?"

"Knock it off," Alan said gruffly. "You were a great father. That's not what I meant. We were never the type, either of us, for those man-boy fishing or camping trips. Somehow, Dad," he said lightly, "I just can't picture you as a Scout leader. Or, for that matter, myself as a Boy Scout. I think of you as somebody I've always looked up to and liked, as well as loved."

334

For a moment Peter looked like his old happy, confident self. "I can't think of anything I'd like more than for you to make this trip with me," he said. "I want you to know Elizabeth well and I want her to know you. Charlene, too. You'll all like each other. I'm going to be very proud to show you off to them."

Alan had almost forgotten about Charlene in his absorption to get Peter to the Coast for a talk with Elizabeth. How would he feel about seeing Toni's mother? He somehow couldn't think of her as his aunt or even his mother's sister. More importantly, how would she feel about him? She must know what he and her daughter had felt for each other, what, for that matter, Alan still felt. He wondered whether Elizabeth's suggestion that he come to California might have something to do with her wanting him and Charlene to meet. But why? Toni had been married nearly four months and apparently happily. Why would Elizabeth want to stir up old hurts? What possible motive could she have for wanting him and Charlene to know each other now?

He dismissed this train of thought as ridiculous. His grandmother wanted to know *him*. That was only natural since she might never have another chance. And perhaps she thought he could help Peter see his painful duty. As she'd said, his presence there "couldn't hurt." There was nothing more to it than that.

Only to Joanne did he confide what he'd done. She highly approved. "God knows, it's worth a chance," she said. "He may listen to Elizabeth if she's even half as sensible and convincing as I imagine her to be. I'm glad you're going with Dad, Alan. I think you and Elizabeth will be a strong team. I envy you." she added. "That's one lady I always wanted to know. I guess I never will. How old is she?"

"Middle seventies, I think. But hearing her on the

335

phone, she sounds like a young woman. She'll probably be around for a long time, Jo. Maybe you will meet her again one day."

He thought of that conversation as he and his father approached Elizabeth's house a few days later. It's unfair that we've been such a divided family. Unfair and unnecessary. If it hadn't been for Ann, so many things would have been different. He tried hard to be tolerant of his mother's actions but it was impossible. He didn't love her but he didn't hate her. He felt the most terrible emotion of all—indifference to her as a person. Time had softened the edges of his outrage over what she'd done to him and Toni, had even subdued some of the bitterness he felt about her actions toward her own family. He was totally committed now to saving what could still be saved: the remnants of his father's life. All the other things were over and unchangeable, but Ann must not be allowed to add Peter Richards to the list of those whose lives she had tried to mold in her malicious way. There was still hope for Peter, and Alan meant him to have a last chance at happiness. Despite Ann, Charlene and Jim and Toni had found it. So, in their own ways, had Joanne and Pete. Even I, Alan thought, am young enough to find my own way. But if we don't help Dad he'll drown in his own misery.

Elizabeth was smiling up at him now from her wheelchair, looking startlingly beautiful and alert, her eyes dancing with happiness at the sight of him.

"Alan. You're what I expected. Maybe even more. I wish I could jump up and throw my arms around you! Lacking that, come and give me a great hug and a kiss."

He went to her as easily as though he'd been embracing her every day for twenty-six years. She felt soft and warm in his arms, smelling sweetly of some light cologne, her cheek cool and smooth against his own.

336

Peter and the woman introduced to him as Laurel stood in the background, their pleasure unmistakable.

"I take it he passes inspection," Peter said at last.

"You did well, Peter. He's very like you."

"That's what Charlene said when she saw Alan's photograph on the jacket of his book: that he looks the way I did when she first met me."

"It's more than a look," Elizabeth said. "It's the inside goodness showing through." She turned to Alan. "By the way, it's a good book, Alan. We're all very proud of you."

He'd not uttered a word since they came into the house. His eyes had been riveted on this gentle lady he'd waited so long to see again. Now, almost as though he were coming out of a trance, he looked around the big sunny living room, seeing the delicate, tasteful touches, the objets d'art, the casually but lovingly arranged flowers, the books that were everywhere. But something was missing. For a while he could not figure out what it was the room seemed to call for. And then he realized what it was: photographs. There were no pictures of people anywhere.

"This is a lovely room, Grandmother. It suits you. I remember it this way, warm and gracious and serene."

"I hope you'll find the rest of the house just as pleasing. I've put you and your father in the big room down the hall where you can wake up and see my view. Speaking of which, you two must be dying to freshen up after that plane ride. Laurel, dear, will you show them the way? I'm going to have a bit of a rest. We'll meet for cocktails, all right?"

The two men nodded.

"By the way," Elizabeth said, "Charlene is joining us. She's sorry she couldn't meet you at the airport, Peter. Some fearfully important meeting at the Pasadena

337

museum. But she'll stay over while you and Alan are here."

Laurel led them to the spacious, comfortable guest room. At the doorway, Peter turned to her.

"How is she, Laurel? Physically, I mean. She looks well, but I've never known Elizabeth to talk about resting in mid-afternoon."

"We're all slowing down, Peter. We had a little scare last month. A heart flutter. The doctor said it wasn't serious but she does have to take it a bit easier. The afternoon rest is part of the regimen. And believe me, she fights it every inch of the way!"

Peter looked concerned. "Are you sure that's all it was—just a flutter? What does Charlene think?"

"She doesn't know. Elizabeth didn't want to worry her. Charley's had enough in the last six months."

As the door closed, Alan turned to his father. "You think it's serious?"

"Not necessarily. Elizabeth's very strong and reluctantly sensible as you can see. She loves life, Alan. She'll fight for every second of it."

Silently they began to unpack.

"Dad?"

"Yep?"

"This is going to sound far out, but I'm curious. In that big, beautiful, very personal living room, there's not a single photograph. I don't know why it struck me, but it did. I guess I expected to see pictures of all the family. Toni and her parents. Grandmother's husband. Uncle Quigly. Maybe even us. Do you know why there aren't any? It seems out of character."

Peter stared at him. "Frankly I never thought of it, but you're right. People usually have pictures of those they love. Particularly those who are gone. Most likely Elizabeth keeps them in her bedroom, Alan. What a strange thing for you to pick up in those few minutes."

"I know. It was spooky and probably stupid. Lots of people don't keep personal pictures in public rooms. I just had this crazy feeling that it wasn't an ordinary omission."

"Maybe it isn't," Peter said slowly. "Now that I think of it, pictures are lifeless, and to Elizabeth no one ever loses life. All the people she loves are constantly with her, even those who've died, like Jim Jenkins and Tony Alexander. I think she doesn't need frozen faces in a frame, Alan. Not when she can see the real thing every day." He paused. "I also know why you noticed the absence of photographs. You were looking for a picture of Charlene, weren't you? Don't be uneasy about meeting her again. She's as lovely as her mother. *And* her daughter."

I suppose he's right, Alan thought. I *was* looking for a glimpse of Charlene. Maybe I wanted to see Toni's father, too. But perhaps most of all, pictures of Toni. I've never had a picture of her. Except the one that's always in my mind.

Chapter 24

In the guest room of her mother's house, Charlene lay
awake thinking of the evening she'd just spent. Alan
would never know that she'd been as nervous about meeting him as he'd been about coming face to face with her.
They'd both been unnecessarily apprehensive. From the
moment she arrived at Elizabeth's and seen her nephew
again she'd felt drawn to him. It was more than his good
looks. He had the manner of a dependable man, a soft
and gentle man who would make a woman feel beautiful
and protected, even while he let her know that he considered her a person in her own right.

He's very much like Jim, Charlene mused. She understood now how Toni could have fallen in love with him,
instantly and irrevocably. I don't think I could have given
him up, Charlene thought. Toni must have more conscience, more self-discipline than I. She was strong in a
way I never could have been. I hope she wasn't wrong.
Bryce Sumner had all the appearance of an ideal husband, and Toni's letters in these last months seemed reas-
suringly happy. But Charlene sensed now that Bryce
could never give her what Alan could. Bryce did not have

the depth of feeling, the capacity for unselfish love and understanding that was recognizable in the young man she'd just met. Cousin or not, Ann's threats be damned, Toni should have married him. Since she planned to remain childless, it would have been better to build her life around this sensitive human being than the one she had chosen. Not that I have any reason to dislike Bryce, Charlene thought, but there is something I can't trust. How ironic and terrible, she thought, if he were keeping a secret from Toni, just as she was foolishly hiding one from him.

Charlene turned over and punched her pillow, trying to settle down. She wondered if she'd ever get used to sleeping alone. It seemed to her that she hadn't had a good night's rest since Jim died. I'm not like Elizabeth, she thought. I can't survive without the physical nearness of someone I love.

Her thoughts turned to Ann and Peter. Elizabeth had told her what was happening and she could imagine the atmosphere of that New York apartment: Peter lonely and full of self-condemnation, Ann turning rapidly from hostility to paranoia. Charlene didn't know what her mother planned to say to Peter but it seemed unlikely, from the little they knew, that there was any way to make him see reason. If he felt himself responsible for Ann's condition he would cling to his self-imposed punishment. And in her lucid moments, Ann would take pleasure in his suffering.

The first light of dawn was breaking before Charlene finally fell asleep. Her dreams were disconnected and troubled, like little one-act plays in which the people she loved were all trapped and tragic figures.

After breakfast, Elizabeth asked Alan what he'd like to do. "Your father and I have some business to go over,"

341

she said. "I'm sure Charlene would be glad to drive you around and show you our part of the world. Or you can just stay here and loaf."

"I'd like to see something of this area if it's not too much trouble." Alan said. "If I'm lucky, I may be out here for a while next year. We think we've sold *Summer Romance* as a screenplay. If so, I hope to do the film adaptation." He smiled at Charlene. "I may end up on your doorstep yet."

"Hollywood isn't exactly my doorstep," she said, "but your being in California is a nice idea. Come on. I'll show you where the beautiful people hang out in Beverly Hills."

When they'd gone, Elizabeth took Peter into the study.

"I like your boy," she said. "I told Toni long ago that I would. He's kind and levelheaded and he faces facts." She took a deep breath. "Which is more than you seem to be doing, Peter."

Her son-in-law didn't answer.

"Long ago, when I first wrote to you about Toni, I told you that I was exercising the right to use an old lady's 'meddler's license,' poking my nose into things that really were not my business. I'm going to do it again. Peter, tell me the truth. How far gone is Ann? Is she really out of her mind?"

He looked surprised. "How did you know?"

"Never mind. It's not important how I know." Elizabeth reconsidered. "No, I take that back. It *is* important. I know because Alan called to tell me how bad she was and how you've reacted to her illness. Can you imagine what courage it took for him to do that? Can't you see how much he loves you and how desperately unhappy he is for you? He didn't know what to do, where to turn to find help for you. He took a chance that his remote grandmother wouldn't turn her back on him, or on you

342

and Ann. Peter, that kind of devotion deserves something in return. You fancy that your only obligation is to Ann, but it isn't. It's also to your children and yourself. If Ann is unbalanced, you must do everything you can for her, but not at the expense of all the other lives involved. You have the right to throw away your own if that is your choice. But you don't have the right to make Alan and the others sick with worry for you."

"They're young," Peter said. "They don't live at home. This doesn't really affect them. They have their own lives, Elizabeth. I'm the one who's driven Ann to this point and I'm the only one who has to pay for it."

She slapped her palms impatiently on the arms of the wheelchair. "I never heard such nonsense! Of course they're affected. I know Alan is. I'm sure Joanne and Peter are too, even if they haven't taken the action Alan has. You must think of them. But even more importantly you must think of Ann."

"That's what I'm trying to do."

"And making a damned bad job of it, if you ask me."

Peter looked at her. "Elizabeth, there's only one answer to all this. I'd have to send Ann away. Can you really advise me to put your daughter in an institution?"

She didn't waver. "Yes, dear, I can. Not because I don't love her but because I *do*. I want her to have help, Peter, before it's too late for her sake and everyone else's." Elizabeth looked wretched. "Do you think it's easy for me to recommend that my child be sent away? I gave her life. She was my firstborn. Do you think I like to admit that she is not well and beautiful and perfect? It makes my insides go into knots to think about her. But I can't hide from the truth, any more than I could finally avoid facing the fact that her father was insane. And later her brother. I've been through it, Peter. I know all the self-doubts, the blame I put on myself, the years I stood

343

by, trying to right a mind gone wrong, a mind that I, too, thought had been warped by something I'd done. But I hadn't done it, Peter. And neither have you. Ann, like her father and Quigly, has brought about her own self-destruction. She's been angry since she was a child and that anger has grown until she hates the world. She's been hostile and devious and selfish all her life. You had nothing to do with it. You couldn't have changed her if you'd been the world's most faithful and devoted husband. She's been heading down this path since the day she was born."

Peter shook his head. "I just don't know. I want to believe you, Elizabeth. I want to help Ann but she won't accept help."

"Neither would her father. That's why you have to be strong and make the decision for her. Alan Whitman died with his anger and his refusal to admit that he couldn't handle his life. Maybe he could have been saved if I'd taken drastic measures. I'll never know. I ran away to save my children and myself when I couldn't stand it any longer. Maybe if I'd forced help on him it would all have been different. Maybe even Ann would be a different kind of woman today. I can't be sure of any of that, but it seems pointless to blame myself for what I had to do at the time. For all I know, Ann's breakdown is more my fault than yours. But I can't speculate on what caused it. It's too complex and useless. All we can do is face the present and hope for the future. Not punish ourselves for the real or imagined mistakes of the past."

"You're telling me that in a mixed-up way I'm being selfish. That Ann's paying for my bad conscience."

"Yes," Elizabeth said. "Ann's paying and so are all the people who love both of you."

He began to pace the room. "God! I'm such a coward! I can't bear to think of her locked up!"

Elizabeth's heart went out to him. "She's more locked

344

up now, Peter, than she might be in a place where she could be helped. She's living in her own kind of purgatory, whether she realizes it or not. Ann has built her own prison and only you have the key to let her out. She can't break down the door. You must help her open it."

She could have lessened his guilt even more. She could have told him how Ann had deliberately trapped him into marriage by playing on his honor, by scheming to have him seduce a virgin. She could have told him all the cruel, hateful things Ann had said and done in her early years, the accusations of disloyalty she'd hurled at her mother, the sordid things she refused to recognize about her father. These things might help Peter justify his inevitable course, but they were not the reasons he had to do what he couldn't face. He had to deal with the actualities of the moment and leave the underlying background reasons for Ann's illness in the hands of psychiatrists who might make her understand them.

Peter came to stand quietly in front of her. "Do you know she has to be watched day and night, Elizabeth? Do you know that in November she ran naked out into the street, screaming that she was being held prisoner? Christmas Eve she set fire to the curtains in her room. Accidentally or deliberately, I don't know. And yet, at moments, she's as lucid as you or I. She sometimes goes along for days acting as she always did, remote and sarcastic with me, but making perfect sense. Then she'll break out and do something insane."

Elizabeth didn't want to listen. He was talking about her child. The pain of it stabbed her and yet there was a strange kind of consolation in hearing these awful facts. Ann was not responsible for her actions. Hadn't been for years. All the hurt to Charlene and Jim, all the tragedy she'd created for Toni and Alan, these had been the work of a diseased mind. It was easier to forgive her, knowing that.

"Help her, Peter," Elizabeth said. "Help her family."

"Yes," he said. "I see that I have to, God help us all."

While his father and grandmother were having their difficult talk, Alan and Charlene were making polite, guarded conversations over lunch in the Polo Lounge of the Beverly Hills Hotel. He told her about Paris, and about his decision to become a full-time writer, the only work he really wanted to do.

"I hope I can make it," he said. "The first book did well. I have my fingers crossed about the second." He paused. "Aunt Charlene?"

She smiled. "Please drop the 'aunt.' It makes me sound terribly forbidding."

"*That* you could never be, but thanks. I prefer 'Charlene.' What I was going to say was that the second book is based on Toni. I hope you and she won't mind."

Charlene raised her eyebrows. "Oh? Tell me about it."

"It's my idea of what goes on in the mind of a beautiful young girl of mixed parentage. The searching and wondering about where she belongs, the feeling of being uncertain of her place in the scheme of things and the fear of rejection that sometimes makes her feel very lost. She's in a kind of constant suspension, hovering between what she knows is right and what our stupid civilization condemns as wrong. She lives somewhere between two worlds. That's why I call the book *Limbo*."

"It's not a pretty word," Charlene said.

"It's not a pretty life for a thin-skinned girl like that."

For a moment Charlene was angry. How dare he write about what he did not even begin to know? What gall to presume that he could get inside Toni's head and conclude that she was lost and uncertain! And then she knew

346

that the book was really Alan's cry of despair more than Toni's. In fiction he hoped to express his understanding and love as he had been unable to do in fact. He would handle it sensitively without treading on the heart of the girl he loved.

"I think Toni will be pleased," she said. "I'm sure I will be."

"I've tried hard to portray her as I believe she is. It was a wrenching book to write, Charlene. I know her so well and so little and I still care for her so much."

Charlene was silent.

"How is she?" Alan asked. "Is she happy? When did you see her last?" The questions came out eagerly.

"She's fine," Charlene said. "I saw her in New York in October when she and Bryce were married. Her letters sound quite content. She's busy, still doing free-lance work, and she's started to paint quite seriously."

He nodded. "That's good." There was so much more he wanted to ask and he dared not.

Charlene took pity on him. "Bryce Sumner is a good man," she said. "He's devoted to Toni and she to him." And then, in a rush of compassion, she said, "I know she doesn't love Bryce the way she loved you, Alan. I don't think she'll ever love anyone that way again. That's small comfort, perhaps, but it's good to know that someone once adored you enough to run from the risk of spoiling a perfect relationship. That kind of unselfish devotion doesn't come along very often."

"I know. I understand it now. I didn't at the time. That's what the book's all about, Charlene: the boundless self-sacrificing love of a troubled, thoughtful woman."

They were quiet for a moment. Then realization struck Alan. Charlene hadn't seen her daughter since October and it was nearly February.

"Didn't they come out for Christmas?"

"No. Bryce couldn't get away."

That didn't ring true. Alan had been in the advertising business. He knew that from the middle of December to early January both the agency and its clients were practically on holiday. Printers and suppliers shut down and business almost ground to a halt. It was the time, in fact, when most advertising men took vacation, an idle, unproductive time of year. Sumner, who owned his own shop, could leave *any* time he liked, for that matter. There must be another reason Toni and her new husband had not come home. She would certainly want him to meet Elizabeth. The truth dawned on him.

"Charlene, Toni hasn't told Sumner about your husband, has she?"

She didn't answer.

"I'm sorry," Alan apologized. "That was out of line. It's none of my business."

"That's right," Charlene said not unkindly. "It's Toni's. Let's let it go at that, shall we, Alan?"

It was not until they were on their way back to New York that Peter told Alan of his decision to put Ann into a sanitarium. When he haltingly got the words out, he looked almost pathetically at his son for confirmation that he was doing the right thing. Alan put his hand on his father's arm.

"I'm glad you've made the decision, Dad. It's the only one. I can only imagine how tough it is for you."

"But you don't seem surprised," Peter said.

"No. It had to come to this. For her sake most of all."

"Your grandmother made me see that." Peter sighed. "You knew what the purpose of this mission was. Elizabeth told me you called her. I'm very grateful, Alan. It couldn't have been easy for you."

"I couldn't let you go on that way, Dad. I could only

gamble that if anyone could make you understand what you were doing, Grandmother could."

"It's going to be a nightmare. Your mother probably will have to be taken forcibly."

"I know."

"Will you do one more thing for me, Alan? Will you stay at the apartment for a couple of days until it's . . . until I can make arrangements?"

"I'll do better. Why don't I move in and batch it with you, at least until I go to the Coast? Seems silly for us both to be rattling around in separate apartments. I might as well let you pay my rent."

Peter clutched his son's hand. "You've got a deal," he said.

Though she had sounded positive and convincing in her talk with Peter, Elizabeth went into a depressed state at the thought of her daughter being institutionalized. Remembering Ann's father, recalling the progressive madness, she gave in to a dull, despairing conviction that this would be the end of Ann's contact with the outside world. And she felt, as she'd told Peter, a degree of responsibility for the warped thinking that consumed Ann. There was also the dreaded thought that some hereditary strain of insanity was being passed down from Alan Whitman's family to his children and, God forbid, his grandchildren. After all, there was Quigly too. None of the others, not Charlene or Toni or, apparently, Ann's children showed any sign of imbalance. Elizabeth convinced herself that this area of her fears, at least, was groundless. Neither father nor the children seemed to her to be "classic" cases of genetic madness. All three had slowly and steadily moved toward their breakdowns with irrational anger.

Elizabeth had succeeded in convincing Peter that Ann's

only chance of recovery was professional care; that he owed it to her and to their children to impose this help on her. She believed the latter reason was right; she had less real hope for the former.

Laurel and Charlene, watching her in those next few days, were alarmed. It was unlike Elizabeth to be despondent, understandable as the reason was. Charlene, even more than Laurel, identified and sympathized with Elizabeth's misery. As a mother, what would I do if I had to advise Bryce to commit Toni? Could I do it, even if I knew it was the only answer?

She and Laurel quietly discussed the problem, coming up at last with a desperate, alternative plan. If Elizabeth wanted, they would try to get Ann to California. Charlene would move into her mother's house and perhaps, between the three of them, they could somehow get through to Ann. Maybe away from Peter and her own children she might find some kind of peace within herself. It was a slim and impractical idea and Elizabeth knew it even better than they.

"No," she said, "it's not the answer. Not only because it wouldn't work for Ann, who despises me more than anyone else, but because I won't let you and Laurel turn yourselves into round-the-clock keepers. You're dear, both of you, to offer to take on this burden for my sake. If I thought there was even a remote chance of its working I might be tempted to take you up on it. But it isn't the solution. Ann's only hope lies in the hands of doctors." She smiled lovingly at the concerned women. "Don't worry. I'll be all right. I have to believe that I'm doing the best for Ann by convincing Peter to put her where she can get the right care. I *do* believe it, but I can't pretend to be lighthearted about it. You don't expect *that* of me, do you?"

Peter and Alan returned to a hushed, darkened apartment. The night nurse explained that Mrs. Richards had had one of her "spells" and the doctor had been called to give her a sedative.

"She'll sleep through until the morning," the nurse said, "but the doctor left word he'd like to speak with you when you returned, Mr. Richards."

Peter nodded. He knew what the doctor would say: the same thing he'd said many times before. Only this time Peter would give him a different answer.

Alan went to bed in the guest room and Peter quietly opened the door to the room where Ann was lying in a drugged sleep. He stood by the bed, looking down at her. At this moment she looked young and vulnerable, like the girl he had thought himself in love with so many years before. For a moment he wavered. He couldn't send her away. But he had to.

He closed the door noiselessly. Tomorrow he would discuss the terrible arrangements with the doctor. And then he'd tell Joanne and Pete what he'd decided.

The doctor was matter-of-fact but kind. "I'm relieved that you've finally reached this decision, Mr. Richards," he said. "I know how hard it is for you. But Hillview is a lovely place, if such places can be said to be lovely. You're fortunate that Mrs. Richards can have the best care in the most luxurious surroundings. Believe me, it's the only answer for her. She's retrogressing rapidly. I'm glad you weren't around last night. Let me put it on the line. She's like a murderous child. She could do bodily harm to herself or to someone in the household. It's reached that point."

"When can they take her?" Peter's voice was numb.

"Almost immediately, I'd think. I'll call right away.

Meantime, I want you to keep those nurses round the clock."

"How . . ." Peter's voice broke. "How is this handled, Doctor? My son is with me. Do we drive her to Hillview?"

"Don't punish yourself more than you have to, Mr. Richards. You and I will sign some papers, and then you can try to talk to your wife. I'll be with you, if you like. After that, it would be better if you let Hillview send a private ambulance and attendants while you're out of the house."

"No! I can't do that! I'll go with her. My God, Doctor, at least I can do that much!"

"All right. But I warn you, it might not be pretty. She may make a terrible scene. I'll give her something to calm her down, but you could be in for an inhuman emotional beating."

"Nothing compared to what she'll be going through," Peter said.

"Perhaps. Perhaps not. She's not often lucid, Mr. Richards. She may not even realize what is happening." The doctor frowned. "I'm not certain she'll understand when you try to talk to her. Perhaps it would be wiser to say nothing until the time comes and hope that she'll accept the transfer passively. Patients like these are hard to predict. If she was totally unaware, it would be easier. Let's hope we catch her in one of those unreal periods."

Peter smiled, an unhappy smile. "Ann will never be passive. She'll know what I'm doing to her."

"Not *to* her, Mr. Richards. *For* her."

That afternoon Peter went in to see his wife. She lay on a chaise, staring vacantly out the window. The nurses were keeping her lightly sedated and her eyes had the glassy, vacant stare of the half-drugged. She turned when

Peter came in, trying to focus on his face. He sat on the edge of the chaise and reached for her hand.

"Ann, dear, it's me, Peter."

She drew away from him. "Get away," she said. "Don't come near me!"

He pulled up a chair.

"We have to talk honey. You're sick. Very sick. The doctor and I want you to go away for a rest. Just for a little while."

Her eyes narrowed suspiciously. "I'm not sick. And I'm not going anywhere. This is my house."

"Of course it is. And it always will be. But you need a change, dear. There's a lovely health farm that I know you'll enjoy. A beautiful place. I want you to go for a little visit. Get your strength back. Be pampered and fussed over. You always like that."

"No."

Peter clenched his fist, fighting for control. "I'm sorry, darling, but I must insist. You need peace and quiet."

She turned on him suddenly. "You mean *you* need peace and quiet! You're just dying to have this place all to yourself so you can have a different woman here every night! You don't want to be bothered with me, do you? I'm in your way. I always have been, haven't I?" She laughed. "Health farm! I know where you want to send me: to an insane asylum! Well, you won't do it! There's nothing wrong with me. It's you who are crazy. You and those doctors and those terrible women you get to watch me!" She laughed again, more loudly, a frightening sound. "You can't make me go anywhere. You're stuck with me!"

He felt sick but he couldn't back down. "Ann, dear, it's not that way. You've had a breakdown. You can be cured. That's all it is. Please, please, try to help yourself. If not for my sake, then for the children's."

She looked at him slyly. "Oh, no, you don't," she said. "Don't try to trick me. I don't have children. I'm twenty-five years old and barren. That's why you go to other women. You hate me because I can't have children. My father said you'd be like that." She began to cry. "Why didn't I listen to my daddy? I want my daddy!"

The brief, semi-lucid moment had passed. She had gone back into that dim, childish world where no one could reach her. Peter got up from his chair and stroked her shoulder. She cringed at his touch.

"It's all right, Annie," he said softly. "We're going to take you to your daddy."

She smiled radiantly. "Really? When?"

"Tomorrow," Peter said.

That evening he called Joanne and young Peter and said he had something very important to tell them. "Come over about nine o'clock," he said, knowing Ann would be asleep by then. "Alan will be here, too. He's staying in the apartment for a while."

They tried to question him but he put them off. "I'll explain it when you get here. I want us all together."

When they gathered in the study he told them, as calmly as he could that their mother was going to a sanitarium. He detailed her rapidly deteriorating condition, emphasizing that it was not hopeless but that the doctors had agreed that she must be where she could get constant care. "I hope it won't be forever," Peter said, "but there's no way of knowing. The only thing I'm sure of is that I can do nothing for her. Maybe someone else can."

Joanne began to cry softly, tears of agreement. "It's the right thing, Dad," she said. "It's so sad, so terrible. But I know it has to be. We'll all stand by. You know that."

"Of course I do, Jo. I know this is as hard on you kids as it is on me."

354

Young Peter frowned. "Are you sure you've given this enough thought? Maybe we should call in specialists. At least try to keep her home! The idea of Mother in an institution ... that's a pretty drastic step. I think there should be more consultations before you go that far."

The pompous words angered Alan. "Easy for you to say, Pete. You haven't lived with this for years, the way Dad has. He's already consulted the best men in the field. My God, you don't think he'd do this if there was any alternative! He doesn't want to send Mother away even now, but he must. To save her if he can. And yes, damn it, to save himself, too. What do you prefer, Pete? Two ruined lives instead of one? Look, we even went to California to talk this over with our mother's mother. *She* understood and it's her child! She knows Dad is in agony over this. We all are. But *we* have to live, too!"

Pete subsided but he continued to stare accusatorily at his father. Peter reached for a book on the table beside him.

"When Alan and I were in California talking this over with your grandmother, she gave me a book with a passage marked. It helped me realize that I must preserve what I can, no matter what my guilts or my wishes. I'd like to read you something from it, something old and wise, a Tibetan aphorism." He opened a marked page and spoke the few words on it:

"All desires should be abandoned, but if you cannot abandon them, let your desire be for salvation. That is the cure for it."

He closed the book. "I know this Buddhist doctrine is referring to very different kinds of desires and salvation, but the words seemed to say something to me about my own predicament. My desire is to keep your mother with me, but my salvation and hers is to abandon that desire." He tried to smile. "Let's say I've taken a little poetic li-

355

cense with ancient wisdom. Salvation is self-preservation. My sanity must be maintained while hopefully hers is restored. I don't know how to put it to you any other way. I beg for your understanding and forgiveness, if you think I need it. But mostly I beg for your faith and love."

Joanne came to him and put her arms around her father. "We all understand, Dad. We do have faith and love." She looked expectantly at Pete.

"Jo's right," he said reluctantly. "We're with you."

Alan breathed a sigh of relief. Terrible moments lay ahead, but at least Peter Richards had the support of all the people who mattered to him. Alan thought of Elizabeth and knew how she, too, must be suffering. He sent her a silent message: Thank you, Grandmother. Without your strength he couldn't have done it.

Chapter 25

The contentment of being Mrs. Bryce Sumner came almost as a surprise to Toni. At the last moment she had hesitated, privately questioning her motives for rushing into this marriage. She was devoted to Bryce in a quiet, very solid way, but that did not account for this feeling of urgency. Was it her old search for identity, desperate wish to be a "new person"? Was it the ego-building effect of Bryce's adoration contrasted, perhaps, with the silent withdrawal of a less aggressive Alan? Did she, as her mother had suggested, hope to remove herself forever from the possibility of running to her real love? Or could this be defiance in the face of Charlene's disapproval of her daughter's lack of candor with her husband-to-be?

Whatever the reasons, Toni was glad she'd married Bryce. He was the most considerate and ardent of husbands and his pride in her was almost touching, whether he was boasting about her skill as an artist or as a hostess. They were living in Bryce's apartment while Toni searched for a bigger one. Her days were full and happy. She continued to take free-lance illustration jobs and began to dabble in serious painting. She looked at co-op apartments and town houses, appalled at the prices asked, but Bryce didn't blink an eye when she reported them.

"Things are good, honey," he said. "We can afford to live like the rich folk. In fact, it's important for my business that we look prosperous. I want to do even more home entertaining of clients and this apartment really isn't big enough. Besides, it's all tax deductible."

Most of the people they saw were those with whom Bryce did business, or prospective accounts he hoped to capture. Toni enjoyed giving dinner parties, liked planning the menus, arranging the flowers and engaging the "outside help." It was a kind of life she'd never known and she had a natural talent for graciousness enhanced by the trappings of luxury.

Her sex life with Bryce was even more uninhibited than it had been during the period of their affair. She supposed that she had little talent for the illicit. She was much more at ease, much more outgoing in her conventional status. Being a wife agrees with me, she thought, and said so contentedly one night as she lay in Bryce's arms after a long, satisfying period of lovemaking. He held her close.

"So much love in that little body," Bryce said. "I find more every time. Is there no end to it, I hope?"

"No end," she said. "And *all* of it for you."

He knew what she meant. They'd talked about children before their marriage. Toni had been sweetly firm about not wanting them. He hadn't known her reasons were lies.

"I don't think I'd be very good as a mother," she'd said. "Not that I don't like children. I do. I suppose if my drives were different or if we were people with another kind of life style I'd think we should have a family. But I don't want the responsibility of children. Not right now, anyway. I want to keep on working, and be free to travel with you anytime, anywhere. I know it's incredibly selfish of me, darling, but children can be heartache and trouble, for all the joy they can bring. I know. I was a child once myself."

He'd laughed. "You're still a child and I'm sure you never brought a moment's heartache or trouble. But if that's the way you feel, I'm satisfied. We're well mated. I have no burning desire for immortality. The paternalistic urge in me is no stronger than the maternalistic one in you. We have each other, my love. That's as much happiness as I could wish for. Maybe more than I'm entitled to."

He believed it was true. He supposed he wouldn't have minded if Toni had had a baby, but he was no more eager for it, for different reasons, than she. Maybe later they'd both feel differently, but the memories of his own childhood, of a crowded, ugly shack overrun with bickering brothers and sisters, still haunted him too vividly. He hated all those crude, loud products of his father's lust and his mother's ignorance. Though it was another world, in no way comparable to a family he might have with Toni, the smell and sound and presence of children symbolized the unhappy first years of his life. He was glad his wife also opted for a childless marriage. There were enough other people contributing to overpopulation. Besides, Toni was right. There were things she wanted to accomplish. She was becoming quite a good painter and had even begun to talk of having a show. And there would be more travel as the agency grew. He hoped to make arrangements with other agencies overseas, to expand his operations, which would mean much time out of the country. He wanted her with him every minute. They had done no traveling so far, not even to California, but he had great plans for the future.

Their only ventures out of the city that winter were ski weekends in New England. Toni was a good skier. It was an easy drive from Pasadena to the mountains and she'd

359

gone skiing often on weekends as a very young girl. Bryce had never tried, but he took to it immediately. They rented a tiny house in Vermont and drove up almost every weekend. These were idyllic times. They spent the days in the clean, crisp air and the nights making love. A "hired woman" came in during the week to clean. Otherwise they "roughed it," devoting a minimum of time to tidying up and cooking. Toni was quite expert in the kitchen, Bryce discovered. They ate well, relaxed thoroughly and looked forward to the Fridays that Bryce could leave the office at noon for the long drive to the deep-snow country.

As the months went by, Toni grew more content. She thought less often of Alan, unaware of the tragedy that had taken place in his family. Charlene had said nothing about her sister's commitment in her letters. It seemed pointless to rouse old memories of Ann. It might even be cruel to let Toni know that Alan had been right: that his mother was deranged and that had Toni listened to him her life might have been quite different. She did mention, casually, in one of her letters that Alan and his father had come to California to discuss business with Elizabeth.

"He's a nice young man," Charlene wrote, "and apparently a talented one. Did you read *Summer Romance?* I found it delightful. Grandmother did, too."

She did not tell Toni about the forthcoming book. She guessed her daughter would read *Limbo* when publication was announced, but that was still six months away. Toni would have been securely married to Bryce for a year and better able to handle the poignant reminders that Charlene suspected were in the pages of Alan's second novel.

Toni had not read *Summer Romance*. She'd been tempted to buy it and afraid to. She would hear Alan's voice in every line of dialogue. She remembered that Peter had given a copy to Charlene when she was in New

York in October, but Charlene had put it quickly into her suitcase, saying nothing, sensitive to the knowledge that any mention of Alan would hurt. It was only now, nearly six months later, that Charlene apparently felt her daughter could handle even the slightest reference to him.

The diagnosis was correct. Toni could read his name with only a little stab of sorrow. She blessed Bryce for that. He had made her happy. Her only regret was that she could not take him to visit Elizabeth. She dared not let Bryce come in contact with any part of her early life. Charlene, even disapproving, could be counted on to keep her secret. So, Toni supposed, could Elizabeth. But there were too many others in California who would want to meet Toni's husband, too many who had known and loved Jim Jenkins and would, in all innocence, want to tell Bryce about him.

It saddened Toni to think she might not see her grandmother again. Elizabeth was getting old. Who knew how much time she had? Toni made up her mind to find a way of visiting her without Bryce. Perhaps he would have to make a prolonged business trip soon. She'd use his absence as an excuse to go home instead of tagging along to Chicago or Dallas or some less than exotic spot.

Meantime, she gave thanks for her good life, for a husband who shamelessly indulged her in everything from extravagant furs to the rustic, charming lodge in Vermont. She smiled, remembering how awkward Bryce had been when he first learned to navigate on skis. "Only for you," he'd said, "would I risk my neck on these damned treacherous things!" But now he loved the sport and looked forward even more eagerly than she to the peaceful remoteness of their brief escapes from the frenetic pace of his business life.

One weekend in early March they had not planned to go to Vermont. Bryce had an important client meeting on

Saturday, but at ten o'clock on Friday morning he called her from the office and told her that his date was canceled.

"Throw a few things in a bag for both of us, honey," he said. "I'll get the car and be in front of the apartment in an hour."

Delighted, she was waiting downstairs when he arrived.

"Remember to pack everything we need?"

"I hope so. You didn't give me much time to get organized."

"Anything you forgot we can pick up in the village."

It was not until she unpacked her cosmetic case that Toni discovered she'd forgotten something she couldn't buy at the local emporium: her supply of the pill. Apologetically, she reported her oversight to Bryce.

"Darling, it's so dumb of me! Damn! I've spoiled the whole weekend."

He laughed. "Come on, it's not all that tragic. We can try a celibate weekend. Might do us both good."

"I don't want a celibate weekend."

"Sex maniac."

He was so sweet. She knew he looked forward to these totally carefree days and nights as much as she. How stupid of her!

The sight of her downcast face amused him. "Look, love, it really isn't the end of the world. Being a senior citizen, I was brought up in a pre-pill world. I know how to hop down to the drugstore and take over the job of precautions."

Toni wrinkled her nose. "No. I think I'd hate that."

"Well then, my darling bride, I suggest that we have no choice except to restrain ourselves. Unless you trust *me* to do all the restraining. I know about that way, too."

She hesitated. They were passionate lovers. What if Bryce forgot to be cautious? Anyway, it was an unnatural, unfulfilling idea for him to withdraw at the moment of climax. I could take a chance, she thought. After all, there are only three days out of the month that I can get pregnant. She didn't know when her period of fertility was, but the odds seemed good that they could get away with it. Almost with embarrassment, she explained her thinking.

"No way!" he said. "That's stupidly risky. Darling, a little deprivation isn't going to kill us. Thank God you were pure until you met me! You'd probably have ended up in a home for unwed mothers!" He was laughing. "You can trust me, honey. I promise I'll leave you at the crucial moment."

She laughed with him. "You're right. I'm being silly. I'd rather have an interrupted love life with you than no love life at all."

On Friday night they made love very carefully, but when Bryce kept his word Toni felt unsatisfied and angry with herself for forgetting the pills. On Saturday morning she woke him with a kiss and a caress. As he always did, he reached for her, half asleep, and she came to him quickly, almost fiercely. As he felt the moment of completion nearing, he tried to draw away, but Toni held him with superhuman, determined strength.

When it was over he looked at her, troubled. "Sweetheart, why? That was a damned fool thing to do! You know what we agreed last night."

"But last night wasn't us," she said. "Not the way we always are. I wanted you to make love to me the way you should." She kissed him. "Don't be such a disapproving husband. Nothing will happen."

She sounded more lighthearted than she felt. She didn't know why she had done it, why she had locked herself around him so that he couldn't escape. Maybe I really do want a baby, she thought. Maybe, subconsciously, I want

363

to be found out. Freudian nonsense, she told herself. You just wanted to be totally taken, to make Bryce happy, to make up for your own carelessness. It would be too absurd, too diabolical that she would conceive. This weekend simply couldn't encompass the seventy-two hours that she could get pregnant.

He continued to look worried. "You're a crazy, beautiful lady. And just for that, no more nonsense. Today I march myself to the local pharmacy and take care of the rest of this weekend!"

She acquiesced meekly. And as she knew, she hated the whole preplanned process. At least it taught me a lesson, Toni thought. From now on I leave a supply of pills here with my ski clothes. She refused to think there'd be no need.

At first, when she began to suspect her pregnancy, Toni was so disbelieving that she said nothing to Bryce. Every morning when she woke, her first thought was that perhaps this was the day her fears would prove groundless. It couldn't be. Not just that once! Not when she had, for whatever motives, been deliberately reckless. But after six weeks she went to the doctor to hear officially what she already knew: she would have a baby in December.

That evening she told Bryce. Before he could answer, Toni said firmly, "It's all my fault and my responsibility. I'm going to have an abortion."

To her surprise, he didn't answer.

"Darling," Toni said, "this isn't exactly what you'd call planned parenthood. I haven't changed my mind about having children. Have you?"

"I'm not sure," he said slowly. "I think maybe you want a baby, Toni. And if *you* do, *I* do."

"No, I don't. Really I don't, Bryce."

"All right, sweetheart. It's your decision."

She looked at him curiously. "I think you really want me to have it."

There was a little pause and then he said, "Yes, I do, now that it's been conceived. I was perfectly content with the *theory* of no children, but now that the beginning of one exists, I don't feel quite as clinical about the subject. We're suddenly dealing with a real thing. Part of both of us." He took her in his arms. "It's not a moral issue, love. Right or wrong, I take the position that at this stage it's not really a baby. I'd like us to have a child, Toni, but if you feel otherwise, believe me, I'll go along with that. It's only a fetus, not yet a person. I don't have any hang-ups about our 'taking a life.'"

But, God help me, *I* do, Toni realized. I don't know why I deliberately exposed myself to this but it is as though it was meant to be. I can't destroy anything as precious as life. Not even if it ends the masquerade.

If only I could tell Bryce the truth, she thought. If only I dared tell him that this child's blood will be one-quarter black. For a moment she played with the idea, trusting in his love, gambling on his ability to understand why she had lied to him from the start. She dared not. Even her mother and grandmother could not comprehend the heavy responsibility she felt toward Jim Jenkins' wishes. They did not believe, as she still did, that her father had died to protect her secret. And now she was going to give life that could make his sacrifice a farce. She was going to have a baby who might emerge as living proof of her deceit. And she had to do it. I've been a liar and a cheat, she told herself, but I cannot be a murderer.

The right, the honorable thing to do would be to tell Bryce everything now. Let him choose. Let him decide whether he wanted a baby with mixed blood and, for that matter, a wife with an even greater amount of it. I'm too cowardly, she thought. Even if it's wrong, it's too late now to tell Bryce I married him under false pretenses. If he recoiled, I think I'd die. I couldn't stand to see contempt or accusation in eyes which have only shown me love.

I want the baby, she thought. I must have wanted it all along. Maybe because I don't have the courage to admit the truth I'm hoping that this third person, as yet unborn, will put an end to the dissembling. And in the same breath, contradictorily, hating herself for her values, she told herself that maybe even after the child came Bryce would not have to know. She did not look Negroid. Her child should be less likely to be recognizably black. Bryce was amazingly happy at the prospect of fatherhood. She'd have to take a chance. She owed it to *him,* as well as to the growing life within her.

Bryce had no idea what was really in her mind. He simply waited hopefully for her decision. She looked at him lovingly.

"Okay, darling," she said. "Get ready for the most important Christmas present of your life."

He kissed the tips of her fingers. "You're sure, Toni? You're really sure? You're not doing this just for me?"

She shook her head. "Not for you. For us."

When Charlene received Toni's letter, she didn't know whether to feel happy or sad. She could imagine what Toni would be going through between April and December. Not the physical discomfort; the mental anguish. She debated whether to keep the news quiet for a while so as not to disturb Elizabeth, who seemed to be failing rapidly. The combination of Jim's accident and Ann's tragedy had transformed her from an ageless, blithe spirit to a saddened, thoughtful, elderly lady. Even her own beloved husband's death had not left such visible scars on Elizabeth. Not that they did not exist inside, Charlene knew, but she had borne that tragedy with greater outward courage. She's getting old, Charlene thought. I keep forgetting that.

Still there was no point in keeping this new, possibly disquieting information from her. Charlene had told Elizabeth everything, all of which Elizabeth already knew, about Toni's belief in Jim's suicide and her determination to make his sacrifice worthwhile. They'd had a long talk when Charlene returned from the wedding in New York and Elizabeth had shaken her head sadly.

"Poor child," she'd said. "So torn. So troubled and foolishly guilty. Thank God Jim doesn't know what he unintentionally did to her. You don't believe that his death was planned, do you, Charlene?"

"No, Mother. I never will."

"Nor I. I'm not sure Toni really believes it herself. It seems more like a subconscious desire to go along with that early conversation of theirs . . . to follow her father's wishes. His death gave her an acceptable rationale for it. Something she could live with. But dear God, what a burden! Imagine living with that kind of secret." Elizabeth looked pained. "And I'll never meet Toni's husband, will I? She won't dare bring him to California."

Charlene had tried to cheer her up. "There's no reason why you and I can't visit them in New York."

"No, thanks. I have no wish to go in a wheelchair down streets that I used to fly through with such excitement when I was young. Well, no help for it. Perhaps Toni will manage to come alone. I miss her, Charlene, almost as much as you do."

That had been in October. In January, Elizabeth had been faced with the anguish of Ann's illness. She had been strong for Peter but she had literally collapsed and cried in Charlene's arms when Alan wrote and told them that his mother was in a private sanitarium.

"It wasn't easy," he wrote in vast understatement, "but

367

we know it's best. Thank you, Grandmother, for the courage you gave Dad. I can't begin to guess what that decision must have cost you."

And now it was April and Charlene arrived with Toni's letter in hand.

"There's good news and there's bad news," she said.

"Let's have the good first."

"Toni's going to have a baby in December."

Elizabeth's face lit up. "That's wonderful! But it's also surprising. You told me she and Bryce had decided not to have children."

"They had. This was a happy accident. At least I *hope* it's happy. That's the bad news."

"She doesn't want it?"

"Not that," Charlene said. "She does want it, but she's terrified of . . . of its color."

Elizabeth was aghast. "You mean she still hasn't told Bryce?"

"No and apparently she doesn't intend to. She's hoping that the child will look like every other white baby." Charlene looked troubled. "Let me read you what she says."

It was a long letter that attempted to be light and happy and which revealed panic in almost every line. Trying to make it sound humorous, Toni told her mother where and how the child was conceived.

"It's a wonder Eskimos aren't even more prolific," she wrote. "They've always stuck me as very stupid, and that, combined with the necessity to bundle a lot, should have produced an overpopulation of papooses! I should know! I was as stupid in the Antarctic atmosphere of Vermont as any uninformed lady in an igloo!

"You know I never planned to have children, Mother, and you know the reasons why. But now that it has happened I'm really glad. If I can give my child even an iota
368

of what you and Dad gave me, all the trepidation—and I'm full of it—will be worthwhile. Bryce doesn't know about his wife's heritage and, consequently, his child's. I am praying that little what's-its-name will be my co-conspirator. I'm sure you won't agree with that. You didn't from the start. Neither, last summer, did Grandmother. But there's no turning back now. I chose the course. It's a little late to spring surprises on the dearest, most wonderful husband who ever lived. I'm hardly an admirable woman. Maybe I can be forgiven because I think I'm being a considerate one. Why burden Bryce with all this before—God forbid—there's a need? What would be accomplished by confessing everything now? I'd hurt him terribly. I know I would. And, selfishly, I don't want him to turn away from me. I'm much too happy, and part of my happiness is watching his own. Now that the baby's coming I sometimes wish I'd done things differently. But then I realize that if I'd done things differently I might not be married to Bryce and have a baby coming.

"Anyway, darling, join me in some prayers for the next seven months, will you? Keep holding good thoughts of a little pink-and-white thing. It's what I want, and I know it's what Dad would have wanted."

There was more about Bryce, how he was strutting like a peacock, how they were now seriously apartment hunting for a place big enough for a nursery and a live-in nurse.

"I'm determined to give my child love and security," Toni went on, "but after he's born (we're sure it will be a boy!) I want to keep working and be free to travel with Bryce whenever he wants me to. Thank goodness we can afford a nanny. How about that? I've come a long way from Pasadena and grade school and Nadine Thompson, haven't I?"

Elizabeth looked puzzled. "Who on earth is Nadine Thompson?"

"You've forgotten her name, Mother. She was that terrible child in the second grade who first made Toni aware that she was 'different.' "

"Ah, yes. I'd almost forgotten the whole incident. But Toni obviously hasn't."

"No," Charlene said. "That was the beginning of it all, I think. Not that it wouldn't have happened sooner or later, but it was a cruel way for Toni to learn about herself." Charlene's eyes misted. "I remember how marvelous Jim was that night. So direct and yet gentle with Toni, and so irrationally angry with himself for having brought this on her. He always felt that guilt. Strange. I never have."

Elizabeth looked out across "her" mountains. "Don't forget that Toni is Jim's child, Charlene. That part of him creates anxieties in her that neither you nor I can ever fully understand. She has guilts like smoldering volcanoes, always there beneath the surface. You never know where and when they'll erupt and how much damage they'll do. Toni's like her father. She keeps her emotions bottled up but the seething never stops, I suppose. It's the only way we can accept the way she thinks, the way she's chosen to live her life." She looked searchingly at Charlene. "So now we must pray for a very specific kind of snow-white baby. Can you do that, dear?"

"I don't know," Charlene said. "I suppose I can pray for anything that Toni wants."

In late December 1971, Toni opened her eyes to see her husband standing over her hospital bed. There was no mistaking the joy in his eyes as he leaned down and kissed her. It's all right, Toni thought drowsily. Thank God, it's all right.

"Sweetheart, it's all over. You had a bad time. They had to knock you out finally, but everything's okay. You *and* the baby."

"Is he perfect, Bryce?"

"In every way, darling. Except he is she. We have a little girl." He turned to the woman who stood in the shadows of the room. "Charlene, tell your daughter what a gorgeous creature she's produced."

Charlene came over and kissed her. She'd been with Toni and Bryce for the past two weeks, sharing as best she could Toni's last-minute anxiety heightened by the torment she could confide only to her mother.

"She's beautiful, Toni," Charlene said. And then, significantly, "Everything you wanted. She's like pale French porcelain."

Bryce was beaming. "What shall we call her? We have a raft of boys' names, but no girls'."

"May I make a suggestion?" Charlene asked. "It would be lovely to name her for her grandmother."

"I think so, too," Bryce agreed. "Elizabeth's a good choice. What do you think, darling?"

Toni looked at her mother. "I'd like that. But Mother says she *looks* like porcelain. Maybe she should *sound* just as fragile and romantic. There's a name I've always loved. I think it's a French derivation of Elizabeth. Bryce, could we call her Elieth?"

"Elieth Sumner," he repeated. "Pretty. 'My daughter Elieth.' My God, that sounds good!"

They brought Elieth to her and Toni and looked wonderingly at the tiny little pink baby in her arms. "You didn't betray me, Elieth," she said silently. And then, unreasonably, "Maybe it would have been better if you had."

Chapter 26

Elieth was pure joy from the moment of her birth. Toni saw in her much more than just a beautiful, healthy baby. She was, in a strange way, her mother's vindication. After that first, fleeting moment in the hospital when she'd almost wished Elieth had forced the truth, Toni became euphoric. She'd been right not to tell Bryce about Jim. She'd been right to have this child who need never know the anguish of divided loyalties. They'd be a happy, untroubled family. All the sins of omission—for that's what they were, really, not lies—Toni had committed seemed worthwhile when she looked at this laughing infant who'd have the best of everything.

Bryce was mad about her. He rushed home from the office every evening as early as he could and sat with Toni in the nursery, watching her breast-feed Elieth. She'd wanted to do that for a while. She wanted to give this little girl a feeling of closeness to her mother, the security of being held and protected. It was a new and marvelous experience for Toni and Bryce. Toni, an only child, had never watched a new baby contentedly drawing nourishment from its mother, and Bryce, the youngest of his family, had also been deprived of this special sight. He thought sometimes of his own mother, imagining how often she had sat patiently with a greedy mouth at her breast. It must have been a far different picture. He could still see Hannah, her bosom sagging from too many little mouths seeking sustenance, and he felt again the old anger at his father, who, characteristically, would have accepted her life-giving act as part of "woman's work" if, indeed, he had ever bothered to watch.

Thank God it will never be like that for Toni, he told himself. Her beautiful breasts will be withdrawn in a few weeks from this natural demand. She would be the same slim, girlish-figured young woman she'd been before her pregnancy, thanks to the life he could give her, the help he was able to afford, from a nursemaid to the firming exercises she planned to start at Elizabeth Arden. Toni would never be poor and put upon and old before her time as Hannah Sumner had been.

"Think maybe we should have a couple more?" Toni asked one evening. "Being an only child isn't all it's cracked up to be."

He knew she was thinking of Charlene. Toni felt the heavy responsibility of being all that her mother had. She wished, perhaps, for brothers and sisters who would have helped divert Charlene's attention, now that she was so alone. But Bryce wanted no more children. He adored the one he had but the old recollections of a houseful of screaming brats plagued him. He had never told Toni the truth about his family. He had resorted to evasions when the subject came up. He did not want her to know about the slovenly brothers and sisters, the sordid atmosphere in which he'd spent the first years of his life. He wished he could forget them completely, that he could put all the memories of those early days behind him forever. He felt guilty about keeping secrets from Toni, but he would

373

never allow the skeletons to come out of that long-closed closet.

"It's your *daughter* who's greedy," he'd said lightly, "Not your *husband*. I'm content with what we have, darling. How much conversion to fatherhood do you think I can handle?"

She laughed, feeling a sense of relief. The possibilities she'd imagined during her pregnancy were not ones she looked forward to enduring again. The game must go on and she'd be a fool to take another chance with the odds. She'd been lucky. What would Bryce have done if she'd produced a dark-skinned baby? Nothing, Toni told herself firmly. He'd have loved it as he loves Elieth. He'd have been able to see why I did what I did. But she was not as sure as she tried to pretend. He was a good man, honorable and loving, but there were moments when she'd had a disquieting insight into the ingrained prejudices she supposed came from his upbringing. She knew surprisingly little about his family or his early life. She did know that he'd come from poor Texas stock, and she was aware of how many people in all parts of the world felt about Negroes. Bryce innocently revealed his deep feelings when he complained about the pressure brought to bear on the agency to hire blacks. She cringed inwardly when he thoughtlessly used the words "black bastards," but only once did she speak out in defense of what sounded like a qualified Negro employee.

"Aren't you being unfair?" she'd asked. "If the man is right for the job, what difference does his color make?"

"None, I guess. But that's a big 'if.' I've never found blacks intellectually equal to whites. Of course there are exceptions. Any liberal can name a dozen. But by and large, they don't have the white man's mind. Maybe someday they will. Maybe future generations will develop with time and the opportunity for education and social

374

adjustment. But right now, baby, they're inferiors, being forced down our throats. They're not ready for us and we're not ready for them."

She'd permitted herself indignation. "You disappoint me. It's not like you to generalize."

"I know. It's wrong. But, honey, I was brought up in a different milieu than you. In my part of the world I saw nothing but lazy, ignorant, conniving Negroes. I know it's unfair to condemn *all* blacks because of those I've known. I wish I *could* kick those racial hang-ups, but I still think God's a white man."

She'd fallen silent, ashamed of him, even more ashamed of being less honest than he. Dad was right, she thought again. It doesn't change. Not even with decent men like Bryce. She deplored his prejudice but, because she was her father's child, she sadly understood it. Bryce was the product of his early influences. Just as she was the product of hers. She remembered her Aunt Clara, urging her to do the right thing for the race in which she held half membership. And then she remembered Jim and his fervent plea for realism and the act which he'd believed would make her honor his wishes, as indeed it had. Feeling like a traitor to everyone, she continued to keep quiet.

Quite often since Elieth's birth she'd thought of Alan, wondering what would have happened had they dared marry and even accidentally had a child as she and Bryce had. She'd read *Limbo* and recognized what he'd tried to say to her. But he knew so little of the real story. His was a fantasy, far removed from the harsh realities of the situation. She did not show the book to Bryce, did not want to discuss it or the author with anyone. She paused a long time over the dedication. "For the girl on Christopher Street," it said. She wondered whether Sarah and Amy had read *Limbo*. They would know to whom it was dedicated, though they had no idea how drastically Christopher Street had changed her life.

Toni heard nothing of Alan or his family directly. Charlene offered no information and Toni could not bring herself to ask. She read the reviews of the book, which were generally favorable, and once, for lack of anything to do, she turned on television to watch an afternoon talk show. By a crazy coincidence, Alan was one of the guests, part of a panel discussion on interracial marriage. She sat transfixed, watching the serious face, hearing the easy, sensible voice begging for the acceptance of people as people.

"My grandmother in California," Alan said, "is fond of quoting obscure passages from Eastern religions. One of her favorites is from the sayings of Sri Ramakrishna: 'Man is like a pillowcase. The color of one may be red, of another blue, of a third black, but all contain the same cotton. So it is with man: One is beautiful, another is black, a third holy, a fourth wicked, but the divine One dwells in them all.' "

Toni turned off the heated debate that followed. I still love him, she thought. God help me, I still do. Without thinking she ran to the nursery and picked up Elieth, who was gurgling happily in her bassinet. Toni held her tightly as if to reassure herself that this was reality. This was her child. And Bryce's.

In March, Bryce had to make a trip to Brazil and he wanted Toni to come along.

"You've never seen Rio," he said, "It's one of the most exciting, beautiful cities in the world. Come with me, darling. Elieth will be all right. Miss Yardley—damn, I can never bring myself to say 'Nanny'—will take good care of her. We'll only be gone a couple of weeks."

Toni felt as though she was letting him down. She'd

been determined not to let the baby's arrival interfere with the things she and Bryce did together. And she would have loved to go to South America. In almost a year and a half of marriage they'd never been able to take a long trip together. It would be like a delayed honeymoon, and she knew that the dependable Miss Yardley, who'd been with them since Toni came home with Elieth, would be completely responsible. Toni wouldn't have a moment's worry about her child and she was sensible enough to know that a three-month-old baby wouldn't miss her. I've even been replaced by a bottle, Toni thought, with amusement. But she saw a chance to do something else she felt even more obliged to do, wanted to do. Bryce's trip would give her an easy opportunity to go alone to California. It was a chance for Elieth to see her great-grandmother. Or, more correctly, for Elizabeth to see her great-grandchild.

Charlene's letters always cheerful and full of small talk, had not overtly shown her concern for Elizabeth, but Toni read between the lines. Her grandmother was getting on. Toni couldn't bear the idea that someday Elizabeth would die. In her mind, Elizabeth was indestructible, eternal. But of course she wasn't. One day she'd be gone. And Toni couldn't let that happen without seeing her again.

"I'd love to go to Rio with you, darling," she'd said, "but I wonder if this wouldn't be a good time for me to make a quick trip home. I haven't seen Mother in three months and Grandmother in nearly two years."

He looked disappointed. "Why do you have to go now? I promise I'll pry some time loose in a couple of months and we'll go together."

"You and your promises," Toni teased. "Your business takes you in every other direction. Lord knows when you'll make it to California!" She sobered. "Besides,

Bryce, Grandmother is getting on. Every day counts. And I do want her to see Elieth."

"Okay," he said unwillingly, "if you think that's what you should do. Personally, I'm a little jealous. I think the real reason you won't go to Rio with me is because you can't bear to be separated from the baby."

"Not true. You come first. I'm not one of those fatuous new mothers who forget they have husbands! No, I just think it's a good time. You'll be busy in Rio and I'll be back by the time you are. It makes sense, Bryce. It really does."

"You'll take Yardley with you?"

"No. There wouldn't be anything for her to do and I think that four clucking females, including Laurel, are just about all that poor little baby can stand." She smiled. "Seriously, the real reason is that I'd like to stay at Mother's and there just isn't room for all of us. Nanny can have a couple of weeks off. She deserves it, Lord knows. She's been on twenty-four-hour duty for months!"

She arranged a flight that left before Bryce's so that he could take her and Elieth to the airport. At the gate he held her close and kissed her.

"It's our first separation," he said, "and I don't like it. Last time you went to California I thought I'd lost you. Don't forget to come back, will you?"

"Never, darling. I came back to you before and I will again. Don't *you* get carried away by some sexy Brazilian beauty and forget to come back to *me!*"

"I can't," Bryce said solemnly. "You're holding my kid for ransom."

Smiling, he watched her go through the gate, waving as she and Elieth disappeared. Then he turned away with a frown. Instinct told him that for some reason Toni didn't want him to come to California. He put aside a nagging, unworthy thought. He'd read in a column that Alan

Richards was in Hollywood writing the screenplay of *Summer Romance*. He hadn't mentioned it to Toni, nor had she to him. You have an ugly, suspicious mind, he told himself. Toni probably doesn't know that cousin of hers is there. And what if she does? That romantic nonsense ended years ago.

There were moments, too many of them, when Alan wondered where his life was going. It was a strange attitude for a man only in his mid-twenties, and no one knew that better than he. He seemed to have everything: success, money, good looks and robust health. And yet he felt displaced, purposeless. He supposed it was because he really didn't feel needed. Lord knows, his brother didn't need him or anyone. Joanne, always fiercely independent, had a full life among fashion people who were foreign to him. He'd cut his ties with the advertising world when he'd quit to write his books, and though he had no wish to go back into that frenetic business, he'd had, at least, the feeling of being necessary on a day-to-day basis, no matter how stupid and shallow the work was.

For a year he'd stayed with his father and for the first six months he had felt as though he was making some kind of contribution to Peter Richards. Ann's commitment had been a nightmare. She had known what was happening to her, had yelled and scratched and screamed as they took her to the waiting ambulance, had shouted obscene things at her husband and her son as they rode with her to the upstate private sanitarium which was, after all, nothing more than a luxurious prison. It was all Peter could do not to order the ambulance to turn around and take her home. Only Alan's steady hand on his father's arm, his quiet, measured words kept Peter Richards from collapsing as he watched his wife being taken away to the room that probably would be her home for the rest of her life.

For weeks after, Peter clung to Alan, looking to him for reassurance that he had done the only possible thing. In that period their roles had been reversed; the child had become the protective one, the father lost and helpless. In time, of course, the pain and self-doubt in Peter began to ease. Slowly, he became once again the calm, strong man he'd always been. He went religiously, every Sunday, to see Ann. Sometimes she didn't know him, but at other times she recognized him and was pathetically sweet, tearfully begging him to take her home. Those were the hardest visits of all. Alan knew when they happened. He could hear his father pacing the library half the night after he'd been through one of those sessions. Finally, Alan would get up and join him. They talked little in those worst hours before dawn. Mostly they sat drinking in silence until Peter would look at his son and say, "Thanks, Alan. Let's both try to catch a little shut-eye." He'd watch his father wander slowly off to bed, knowing that there'd be no sleep for either of them that night.

Once or twice Alan went with Peter to visit Ann, but the sight of her son seemed to agitate her and he soon stopped going. She was, despite the doctors' insistence to the contrary, making no progress, as far as Peter could see. There were the same lucid moments and the same ungovernable rages. He didn't believe the psychiatrists when they said that in a few months she might be able to come home for short visits. He knew that they were only trying to give him hope, to make it possible for him to live with himself.

Eventually Peter learned to accept and adjust. Once again he could concentrate on his work and slowly, tentatively, he began to accept the previously rejected dinner invitations of concerned friends. Alan watched the return to normalcy and was glad for his father, but his own momentary sense of being essential was fading. Peter could make it alone now. In all likelihood, Ann would never come out of the hospital, but Peter had really been alone for years in his marriage. Now, at least, he could come home to some sort of serenity, begin to rebuild his life with his peers. By the end of the year Alan knew it was time for him to move on. *Limbo* was doing well, a third book was under contract and *Summer Romance* had finally been sold to Hollywood. His agent also had been able to sell him as the one to do the film adaptation, a neat trick since Alan's only experience with this kind of writing had been thirty- and sixty-second commercials for soap powders and perfumes.

He spent Christmas with Peter. They drove up to see Ann but it was one of her bad days. She refused to see Alan and wouldn't even look at the gifts Peter brought. He tried to explain that young Pete was home with his own family and Joanne had gone to the Virgin Islands for the holidays.

"They send you their love, dear," Peter said.

Ann turned away. "Like hell."

He sat silent for a moment, wondering whether he dared give her the Christmas message from Elizabeth. He decided against it. Elizabeth had written to her daughter every week since this tragedy but Peter had shown Ann only the first letter. It had been a mistake that he'd never repeated. She'd refused to touch it, wouldn't let him read it aloud to her, had become hysterical when he told her that Elizabeth wanted to communicate with her, that she loved her and wanted her daughter to know that.

"Goddamned sanctimonious bitch!" Ann's voice could be heard all the way down the hall. "Ugly old meddling woman!"

Peter had tried to calm her. He'd thought it was one of

her more rational days, that she might even be touched by the tender words her mother had sent. He'd been wrong. The very mention of Elizabeth had sent her off into a wild outburst. He'd put the letter away and lied to the writer about its reception.

"Ann was glad to hear from you, dear," he'd written. "I read your wise, loving words to her and I think she understood." He hoped that the considerate falsehood would bring comfort to Elizabeth. Apparently it did. She had written every week to Ann since then, and Peter had read the heartfelt, generous phrases and added the letters to the growing pile his wife never saw. He continued the pretense for Elizabeth's sake, telling her how much her words meant to Ann and him, how sorry he was that her daughter could not yet reply herself, holding out hope that Ann would recover and saying that Elizabeth's love would speed the process.

He sighed now. Christmas was the worst time. Families should be together and here he was, sitting in a room devoid even of holiday decorations. Ann had received a dozen plants, including a beautiful white poinsettia from Elizabeth. She would have none of them, screaming at the nurses to take them away when those kind women appeared, ooh-ing and ah-ing over the thoughtfulness of Mrs. Richards' friends.

He wasn't sure Ann knew it was Christmas. Or cared. She was retreating further and further from this world and those in it. Aside from an occasional angry outburst, she was more like a pensive child. She didn't understand who Peter meant when he talked of Joanne and Ditto. The only name that seemed to strike a response was Alan's. Her face had lit up today when Peter said that Alan wanted to see her. She thought he meant her father.

"Daddy's here? Where is he?"

Peter's fumbling attempts at explanation only confused

her and finally made her cry with frustration. He'd tried to comfort her and had received a stinging blow on the cheek for his efforts. Alan saw the red mark and said nothing. On the long drive back to town, he and his father did not exchange a single word.

A few weeks later Alan left for California. He rented a small house in the Hollywood Hills, met more people than he cared to and went to a handful of celebrity-studded parties which bored him to distraction. He was besieged by invitations but he kept to himself, working on the screen adaptation and outlining a new book.

The best and easiest moments were those he spent with Elizabeth and Charlene, singly or together. They gave him a much needed sense of belonging and he felt closer to them than he did to anyone except Peter and Jo. They took him into their homes and their hearts, knowing he needed love. And he gave as much as he got. Like her mother, Charlene had taken a great fancy to him, inviting him often to the little house in Pasadena for a simple dinner and an easy evening of conversation. He knew he was a replacement for Toni. They talked about her a great deal. Charlene missed her terribly and Alan admitted that seldom a day went by when he did not think of her, too. The news that she'd had a baby gave him, at first, a sinking feeling in the pit of his stomach. It seemed to make her marriage so final, so unrelentingly permanent. And Charlene did not seem quite as elated as he'd have thought she would be.

"I went East when Elieth was born," she said. "She's a beautiful little girl, Alan. Everything Toni prayed for. Blue-eyed, light-haired. With skin like ivory."

The last words alerted him—to what, he didn't know—but something about the arrival of this child was worrying Charlene. He wouldn't presume to push her. Instead he said, "I'm happy for her. She'll make a wonder-

383

ful mother." And then, feeling free to say what was in his mind, "If she'd married me I don't think she would dared have children."

With equal candor Charlene said, "She didn't mean to have this one." There was a long pause. "She was terrified that Elieth would have her grandfather's color."

It took a moment for him to realize what she was saying. Toni hadn't told Bryce Sumner about Jim. Alan felt shock and bewilderment. Then he tried to sound unconcerned.

"You mean Sumner still doesn't know about your husband."

Charlene nodded.

"I'm sure Toni has her reasons," Alan said. "I know how much she loved her father. Idolized him. If she hasn't told Sumner it isn't because she's ashamed of Jim Jenkins. She thought he was the most wonderful man who ever lived. There must be something else, something very important to her."

"There is. A responsibility she's invented. Alan, you're family and you love Toni. I've never discussed this with anyone but Toni and Elizabeth, but I'd like to tell you."

He heard it all then, all the background that added up to the "debt" Toni believed she owed a dead father.

"She's wrong about it, of course," Charlene said. "Wrong in believing that Jim killed himself. Wrong in not telling Bryce the truth. It will all come out one day, Alan, and she'll be terribly hurt."

He shook his head. "It doesn't make sense. Toni's too intelligent."

Charlene gave a wistful smile. "She's also too loyal and too emotional. Have you forgotten how she ran away from you because she couldn't bear to think she might cause Ann's death? There's a parallel with Jim. She thinks she has to keep the secret she believes he died for.

384

And she didn't want to do either thing. She felt she had to. You know," she said slowly, "if I didn't understand my daughter so well, I'd almost resent this unconscious egotism. If I heard the same things about a stranger I'd say, 'My God, what makes her think she's so important that a woman would attempt suicide and a man would accomplish it because of her?' I know how much Jim loved Toni, but I also know how much he loved me. If he felt as strongly as she believes, he'd have found some other way around it. He'd never have left me for such a reason. If I thought that, I'd hate him for it. But I knew him much better than Toni did. I knew the way his mind worked. Just as you and I knew the way your mother's worked. In her case, we were proved right. Even Toni would admit that if she knew what's happened to Ann. But Jim's another matter. There's no earthly way we could convince Toni that her father didn't make the ultimate sacrifice for her. I tried to talk her out of this false responsibility. So did her grandmother. She couldn't listen. Right up to the eve of her wedding I begged her to tell Bryce. I said if he loved her he'd understand. But she wouldn't do it. She was afraid of letting her father down."

Alan was stunned. "*Did* you believe Bryce would understand, Charlene?"

She looked at him directly. "No. I thought he'd back out."

"You didn't want her to marry him."

"No," Charlene said again. "I wanted her to marry you."

Chapter 27

The early light filtered slowly, softly into Elizabeth's room and she lay very still, watching the arrival of another day. It was not yet six o'clock, but she always slept lightly and awakened early. It came from habit, from years of half listening in one's sleep. Early on, her ears had been attuned to the stirrings of children. A bit later she'd waited fearfully for the dawn arrival of a drunken husband, out all night, God knows where. And after that, early rising had become a necessity when she'd had to organize her household before she went to work. Now that she had no need to get up, indeed could not until Laurel came to help her, she still woke long before the rest of the household.

She didn't mind. She was a "morning person," her mind always clearest in the first hours of the day. And now that there were no demands on her, she used this time to simply lie in bed and think. In the peaceful silence she did not hurry herself into full consciousness. She let her thoughts emerge slowly, like floating fragments that came together finally into a recognizable totality.

Idly, she switched on the bedside clock-radio, turned to

a soft-music station. The button activated the small percolator plugged into the radio. Her Rube Goldberg arrangement, Laurel called it. The music started the coffeepot perking and in less than five minutes she was sipping the strong, hot brew from the cup which was also on the table. She could never fully wake up until she had her coffee, two big cups of it.

She propped herself up in the big bed, took a swallow and lit a cigarette. In two seconds, she thought with amusement, I've violated two medical and one household rule. Both the coffee and the cigarettes were forbidden, at *any* time, by the doctor. Smoking in bed was a habit Laurel begged her to abandon, not only for health but for safety. She'd solemnly agreed with the supplicants and proceeded to ignore them. She wasn't going to fall back to sleep and burn the house down. Once awake, she was awake for the day. As for the harmful effects of nicotine and caffeine, it was a little late to start worrying about a heart attack or lung cancer or whatever the doctor thought was so dangerous. "I've passed my allotted threescore and ten," Elizabeth had told him. "That's outmoded thinking," he'd answered. "Take care of yourself and you're good for another ten years. Maybe more."

He would have been shocked and disbelieving if she'd told him that she had no wish to be eighty or ninety. Everybody was supposed to want to hang on to life as long as they could, no matter how useless or helpless they were. Elizabeth did not subscribe to that. As long as she was mentally alert, as long as her conversation made sense and her experience was of some value to those she loved, she was willing to stay around. But she was more tired than she let any of them know. She'd had a long, full life, much of it wonderful, some of it terrible, all of it interesting. She'd done the best she could, making her share of mistakes but somehow blundering through. It

387

was enough. She wouldn't care if she didn't see the next sunrise because she believed she would be part of it.

There was nothing morbid of self-pitying in these thoughts, no real "death wish" as such. It was just that she'd done all she could for those she loved and most had given her even more in return. She felt complete. Not satisfied, but in a state of willing surrender.

She thought sadly of Ann. Peter had not fooled her with his transparent lies about how much her mother's letters meant to Ann. Elizabeth had known from the start that only Peter read them and she deliberately wrote them that way, hoping to bring him some measure of comfort. Her recent talks with Alan had confirmed what she knew. Her daughter was incurable. Never mind what the doctors said; Elizabeth had seen a mind like that before. It never healed itself. I wish she would slip off quietly in her sleep, Elizabeth thought. It would be merciful for her and the others. But she wouldn't. That was the bitter part of it. She'd go on for years, being a nothing, holding her children and Peter in terrible, futile bondage.

Elizabeth poured another cup of coffee and lit the second cigarette that was its routine companion. Thank God Charlene is all right. If only she'd meet someone she could love. It wasn't easy. Available men in their forties and fifties were rare commodities. They were all married, or if they got divorces it was because they already had the next wife picked out. Never mind, she told herself. What will be, will be. If Charlene is meant to marry again the man will appear.

Her mind skipped to the next generation. Alan had reappeared late in her life, a delayed blessing. He was a fine man. She hoped he'd find a young woman worthy of him. Like Charlene, she wished it had been Toni. To hell with all the blood-relationship problems! If ever two people were suited to each other, these two were. But no use brooding over that. Toni was married and living her life the way she had to. Elizabeth wondered whether she'd ever meet Bryce Sumner. Probably not. But at least she'd seen Bryce's child. Toni had arrived with Elieth two days ago. The memory made her smile. She'd taken the infant in her arms and it had been like looking down at Charlene. The baby had gurgled and reached a tiny hand up toward Elizabeth's gleaming white hair, catching a strand between the little fingers.

"Elieth! Don't pull Great-grandmother's hair!" Toni had spoken as though the baby could understand, and then she'd joined the others in their laughter, realizing how ridiculous her admonition was.

"Great-grandmother," Elizabeth thought. It seems impossible. I don't feel that old. I don't think I'll ever feel old. Just world-weary. Ready to step aside and make room for the new ones. Ready to find the spark that's my Tony.

As though some mysterious force heard her, she felt a great searing pain in her chest. A hot poker ran down her arm with a huge thrust that left her gasping for breath. Then it subsided. In a reflex action she carefully stubbed out the cigarette and lay back on the pillows, waiting.

There was no sound in the room except the soft music from the radio. The sun had risen higher now and it sparkled on Elizabeth's bed with greater intensity than ever before, for now it had been joined by one more dancing dot of light.

Laurel found her an hour later. She called Charlene and then the doctor, and while she waited she sat beside Elizabeth, too crushed even to weep. So many years, Laurel thought. So many good years. They'd been friends since they were very young women. She had lived through Elizabeth's divorce, remarriage and widowhood, had watched her children grow up, had come to California when Tony died and Elizabeth had her stroke. She'd run the business, run the house. But she'd never run Elizabeth. Elizabeth was staunchly, personally her own woman. A giving, loving woman, refusing pity just as she refused orders. Laurel's eyes wandered to the bedside ash tray with the two snuffed-out cigarettes. Right to the end, she thought. You did it your own strong way right to the end. Damn you, there'll never be another like you!

Only then did the tears come. She put her face on the coverlet next to Elizabeth's hand and gave in to the realization of her loss.

As Elizabeth had been strong for her, so Charlene now was for the mother she loved so much.

"It was quick and almost painless," the doctor said. "She didn't suffer."

Not in dying, Charlene thought. God knows how much in living. She turned away from those thoughts. Elizabeth would have hated maudlin sympathy as much in death as she did in life. Her wishes were known to all of them. They were the same as for Tony and Jim. Charlene, her back straight, her eyes clear, began to give orders.

"Toni, you'll find Alan Richards' number in that little book over there. Call him. Tell him what's happened and ask him to notify Peter immediately."

There was a second's hesitation as Toni and her mother looked at each other.

"He's here," Charlene said, "living in Hollywood. We've become very close. He adored your grandmother, and it was mutual. He's become very dear to all of us." She waited a moment and then said evenly, "This is no time to think of yourself, Toni. Make the call."

Obediently, Toni did as she was told. She gave him no time to say anything. As soon as he answered the phone she said, "Alan, it's Toni. Grandmother died this morning. Mother wants you to call your father."

She heard his quick intake of breath. Shock at the news of Elizabeth? Surprise at hearing her voice? Both, probably, but the slight gasp immediately gave way to concern.

"I'll call right away. When did it happen? How is Charlene?"

"The doctor says it was a heart attack. Probably about three hours ago. Mother's being wonderful. Laurel, too."

"And you?"

"I'm trying to follow their example."

"I'll be there as soon as I can."

Toni replaced the receiver and stood very still. Memories of her father's death flooded over her. She remembered Bryce's voice at the time, insisting he should come, pointing out that there was no man to take charge. She recalled how surprised she was, realizing it was true. It was not true now. Alan was on the way to give Charlene the shoulder she needed to lean on. And Peter would arrive soon. There were men this time, strong ones. Including Bryce, who now had a right to be at her side. She dug into her purse for a copy of his itinerary and then she picked up the phone again and dialed long-distance.

"Operator," she said, "I'd like to place a call to Mr. Bryce Sumner at the Copacabana Hotel in Rio de Janeiro, Brazil."

The next few days were a blur to Toni. She moved through them automatically There was an unreal quality about everything, like watching another person in her skin go about the hundred necessary things that had to be done. She remembered Alan arriving and only for a fleeting moment as he took her hand did she feel the anguish of that other loss. Then he moved away to Charlene and she to her assigned duties. Somewhere she called an agency and got a nurse to come and stay with Elieth. Sometime she was reintroduced to a handsome, stricken Peter Richards. She vaguely knew that she had called Fred and Addie Jenkins in Denver and had heard the sorrow in their voices. She heard sorrow in many voices as she notified people her mother told her to call: the manager of the decorating shop; the president of the aviation company, who had kept in touch with Charlene and Elizabeth after Jim's death; even Karen Golden, Toni's childhood friend whom she hadn't seen in nearly two years but who'd thought of Elizabeth as her "adopted grandmother."

She told them all the same thing. It had been quick and peaceful. Services would be private. There'd be a quiet tribute to Elizabeth in her own house in a few days. Her cousin, Alan Richards, would speak a few words. Automatic. In control. Saying all the right things, thanking them for their condolences, promising to relay their words to her mother.

She kept putting aside the knowledge that Bryce was on his way. It took a long time to reach him and she recalled trying to dissuade him, but this time he understandably would have none of it. He'd arrive for the memorial service, see to things there, and then take her and Elieth home.

"There's no need," she'd said. "You didn't know Grandmother and it's pointless to cut short your trip and make the long one out here."

"Darling," he'd said, "you don't think I'd let you and Charlene try to handle things alone at a time like this!"

"We won't be alone," she'd said unthinkingly. "Alan Richards and his father will be here."

There was a little silence on the other end. Then Bryce said, "I'm *sure* they will." He cursed himself for letting sarcasm creep into his voice. He hoped Toni hadn't noticed. What a stupid moment to be jealous! He went on hurriedly. "I'm glad they'll be there, sweetheart, but that doesn't mean I shouldn't be. You sound calm but I know you're going on your nerves. I want to be around when this really hits you. How's Elieth?"

"Fine. I found a nurse to look after her."

"You could have sent for Yardley."

"Yes, I suppose I could have. I didn't think of it. There's been so much to do." Her voice broke finally. "Oh, Bryce, I can't believe she's dead!"

"I know love. But isn't it miraculous that you didn't make this trip with me? What a blessing you were there when it happened and that you could see her once more."

"Yes. And that she saw Elieth." She choked again. "She thought Elieth was wonderful."

"Hang on, darling. I'll be there in a couple of days. Kiss the baby for me. And my love to Charlene."

She hung up, momentarily bolstered by his strength. For a little while she'd forgotten why she didn't want Bryce ever to come to California. She remembered now, but somehow it didn't matter. She'd tried, really tried, to do what Jim Jenkins wanted. Charlene had said she was wrong, that it would come out one day no matter how hard she tried to keep the secret. Toni wearily supposed that this could be the time. She was too tired to care. She'd done her best for her father. She believed she'd been right, no matter what anyone said. Fate had taken its time to have its way. If it had chosen death as the instrument of truth, perhaps that was fitting. Perhaps death was the only inescapable reality of life.

They were living it all over again, differently this time, more logically acceptable than Jim's death but no less sad to those who gathered at Elizabeth's a week later to remember her. There were three little mounds under the

393

great tree now, a new one for the great branches to shelter and the warm earth to take back to itself.

Toni sat between Charlene and Bryce, firmly holding a hand of each. Bryce's grasp was strong and supportive; Charlene's passive and soft. In a continuing link, as though they were drawing strength from each other, Peter Richards held Charlene's hand in one of his and Laurel's in the other. Inane thoughts ran through Toni's tired mind. "Dearly beloved, we are gathered together . . ." No, that was the wedding ceremony. And yet it fit. Elizabeth was joined once again with her bridegroom.

There was no humming sound in the big living room this time, no recording of Alan's words as there had been of Elizabeth's when she spoke of Jim. We should have recorded it, Toni thought. It's beautiful. Elizabeth would have appreciated the beauty.

The depths of her grandson's feeling came through in the strong, unfaltering voice. He talked of how briefly he had known Elizabeth, but how well. He spoke of her wisdom and strength, of the bottomless well of love from which they all drank, and of how arid the world would be without it.

"She was far too intelligent to be eternally, uninterruptedly, vacuously happy. She had her moments of sadness and disillusion, her disappointments, her fears and doubts. But she came to terms with life. She saw more joy than sadness, more good than evil, more upturned mouths than downcast eyes. She lived fully and well. She gave and received. And above all she believed in the inherent goodness of people, not blindly but with compassion and regret for the sadness they inflicted on themselves and others."

He was thinking of Ann, understanding that Elizabeth had known she was powerless to help her daughter, pitied

Ann for her poor, lost self, forgave her for those things that no one could change.

"God knows even better than we that Elizabeth was no saint. But God knows, as we do, that she had saintly qualities. She did not presume to judge, nor to condemn, nor ever to impose her will or her wishes on others. She lived her life trying not to hurt even a stranger. She had her own code of morals, her own standard of ethics, her own fierce loyalties and her blessed independence. She had her faults, her weak spots, but because she knew them she was an extraordinary woman and a complete person. And so she will always be to those of us who knew this graceful lady.

"She left life the way she lived it—serenely, confidently, with a smile and a quiet wave of her hand." He paused and looked directly at Charlene and Toni. "She left us richer in spirit, stronger in awareness, better for having touched her. Our hearts and souls are full of gentle gifts from Elizabeth."

And then it was over, the small assemblage quietly dispersing. Charlene went to Alan and took his face between her hands.

"Mother would have liked that," she said. "Particularly the part about her faults and weak spots. She could never bear perfect people; only perfect intentions."

Toni approached with Bryce. "Thank you, Alan. You did it just right."

"I wish I could have done it better." He looked at Bryce. "We haven't met," Alan said, extending his hand, "but I want to congratulate you."

Bryce shook hands firmly. "I only arrived this morning," he said. "Thank you. For the congratulations and for such a moving tribute to Toni's grandmother. I'm only sorry I never knew her." He looked at Toni. "Honey, I know you and Charlene want to speak to people. I'll wait for you out on the porch."

He left her alone with Alan. It was the first time they had been even this much alone since Elizabeth's death. Deliberately? Unavoidably? Neither of them really knew.

"Seems like a nice man," Alan said. "Are you happy, Toni?"

"With Bryce? Yes. I have a beautiful little girl, a good, solid, uncomplicated marriage. My husband loves me very much. I'm fortunate. And you, Alan?"

"None of those good things, but a good life nonetheless. My work's going well and I like California."

"Will you stay here?"

"For a while. Until the picture's finished. But it won't be the same. Not for any of us."

"No," Toni said softly, "not for any of us." She took his hand. "I'm glad you and Grandmother got to know each other. Mother told me how much she loved you. Mother loves you, too."

Involuntarily he said, "And you?" Then he looked ashamed. "I'm sorry, Toni. Forgive me. That's rotten taste. This is not the time or place for a question like that. It just came out."

She held on to his hand. "I think Grandmother would have understood and probably approved. I know she'd want me to give you an honest answer. I still love you." She withdrew her hand and turned to speak to the people who were waiting.

Bryce leaned against the terrace railing, smoking a cigarette. He was tired. It had been a long trip from Brazil but he'd have gone to the end of the earth to be with Toni at this time. He hoped everybody would leave soon. He was very much aware that he was a stranger, almost an intruder, here. He knew no one except Charlene, and he was in no mood for introductions. Except to Alan

Richards. Bryce had always been curious about the cousin Toni once planned to marry. Damned good-looking guy. Probably decent, too. But thank God it hadn't worked out. Bryce was deeply in love with his wife, more sexually attracted to her now than when they first met. A little ashamed, he felt strong desire. Aroused, he closed his eyes and the picture of their lovemaking swam before him. No one had ever been able to excite him as this slim, golden girl always did.

"Beg pardon," a man's voice said, "but aren't you Toni's husband?"

Bryce opened his eyes to see an elderly man standing beside him. He hadn't even heard him approach.

He nodded. "Right. Bryce Sumner."

"Joseph Bleeker. President of McVane Aircraft. Toni's father worked for me." They shook hands. "Sad thing," Bleeker said. "Elizabeth was a wonderful woman. Not that her passing was untimely. She lived her span. But none of us ever thought of her dying. Odd. It was almost more of a shock to me than Jim Jenkins' death. Not literally, of course, but it's even harder because it's been such a relatively short time since Jim went." He shook his head. "Poor Charlene and Toni. They've had an awful lot of sadness in the last couple of years."

Bryce didn't know what to say but his silence went unnoticed as Joe Bleeker talked on.

"Never forget how proud they all were the day we inaugurated the KJ-16. Happiest family I ever saw, in spite of all the odds. Yes, sir, they were an inspiration, that family. People think they're so liberal these days, but when it comes to black marrying white most of 'em can't handle it. Elizabeth and Charlene and Toni sure were the exceptions. In their eyes Jim Jenkins was as white as snow. In mine, too. I guess most of us at the plant admired him so much as an engineer that we seldom

397

thought about the fact that he was a Negro. Of course, it was easier for us. He wasn't part of our households."

For a moment Bryce couldn't grasp what he was hearing. It was seconds before the full facts hit him. Toni's father was a Negro. Bryce Sumner had married a mulatto. It was impossible. There must be some mistake. Toni would have told him. This old fool must be mixed up. He was thinking of someone else. He had to be. Years of facing clients had taught Bryce never to show surprise at the unexpected. The experience stood him in good stead now. His expression didn't change.

"You employ many Negro engineers at McVane?"

"Have one now. But for almost twenty years Jim Jenkins was the only black man on an executive level. Not that we considered him a 'token,' mind you. Hell, I hired him long before all this business about 'equal opportunity.' Jim was the best aeronautical engineer I've seen before or since. He could have been pea green as far as I was concerned. And not only talented. He was one helluva man. Well educated. Good athlete. Bright, polished, amusing. Damned shame you never knew him, Sumner. You two would have gotten along. He loved his wife and daughter like I hear you love yours."

Bryce nodded, turned away and saw behind him a small, attentive figure in the doorway. Toni. How long had she been standing there listening to an innocent Bleeker extol the virtues of her black father? Bryce couldn't tell. The face was impassive, but the tautness of her body told him she'd heard enough. She was waiting now for him to accept or reject her. Whatever I say now, Bryce thought, will determine our future. He moved toward her.

"Are you all right, sweetheart?"

There was no mistaking the gentle lovingness in his voice. An almost pathetic look of relief came over Toni's

398

face. Bryce knew and it didn't make any difference to him. All her dissembling had been unnecessary, all the self-reproach for deceiving him could be put behind her. She felt free for the first time since they'd met. He hadn't failed her. He was every bit the man she'd hoped. I've never loved him as much as I do at this moment, Toni thought. Thank you, God, for not letting it matter.

"I'm all right, darling," she said. "Just about everyone has gone. I came looking for you."

Joe Bleeker looked at his watch. "Good Lord, I didn't realize it was so late! Your husband and I have been having a good talk, Toni. You picked a fine man."

She smiled. "I know, Mr. Bleeker." Her glance traveled beyond him to Bryce. I'm glad you know, it said, and I humbly beg your forgiveness for letting you find out this way. I adore you for understanding.

Bryce returned the smile, as though he read her thoughts. He put his arm around her. "You must be exhausted," he said.

"She certainly must," Bleeker agreed. "Take care of her, Sumner. She's quite a girl. Goodbye, Toni, I hope I'll see you both before you go back to New York."

"Goodbye, Mr. Bleeker," she answered. "Thank you for everything."

He brushed aside the misunderstood statement. "I didn't do anything. Wish I could have. Anyway, I'll keep in touch with Charlene, you can count on that."

They stood silently for a few seconds after he left.

"Then Toni looked up at her husband.

"I should have told you before," she said. "There were reasons why I felt I couldn't. You see, I believed my father . . ."

Bryce put his hand over her mouth. "Hush, love. Not now. We'll talk later if you want to. But it's all right, darling. I love you very much and I want you terribly."

399

Toni's heart rose even higher. She could hardly wait for them to be alone. I'll make love to you the way I never have before, she thought. It would not be disrespectful to Elizabeth. On the contrary, her grandmother would have been happy to know that the truth had finally come out, enriching them and strengthening their devotion.

They were all staying in Elizabeth's house, Charlene, Toni and Elieth had been there since the morning Elizabeth died and now Bryce would join Toni in the guest room next to the baby's. Peter was at the Beverly Hills Hotel. He would stay in California long enough to get Elizabeth's affairs in order. They had not yet had time to think about what Laurel would do or where Charlene would go after Toni and Bryce left. Perhaps, Toni thought, she'll move here with Laurel. It would be the best, most sensible arrangement.

But right now she couldn't think that far ahead. None of them could. Laurel and Charlene were completely drained of their last reserve of strength. After a light, early supper, Toni literally put them both to bed, insisting that each take a sleeping pill. Then she and Bryce looked in on Elieth. Bryce took the baby in his arms and held her tenderly, whispering to her, kissing her lightly as the nurse looked on approvingly.

"I swear she's gotten pounds heavier! And twice as beautiful!"

Toni laughed. "Darling, it's been less than a week since you've seen her!"

"Irrelevant," he said. "I know what I see and feel."

His own words echoed in his ears. Do I? Bryce wondered. Do I really know? I love this child. She's mine. But will I always think, as I hold her, that part of her is black? Will I find this same uncertainty when I hold the body of her mother?

He put Elieth back into her crib. Don't, he begged an unseen Being. Don't let the old childhood prejudices come back to haunt me after all these years. Please, please, don't let me be Hank Sumner's son.

Chapter 28

Hand in hand, Bryce and Toni went into the big guest room next door. Inside, Toni turned to him and held out her arms. He went to her and pulled her close to him, kissing her, feeling the softness of her body under her clothes, touching all the loved and remembered outlines. Desire was in his head but not in his body.

"You're not too tired?"

"Darling," she said. "I want you. Oh, Bryce, I love you so much!"

That was the way he'd felt standing on the terrace, filled with a physical ache for her. But that was before he knew. Before Bleeker had inadvertently told him whom he'd married. It doesn't matter, Bryce told himself. She's the same glorious woman, the same sensitive, superb creature who fills me with such passion.

"Do you remember what you did the first night we made love?" he asked. "Way back when you were a frightened but determined little virgin?"

Toni nodded.

"Do it again," he whispered.

Almost solemnly she backed away and slowly, with the

same natural seductiveness, stepped out of her clothes, her eyes never leaving his. She stood beautiful and naked before him, the body as slim and firm and golden as it had been then.

Bryce felt, joyfully, his own physical response. He undressed rapidly, scooped her up in his arms and carried her to the big bed. But as quickly as desire came, it left. No matter what either of them did, he could not consummate their reunion. After a long while they lay quietly in each other's arms.

"Sweetheart, I'm sorry," Bryce said. "I must be exhausted from the trip. I feel like hell, failing you this way. I'll make up for it tomorrow, you can bet on that. All I need is a good night's rest."

She stroked his cheek. "Of course, darling. It's perfectly understandable. I'm tired, too. Good night, my love. Sleep well."

"You, too. Do you want me to get you a sleeping pill?"

"No, I'll be fine."

"I'm sorry," he said again. "God knows, I'm as disappointed as you. Probably more. It's ridiculous! Bloody damn time changes! If God had wanted man to fly he'd have given him a better internal clock!"

She smiled, a sad, dignified smile. "It's all right, Bryce, dear. Get some sleep."

He turned on his side, his back to her. But he didn't sleep. His mind unwillingly reached back to Texas. He could hear Hank Sumner's terrible voice gloatingly describing the lynching of a black man who'd dared have sex with a white woman. The woman had been a tart and willing, but that made no difference to the ugly, angry white trash. It was as though he were back in his adolescent world listening to his father and his brothers talk about Negro girls. They were not averse to a "piece of black ass," as they called it. That was okay. Every white

403

man had his fun with the "nigras" and many a mulatto baby was born as a result of it. But no white man, no matter how low or shiftless or stupid, ever married a black woman. Or even a mulatto. They were animals, Hank Sumner said, right out of the goddamn African jungle. No matter how high and mighty they thought they were, they were not fit for anything but cleaning white women's houses and screwing any white man who decided he wanted them, in their dirty shacks or back in the bushes.

But I'm not like that! Bryce screamed inside his head. I despise that prejudice, that unbelievable ignorance! No part of it could have stayed with me. I love my wife. I don't care that she's a mullato. It can't be true that somewhere deep inside I'm unable to accept her because she's half black!

And yet, why couldn't I make love to her tonight? On the terrace, before I met Joe Bleeker, I was ready to throw her to the floor in front of everybody and lose myself in that beautiful body. And when it was offered, with all its love and warmth, something in me was repelled.

No, Bryce told himself. It isn't that way. I'm just tired. I've been flying for hours. It's pure physical fatigue plus the emotion of this day. It's affected us both. Tomorrow morning when we wake everything will be as it always has been. Toni believes that. So do I.

But Toni did not believe it. She, too, lay pretending to sleep, but wide awake, her mind filled with terrible certain fears. Bryce was not too tired for sex. Ever since he'd arrived that morning he'd been subtly touching her, looking at her in that private way they had when they knew they wanted each other. But though his kiss when he'd come into their room had been deep and hungry, Toni had sensed a difference, one he was unwilling to admit. He'd asked her to deliberately seduce him, like some strange

404

girl he'd wanted to arouse him; not like the wife with whom he always went easily and joyfully to bed.

Knowing about her *did* make a difference. She was sure he didn't want it to, that he couldn't help it, that he probably hated himself for it. Poor Bryce, she thought. I don't know what they taught you in those early days in Texas, but God help us, I'm afraid it stuck.

She tried to tell herself, lying sleepless in the dark, that she was wrong. Perhaps he *was* simply exhausted. Perhaps she was also more drained than she knew, still too deep in her grief that night to respond as she should. That had to be what it was. For his sake and hers and Elieth's. I mustn't read anything significant into the fact that Bryce couldn't make love to me one night. It happens now and then to all married people, under even less trying circumstances than those they'd both gone through. It will be different in the morning, she told herself firmly. I must get some rest. I must be fresh and desirable to Bryce when he wakens. A long while later she finally fell into a troubled, exhausted sleep.

The touch of Bryce's hand on her breast awakened her at dawn. He leaned over her, looking lovingly into her face, his eyes still half filled with sleep. She reached for him and held his body against her own.

And once again, nothing happened.

His remorse was terrible to see. In the three days and nights that followed, before they returned to New York, he tried time and again to make love to her, always without success. It was the same in New York, night after night of failure until at last Bryce was so anxious and Toni so heartsick that they could no longer pretend it was a temporary thing.

She was very gentle as she finally said, "Bryce, what are we going to do?"

He sat on the side of the bed forlornly, almost in tears.

"I don't know. I don't understand it."

Toni spoke very softly. "Don't you, dear? Don't you really?"

"No! I love you, Toni. You know that. There must be something physically wrong with me. A man doesn't just become impotent overnight, especially when he's as much in love as I am. I'll go and get a checkup. Find out what the hell's the matter with me."

She didn't answer for a moment. Then, very tenderly, she said, "You know it started the day you discovered that I'm half Negro. I think that's what it is, Bryce. I don't blame you, darling. It was wrong of me not to have told you at the beginning. I know you love me. But somewhere, buried deep, knowing what I am has made a difference. It's not your fault. Many men can't help feeling that way. Even the most wonderful men. My father knew that." She told him about Jim then: the early, begged-for promises, the "accident" that happened the day after he heard she planned to marry Bryce. All of it: Charlene's disapproval of her actions, Elizabeth's conviction that she was wrong. "Can you see, darling, why I felt I couldn't tell you? Why I never intended you to come to California to meet any of the people I'd ever known? I felt I owed it to Dad." She laughed mirthlessly. "And Elizabeth blew it sky high. I'm sorry I lied to you, Bryce. I was wrong. Please forgive me, if you can."

There were real tears in his eyes now. "I've lied to you, too, Toni. And I've lied even more to myself." It was his turn for confession. He poured out all the things he'd told no one: the story of his boyhood, the bestiality of his father, the helplessness of Hannah Sumner. He talked about the attitudes of his brothers and sisters and of the people around him as he grew up. Bit by bit, the racism emerged and he spat it out with scorn for it, revulsion for those

406

who thought that way. "I don't believe that such despicable prejudices could stay with me. It makes no sense. I can't accept it. It's impossible that somewhere inside me there's bigotry I reject with my intellect and don't know how to beat with my emotions. Toni, I've been so much more cruel to you than you have to me. Your lies were loyal ones. Mine were inspired by shame and vanity. And now this. You're suggesting a terrible mental block I don't even believe in!"

She put her arms around him. "Sweetheart, let's not give up. We're hiding nothing from each other now and that's a good beginning. Let's get help. We're confused, each in his own way. But maybe with psychiatry we can get straightened out, now that we've been honest. We loved each other so passionately once. Surely we can again if we understand our guilts and complexes. We can still have a complete life together, Bryce. I want it now more than ever. Do you?"

"You know I do, but what if I don't come out of this, Toni? I can't expect you to spend the rest of your life with a man who simply worships you from a distance. I can't spend my life that way, either."

"No, we can't live that way forever," she said, "but before we accept that, shouldn't we make an effort to save something very good?"

Bryce nodded. "Yes, of course. First I'm going to have that physical checkup. But if that proves nothing, do you really think a head doctor is the answer?"

"For both of us," Toni said. "I've been on the wrong track, too. And I'm not off of it yet."

He looked dubious. "I've never had much faith in shrinks, Toni."

"I've never had any experience with them, dear. I grew up in a family of common-sense people. We always tried to talk out our problems together. But since Dad's death

407

I've been blind and obstinate, Bryce, and I'd like to know why."

"You think you need analysis to understand why you lied to me? I don't think that takes too much figuring out, darling."

"I think it does," Toni said. "I think I was feeling like the bearer of a divine obligation rather than the instrument of an intelligent, realistic cynic, the daughter of a man who loved me, as the saying goes, not wisely but too well."

"You sound as though you're angry at your father."

The perceptiveness of the remark startled her.

"Perhaps I am," she said. "That's one of the things I have to find out." She thought of Clara Jenkins. Perhaps there was more insight in the things her aunt had said to her than Toni had been able to see. And Charlene. Charlene must have sensed that Toni's motivations were, in a strange way, selfish, though their owner honestly thought them—she cringed from the word—noble. There were other things too. Her blind, determinedly self-sacrificing attitude about Alan and Ann. She'd made so many blunders that had affected not only her life but those of others.

She did not say any of this to Bryce. She was afraid he wouldn't be able to accept the need for therapy. He was troubled about his feelings, but more concerned about his loss of "manhood," his sudden lack of virility. Toni knew he was putting his faith in finding a physiological cause. He could not, even now, countenance the idea that early prejudices, unwillingly learned, were still with him, and that the subconscious could affect his physical performance. Could he ever face the fact that psychologically he still "looked down" on black people and was unknowingly horrified that he'd married one? She felt sad for him. And for Elieth and herself.

Peter Richards returned to New York a week after the memorial service for Elizabeth. It had been a busy week, entering the will for probate, discussing with Charlene and Laurel their options for the future. They'd left the latter undecided. It was too soon for either woman to know whether they should continue the decorating business or sell it. Charlene didn't even know whether she'd stay in her familiar little house in Pasadena or move to the big place which belonged to Laurel for her lifetime. Peter urged them both to take time before making any step.

"There's no rush," he told Charlene one night over dinner in her house. "You're a rich woman now, Charley, whether you keep the business or sell it. As for moving in with Laurel, I know how devoted you are to each other, but you're two generations. Be very sure you want to live under the same roof."

She'd agreed. She needed time to think about the course of her life. She realized how much she'd depended on Elizabeth and how lost and lonely she felt without her. Sometimes she couldn't believe her mother was dead. She found herself starting to the telephone to call her, as she had for so many years. And then she'd stop, sickened with the awareness that the lilting voice would not answer. Charlene had not gone into the terrible shock she'd suffered when Jim died. This was more of an emptiness, a constant, dull ache. Thank God for Peter. Elizabeth had been so wise to name him co-executor. He was not only a good lawyer, he was a warm, dear man. He had been with her almost constantly this past week. Most nights they and Laurel and Alan dined together quietly, but on two evenings she and Peter had been alone, comforted by and comfortable with each other. This was one of those evenings, the last before Peter's return to New York. Charlene hated to see him leave and she couldn't resist telling him so.

"You don't dread my departure half as much as I do," he said. "In spite of the sadness, I feel serene here. I never do in New York."

She knew he was thinking of Ann, of the dreaded weekly visits to the hospital which he felt duty-bound to make. He must be lonely, too, Charlene thought. Even a "social life" could be empty and boring without someone you loved, and Peter had lived that way for years, long before his literal separation from Ann.

They had spoken little of his wife in these days of mourning. When Peter arrived, Charlene had asked him whether her sister had been told about Elizabeth.

"I tried to tell her," he'd said. "I drove up there before I caught the plane. She . . . she didn't know what I was talking about. It meant nothing to her. Nothing at all."

They hadn't discussed Ann since, but on this last evening Charlene quietly pressed him for more information.

"She's incurable," Peter said flatly. "Even the doctors now admit that only a miracle could make her well. Physically, she's strong. They've built her up with good food and outdoor exercise. And of course she can't get hold of liquor any more. But the schizophrenia continues and will as long as she lives. Therapy, shock treatments, nothing has helped." He pronounced the words slowly. "She's totally, irrevocably insane."

Charlene shuddered. "Does she know you, Peter?"

"Sometimes. Most times, no. Strangely enough, she seems quite happy. She has flashes of recall, always about her father. But they're brief and childish. I'm taking her the letter Elizabeth left her, the one from FDR to your father. God knows whether she'll understand what it is, but Elizabeth wanted her to have it. Maybe they'll let her hang it on the wall of her room."

410

He sounded so defeated, so hopeless. We're both lost, Charlene thought, but Peter's more lost than I. He doesn't have beautiful things to remember. He's not even allowed the healing adjustment that time mercifully gives the bereaved. I'll never forget Jim, but I've been forced to accept the fact that he's gone. That's easier than being bound to a woman who's living but not alive.

It was a stupid question, but Charlene had to ask it. "What are you going to do, Peter? You still have your life."

"I haven't had a life for a long time, Charley." He smiled. "Sounds remarkably like 'poor-little-me,' doesn't it? I didn't mean to sound sorry for myself." Then he frowned. "Damn it, that's a lie. I do feel sorry for myself. I'm wallowing in stupid, futile self-pity and I can't help it. I can't stand seeing the rest of my life go down the drain, especially when I know there are women like you in this world!" He stopped, aghast at what he'd said. He hadn't meant to even hint at how much he loved her, how much, he knew now, he'd always loved her. She'd be disgusted with him. Her own sister's husband practically admitting that he wanted her!

But Charlene's expression did not change to shock or revulsion. If anything, her eyes softened with sympathy.

"I don't pity you," she said. "I don't think you want pity from anyone. But I understand self-preservation, Peter. It's human to fight for it. I think you should. I think the day will come when you will have to."

There was a moment of complete communication before they went on to talk of Alan's career. Toni's happiness and the wonderful advent of Elieth. Charlene knew nothing of her daughter's difficulties with Bryce.

"I suppose that worked out for the best," she said. "I mean Toni and Alan."

"You don't sound entirely sure."

Charlene smiled. "I'd have preferred it differently. I even told Alan so. But I once told Toni something else: 'Never interfere with a good Scriptwriter.' I have to stick with that belief, Peter. I guess this is the way it's meant to be, for all of us, until God decides to write the script."

He drove back to the hotel still hearing her words and wondering when, if ever, God would rewrite the tragicomedy that was his life.

Alan Richards had had a hard time keeping his mind on his work in the past week. Elizabeth's death hit him hard. He'd grown to love her, fascinated by her mind and enchanted by her uniqueness. It seemed unfair that he should have really known her for so brief a time. He wished Joanne could have met her. She was the kind of gutsy female Jo would have admired, the kind of emancipated, high-spirited and feminine woman his sister wanted to be.

And seeing Toni had thrown him. Aside from the few seconds they'd had alone, the incredible seconds in which she said she still loved him, he'd scrupulously avoided any contact with her while she was there with her husband and child. She looked more beautiful, more desirable than ever. From the shy, wonderful girl she had grown into a poised and lovely woman. Reluctantly, he gave much of the credit to Bryce Sumner. He wished he could hate him. God knows, he was jealous of him. But he couldn't hate anybody who made Toni happy.

I'm glad one of us is happy, Alan thought wryly. Dad is miserable, Charlene and Laurel are like abandoned souls, and I have nothing in my life but my work and a series of transient, meaningless affairs. Even the charm of California was beginning to wear thin. It must have been wonderful in the old, glamorous days of Hollywood. But now it's not even Tinsel Town. More like a determined dowager who's had her face lifted once too often. The party's moved on, but the old girl still sits waiting for invitations that never come.

He rolled a sheet of paper into the typewriter. The film script, endlessly revised, had begun to bore him and he was relieved that in another week or two he'd be finished with it. But then what? Should he stay in California to write the next book? Despite his disenchantment with Hollywood, life was easier here, the climate good and the pace less frenetic than in New York. But it was also less stimulating and more lonely without Elizabeth. If he left he'd miss Charlene but he knew that in a way his visits to her were masochistic; every one reminded him of Toni. Will I never stop loving her? Alan wondered. What will it take to make me quit? Not even the affair in Paris or those that followed had erased Toni from his heart.

Geography certainly was not his answer. Wherever he was he had to find inner peace. He needed someone to care for, a "meaningful relationship," he thought, vaguely amused at his easy use of the current cliché. But the only one he wanted endlessly eluded him. Toni didn't need him.

Only Peter did. There was nothing Alan could do for his mother, nothing anyone could do. But his father seemed so defeated, so spirtless. He needs any kind of affection, Alan thought. Even mine.

He made up his mind to go home soon. What difference did it make to him where he lived? I'm a man without purpose. Someone who doesn't know what tomorrow will bring and who isn't even interested.

Chapter 29

"Doctor, what is reality?"

"What do you think it is, Mrs. Sumner?"

Toni leaned back in the chair facing Dr. Morrisy's desk. Thank God her sessions with the therapist were spent sitting up, not lying like a talking doll tossed carelessly on a couch, its mechanical voice whining over and over, "Ma-ma, Ma-ma." It helped her to watch the psychiatrist's face as she talked. Not that he reacted openly, but it made the whole thing seem less grotesque, more like a conversation with a friend than an outpouring directed toward a note taker who sat behind her and answered in disembodied syllables. She smiled at the doctor.

"You really should have had a career on Seventh Avenue," Toni said. "That's the way they talk. 'How's business?' 'How should it be?' In the garment center they always answer a question with a question. It's probably a very relaxed way to live, now that I think of it. Are you relaxed, Doctor?"

The corners of his mouth turned up slightly. "Are *you*, Mrs. Sumner?"

She laughed. "Okay. Touché." She thought back for a

moment. "I suppose reality is part acceptance and part hope," she said. "I think it's knowing when you've been wrong, and believing you've learned from it, so you can do better next time. It's understanding what you *can* handle and what you *can't*. And in both cases, *why*." She looked at him carefully. "Does that make any sense?"

"Quite a lot, especially in your case."

Toni pretended shock. "Doctor, you made a statement!"

Morrisy laughed. "I figured after six months you were entitled to one. So now you've scored a point. What comes next?"

"For me?"

"For you and the people you care about."

Toni hesitated. "I don't know for sure, but I do believe I don't have much else to say to you. I guess you've helped me all you can, Doctor."

He nodded. "I agree. But you had to say you were ready to discharge *yourself*, because you've done it for yourself, Mrs. Sumner. You've talked it out, five days a week for six months. You knew it all before you came, really. You just had to think it through out loud, with a stranger. You know where the guilts began and how they grew and why they led you where they did. And you understand yourself—as much as people ever can understand themselves. Psychiatry isn't a magic cure. It's more like the adult spring housecleaning of a childish mind." He studied her closely. "You've grown up. I'm sorry your husband has refused help, Mrs. Sumner. Sweeping away your early cobwebs unfortunately won't necessarily take the broom to his."

"I know. But at least I may have a better perspective on Bryce's problems now that I have some knowledge of my own." She stood up. "Goodbye, Doctor. Thank you."

He rose and shook hands. "Goodbye, Mrs. Sumner."

At the door, she paused. "Wish me luck?"

"I don't put much trust in that fickle lady. I'd rather wish you courage."

She walked slowly down Park Avenue in the crisp October sunshine, hearing his kind, sensible words. She hadn't answered his last question about what came next, but she knew the answer. If Bryce wouldn't get help, she'd have to leave. He'd become a different man in this half year since Elizabeth's death. He was still gentle, still kind, still, Toni believed, remorseful and in love with her. But they had no marriage. Bryce had been to doctor after doctor, seeking a physical reason for his impotence, refusing to admit that it was caused by his involuntary rejection of his wife. There had been no scenes, no accusations, but they grew further and more politely apart. The marriage had simply expired one golden afternoon on a terrace in California.

Bryce stubbornly refused to believe in its demise. Time and again he tried futilely, almost angrily, to make love to her. She accepted her humiliation and his with understanding and silence. But she did, often, beg him to go, as she was going, for psychiatric help. He flatly refused.

"It's nonsense," he said. "This can't be in my head. I love you, Toni; so there *has* to be a medical reason." But even as he said it, he knew it was a lie. A month before, acting on a doctor's advice, he had gone to a posh call house on the West Side, and there, with a blonde Norwegian girl, he had been as virile as ever. The realization plunged him into despair, increased his hopelessness and self-hatred, and confirmed his belief that no doctor could undo what was bred into his bones. He could not bear the idea of losing Toni and Elieth with her, but he knew she could not live this way. She was twenty-one, passionate and faithful. He could find sex outside his home and remain married. Toni could not, would not, must not even be asked for such a sacrifice. He waited, in pain, for the inevitable. It came the evening after her final visit with Dr. Morrisy.

They kissed Elieth good night and went into the library for their pre-dinner cocktail.

"Dr. Morrisy discharged me today," Toni said. "Or, rather, I discharged myself."

"Oh? Good, honey. Then you think he's helped you?"

"He's helped me help myself, Bryce. It hasn't changed any of the things I've done or given me absolution for them, but it's made me face why I did them. I know my problems started very early." She hestitated. "As yours did, darling."

Bryce busied himself mixing martinis.

"Bryce, look at me," she said. "We both know what's at the root of our problem. Won't you *please* go and talk it out with someone? Please. You say you love me. Do this for my sake and Elieth's if you won't do it for your own."

He came and sat beside her, putting the drinks carefully on the cocktail table.

"I can't, Toni. I just can't. I can't go digging back into those old memories. It would drive me crazy and it wouldn't change anything. Those first fifteen years of my life can't be removed like a tattoo I'm sorry I had. No shrink can help. I'd just end up hating myself even more than I do. And God help me, I'd hate you for making me relive everything I've devoted my life to forgetting. Be patient. We'll work this out."

It was the first time in all these months he'd admitted the real cause of the problem. Toni felt a little surge of hope. At least he wasn't pretending any more. That was something. If only she could persuade him to understand how the racial bias began and convince him it wasn't a chronic, incurable illness.

417

"Darling, I know it would be terribly painful for you. Excruciatingly painful. But isn't it worth it to save us?"

"It would be if it would work, but it won't."

Toni was wild with frustration. They'd been over this a hundred times with the same lack of result. "But you don't know that! You've got to try, Bryce! How can you sit there and say it won't work unless you give it a chance? My God, you're much too intelligent for that!"

He turned on her angrily. "Damn it, Toni, I know how I feel! I feel it every day at the office watching those black upstarts smirking behind my back, just like they laughed at me when I was a kid in Texas! Don't you see? I love you as a woman but I can't touch you as a black woman. Jesus, I know you had nothing to do with what you are, but every time I imagine Charlene in bed with your father my stomach knots up because I know you're the result of it!"

He stopped, horrified by what he'd said. He was remembering a black tart he'd once approached out of bravado, wanting to prove something to his father. He recalled how she'd sneered at him, told him to "go 'way, kid, and come back when you grow up." He'd hated them all then. And he'd never stopped. Now the bigotry he couldn't face, the prejudice he couldn't conquer and the rejection he'd never forget had come back to wound this girl who was fighting to save their marriage. He'd unjustly equated her with ignorance and inferiority and cruelty, when it was he who was ignorant and inferior and cruel. He wanted to beg her forgiveness, plead for mercy. But it was too late and they both knew it.

He hoped she'd scream at him, throw something, call him every dirty name he deserved. If there was a gun nearby she should pick it up and kill me, Bryce thought. I deserve to die for saying those things, but God help me, they're true. I do see Charlene and Jim Jenkins screwing

418

when I try to come near Toni. I do believe that black blood is tainted blood. No head doctor can change that. Nothing can.

Toni said nothing for a long while. She sat stony-still, silent as a statue. At last she reached out and touched his face, lightly, affectionately.

"I'm so sorry for you, Bryce. So desperately sorry."

He couldn't bear her pity, her understanding. Not looking at her, he said, "What do you want to do?"

"I don't think we have much choice, do we? It's no good for you, living like this. And no good for me."

"What about Elieth?"

She wanted to say, bitterly, that he must also feel repelled by his own child. But she couldn't punish him any more than he would forever punish himself. He wasn't responsible for the way he felt. She knew, long before Dr. Morrisy, that she'd been unfair to Bryce by being less than honest before their marriage. Part of this was her fault. But most of all, Bryce didn't need counter-accusations or a vicious striking out at him. He would inflict his own soul lashing, more terrible than anything she could muster. There'd never be a day the rest of his life when he'd forget what he'd said tonight.

"Elieth?" Toni said now. "It would be wrong of us to let her grow up in a house where there is so much torment on both sides. A child can be destroyed by its parents." She wanted to say, "You were," but she refrained. "I want her to come with me, Bryce, but after the . . . after the divorce you'll see her any time you want, of course."

Divorce. The word had a terrible sound of failure, a clanking finality that filled Bryce with actual nausea. He knew it must be the same for Toni, though she held herself tightly in check. No hysterics, he thought. Not a word of hatred or reproach. She had such pride. Hannah Sumner would have called it "Quality." How unspeakable that he should be the one hurling insults at her and her parents when she was the one who'd married the warped offspring of poor white trash! He'd have given his soul to take back the terrible things he'd said, to implore her to give him another chance. He'd go to a psychiatrist, do anything to keep her, even though he didn't believe for a moment that treatment could change the way he felt.

"Toni, please don't say that. Don't talk of divorce. I'll do anything you want. Including seeing a doctor."

"It's not what *I* want, Bryce. It's what *you* have to want. Psychiatry won't help you unless you believe in it. And you don't. You never will. You're not at the point where you feel unable to cope, and that's where you have to be to make it work."

He pleaded with her. "All right, maybe I don't think psychiatry is the answer, but just saying those terrible things aloud to you made me know how insane they are. I can lick it now, Toni. I know I can. Just give me a chance."

She shook her head. "One of the things I've learned is that I'm not superhuman. I can't forget what you said tonight. I'm vulnerable, Bryce. I have feelings. I can't go on living with a man who feels as you do. I am sorry for you, that's true. But I'm sorry for myself as well. I deserve better than this. And so does Elieth. It won't work, Bryce. Too much of the real Bryce Sumner has come out. We can't pretend any more. I wanted our marriage because I loved you. In a way I still do. But I think if you touched me now, I'd be sick."

There was no argument. She couldn't change her mind. She would forgive because she had a heritage of compassion and basic wisdom. And not just for Elizabeth and Charlene, Bryce realized. Part of that containment must

420

have come from Jim Jenkins. God, lend me a little of that pride, he begged. Just enough to get me through this.

"I can't blame you for feeling as you do," he said. "I despise myself. You must despise me, too."

"No, but I've never understood your refusal to help yourself. I know now that it's some very complicated part of you. It's something I can't deal with, Bryce."

He knew he was beaten. "Do you want me to go to a hotel tonight?"

"No need. We have a guest room. Tomorrow we can make other arrangements. Just tell Maria I won't want dinner, will you?" She managed a smile. "I'm not very hungry."

He sat for hours after she left the room, staring at nothing, trying to comprehend that it was over. He remembered all the laughter, the shared jokes, the love-making, the morning in Vermont when Elieth was conceived. He thought back to the night she was born, and understood for the first time what Charlene had meant when she emphasized to Toni that her baby was "everything she'd hoped for . . . like pale porcelain." For an instant he was angry. They'd duped him, made a fool of him. And then he thought, no. I've made a fool of myself.

He was very tired. He looked at his watch. Three o'clock in the morning. He'd been sitting for hours. He made his way to the guest room, passing the nursery. On impulse he opened the door noiselessly and tiptoed to the bassinet. The tiny night light enabled him to make out the innocent, beautiful face of his daughter.

"Poor little girl," he said. "You deserved a better father."

Softly he dropped a kiss on the delicate, curved cheek. "Goodbye, Elieth. Take care of your mommy."

He'd already left the house next morning when Toni came out of what had been their room. She'd slept barely at all. She'd heard Bryce come down the hall and knew he was stopping in the baby's room. For a moment she had almost weakened, her heart wrapped in pain at the mental image of him going in to look at the child he loved so much. A few months before she might have called out to him, might have given him the final chance he'd asked for. But with Dr. Morrisy's help she'd stopped unconsciously thinking of herself as some eternally forbearing creature whose only mission in life was to make everybody else happy. She'd learned a kind of healthy selfishness, not goddess-like, perhaps, but infinitely more real.

Clenching her fists, she'd let him go on to the guest room. And then she lay sleepless, as she had that night six months before in Elizabeth's house. But this time there was no pathetic self-delusion, no stubborn refusal to face the truth.

Her mind had reached back to her childhood, remembering how her father had talked to her after a cruel Nadine Thompson had called Jim a "nigger." What had he said? Something about none of them being any different than they'd been before; that no words could change the essence of people's actions or behavior. She wished Bryce could have heard Jim Jenkins. She was the same woman she'd been when Bryce had found her so physically desirable. She hadn't changed except in her husband's mind. He had rejected her as the epitome of all he despised and looked down on. He hadn't rejected Toni Jenkins; only a half-black woman who wore her skin.

Was it only this afternoon that she'd given Dr. Morrisy a capsule description of reality? It seemed she was bracing herself even then for what was to come. I *have* learned from my mistakes, she told herself fiercely. I *do* know what I can handle and what I can't. God willing, I'll do better from here on. I'll never do to Elieth what my beloved, mistaken father unwittingly did to me.

Only then had she allowed the tears to come. They slid silently from her wide-open eyes and she welcomed the release they brought. She'd lost the only two men she'd truly loved—through stupid self-sacrifice, through an imagined obligation. No more, Toni thought. If there's ever another chance for me I'll meet it like a woman. Courage, the doctor had said. He was right. She'd depended too long and too childishly on luck.

In the morning she found Bryce's note waiting for her.

"Darling," he wrote, "I won't try to excuse myself for the way I behaved last night. I won't ask you to forgive me. But I do beg for time before you take a step as final as divorce. Let me try to come to my senses, somehow, before we rip up our lives and Elieth's. I'm moving to the Plaza today. You stay in the apartment. Everything will be taken care of as usual—you have no money problems, at least. Please agree to this 'trial separation' for a little while. Bear with me just a little longer because I love you so much. Bryce."

She read the words twice, thoughtfully, wondering how Bryce expected to "come to his senses, somehow." There was no way he could. He'd never really change. The man who'd spewed such venom last night had been weaned on hatred. His insecurity—for all the surface poise—was so deeply ingrained that he'd never rise above it. Nor could she. Bryce Sumner could never again regain his wife's admiration and respect. And without those things he'd never regain her love.

She would go along with his plea for time before she divorced him. But it was only a game being played for his peace of mind in the next few anguished weeks. He could have his "trial separation" if it meant so much to him. She was in no hurry to divorce him. There was no one else she intended to marry. But it was finished. Toni knew it, just as, in his heart, Bryce knew it too. He was only playing for time, unwilling to face failure of any kind, as he'd always been unwilling to face it.

Time was a small gift she could give him, wrapped in a tissue of polite lies. Inevitably, though she'd be an Indian giver, she'd have to take back this final present. It was only a question of when.

Unaware of Toni's marital problems, Charlene was surprised when her daughter called to say that she and Bryce had separated. Toni sounded very calm, almost passive as she broke the news. She gave Charlene only the bare facts.

"There's so much to tell you, Mother," she'd said, "but I'll wait until we're together. I'm not filing for divorce yet. Bryce has asked me not to rush into that and I won't, although we both know it will be the eventual outcome."

"I'm sorry, darling. Are you all right?"

"Yes, I really am. A little sad, a lot regretful, but I'm okay. It was, as the saying goes, an amicable parting."

"What are your plans? Are you going to stay there?"

"For the moment. Bryce is living at the Plaza. What about you? Have you and Laurel reached any decision about the business?"

"We were talking about it only last night," Charlene said. "We've had a good offer and I think we're going to sell. Laurel's getting on. She's only a few years younger than your grandmother was, you know. And I have no talent for business." A thought struck Charlene. "I don't suppose you'd like to come out here and learn how to run it, would you? Maybe the timing is just right."

"No," Toni said, "I don't think so. I'm not really interested in that kind of thing either. I'm not sure I want to stay in New York, but things have happened too fast for me to know exactly where I want to be. Maybe California, but not in the decorating business. Maybe some place totally different. I just don't know right now."

"I understand, dear. You're wise to take your time. That was Peter's advice to me and I'm glad I took it. Like I'm glad I've stayed here in Pasadena. Much as I love Laurel, I never could live with her. Nor she with me. Two grown-up women under one roof is an invitation to disaster."

The implication was clear. Charlene did not expect her to come home, nor would she ever consider moving in with her daughter. She was making that known to Toni, in a thoughtful way, reassuring the soon-to-be-divorced daughter that she need feel no obligation to live with the widowed mother. Once again Charlene was affirming Toni's right to a free choice, as she had after Jim died. Toni was touched by the tactful, subtle message.

"How about coming for a visit, Mom? I haven't seen you in more than six months and you haven't seen your growing granddaughter. She's almost ready to walk, believe it or not! If you don't hurry up, she'll be playing hopscotch in Central Park!" Toni's voice sobered. "Seriously, would you come for a little while as soon as you can? I need you."

Charlene realized again, as she often had before, that Toni really had no close friends. She knew dozens of women, but had taken none of them as a dear and trusted confidante. Not since childhood had Toni had a "best friend," someone to whom she could talk freely and with certainty that her secrets would be kept. I'm a fine one to criticize, Charlene thought. After childhood, I never had a close woman friend either. But I had more valid reasons. I never dared hope that another woman would understand my marriage. I wish I had such a friend now, she thought.

425

I wish Toni had one. Elizabeth was luckier than we; she had Laurel.

"Mother? Are you still there?"

"Yes, darling, I'm here. Just thinking about your invitation. I'd love to come, Toni. Might be a very good time, as a matter of fact. I need to talk to Peter about this business offer. I can save him a trip out here."

Toni's relief and pleasure came through. "That's marvelous! When shall I expect you?"

"In about a week. And, Toni, would you call Peter at his office and tell him I'll be in town next Thursday? You don't mind, do you, now that you've met him?"

"No, of course not. Shall I ask him to dinner?"

"That would be lovely." Charlene paused. "You're really okay, kitten?"

"I really am. You'll see when you get here."

Chapter 30

Joanne Richards sat back in the upholstered swivel desk chair and looked with satisfaction at her beautiful new office. It had been one of her demands when she took the job as fashion editor of *Enchantress,* moving after almost ten years at *Glamour.* Ambiance and money, with a generous dollop of status thrown in. That's where it was for her, at least in the career department. She liked being well known in the international fashion world. She liked being important at the magazine and commanding a large, super-chic office, expensively decorated and personalized with pictures and knickknacks that had nothing to do with business. She could work well only in such an atmosphere. Apparently she needed the security of glamorous surroundings to reinforce her belief in her own ability.

A devoted lover would have helped, too. Unfortunately, they were not as easy to come by as rosewood desks and Louis XIV side chairs. Not that Joanne didn't have her share of escorts and lovers. At thirty, she was good-looking, amusing and successful. Too successful, she sometimes thought. Her high-poweredness scared away the kind of men she really liked, the ones with whom she could have considered some kind of permanent or even semi-permanent arrangement. She had her occasional flings. Sex was an enjoyable and necessary part of a well-rounded life and she liked the men she slept with. She just didn't love them.

Glancing idly through the morning mail, she thought of her mother. It was one of Ann's aberrations that Joanne was a tramp. It wasn't true, of course. Jo was simply part of the "new morality" that took a sensible, realistic, discriminating attitude about sex. You took love from those who gave you pleasure and you reciprocated. Simple as that. You didn't get hung up in possessiveness and jealousy and demands for eternal faithfulness. You made love, enjoyed it and felt relaxed and free. Or so, at least, you convinced yourself, most of the time. Ann would never have understood that. Not even when she was capable of understanding anything.

Funny, Joanne mused. Ann was light-years away from her mother, just as I am from her. From all she'd heard of her grandmother, Elizabeth had been a free spirit. She'd broken all the rules. She'd had a married lover once, and later a husband years younger than herself with whom she'd been happy. She'd left a rotten first husband and struck out on her own, taking her children with her. She was her own person, even way back in the 1930s when it was much tougher for women to support themselves. Jo had heard a lot about her from Peter, who'd known her early, and more from Alan, who'd met her late. At least Alan knew her, Jo thought. I wish I'd had that chance. Maybe I'd understand how she could have produced two such different daughters: Ann so priggish and conventional; Charlene, who sounded so loving and so secure that she could marry a black man and never apologize for it. I wish Elizabeth and I could have swapped philosophies. I'm sure she must have been

428

amused by all this talk of "liberation"; she was a liberated woman long before it became fashionable to be one.

The intercom buzzed and Jo's secretary said, "Your father's on the line, Miss Richards."

Jo picked up the phone. "Hi, sweetie," she said. "How are the habeases corpusing this morning?"

She loved to hear him laugh as he did now, briefly, affectionately.

"Is that the extent of your Latin, God help us?"

"Yes. It's like my menu French. Get me past *veau* and I'm a dead veal. What's going on?"

"I have a dinner invitation for you," Peter said.

"Great. Is he married or gay?"

"Aren't there any other choices?"

"Not in my age bracket."

"As a matter of fact, it's not a man I want you to meet, it's a woman. More correctly, two women. Your Aunt Charlent is arriving next week. Toni called to ask me to dinner Friday evening and I asked if I could bring you, if you're free. I'd like you to know them, Jo. Charlene is a very special lady, and though I've hardly said a dozen words to Toni, I think she's special, too. At any rate, she sounded warm and cordial and eager to see both of us."

"I guess her mother is coming because of the separation, huh?"

Peter was surprised. "How on earth did you know about that? Toni was very forthright about it when she called me but it only happened a couple of days ago."

"Darling, New York is one big telephone party line. There are no secrets from the people on it. As it happens, my secretary's roommate works at Bryce Sumner's agency. The feedback is that the great man is sulking in his tent at the Plaza and the marriage has gone 'Tilt.' I'm sorry for Toni. That is, I guess I am. I never had a lofty regard for the great Bryce Sumner. In fact, I think they coined the word 'superficial' in his honor. Deep down he's really shallow."

Peter ignored the little joke. "I didn't know you knew him."

"Don't, really, except through business. But I've seen and heard enough to decide that guys like that are all right but I wouldn't want my daughter to marry one." Jo paused. "I gather Toni's taking it in stride."

"I wouldn't know, honey. She sounded very composed and she came right out and said that Bryce wouldn't be there Friday because they'd separated. I suppose she wanted to spare us any awkward questions. But I don't know any more than that and I don't know Toni well enough to ask questions."

"Didn't you get to know her when you were in California?"

"Not really. She and Bryce only stayed a couple of days and Alan and I didn't intrude, for obvious reasons. Of course, I've heard a great deal about Toni from Charlene."

Jo barely heard the last sentence. She hadn't thought about Alan when she'd heard of Toni's separation. He was still mad about her. She knew that from his letters. Maybe now . . . Hell, she was thinking like a soap opera! Toni had been separated from her husband for two days and already Jo was reuniting her with her lost love.

"I'd love to go Friday," she said now. "Shall I call Toni and tell her I'll be delighted?"

"No. I said if I didn't call back we'd both be there about seven-thirty. Very informal. Just the four of us."

"Peter Richards and his harem."

The low laugh came again. "Well, I'll tell you, if I had to choose three ladies I'd most like to be with I couldn't do better than this all-star cast. Pick you up about seven?"

"Fine." She hesitated. "How's Mother?"

"No change," he said. "Goodbye, darling."

No change. Jo felt as though she'd been hearing those words all her life, as though she would hear them the rest of her life. It had been more than a year since she'd even gone through the motions of visiting Ann. This strange, brooding woman who was her mother had not even known her the last time she went with Peter to the sanitarium. Even then she'd only gone to keep him company. Why didn't you let me love you? Jo silently asked Ann Richards. Why were you always so angry? Didn't you ever care for any of us?

Looking toward Charlene at the other end of the table, Toni thought she'd never seen her mother more beautiful. In the soft flickering glow of the candlelight, she reminded Toni of a young Elizabeth, smiling, gracious, involving Peter, who sat at her left, and Joanne at her right in easy, undemanding conversation.

Though it had been her own idea to invite Peter to dinner, Toni had felt uneasy about the involuntary suggestion. He was her uncle, but he was, first of all, Alan's father. He'd been charming on the phone, never missing a beat even when she told him, as she felt she had to, why Bryce wouldn't be with them. When Peter had asked politely if he might bring his daughter, Toni had instantly and enthusiastically said yes, and then had been even more apprehensive about that. She'd at least seen Peter briefly when Elizabeth died, but Joanne was still only a voice on the telephone from the hospital that awful morning when Ann tried to kill herself. Or pretended to try. Joanne had been warm and friendly in those few moments long ago. She did not sound like the big lady executive Toni knew her to be. She'd seemed genuinely happy that Alan had found the girl he wanted.

How will she feel about me now? Toni wondered, putting down the phone after her conversation with Peter. Will she hate me for hurting her brother, for running away like a stupid, selfish little coward? Or will she understand?

It was obvious from the moment she came in not only that she understood but that she truly wanted to be friends. She didn't give Toni one of those phony "cat-pack kisses" as *Women's Wear Daily* called them. She took her cousin's hand warmly, looked straight into her eyes and said, "Toni. At long last. I'm so very glad to see you."

Joanne had set the tone for the evening with those simple, sincere words. Sitting at the head of her table, Toni felt that she was with her family. It was a good feeling, safe and peaceful. For a few hours there was no Ann Richards, no Bryce Sumner for any of them. The talk was light and cheerful.

Joanne was hilariously funny about her job, regaling them with anecdotes about the mad creatures at *Enchantress*.

"Did you know that Laurel Lane was once editor of that magazine?" Charlene asked her.

For a moment Joanne looked blank. "Laurel Lane? Oh yes, of course. I've seen her name on the masthead of some of the old issues. She was there very early, wasn't she?"

"In the forties," Charlene said. "She was your grandmother's best friend. She left the magazine to go into Elizabeth and Tony's decorating business. She's run it ever since. Since Mother had her stroke, I mean. And even now." For a moment Charlene looked troubled. "I hope we're doing the right thing, selling the business. I don't know what Laurel will do without it."

Peter leaned over and patted her hand. "Laurel will be fine. You know she'll keep busy, Charley. She'll be into

432

all kinds of projects. I think she'll be glad to be relieved of that enormous responsibility."

Charlene looked at him gratefully.

"How strange that I should end up on the same magazine," Jo said. "The fashion business must have been even crazier in those days."

Charlene laughed, her anxiety dissipated by Peter's reassurance. "I'm sure it was. Laurel and Mother used to tell some of the wildest stories about their early days in New York."

They began to talk easily about Elizabeth. Charlene and Peter carried most of the conversation, some of it going back to the days when Charlene was a little girl, hopelessly smitten, she said humorously, with the glamorous grown-up man her sister married. But they did not dwell on Ann. They talked affectionately of Elizabeth, remembering little incidents that happened long before Toni was born, some of them even before Joanne.

"Do you remember the day?" Peter would ask Charlene, launching into some mischievous escapade of Elizabeth's. Charlene would nod and respond with "And how about the time . . ." recalling some endearing, outrageous incident.

The two young women listened, enraptured. Toni had heard some of the stories, but many were new to her. She felt again the pangs of love and longing for Elizabeth, happy she had shared some of the courage and humor of that remarkable woman, sorry that Joanne had not had the same privilege. Jo obviously felt the same.

"She sounds like the original Auntie Mame," Joanne said almost wistfully. "She must have been wonderful."

"She was," Charlene said. "Wonderful and gentle and funny and so damned brave." She looked at Peter. "Mother would love to know that we're sitting here remembering her with laughter. Lord, how she'd hate a

433

tableful of mournful faces!" She turned to Jo. "She'd have so much liked to know you as an adult, Joanne. She adored Alan. I used to find them giggling together like two kids. It was delightful to see. I could never think of them as grandmother and grandson. They were more like two happy, conspiratorial equals. She was that way with everyone she loved. I don't think she ever thought about age differences. And yet she'd lived long enough and hard enough to support all of us with her wisdom and her faith."

There was a little silence and then Charlene said briskly, "Well, now, enough of that! I feel as though Mother is right here, probably criticizing your centerpiece, Toni, beautiful as it is."

Toni smiled. "I know. She'd have said, 'Too sterile, Toni, my love. Flowers shouldn't look posed, all rigidly arranged like a well-choreographed ballet! They should be allowed to fall into graceful positions, like prima ballerinas!' I feel guilty every time I put a done-up centerpiece on my table. I remember how many of them Grandmother pulled apart and redid and how much more beautiful they were that way. But the best, of course, came from her own garden. In New York I miss the luxury of growing my own."

"I always would," Charlene said. "I don't think I could ever live where things didn't grow outside my window."

"You two flower lovers should come with me at the beginning of December," Joanne said suddenly. "I'm going to Haiti with a troupe of models and a photographer to find some lush green backgrounds. We have to photograph early-summer clothes in the tropics before Christmas to get them on the newsstands in the April issue."

"Haiti?" Peter asked. "Is that safe, Jo?"

"A lot safer than Central Park from what I hear. Now that the new government is in, people are flocking back

434

there. It's a beautiful island, still unspoiled, but probably not for long, thanks to horrors like me who'll begin to publicize it in fashion pictures."

"I sounds exciting," Toni said. "Voodoo and jungle drums and every other person a spy."

Jo laughed. "I'm not so sure about that. Most of the voodoo is a phony performance specially set up for the tourists and there's been some talk that the bongo drums have goat hair that spreads some kind of awful disease. As for the spies, I think you've read one too many Graham Greene novels. But it really is a great spot. Perfect weather. Marvelous hotels. No crime, no drugs." She looked squarely at Toni. "And it's becoming *the* place for painless divorce."

Her head-on recognition of Toni's problem surprised her companions. They'd all been careful to avoid any mention of Bryce just as, Toni realized, there'd been only passing references to Alan. Charlene had been the only one to even mention him. They were tiptoeing around the delicate areas of their lives. It was wrong. They were all the family that was left unless you counted Peter's other son, who seemed not to have come into the conversation either.

Toni returned Joanne's gaze calmly. "That's something to think about," she said. "Maybe we could have lunch next week and talk about it?"

"You're on," Jo said. "Name the spot. My expense account has no conscience."

"Like them?" Charlene asked after Peter and Joanne left.

"Very much. He's a terrific man, Mom. And he's obviously crazy about you."

"Don't be tasteless, Toni! He's my sister's husband!"

She was a little girl again, gently but firmly repri-

435

manded. I'll always be a little girl to Mother, Toni thought. Even if I'm seventy-five and a grandmother myself.

"I'm sorry," she said. "I didn't mean . . ."

It was Charlene's turn to be repentant. "No, *I'm* the one who's sorry, for snapping at you that way. I don't know what's the matter with me lately. Too much time to think about myself, I guess. I seem to take offense at every little thing. I can remember feeling like this only once before, when your father was so involved with the KJ-16 that he hardly knew I was alive. I was jealous of that damned airplane. It was more demanding than a mistress." She smiled. "And now if I could only have him back I wouldn't care if he was working on six new airplanes. Being alone is no good, Toni, and I haven't adjusted to it. I will because I must, but I miss a man. Not just physically. For the way he fills a house and a life." She looked searchingly at her daughter. "I'm sorry you're going to be alone, baby. You are, aren't you? This is no trial separation in your mind. You're never going back to Bryce."

Toni had been truthful with her about the reason for the breakup. She had spared Charlene the ugly repetition of Bryce's helpless hatred for all Negroes, but she had to tell her that Bryce's discovery of her heritage had led to impotence, an impotence that he refused to believe was psychogenic. She could not tell her mother that even if Bryce changed his mind about analysis, it was too late for a reconcilliation. She had stopped loving him the night he aired his thoughts about Charlene and Jim and herself. Could you stop loving someone just like that? she wondered. Perhaps she had never really loved Bryce Sumner at all. She'd never quite admitted that, not even to Dr. Morrisy. She'd always talked about how much *he* loved *her,* how good he was to her, how grateful she was to him for giving her Elieth. In their moments of passion she'd told Bryce she loved him and believed it. But she knew that love was much more than sex. That was only part of it. It she was in love with her husband, she'd stay with him, even if he never touched her again. She'd treat the impotence like some crippling disease, feel about it as she would if the man she loved lost his arms or legs. You don't abandon a cripple you really love, Toni thought. That's what Bryce is, an emotional cripple. And I don't love him enough to be his nurse.

"Thank God for one thing," Charlene said, "you're young enough to start a new life. I'm grateful this didn't happen to you twenty years from now. You'll meet someone else, Toni, even if you don't want to think about that right now."

Charlene was right. Toni didn't want to think about it. But she was certain of one thing. If she ever did meet a man she could love she'd hold back nothing from him. Dr. Morrisy had helped her see how infantile her reasoning had been. Charlene had told her from the start that she should be honest, but she'd been too caught up in her crusade to listen to her mother. Or her grandmother.

"I'm grateful to you for so many things, Mother, and right now I'm especially grateful for one."

"What's that, darling?"

"You have the good grace not to say 'I told you so.'"

Two days later, Joanne rang up.

"I called to make my manners," she said. "It was one of the better evenings, Toni." Without waiting for an answer, she rushed on in her brisk, decisive way. "Also, I really meant it about Haiti. Can you have lunch tomorrow and talk about it?"

"I'd love to have lunch. As for Haiti, well, I'm not so sure about that, but we'll see."

"Fair enough. Grenouille at one o'clock?"

Toni hesitated. Not La Grenouille. La Grenouille was Bryce. The place where their romance began, the romantic, flower-filled restaurant that had seemed to symbolize a happy future was not the spot in which she wished to discuss its end. She hadn't been there since she and Bryce returned from California.

"How about Orsini's instead?" Toni asked. "I assume you have enough influence to get a reservation only twenty-four hours ahead."

Jo laughed. "Kiddo, with *Enchantress* behind me I have enough influence to even name the table. See you then."

Toni dressed carefully for her luncheon date. Until six months ago she'd kept up to date on fashion through her free-lance assignments, but since the trouble began she'd not accepted any jobs. She blamed it on lack of time. There were the sessions with Dr. Morrisy that cut into her day, and she told herself she wanted to spend more time with Elieth, who was now getting to an alert, interesting stage. Neither was a valid excuse. She simply was too filled with anxiety to concentrate on making appointments, taking on work that had to be rapidly and expertly executed. She even thought that a full-time wife and mother, rested and relaxed at the end of the day instead of rushed and harried, might ease Bryce's attitude. It was a ridiculous, convoluted thought. Her work had nothing to do with their problems, but she'd grasped at anything that might indicate how hard she was trying to hold her marriage together.

This desperate thinking went through her mind now as she prepared to meet Joanne. She'd not been immersed in fashion, but she was still aware of it. It was important to look well when you lunched with the most important fashion editor in America, maybe in the world. Orsini's was a gathering place for retailers, manufacturers and members of the fashion press. She didn't want to "disgrace" her hostess by looking like a "country cousin." The phrase made her smile. She had almost forgotten that they really were cousins. Jo seemed more like what Toni had always wished for—a good woman friend.

Charlene came in as Toni stood staring at her closet, trying to decide what to wear.

"You have the intent look of a woman dressing for a big date instead of a girls' lunch," Charlene said easily.

"In a way it *is* a big date. We're going to Orsini's and if I know anything, Eugenia Shepard may be there making notes for her column and the *Women's Wear* photographer will be hanging around the entrance. Not that they care about me, but Joanne is news wherever she appears. I want to look right."

Charlene tried to look impressed. "I had no idea it was so important. I figured you could eat fettuccine wearing just about anything. So what's it going to be—your St. Laurent pants suit or your Bill Blass dress?"

"Neither." Toni grinned. "It's Anne Klein all the way. Skirt and blazer. Understated and casual. Well, maybe just a little status, like the Gucci shoes and the Hermés bag."

"And the Givenchy scarf and Cartier watch."

"Rat!" Toni said affectionately. "You know I'm a phony, don't you?"

"I think you're the realest young woman I know. I also think you're giving a lot of serious thought to an easy divorce in Haiti."

"Would you approve, Mom?"

"Don't ask me to help you make that decision. That's between you and Bryce. I told you the other night I don't think you're going back to him, but you did promise to give him time. It's only been a couple of weeks, Toni."

"I know. But we haven't even spoken on the phone. I thought he'd want to come and see Elieth by now."

"Maybe he needs time to sort out his thinking before he sees either of you. I suspect he's not a man to put himself in a vulnerable spot. Not until he's had time to consider all the pros and cons. He wants to make the final decisions. He might even contest a divorce if you asked for one now."

Toni looked at her inquiringly.

"I spoke to Peter yesterday," Charlene said. "He advises you to go slowly. A Haitian divorce might not stand up one day if you do it without mutual consent. Bryce could even make a claim on Elieth if he chose, if not now, sometime in the future."

"Oh, no!"

"Well, nobody's sure about these out-of-the-country divorces, dear. Just promise me you'll check it all out thoroughly before you take any giant steps. After all, you're not really in a rush, are you?"

"No," Toni said slowly, "not really. It's just that I hate loose ends, unfinished business. It makes my life seem messy to be married but not really married. I know it's physically and emotionally finished, so why not legally, so that Bryce and I can get on with the business of our separate lives? Anyway, at the moment I couldn't do anything without talking to him. And who knows? He may already have decided he wants a divorce."

"You'd better get dressed," Charlene said. "It's quarter past twelve. I'm going to borrow my granddaughter this afternoon, if that's okay. I thought we'd go to the park and visit the seals. They're so marvelously uncomplicated."

It was five minutes past one when Toni stumbled into the blackness that pervaded the foyer of Orsini's. It always irritated her that the restaurant was so dimly lit that you could break your neck on the little steps inside the door because your eyes hadn't adjusted from the brightness of the outside world. She groped her way to the stairs that led to the second floor, the "in" room for lunching. Tino, the handsome young maître d' with a prodigious memory, greeted her by her name.

"Signora Summer! Nice to see you! Whom are you meeting?"

She shook hands warmly with him. "I'm lunching with Miss Richards."

"But of course. I have her table by the window. You are first. Would you like to be seated?"

She followed him down the narrow aisle, past the rows of already filled tables. She recognized the lady president of a smart specialty store, the fashion editor of *Women's Wear*, two limp-wristed Seventh Avenue designers and Eugenia Shepard with the wife of a cosmetics tycoon. None of them gave her more than a passing glance. They would respond quite differently when Joanne came sailing in.

She did, ten minutes later, stopping at all the tables, having her hand grabbed at, shaken or kissed, depending upon the proclivity of the men who greeted her. She exchanged little in-the-air kisses with some of the women, waved airily at others and arrived on the banquette next to Toni full of apologies.

"Sorry you had to wait," Jo said. "I detest people who are late, but it couldn't be helped. Last-minute crisis. I hope you ordered a drink."

"I've only been here a few minutes myself. No problem."

They ordered Campari and Jo settled back. "Well now, Cousin. What are we going to do about you?"

Toni laughed. "Do you always go at things so directly?"

441

"Not always. I just have the feeling that with you I can." She dropped the flippancy. "You see, Toni, I know a lot about you. From Alan. I like everything I've heard. I even had to respect you when you let my mother's act put you off. Frankly, I thought you were dumb to buy it, but I could see how any decent girl with a conscience might. Alan made me understand that and a lot of other things. He loved you very much."

The past tense made Toni feel unreasonably sad. "How is he, Joanne?"

"All right, I guess. I haven't seen him in months but we keep in touch. I'm very close to my baby brother, and very proud of him. Both his books have done well and he's moving along on the third one, now that the screen adaptation on the first is just about complete." She looked searchingly at Toni. "Did you read *Limbo?*"

"Yes. It was a lovely story."

"Story my derriere! It was a love letter to you."

Toni couldn't bear it. She didn't want to talk about Alan or any of that. She didn't want to think how she'd blundered in the past, how she'd never have another chance. He'd loved her, Jo had said. Which meant he must be over it now. Why not, for God's sake? Did she expect him to mope around forever while she got married and had a baby? She remembered those few minutes at Elizabeth's memorial service. He hadn't said he still loved her; it had been the other way around.

"Tell me about you," Toni said, determined to get off the subject of Alan.

Jo gave her a what's-with-that-cliché look and then said kindly. "Not much to tell, Toni. Business life sensational. Sex life adequate. Love life nil. My story in three sentences."

"What about your mother? And your other brother?"

Jo looked pensive. "I guess my reaction to them is

442

numbness. That sounds awful, doesn't it? But it's true. I can't grieve for Mother because she never was the way I thought mothers should be—warm and loving and understanding. I can't remember her ever kissing me. Isn't that strange? She's just a poor, sad woman I don't see and try not to think about. I've missed a lot, but then so has she. As for Peter Richards the Third, he's a bloody bore. So is his wife. So, probably, is his son. I feel no obligation toward them. Just because he's my brother I don't feel that I have to love him, or even like him. The way I look at it, given a choice I'd never pick him as a friend. Now Dad's a different story. I've only really gotten to know him in the last few years and God does he have guts! And integrity. And so much love with nowhere to lavish it. He's a terrific human being. Better than any of the rest of us, except maybe Alan."

They were getting back to it again.

"Tell me about the Haiti trip," Toni said hurriedly.

"Not much more to tell than what you heard at dinner. I'm leaving December fifth with three models and a photographer. We'll be gone about ten days, taking pictures for the summer issues. I'm driving Seventh Avenue crazy nudging them for summer clothes while they're still showing resort and spring, but they'll come through. You want to go along? I think you could even do some modeling if you want to, so the trip would be on *Enchantress*."

"It would be fun," Toni said wistfully, "but I'm not sure I should. Not just yet."

"If you're thinking about the divorce thing, forget it. I can see you're not ready for that decision. I was being my usual untactful self. Why don't you come just for kicks? Seems to me after all you've gone through in the past couple of years you could use a vacation."

Toni wavered. Jo was right. She did need to get away, but there were other things to consider.

"I don't know. There's Elieth."

"Hell, Toni, it's only ten days. You have a good nurse. Or if you don't feel comfortable leaving Elieth with her, I bet Charlene would love to take care of her, either here or in California."

"All right," Toni said suddenly, "I'll do it! I'd love to! But I don't want to do any modeling. I'll just be happy to tag along with the group. I need a change, and I'd never go anywhere alone."

"Good girl! I'll have them make a reservation for you at the Oloffson as soon as I get back to the office."

They chatted amiably through the rest of the lunch, avoiding all the too personal things but knowing that a very special friendship was being born. They felt good about it. It was a relationship both women needed.

Chapter 31

It was the first week in November before Bryce called Toni, nearly a month after he'd moved to the hotel. In the beginning, there had been dozens of times when he'd thought of calling her, but he didn't know what to say. She probably felt he was heartless not to have come to see Elieth or even phoned to ask about her. Bryce took the attitude that if anything was wrong, he'd hear about it. He knew that Toni had plenty of money in her checking account and access to their joint one, so he wasn't worried about her financial condition. He missed her and yet there was a certain peace in being away from her, after all the months of turmoil and soul searching. Bryce didn't like soul searching. There were too many things about himself he did not wish to admit, even to himself.

He could never admit them to a doctor. His certainty of that increased every day. He knew it was probably wrong to feel as he did, but that was something he couldn't help. Toni, on the other hand, had done something she could have helped. She had deceived him, married him under false pretenses. As he searched for self-vindication he even wondered if she'd deliberately forgotten her pills that weekend in Vermont. Perhaps she wanted to have a baby as insurance, something to hold him when he found out what she really was. It even could be that all that stuff about Jim Jenkins had been a fabrication, all that melodramatic outpouring about her father begging her to keep quiet and killing himself to make sure she did. Slowly he began to build the fortress of his self-defense until he really saw himself as the injured party.

Bit by bit he encouraged his own anger and finally began to believe that he had been ill used. He'd even been honest about his background. Too damned honest, he reflected. Toni was the only one in his present world who knew about his past. He couldn't really believe that she'd ever say anything. Still it would have been better if he'd not been so open.

He also succeeded in convincing himself that they had had nothing in common but sex. As he slowly shifted the blame for all that had happened, he rationalized that all he missed was her body. He almost forgot that his feeling of racial superiority had made him unable to enter it for more than six months. Toni was the one who'd caused that, too. He was still lusty and passionate and he went in search of other women. They were not hard to find. He only had to pick up the phone and tell his former bedmates he was on the loose again.

The reaffirmation of his virility with a woman he didn't have to pay gave the assurance he needed. He stopped feeling guilty, almost stopped thinking about his wife and child. He was now certain that the marriage should end, but the businessman side of him told that it was important to make Toni ask for the divorce. Otherwise, it would cost him a fortune. He had left their home, and the law could call that abandonment. And God knows he could never say in court *why* he'd left. He'd be the laughingstock of the town if people found out he'd been duped into marry-

446

ing a mulatto girl and having a child with her. Even the baby now seemed more hers than his.

He'd be willing to make a fair settlement on Toni and insure Elieth's support. She could even keep the damn apartment. But Bryce Sumner was not about to be wiped out financially by some sentimental judge who would award Toni everything he'd worked nearly twenty years to get.

The best thing, he decided finally, was to drift and let Toni suggest the divorce. He discussed this with his lawyer, who agreed that his thinking was sound.

"If you're in no hurry," the lawyer said, "play along. She's very young. She'll find somebody. But meantime, Bryce, watch your own step. If she catches you in bed, she's hit the jackpot. By the way, you don't want to get married again, do you? Now now anyway?"

"God, no! Not *ever*! I've had it, Sol. I don't think I'd have married in the first place if I hadn't thought Toni was going to marry somebody else.

The lawyer smiled. "You're not the first guy to fall for that trick. If it *was* a trick. I'm not sure. I met Toni a few times. She seemed charming and I thought you were both very much in love. She doesn't seem like the kind of woman who'd be devious and spiteful. What the hell happened between you two anyhow?"

Bryce set his jaw firmly. "Call it incompatability, okay?"

"Sure, if you say so. Isn't *everything?*"

His call in November was part of the "playing along." It wouldn't do to let Toni start feeling resentful of his neglect. He knew now what to say: all the proper, concerned things with a slight hint of regret and maybe a tinge of loneliness. He had no clue that Toni would have welcomed his suggestion of a divorce and would have asked for nothing for herself. She did think, if it ever came to

447

that, that he should help support Elieth. As for the rest, she could still earn a respectable living. She didn't believe in alimony in cases such as theirs. She was young, strong and moderately talented. Bryce owed her nothing. She believed she owed him nothing but the time he had asked for.

The sound of his voice made her tremble. Not with desire. She could not want a man who did not want her. But she was too sensitive, too sentimental to feel nothing when she spoke to the man who had been her lover and husband and who was the father of her child. It was difficult to sound cool and composed with so many old memories flooding back in those first few seconds on the daughter.

"How are you?" Bryce asked. "And how's Elieth?"

No reproaches, she warned herself. No overt hurt feelings because he hadn't called earlier to ask about his daughter.

"We're both fine. Mother was here for a couple of weeks. She went home yesterday. How are *you*, Bryce?"

"Managing. It's been hellishly busy at the office. I meant to call sooner."

"It's all right. I know how complicated things get."

It was an overpolite, strained conversation, as nonproductive as a talk between strangers. Toni waited.

"I have to go out of town for a week or so," he said finally. "I wanted to let you know. If you need anything, the office will know where I am. *Do* you need anything, Toni?"

If it hadn't been so sad, she would have laughed. She wanted to say, yes, I need several things. I need someone to love me, knowing what I am. I need warmth and companionship and understanding. And I need freedom from you, Bryce, to try and find them. Instead, she said quietly, "No, there's nothing we need. I appreciate your having your secretary call and tell me to forward the household bills to your office." Damn. It came out sounding like an accusation and he immediately interpreted it that way.

"I suppose you think I should have called you myself."

"No. I didn't mean it that way."

"It certainly sounded like it."

There was a change in him, Toni suddenly realized. The man who had left a month before, pathetically upset and confused, begging her for time, was now almost belligerent. It was as though he was trying to provoke her. Into what? Into asking him to return? Or, the thought dawned slowly, had Bryce decided he wanted out, but wasn't willing to say so?

If the latter were true, that would be his way. He had too much foolish pride to admit that the marriage was a failure and that he wanted to end it. He would need the poor comfort of believing that he had tried to do everything and that Toni had quit. It never occurred to her that Bryce was concerned about what it would cost him in money if he instigated the divorce. She spoke cautiously.

"Is something wrong?"

The voice became testier. "What the hell kind of question is that?"

"I just meant you don't sound like yourself. You seem angry."

"What do you want me to do, Toni, jump for joy? I'm separated from my wife and child. I'm living in a lousy hotel room and eating in restaurants. That doesn't exactly add up to making a man happy."

But the tone had softened. He realized he'd been pushing too hard, sounding too nasty. If he wasn't careful, she'd become suspicious. For that matter she already was. He hoped the sorry-for-himself tone would disguise the fact that he was deliberately trying to provoke her.

"I'm sorry," he said now. "I can't seem to talk to you without going crazy. That's why I haven't called before. I knew I couldn't hear your voice without feeling confused." He sighed. "You do understand, don't you?"

No, Toni thought. I'm not sure I do. I think you're playing some kind of game. But what kind? And why?

"Bryce," she said quietly, "what *are* we waiting for? Are you getting professional help?"

"No."

"And you don't plan to, do you?" Her voice was calm, patient.

He hesitated. "No, I don't. That's not the answer for me. I know enough cocktail-party analysis to understand my problem. I don't need a doctor for that. Isn't that what therapy is all about, Toni? To help you discover the root of your problem? Don't you then have to work it out for yourself when you understand it? The shrink doesn't give you answers, does he? I know my problem. I can't solve it. I just need time to see whether I can live with it."

Anger swept over her. He was making her sound like some inferior thing that he had to decide whether he could lower himself to abide. Maybe a year ago, even six months ago she could have almost humbly accepted that. Before Dr. Morrisy she'd felt apologetic about her mixed blood, perhaps even unconsciously grateful that a white man loved her. But the white man didn't know about her then. And even more significantly, she didn't know herself. Now she no longer felt guilty or inferior. She was a person. Legally an adult, emotionally a woman, proudly a mulatto. There were thousands, millions like her. And there would be more admitting it. Like homosexuals, they were "coming out of the closet," demanding their right to be equal in all things. They did not need tolerance or condescension or special treatment. They needed to deal with people of intellect. And Bryce, for all his keen mind and polished manners and business success, remained ignorant. She felt suddenly free and strong and in control.

"Listen to me, Bryce," she said. "One month or one year won't make any difference. You know what I am and I know what you are. And the choice is not whether *you can* live with it but whether *we both want* to live with it, openly and intelligently. I know we can't. And so do you. I think we should agree to end it. We've both been at fault. God knows, I wish it hadn't worked out this way, but we haven't been borrowing time for *one* month, we've been clutching at it for *seven*. That's long enough."

He was quiet for a moment. "You've given up. You're running out on the problem."

"No. Just the opposite. I've stopped running away from the problem. I'm facing it head on. And there's no solution. Bryce, I want a divorce."

She'd said it. She was almost surprised that she'd been able to speak the words so quietly and with such complete conviction. She wanted to be free. *Really* wanted to be. Until this moment she'd been afraid of the finality. Though she'd talked of divorce a month before, she had not totally accepted the idea, had been vainly waiting for some miraculous solution. No, she told herself, she hadn't hoped for a miracle; she'd wished for a complete change in Bryce, though that in itself would have been a minor miracle.

In any case, there *had* been a change in Bryce, but a different kind. She heard it in his voice, just as she heard the change in her own. A month without contact had given them both a new look at things. If nothing else, it made them aware that they could live without each other. That, indeed, they had to.

"I see," he said slowly. "You're convinced there's no chance for us?"

"Be honest," Toni said. "Aren't you?"

There was an even longer pause. Now that she'd done what he wanted, Bryce's anger had left him. He felt a surge of love and admiration he'd known before. He didn't believe she'd tried to trick him in any way. She was an honest, strangely innocent young woman and he'd been trying, for his own self-protection, to paint her as a cheat and a cheap conniver. But she was right. There was no chance for them because he was incapable of forgetting what she was.

On a deep intake of breath he said, "Yes, I'm sure of that. I'm also sure I'll always love you, Toni, even though the . . . the other thing would always be between us." And then the cautiousness came back. "Have you given any thought to how you want to handle it?"

"Not really. I suppose we should each get a lawyer. I don't want anything from you, Bryce, except for Elieth. I want custody of her and some help from you in providing for her comfort and education. Is that all right?"

"Yes, of course. Will you sue in New York?" He hesitated. "I don't mind that it takes two years here, but I'd like to avoid any publicity. Mostly," he added hastily, "for Elieth's sake. She's only a baby now, but people remember a messy divorce for years. I wouldn't want her to grow up under a cloud of scandal."

Despite the seriousness of the conversation, Toni almost laughed. Surely Bryce didn't think he was fooling her with that nonsense. He didn't want publicity because he'd feel like a fool if it leaked out that he'd married a mulatto, and it well might if some eager columnist or reporter chose to really dig into Mrs. Bryce Sumner's background. Let him think I'm buying his transparent excuse. God knows, I don't wish to destroy him or his foolish pride.

"It wouldn't be messy, but I can go somewhere else for the divorce," she said. "Perhaps out of the country. I understand Haiti specializes in twenty-four-hour procedures. But shouldn't we leave this to the lawyers, Bryce? Will you be using Sol Wyman?"

His voice was very low. "Yes, I suppose so. And you?"

"I'm not sure. I never needed a lawyer before. But whomever I get can get in touch with Sol."

There was another awkward silence and then Toni said, "You know you can see Elieth whenever you like."

"Right. Maybe later."

"I could arrange to be out if that bothers you."

"I'll let you know," Bryce said. There was something of the old sweetness and sadness in his voice. "She's too young to miss me."

"But I always want her to know you. A girl needs to admire her father. I'll see that Elieth does."

"Goodbye, Toni," he said. "Forgive me."

"Goodbye," she said. "And thank you, Bryce, for many things. You changed my life."

"And you mine."

She hung up feeling terribly depressed. No divorce, no matter how inevitable or even how welcome, can be without pain and some sense of self-recrimination. Logic could not overcome the unhappy feeling that there'd been failure on both sides. Toni felt that she, as well as Bryce, might have been more compassionate, more flexible. The marriage was only two years out of their lives, yet for both it had been a period of ecstasy and despair and it could not end unfeelingly. One didn't discard a husband the way one sent clothes to a thrift shop—glad to have the closet uncluttered. You parted with any piece of your life reluctantly, even when it had brought you pain.

She'd had her moments of hating Bryce, resenting him, seeing him as an ignorant, stupid man. She was sure that he'd gone through that kind of same self-preserving rationale about her, probably despising her for her lack of candor, thinking her selfish and cold-blooded. But they both knew, in the end, that they were basically decent human beings who respected each other for their frailties as well as their strengths. They'd once had great love. It was never totally lost, always slightly mourned, endlessly preceded by "If only . . ."

But there were too many unchangeable "If onlys." If was time to wipe the cloud of self-delusion from her eyes. Make a decision. Find a lawyer. Get the divorce in Haiti next month if you can. Automatically she reached for her little brocaded telephone book. She knew only one lawyer. This time when she called Peter Richards it was not to issue a dinner invitation.

Charlene picked up her gardening basket and went out into the sunshine. It was already getting hot, though the hour was still early. She loved the feel of the warmth on her bare arms contrasted with the cool black earth into which she plunged her hands. Her flowers were her comfort, living things that depended on her for survival. Almost the last living things, she thought ruefully, that did. Jim had needed her in so many ways. So, despite her strength and independence, had Elizabeth. It was important to be needed, maybe the single most satisfying thing a woman experienced. Without it, she was one-dimensional.

Thinking of the phone call she'd just received, she unflinchingly faced the fact that even Toni's need for her was more expedient than emotional. Not that her daughter did not love her, but the needs that Charlene could fill for Toni were those that could have been supplied equally well by a competent nursemaid.

Wrong! Charlene told herself, viciously plunging a spade into the damp soil. She does need me. Not just to take care of Elieth while she goes to Haiti for a divorce.

She needs me because she knows I'll give Elieth more than routine care. I'll give my granddaughter the kind of love she can get only from those who see her as part of themselves. Toni knows that Elieth needs to feel secure, just as she did, and I'm the only one, other than herself, who can give that feeling to Elieth while her mother's away. So I'm a baby-sitter? So what? At least I'm an irreplaceable one.

She'd agreed, some weeks before, to come to New York and take care of the baby while Toni took a holiday with Joanne. At that time Toni had agreed not to rush into a divorce, going along with Bryce's plea for time. This morning Toni had told her the dual purpose of the trip.

"I talked to Bryce earlier today," Toni had said. "We've agreed that the separation is pointless. I want a clean break, Mother, and now so does he. He's finally accepted the fact that we can't recover what we had. I don't think he even wants to see Elieth. She's proof of his error in judgment."

The news had not been a surprise. Charlene had known it was coming when she saw Toni in October. Still she felt a pang of regret. She did not subscribe to the fact that it was better to be unhappily married than not married at all, but she knew how lonely life was without a man at your side. Toni and Bryce would be better off without each other, but the girl was so young to have endured all she had: the torment about her father, the hopeless love for her cousin, the optimistic marriage and the disillusionment that came so quickly. She was alone at twenty-one, with a child to raise. She also had to start earning a living. Toni had said she'd accept nothing from Bryce except support for Elieth. She was not even going to keep the apartment when she returned from Haiti.

Charlene (needing to be needed?) had told her not to

worry about money. "I have more than enough for all of us, darling. Your grandmother left me nearly everything for my lifetime and when I die it will go to you and your cousins. A quarter of it will be yours someday anyway. No reason why we can't use it now."

"That's dear of you," Toni had said, "but we'll be all right. I'm going to pick up my work. I can make a decent living at it, and Elieth's needs will be taken care of by Bryce. I'd rather *you* enjoyed the money now, Mother. I wish you'd do more things for yourself. Travel. Buy a lot of beautiful clothes. Have some fun."

Travel? Charlene had thought. Where do I want to go alone? Buy clothes? I get what I want for the life I lead. Have fun? The only fun I've ever known was being part of someone else's life. I'm really a disgustingly old-fashioned woman. I've never had a career or yearned for one. My husband, my child, my unconventional-conventional life was all the fulfillment I ever wanted. I'm past forty but that's not too late to start a new life outside the home. I wonder what Toni really wants. A career? Another marriage? Right now, Charlene supposed, all Toni wanted was a clean slate, and that, with Peter Richards' help, she was going to get.

"I've asked Peter to handle the divorce for me," Toni had said. "You don't mind, do you?"

"Mind? Why should I mind? He was your grandmother's choice as a lawyer and he's always been dear to us as a man."

"He says it's no problem as long as Bryce doesn't contest it. We both get local lawyers to represent us there. Peter's getting in touch with Sol Wyman, Bryce's attorney."

"You sound relieved," Charlene said. "I'm glad. Not glad the marriage didn't work. Glad you're amputating instead of letting it rot away. I know you, Toni. Once you've made up your mind what's right, you never go back."

456

Like you wouldn't go to Alan, Charlene thought. You live by your own set of rules, my darling daughter. I have to admire you, even when I think you're wrong.

"When do you and Joanne leave, exactly?"

"The morning of December fifth. Mom, are you *sure* you want to come here? I could bring Elieth to you for those ten days if it would be easier."

"No, I wouldn't mind a little change and it's much less complicated to transport me than to pack up yourself and the baby and make two round trips. I'll be there on the fourth. Are you excited about the trip?"

"Yes. A little more nervous about it now, of course. Before, I thought of it just as a holiday. Now it will be closing a chapter of my life. I guess everybody who goes through a divorce has some doubts and trepidations, don't they?"

"I'm sure they do. Just remember there are a lot more pages in the book, honey. Keep me up to date on what's happening, will you?"

"Of course. You're absolutely sure you don't mind staying here with Elieth while I'm gone?"

"I'm absolutely sure."

On her knees in the flower bed, Charlene reviewed the conversation. Had Toni really wanted to bring Elieth to California, perhaps in the hope of seeing Alan? Was Alan in her mind, now that freedom was so close? She thought hard. Had she missed the message? Did Toni want her to tell Alan that she was divorcing Bryce? Charlene did not feel inclined to make a point of calling him with the news. He'd probably be in touch with her in the next few days. She could mention it casually then. Maybe it would no longer matter to him. Maybe it didn't even matter to Toni. Charlene could have been reading it all wrong, fantasizing, romanticizing as she so often did. She went back

457

to her digging. Alan would know, in any case. Peter certainly would tell him.

For her part, Toni wondered whether Charlene's insistence on staying with Elieth in New York was based merely on making things easier for her. It did, of course. It would have been hectic, getting ready for the Haitian trip, finalizing the divorce arrangements here, closing up the apartment, flying to California with Elieth and going back again to get her. Still, there was a note of determination in Charlene's voice that seemed to go beyond all that. Maybe it's Peter, Toni suddenly thought. Maybe she'd like to see Peter Richards. No matter that Charlene had seemed offended by Toni's comment on his interest. She likes him a lot. She'll never be anything to him because of Ann. Mother just couldn't do that. But maybe she's lonely for the company of a nice man. Even if it's only that: company.

Chapter 32

"I absolutely despise flying economy." Joanne wriggled restlessly in the seat beside Toni. "It must be my basic insecurity, but it makes me feel like a second-class citizen." She glared at the curtain which discreetly hid the first-class passengers. "I'm always convinced that they're living like royalty up there, waited on hand and foot, slurping champagne and caviar. Maybe having an orgy, for all I know, while the underprivileged are crowded back here in steerage eating with plastic forks."

Toni laughed. "Then why do you do it? I'm sure *Enchantress* would be perfectly willing to have you go first-class, and I'd have been happy to pay the difference in my ticket. It isn't all that much on such a short flight."

"I always make the magazine get me a first-class seat when I'm traveling alone, but they won't go for the extra money for three models, a photographer and his assistant. And beast though I am, I still couldn't sit up *there* and send legal messages back here to the peasants." She blanched at the gray mess presented to them as lunch. "Look at *that*. It shouldn't happen to the editor of *Vogue!*"

"Courage," Toni said. "In another hour we'll be in Haiti. Then you'll start living in the splendor that befits you."

Joanne smiled. "Don't expect the Oloffson to be the Ritz in Madrid. It's marvelous, wonderful, sensational and I could spend the rest of my life there, but the plumbing's not too dependable, room service is nonexistent and there are no telephones except in Al Seitz's office and one in the bar. Also there are a lot of flying, biting things and an occasional creepy, crawly parade all of which the staff fights valiantly with people-choking bug spray."

Toni looked at her with surprise. "I thought you loved the Oloffson."

"I do. I worship it. I told you I could live in that wacky hotel the rest of my life. I haven't told you the wonderful, sensational parts."

"Tell me. Quick."

Joanne's eyes filled with pleasure. "Well, the building looks like a curlicue white wicker doll's house big enough for humans. The rooms are enormous and have marvelous things like comfortable beds and private balconies that can hold cocktails parties of fifty. The public rooms are a combination of Casablanca, Charles Addams and your great-grandmother's Victorian summer home. The food is bliss. The bar is always jumping with writers and agents and publishers and TV stars and actors and incredible local characters. There are two slot machines that seldom pay off. The head barman does everything from make you a wicked rum punch to mail your letters. The staff is beautiful and smiles a lot, mostly because they don't understand a word you're saying and you can't figure out their 'baby French,' which is their own special patois, a combination of the real language and lot of modified words that have crept in over the years. There's an immaculate pool and a bar and you can have the most incredible club sandwich of ham, bacon and avocado sent down for lunch while you lie under the earth's most perfect, cloudless sky, smelling flowers you don't know the names of." She took a breath. "That's for openers."

Toni was smiling now. "More!" she said. "Tell me more."

Joanne leaned back. "Well, let's see. People are always comparing Al, the proprietor, to Ernest Hemingway, but though I didn't know Papa, I suspect Al's a helluva lot sweeter and more considerate. His wife's terrific and so are their kids. Anyway, if Al and Sue like you—and they will—there's nothing they won't do to make you happy."

"And if they *don't* like you?"

"I've heard tell that in cases like that you suddenly find you don't have a reservation. Or there's a mix-up and Barbara Walters is booked into your room day after tomorrow." Jo laughed. "Don't look so alarmed, Toni. It won't happen to you. It's going to be a mutual love affair between you and the Oloffson. I can almost guarantee it. I can also guarantee that you're going to love Haiti itself as much as the hotel."

"Tell me about the island."

"Not now. You'll see it through your own eyes. You're going to have plenty of time on your hands while I'm off all day shooting pretty pictures." She spoke more quietly. "When does the messy business get over with?"

"I'm not sure. I see the lawyer tomorrow. Peter seemed to think the formalities would probably be the same day."

"Funny," Jo said. "I really predicted this the first time we met, didn't I? Not that it took a genius to know you were heading for a divorce, but I just somehow knew you'd come to Haiti to get it."

"It's a crazy coincidence, or maybe not a coincidence at all." Toni was thoughtful. "You started me thinking seriously about how much I didn't want to drag on with the

461

separation. If I hadn't been coming here anyway, I might not have brought up the subject of divorce so soon."

"I'm still amazed that Bryce didn't put up more of a fight."

"So was I, at first," Toni said. "Now I think he knew, even while he was protesting, that he couldn't come back to me and keep his manhood. The whole thing was torture for him. His intellect fought a losing battle with his emotions."

Jo snorted. "Don't be so damned understanding! My God, Toni, Bryce Sumner is up to his eyeballs in ego and prejudice!"

"The latter, yes. But so inbred that he can't help it. It's too late for him to unlearn a lot of things. As for the ego, it's very tenuous. I know it's hackneyed to say that some of the most confident-appearing people are unsure and frightened inside. But in Bryce's case it's true. He isn't secure enough to handle a 'half-breed' wife, either privately or publicly, but he can't admit that, not even to himself. I think he was relieved to have the decision taken out of his hands." Toni frowned. "I'm not trying to be St. Antoinette. I despise him for his weakness and his bigotry. He nearly destroyed me along with himself, but he loved me once, and in my way I loved him. I can't write that off, no matter what he said or did later. And I didn't really play fair with him, Jo. In the beginning, I mean. I didn't tell him about myself. And I married him knowing I really loved someone else."

"Okay," Jo said. "You've both learned from experience. Nothing's ever wasted, is it? Next time you'll be wiser and more realistic."

Almost what I said to Dr. Morrisy, Toni thought. Aloud, she said, "Yes, I'll understand a lot more next time. If there ever is a next time."

Her cousin smiled. "Don't look so depressed, you

462

twenty-one-year-old has-been! There's a future for you. I'd be willing to guarantee that, too."

He stood very straight and tall, his light hair and blue eyes setting him apart from the predominantly black crowd that strained at the outer barriers of the customs gate. God help me if Jo is wrong, Alan thought. He saw the plane land but from this distance he could not make out the figures. The woman he looked for was only one of the crowd of little dots straggling toward the customs shed, one of the faceless, winter-conditioned visitors squinting and already sweating in the scorching heat of the Port-au-Prince airport. Though he was lightly dressed and unencumbered, Alan also was sweating profusely, with nervousness. Jo had been so sure that he should be here waiting for them. He wondered how Toni would take the surprise.

He could identify them now as he looked over the heads of the excited throng waving and calling to arriving friends and relatives. Toni looked so tiny and elegant in her trim little pants suit, laughing up at a much taller, more harassed Joanne, who was urging the other five members of her party on toward a place in the immigration line. He felt sorry for them. He'd gone through the ordeal three days before: the endless wait for the luggage and the minute inspection of each piece by the Haitian customs officials. These stern-looking men did a meticulous job of going through every bag. The island prided itself on being free of drugs and crime. They were not about to let anyone get in with a joint of marijuana or a firearm of any kind. Patience, Alan, he told himself. It will take an hour, at least, for Jo to get her troupe and all the clothes and photographic equipment past "Baby Doc's" watchdogs. Returning natives or relatives of natives seemed to get through much faster. For one thing, they could speak the language. For another, this was the black man's domain. Here *he* tolerated the white who came to his country at his sufferance.

He saw Joanne peer at the crowd and spot him. She gave a little nod of satisfaction but did not raise her hand in greeting. I *am* to be a total surprise, Alan thought. He'd had an idea Jo might decide to prepare Toni on the way down. Apparently she had not, because Toni gave no more than a glance toward the mob awaiting the arrivals. She did not see Alan or notice Jo's subtle recognition of him.

At first he'd resisted when Jo had called him in California and practically demanded that he meet them in Haiti. He'd heard from his father and Charlene about the trial separation but not about the impending divorce. He knew only that his sister and Toni had finally met and liked each other, and that Toni had agreed to go on the photographic junket.

"You're out of your mind," he'd said to Jo. "You don't know Toni. She'd be offended if I showed up like a hovering vulture! Hell, she may be separated but she's still a married woman!"

"Surprise," Jo had said. "She's getting a divorce in Haiti." She let that welcome news sink in. "Listen, Alan, you've blown it before. Don't keep making the same mistake time after time. She's a lovely, desirable, soon to be eligible female. You stake a claim or it'll be too late again."

"Is she interested in someone else? Is that why the sudden divorce?"

"No, dum-dum, but don't give her a chance to *get* interested!"

He'd still hesitated. "I don't know, Jo. It seems crass, chasing after her the first minute she's free."

He heard her sigh three thousand miles away. "Oh,

Lord, where do you those Fauntleroy words? 'Crass,' he says! Alan, don't you *want* her?"

"You know I do."

"Then for Christ's sake get your fanny on a plane and be waiting in Port-au-Prince on the fifth! Put up or shut up, my love. I'm beginning to lose patience with all that polite consideration you and Toni keep stewing around!"

He smiled at the recollection of that conversation. His tough-talking sister was a devout romantic under that glossy exterior. She loved nothing more than a fairy-tale ending and she firmly believed that Alan and Toni would find it. He'd always believed it too. That's why he hadn't married. In spite of Toni's marriage and motherhood, in spite of the long silences and separations, he'd felt they'd end up together. And now when it seemed close and possible he was jumpy and frightened.

He paced restlessly up and down behind the airport crowd. What would Toni's first words to him be? What would he say to her? This was the moment he'd waited three years for. He took out a handkerchief and mopped his brow, sweating with anticipation and an almost superstitious apprehension.

"Hot, isn't it?"

He looked into the deep violet eyes of a pretty blonde girl in pale-blue shorts and halter.

"Murder," he agreed. "I'm glad they take all these precautions at customs, but I wish they'd speed it up a little."

He felt the appraising, approving eyes on him, inviting a pickup. A wild thought ran through his mind: I could bolt right now. One word to this willing girl and I could disappear without Toni ever knowing I was here. My God, I really am scared!

"You meeting someone?" he asked politely.

"Only an old school chum. Nobody special. She doesn't even expect me." The expression grew more hopeful.

465

"What about you?"

He hesitated. "I'm meeting someone very special: my wife."

The girl's face fell. "Oh. Well, nice seeing you."

In that instant, Alan felt wonderful. That impulsive gesture of referring to Toni as his wife, even if it was not the truth, filled him with confidence.

"Thank you," he said to the girl.

She looked at him curiously. "What for?"

He didn't answer. Instead he gave her a jaunty wave and moved toward the gate, smiling happily.

A nut, the girl thought. An absolute nut. The world is full of them.

Joanne, the models, the photographer and his assistant were limp by the time they and all the clothes got through customs. Only Toni, unruffled, seemed to be enjoying it all. She tried to explain to the tall, handsome young inspector what the group was doing with boxes of clothes and shoes and jewelry and mountains of camera equipment and film. He seemed to understand her high-school French but she couldn't grasp a word of his reply. It sounded like some kind of gibberish with a familiar word here and there.

"Don't struggle," Jo finally said peevishly. "Let him paw through the works to his heart's content. *Anything* to get us out of here. We don't have any guns or dope, so it's just a matter of time." She looked suspiciously at the photographer. "You don't by any chance have any uppers or downers with you, do you?"

He gave her a withering look and flipped a limp wrist in her direction. "Dear heart, I have nothing stronger than a box of aspirin and some medicine for whatever is the equivalent of Montezuma's revenge in voodoo land.

466

Marty will vouch for it, won't you, dear? He did all the packing."

The assistant nodded. "That's right, Miss Richards."

Jo nodded. "Okay. Thank God, I think young Hawk-eye is on the last suitcase!" She turned to Toni. "Do you *believe* this performance? It's the only foreign country I've ever been to where they give you a going-over coming *in*. Going *out*, nothing! And at Kennedy they probably won't even open the bags. They know damned well there's nothing you can bring *out* of here." She fanned herself with her passport. "Gad, will I be glad to get to the hotel! Things sure look different from up there!" She watched the official close the last bag. "Okay? *Merci, monsieur. Vous êtes magnifique!* Marty, see what you can do about porters, will you? I think we're finally sprung."

Now that the frenzy was behind them, Jo was happy and excited. She grabbed Toni's arm. "Come on. This gang can get themselves and the luggage into a couple of cabs. Monique has all the instructions. She's the monitor model. You and I have a special chauffeur."

Toni allowed herself to be hurried to the exit. Traveling with Joanne was like being swept along by a tornado. Special chauffeur indeed! Wouldn't you know that Jo would have her own car, if only to make up for the sacrifice of flying economy.

Before she realized what was happening, Jo said, "There he is. Our private transportation. Free. And he speaks pretty good English."

Toni followed the direction of Jo's pointing finger. Alan was walking quickly toward them, his face radiant. For a moment she thought she was imagining it. It was impossible, a mirage. And then he was beside her and it was true, miraculously, ever-so-rightly true. Jo watched her, pleased with her surprise, eager for her reaction.

467

Happiness tangled Toni's tongue. "Alan?" she said incredulously. "Is it really you? How . . . I mean when . . that is, what on earth are you doing here?"

"Waiting for you," he said. "Simple as that." He kissed her lightly. "Welcome. I hope you're as glad to see me as I am to see you. My sister the matchmaker promised me you would be. Are you?"

She was still catching her breath. "I can't believe it!"

"Listen to her," Jo said. "She sounds like all those greedy quiz-show winners who win ugly furniture on TV. 'I can't believe it!' Believe it, Toni, and for God's sake answer the man's question!"

Toni looked deep into the eyes of the only one she'd ever loved. There was no need for an answer.

Chapter 33

Toni felt a little let down as they drove through the downtown area on their way to the hotel. Jo had said he'd love Haiti. How could one love a place where people were so pathetically poor? She sat between Alan and Joanne in the front seat of the rented car. Half of her mind was filled with the man whose thigh brushed her own, whose hand gently reached out now and then as though to reassure himself that she was really there. The other half of Toni's thoughts were on the ragged black people hawking their pitiful wares along the roadway or standing listlessly in the doorways of their hovel-homes. She'd had a picture of people free and happy, gayly dressed, smiling and content in their picturesque paradise. So far she'd seen desperate poverty, dirty streets and unkempt stores and houses. They're no better off than blacks in Harlem, she thought. All they have going for them is a wonderful climate. Beyond that, they're probably worse off than Northern Negroes. At least at home they have a chance to escape, to get an education, a decent job, to move out of the ghetto. Here they're trapped with nowhere to go and no hope of bettering their lives.

Alan seemed to be reading her mind. "Don't let all th[e] get you down too much," he said gently. "I felt the sam[e] way when I arrived. I couldn't bear the sight of so mu[ch] squalor and futility. But I've done a lot of snooping in th[e] three days while I waited for you. The picture is far fro[m] perfect, God knows, but it's getting better. There a[re] schools, believe it or not. And factories springing u[p] which will give employment to the people. A lot of th[e] factories, by the way, are American-owned. The new go[v]ernment is much better than the old regime and a lot [of] foreigners who moved away during Papa Doc's time hav[e] come back. Many of them are remarkable people, doing [a] lot of good here. Don't feel guilty or jump to sad conclu[...]sions, darling. There's a lot to break your heart, b[ut] there's also a good deal to be optimistic about." H[e] smiled. "They're even trying to teach the people conserva[...]tion of the land, though it's pretty hard to convince [a] poor man that it's more important to let a tree stan[d] against soil erosion than to cut it down for the firewoo[d] his wife needs for cooking. But they're trying here, Ton[i.] You'll see."

She squeezed his arm gratefully, saying nothing.

Joanne was less touched, but even more impresse[d.] "You sound like the damned Chamber of Commerc[e.] How have you learned so much so quickly?"

"I don't know very much at all yet, but I'm intereste[d] in the place, and I've talked to some locals who kno[w] what makes it tick. Maybe I'll want to use some of th[e] background in the next book. Besides, Jo, dear, I di[d a] little boning up before I came. Did you know that Haiti [has] been an independent nation since 1804? Would you b[e]lieve that a little group of impoverished slaves, uned[u]cated, armed only with a few stolen weapons, but most[ly] with sticks and hoes, could have thrown out well-arm[ed]

470

ad well-trained European troops and created their own
ountry? It's fascinating! This is the first black republic in
e Western Hemisphere, created eighteen years before
eed American slaves founded Liberia and . . ."

"Hold it!" Jo said. "You're raining on my parade! I
ad this pegged as a romantic reunion, not a history
sson."

"What were you fantasizing?" Alan teased. "A series of
ep sighs and cow-like gazes? Jo, darling, I thank you
r arranging this, but let Toni catch her breath, will you?
can't speak for her, but your passion for romance is
ceeded only by mine for privacy." He smiled. "Don't let
e pedantic talk fool you. I didn't come here for the scen-
y."

Toni looked up at him. "Neither did I."

"Okay, okay," Jo said. "So I'm a shop girl at heart. I'll
y to control my vicarious pleasure, but it won't be easy."

As they left the center of town, the island began to
ok less depressing. They passed the imposing President's
lace and Alan pointed out pictures of Jean-Claude
uvalier, "Baby Doc" as they called him, a hefty, smiling
ack man in his early twenties. An electric sign pro-
aimed: *Vive le président pour la vie.*

"President for life?" Toni translated questioningly.

"Yes," Alan said. "He's 'elected' for life. Haiti is a dic-
torship but they tell me Baby Doc has pardoned thou-
nds of exiled 'troublemakers' and no longer disposes of
s enemies as his father used to do. I hear the only thing
's really uptight about is long-haired young men.
quates them with drug users, I think. Anyway, you won't
e any flowing male tresses except on white visitors."

Toni grinned. "I'm not sure that won't be a relief."

Alan drove carefully and expertly toward the hotel. If
e island was peaceful, Toni thought, the traffic certainly

471

was not. The ground transportation was chaotic, a frenzied clash of taxis, trucks, decrepit cars and small, shar-
the-ride vehicles which she learned were called *publique*
There also were swarming-with-humanity station wago
called *camionettes,* which, Jo explained, would take yo
from Port-au-Prince to Petionville for ten cents. "Sta
away from *all* the jam-packed native rides," she advise
"You'd be squeezed or smothered to death before yo
reached your destination, provided, of course, you kne
where your destination was."

Joanne seemed to have a point. There were no mar
ings on the streets and very few numbered buildings. "M
method," she said, "is to stake out a few recognizab
landmarks like the Holy Trinity Cathedral and take a
my bearings from there. But an even better way is to fi
a dependable driver with his own car."

"Toni won't have that problem," Alan said. "She h
me and my ten-dollar-a-day, ten-cents-a-mile priva
transportation, remember?"

"And I'm thankful," Toni said. "I don't know how yo
do it, Alan! I don't see how anybody drives in this mes
I've only seen one or two traffic cops and about as ma
traffic signals."

"They're suicidally relaxed about all that," he sai
"There don't seem to be any traffic regulations. Y
might get a ticket between eight A.M. and four P.M. f
passing one of their rare red lights. Otherwise, as far as
can figure out there just aren't any rules."

They pulled into the long driveway of the Oloffson.
was as Jo had described it, sprawling, gingerbready, de
cious. Al Seitz greeted them cordially in his cluttered lit
office, pored through his papers and handed Toni
message. She read it quickly and handed it to Alan a
Joanne. The local lawyer had left word for her to me

him the next afternoon at the courthouse and had thoughtfully provided directions on how to get there. The proceedings would take place immediately.

"Your first driving assignment," Toni said dryly.

"I can't think of one I'd rather have."

The spell was broken by the arrival of the rest of Jo's group. Rooms and suites were assigned. The models were comfortably stashed in a huge room in the main house, a spacious accommodation with three daybeds. It opened onto a long balcony from which there were a breathtaking view of the city, the mountains and the harbor with one of the inevitable cruise ships lying in wait for its onshore passengers. The girls were just around the corner from Alan, who occupied the Peter Glenville Studio. All the rooms as well as the suites were named for famous personalities. Jo had the biggest and best, the Sir John Gielgud Suite, while Toni was nearby in a balconied lay-out tagged in honor of Anne Bancroft. The photographer and his assistant were in the James Jones Cottage near the pool.

"I'll leave you kids to get settled," Alan said. "You must be ready for a siesta after this hectic trip. Meet you in the bar about seven?"

Jo and Toni looked after him as he wandered off in the direction of the pool. At the door of her suite, Jo turned to Toni. "You *are* glad I meddled, aren't you? I told you I was impetuous, but there's nothing wrong with my instincts."

Toni hugged her. "You're what I've always wanted," she said, "a really good, close friend."

"And Alan?"

"He's what I've wanted too, since the first crazy night I saw him in Greenwich Village."

"Praise Allah!" Jo said. "Nothing upsets me more than

473

an unsuccessful plot." She smiled. "Unless it's unrequited love. *That* drives me up the wall."

Toni unpacked and stretched out on the big bed in her suite. The balcony doors were open and she could hear the soft voices of the staff on the grounds outside calling to each other in their unintelligible, sweet-sounding language. Above her, a wide-bladed ceiling fan whirred lazily, hypnotically. She watched it for a long while and then dropped off into the first peaceful, dreamless sleep she'd had in a long, long time.

The whole group met for cocktails and dined at a long table in the patio. Jo surveyed the gathering with a look of dismay. "I'm not sure," she whispered to Toni, "that I'll be able to stand ten days of eating with the same eight people every evening. I love you all, but I have a feeling we're going to bore hell out of each other by the third dinner. Let's make a pact. Every man for himself. If I connect with that handsome bearded guy at the bar who's been giving me the eye, I'll get lost with him. And it's for sure that you and Alan are going to want to he alone at least *some* of the time."

Alan, sitting beside Toni, overheard the comment. "Don't worry about us," he said. "I have several evenings already planned. You're welcome to come along, Jo, but I'm no more for traveling with a troupe than you are."

"When it works out, I'll join you," Jo said. "We have to do the gambling casino one night and I have an introduction to an interior decorator who I hear has a fabulous house and who'd like us to come for cocktails. But I think we'll make *those* expeditions a threesome. The five fashion types can find their own fun at night." She pretended to shudder. "I don't even want to *think* what they'll get into! My photographer will probably fall in love with a voodoo priest and end up biting off the head of a live dove." This time she really shuddered.

Toni was wide-eyed. "Do they *do* that?"

"Yes," Alan said, "but only for the tourists. You'll never see real voodoo unless you're here on Christmas Eve and have an in with somebody who can get you to a *real* ceremony. Anyway, I agree with Jo. These ten days belong to us. Let the thrill seekers go where they will. We'll have our own kind of idyllic tropical holiday. I know *I'm* going to enjoy every minute. How can I miss? I'm with the two women I love most in the world." He took Toni's hand and kissed it.

By the time they'd finished dinner the bearded man was nowhere in sight. Jo shrugged philosophically. "Maybe he'll turn up tomorrow night," she said. "Why don't we have a brandy on the porch and make it a quiet evening? We're off early for our photography and Toni has to brace herself for the judge." She stopped, dismayed by her own flippancy. "I'm sorry, Toni. I didn't mean to make it all sound so casual. I know it's a bad moment. It would have to be."

When he left her at the door of her suite, Alan almost echoed those words. "I'm not even going to ask to come in," he said. "God knows I want to. But when we're together, Toni, I want it to be with nothing but ourselves in mind. No ghosts. No guilts. No leftover ties of any kind. Just you and me, darling. The way it was always supposed to be."

He kissed her quickly and strode down the outside balcony to his room.

In a realistic way she was glad he hadn't tried to make love to her this night. And in a most human way, she was disappointed. She fingered the wedding ring she still wore. Alan was right. Until the moment she was no longer Mrs.

Bryce Sumner she couldn't be anyone's lover. Not even Alan's. She undressed slowly and dropped into bed. It was hot but she loved the heat. It made her feel relaxed and sensuous. The way, she thought shamelessly, she'd feel when she was a free woman tomorrow night.

The divorce was granted so quickly, so matter-of-factly that it was a *fait accompli* almost before Toni realized it. She signed a few papers, answered a couple of perfunctory questions and by three o'clock in the afternoon she was no longer married. So this, she thought, is what a "divorce mill" is. She'd heard of them in Mexico and the Dominican Republic, heard of people making a quick plane trip, staying overnight and returning home next day to their renewed single-status lives. She'd never imagined it would be that way for her. But then she'd never imagined herself getting married quickly and quietly, almost secretly, in City Hall in New York, either.

When she was a little girl, she'd always loved pictures of brides in long, flowing white gowns and gossamer veils held with sparkling tiaras. She'd visualized herself looking like that one day. "I'm going to have a big, big, wedding," she'd told Charlene and Jim. "Daddy will be all dressed up and Karen will have a pretty pink dress and I'll throw my bouquet to her so she'll be the next one married."

"And what will I do?" Charlene had asked indulgently.

"Oh, you'll be the most important of all, Mommy! You'll arrange everything!"

As she walked toward the car where Alan waited she could almost hear the voices and see the scene. So long ago. She'd known nothing then, nothing about herself or her heritage, nothing of the burdens that were not of her making, or of those which she took upon herself. I was such a happy child, Toni mused. Secure, loved, always

476

knowing I was wanted. God, what innocence! I didn't understand how society makes us pay.

She stepped into the car and sat quietly beside Alan. He didn't touch her or ask questions. He started the motor and began to drive slowly, waiting for her to speak.

"It was all so clinical," Toni said finally. "No reason why it shouldn't be, I suppose. It was just so routine and impersonal that I felt it was happening to somebody else." She took the gold band off her finger. "I remember reading somewhere once that women who get divorces in Reno had a special place, a bridge or something, where they threw away their wedding rings. I wonder if they have a place like that in Haiti?" Her voice was almost bitter.

Alan stopped the car on a small side street. They had to talk right then. Ragged children playing in a dirt yard looked curiously at the white couple. One little girl, bolder than the others, came up to the window on Toni's side.

"Money, lady?"

Toni looked down into the wide-eyed little black face. Some people begged for love, others for understanding. This child was begging for survival. Toni took the dirty little outstretched hand and held it for a moment in her own. Then she put the wedding ring into it.

"Here's a *lot* of money," she said. "My little girl would want you to have it. I hope it helps."

The child did not understand the words but she broke into a wide grin. Delighted, amazed, she ran into the house, calling out to her mother, Toni supposed, that a crazy white lady had given her a present.

Alan watched, understanding. "I like that better than a bridge," he said.

She could turn to him then, the numbness gone. "So do I, darling." She looked around like someone waking in the middle of sleepwalking. "Where are we? Are we headed some place in particular?"

"Yes. If you feel up to it. I'd like to introduce you to a very special lady. She's the aunt of a college classmate. I looked her up the day after I arrived and we talked a long time. I told her I was going to bring you to meet her."

Toni hesitated. She was not in the mood to make polite conversation with strangers. "I don't know, Alan. I'm not certain I'm up to it today. I'm all right," she added hastily, "but I'd rather be alone with you. Couldn't we meet your friend in a day or two?"

"We could. We will, if you prefer. But I want you to see that people with strength and wisdom and unselfishness still exist. I think this is the moment you need to be near a woman like Martha Cabot. You see, darling, she's the closest thing to Elizabeth I've ever met. Trust me?"

"Yes. Always."

Only then did he take her gently in his arms and kiss her, not superficially as he had at the airport, not reluctantly as he had at the door of her hotel suite, but confidently and passionately. Then he released her and turned the key in the ignition. As the car started, Alan said, "Consider that a sample. Now let's go have tea with Martha."

Later, Toni was to reflect that the short span of her life had been primarily influenced by women. Jim Jenkins, Bryce, Alan, even Dr. Morrisy, each in his way, had altered the course of her actions. But it was the women who had motivated her, from the horrid little Nadine, who had brought the first confrontation with reality, to the demented Ann, who had driven her away from Alan and into the arms of a man who finally could not accept her. Between these two had been the unforgettable example of

478

Elizabeth, the compassionate, strong, humorous grandmother, and Charlene, the loving mother who accepted Toni's decisions without agreeing with them, understanding that her daughter's convictions were not necessarily her own. Toni had learned that women could be evil and women could be good. Karen had taught her the meaning of loyalty, Sarah and Amy the superficiality of acquaintanceship, Joanne the joy of having a friend who deeply cared. Toni had been turned and touched and molded by all these women. But none was to make her see life as clearly as a stranger named Martha Cabot.

At that first meeting, Toni saw why Alan found a resemblance to Elizabeth in this unusual woman. It was more than a physical reminder, though they were both of an age, white-haired and spirited, their eyes showing the wisdom of the world. It was also an attitude of nonpassive acceptance, an independence of thought and action, a willingness to give of oneself that made Martha very like the grandmother Toni and Alan had adored.

On the surface, the two women's lives had been totally different. Martha had never married, though Toni suspected that she had loved deeply. Southern-born, childless, rich with inherited "old money," she had come to Haiti twenty years before on holiday, fallen in love with the island and decided to stay. She'd built a gracious, sprawling house set deep in a wooded area on the outskirts of Port-au-Prince, filled it with simple, comfortable furniture, hundreds of good Haitian paintings and pieces of sculpture and a procession of Haitian children whom she'd "rescued" over the years from their impoverished families. She took these little ones into her home, three or four at a time, saw that they were fed, clothed, educated and prepared for a trade. Over twenty years, she had seen "her children" grow up strong, proud and self-sufficient.

She introduced the "current crop" to Toni and Alan: three solemn, polite black boys aged nine, twelve and fifteen. She was as proud as any natural mother as she told her visitors about the youngsters.

"The little one is quite musical," she said after the boys left the room. "He has a natural talent for the piano. I've found a teacher for him and later I'll send him to the States to study. Emil, the middle one, loves dancing, and is working with Katherine Dunham. My eldest, Henri, I fear has no artistic bent, but he has a head for business." She smiled. "I'm trying to make a 'retailer' out of him. He's working in the shop-factory I've opened in town. The local people sell their handicrafts there—carvings, paintings, woven goods, all kinds of things. Any profits go to help the Haitian people. Henri oversees the selling and supervises the manufacture of things made in a workshop we also have on the premises. He's good with the tourists who come to buy and the locals who come to work or to sell. Someday," she said whimsically, "I expect he'll be a merchandise manager of Bonwit Teller."

"And these three live here with you?" Toni asked.

"Oh my, yes. These and quite a few before them." She looked searchingly at Toni. "You're wondering why I do it, aren't you? Why I choose to live and work on this fairly primitive island. Why I bring strange children into my house. Black ones, at that! And me a well-brought-up Virginia girl!"

"Yes," Toni said honestly, "I really don't understand. I think what you're doing is wonderful, giving these people a chance. But aren't you lonely for your friends and family? Aren't you ever afraid, a lone woman in this foreign place?"

Martha glanced at Alan before she answered. "I see you know nothing about me."

"I've told Toni only two things," Alan said. "One is
480

that you're the aunt of a college classmate. The other is that you're wise and strong and unselfish."

"Well, the first part is true," Martha said. "I can't lay claim to the second, except for the part about strong. Physically, at least. Wise? I'm not sure what wisdom is unless it's what you absorb by osmosis through the very act of living seventy years. Unselfish? No, I'm selfish. The pleasure I get from making some small dent in this wall of ignorance is probably more than whatever I can offer these people. I feel I'm doing something with my life, Toni. Something more important than chairing committees for art museums, or playing bridge with a lot of other old ladies who lost their identities when they lost their husbands.

"I'm an old maid, you know." There was no self-pity in the soft, Southern voice. "I spent the first twenty years of my adult life hopelessly in love with a married man. He was the focus of my life. I used to say, romantically, 'If I knew he was going to die tomorrow, I'd pray to be run over by a truck today!' What nonsense! It was a useless, unrealistic life. I gave nothing to the world, contributed nothing to anyone except a man too selfish and too cowardly to acknowledge me. I thought I lived only for him. I know now that I lived for myself, for my own romantic, overblown vision of myself as a self-sacrificing, undemanding, anxious-to-please puppet.

"And then this love of my life died. And I couldn't even go to his funeral. Think of it. Twenty years down the drain. Twenty pointless, fruitless, barren years of my life, and I was not allowed to say goodbye because another woman had that right. I was past forty. A rich, useless spinster nobody needed.

"A few years later I came here on a cruise. People like me always take cruises, you know. It's all part of living in

481

a lonely, make-believe world. And I saw Haiti. The people. The needs. I could afford in a small way to help them find dignity, but in a more important and selfish way, I saw how I could find dignity for myself. Because I would have purpose in my life."

Martha looked straight at Toni. "For the first time I took a good, hard look at myself. I was a phony. All that baloney about 'sacrificing myself' was just a way of not facing real problems. I used my lover as a shield against responsibility. My 'nobility' was self-indulgence. My 'loyalty' was fear. I had never been a woman, willing to give of myself in any way that counted. I thought my 'back-street life,' as we called it in those days, was brave and generous. I know now that it was weak and self-indulgent. I wasted almost a third of my life deluding myself that I was doing it for someone else. The truth was that I was inflating my own ego, telling myself that someone couldn't live without me. Thank God, I've had a chance to justify my existence even in this minor way. By providing work opportunities, I'm not playing 'lady bountiful.' I'm involved and productive. And by taking kids into my home, I'm not satisfying a subliminal urge for motherhood; I'm doing for them what their parents materially can't. And because they're black, I'm not trying to wipe out the racial prejudice I grew up with. To me they're *poor* people; not poor *black* people. I've been accused of all these things. 'Mother Martha,' some people call me. And it isn't always said in a complimentary fashion, believe me! Many people here think I'm a crazy old do-gooder, bolstering her own ego, looking for replacements for husband and children. Not so. I owe these people much more than they owe me."

They were all quiet for a moment. "And you're happy," Toni said.

"Happy? Child, only morons are totally happy. If I could live my life over, I'd do it quite differently, but since I can't, I'm determined to salvage something good from what's left. I'm content, Toni. I feel needed. I believe that what I do makes a difference in a few lives. And most of all, my dear, I've learned not to care what other people think my motives are. When you're rich and old, you can be eccentric. But at *any* age you can be independent and useful."

Martha glanced at her watch. "Good Lord, I've probably bored you to tears with this endless monologue! Frankly, I don't usually go into the story of my life, but Alan knew some of it and he asked me to tell you. For what reasons, I don't know. But whatever his reasons, I presume they're meaningful to him. And perhaps to you."

Yes, Toni thought, they're meaningful. Like you, I've "meant well." But I've made stupid, frightened self-important decisions. I'm also eager to do something important with my life.

On the drive back to the Oloffson she sat very close to Alan, saying nothing. It was quiet when they entered the hotel. At six o'clock the guests were resting or dressing for cocktails and dinner. The sun was fading but the world was still bright and golden as they made their way through the deserted lobby and up the winding staircase. They had not spoken a word since they left Martha's.

At the door of Toni's suite, Alan said, "Tired?"

She shook her head. "I've never felt so peaceful and exhilarated all at the same time."

He took her hand. "I want to make love to you," he said simply. "Now. In daylight. We've hidden too long in the dark."

His answer was her confident smile.

Two hours later they lay watching darkness settle

483

gently, hearing the sounds of voices below, the rattle of dishes, the discordant trio of musicians on the hotel porch, that energetic, untalented group whom the guests paid to *stop* playing. They had made love in the way neither had ever known it. Gently at first, slowly, almost as though they were afraid to break the spell. It had been wonderment and full realization, a tender, almost awed discovery that what they'd dreamed was really happening. When they came together again it was with joy and confidence and ecstatic abandon, feeling and touching and saying the words that lovers reserve for themselves. The first union was almost a sacred thing; the second was the lusty satisfaction of two young people fulfilling long-awaited desire.

"Three years," Alan said in the twilight. "Three years of waiting and wanting and being afraid to hope."

She didn't answer. All love could be, all a man, a spirit could be, lay in her arms. She tightened them around his strong, receptive body. It was not the moment for regret for precious time lost, or self-reproach for her cowardice or apologies for denying him what had always been rightly his. It was a time for gratitude and looking forward. I'm free, Toni thought. In thought and actions, at last I am free.

For Toni and Alan, the next four days were a magic eraser that rubbed out all the ugly stains of the past. Their happiness was contagious even to those who knew nothing of the background. And to Joanne, who did, the sight of her brother and Toni was like an affirmation that fate could be kind. From the first evening they came down late for dinner, Jo knew they had found each other. They wore the unmistakable look of lovers, the slightly blurred, almost intoxicated expression of people drunk with joy. She recognized that look. She'd seen it once or twice in the mirror. But for her it hadn't lasted. For Alan and Toni, she thought, it would.

In tacit understanding, Joanne and her "crew" left the lovers alone except for those moments when the two indicated they wanted to join the group. They did all dine together in the evening; there was no graceful escape from that. But during the day, the magazine people were off "on location" shooting their pictures, and after dinner Jo and the models sat talking to people in the hotel bar while the photographer and his assistant drove off to God knows where. Toni and Alan, holding hands, went for long unafraid walks down dark, rutted roads, hardly knowing where they were, scarcely noticing the quiet people they passed. They were aware that they had found a special place, special for many reasons. They visited Martha and were endlessly enchanted by her wisdom and her way of life. In the early hours of the morning they lay together in grateful contentment, feeling the soft air drift across their bodies, hearing the brush of palm leaves swaying in the gently stirring breezes before dawn.

Alan had not formally proposed marriage. They simply took it for granted that this would be. Everything that stood in their path had disappeared and this they did discuss, with almost awed gratitude as they examined each discovery. Ann could no longer be hurt, for she had slipped out of reality and gone back into her childhood. She did not even know she had a husband or children, Alan explained, and sad and terrible though it was, it removed from Toni the burden of fear and guilt she'd once felt.

"But what about *our* children?" Toni asked. "I'm afraid for us to have any. It's not fair to deprive you."

"Darling, we have a child. Elieth. I'll love her as though she's my own, because in a way she is. Everything

485

that's part of you is part of me." Alan's face darkened. "And there's something else. Even if I were not so blessed as to have you, I'd never have children of my own. I wouldn't risk it. Our grandfather was insane, Toni. My mother is like him. That's no heredity to pass on to children."

A cold fear swept over her. "You don't think Elieth . . ."

"Of courst not. Bryce Sumner may not come from the best of stock but, from what you've told me, I'm sure there's no true mental illness there. And God knows Charlene is the best-adjusted woman I've ever met. She and you take your characteristics from Elizabeth. No, love, I have no worries about 'our daughter.' Nor about you and me. The genes seemed to have skipped around in this family with most of the bad ones landing on my side, in Mother. I see no signs that anyone else is afflicted, but I wouldn't take a chance on having it crop up in a new generation started by me."

No mention of *her* genes. The black ones.

"I love you so much it scares me."

He held her close. "You're never to be scared again. Never. You've paid your dues."

She lay secure and content in his embrace. Life had never seemed so peaceful. She was with the man she loved. And she had nothing to hide. Yesterday she'd spoken on the phone to Charlene and been assured that Elieth was well and happy. It had been a brief but satisfying conversation, though it had taken hours to get through to New York and then the connection was so bad that they'd cut it short. Toni had not even had time to tell Charlene that Alan was with her. Perhaps her mother knew. She must be seeing Peter, and Alan had told his father where he was going. A little smile touched the corners of Toni's mouth. Charlene would never believe

486

that Toni didn't know Alan was waiting for her in Haiti, but she'd be happy about it. She wished Charlene could be happy, too. Her mother was still young, with, please God, so many good years ahead. It was not enough for her to be mother, grandmother, widow. For all her seeming passivity, Charlene was a lusty woman, a giving one, brave and proud. She had defied the world in her marriage, given up friends, and asked no quarter even now from those who had spurned her and Jim Jenkins. So she was alone. She would return to her little house in Pasadena when Toni and Alan came back to New York. She would have her garden and her small "good works" and Laurel. It isn't enough, Toni thought. She sighed deeply at the injustice of it.

"Problem?" Alan asked.

"I was thinking of Mother. She's paid *her* dues, too, but there's no compensation for her, the way there is for me."

"You're worried about her being lonely, especially with Elizabeth gone."

"Yes. Dad's death was enough, but she had Elizabeth to cling to. Now there's no one."

"I don't think she needs to cling," Alan said. "Charlene is her own person, darling. I've seen more of her than you have in the last year. She's a serene lady."

"But she's so alone," Toni said stubbornly. "She's too young, too interested in life to live like a hermit."

"Would you like her to live with us after we're married? I'd have no problem with that. I love her dearly."

Toni shook her head. "No. *She* wouldn't do it. She doesn't believe in two generations of women under one roof. We discussed that when Dad died. But maybe she'd live *near* us, Alan. Near enough so we could see her often and so that Elieth could know her, the way I knew Elizabeth."

"Why not? Where will it be? New York? California? You're lucky to be hooking up with a mobile man," he said teasingly. "That's one of the best things about being a writer. You can pack up your 'office' and work anywhere in the world. Name your preference, madame."

"How about here?"

Alan propped himself up on one elbow and looked at her in astonishment. "Here? In Haiti?"

"Is it such a crazy idea?" Toni was serious. "You're just said you can write anywhere. We both love the island. It would be wonderful for Elieth, at least until she's old enough for school. And it would be like starting a whole new life. No hangovers, no reminders, no memories of other people, other days . . . other miseries."

"I don't know. I hadn't thought of it."

"I have. Since the day you took me to Martha Cabot. She's doing what I'd like to do, Alan; making life better for people and finding her reward in helping. There's so much to do here. Darling, do you know that only ten per cent of these people are literate? I'm not an educated person but I could open a school and teach children the fundamentals."

He was silent for a moment. Then he said, "How much of this is the racial guilt thing again, sweetheart? Do you want to help blacks by showing them that being part Negro doesn't sentence a person to a life of despair?"

"No. I don't particularly want them to know that I'm half Negro. But this time I'm not hiding it from shame or obligation; I want them to understand that white people care. Because they do. *Thinking* white people care. Look at Martha. Please, Alan. Please let's come back to live. We can find a lovely house for us and one nearby for Mother. Think how happy she'd be gardening in this paradise!"

She was irresistible. "All right, love. We'll spend our

488

four remaining days looking for houses," Alan said. "Let's just hope Charlene likes the idea."

"She will," Toni said. "But even if she didn't, I'd still want to come here, for a few years at least. This is my Garden of Eden. This is where I've been born."

Chapter 34

The sanitarium was very quiet. Only the soft padding of the night nurses' rubber-soled shoes made little sounds outside Ann Richards' room. She looked at the bedside clock. The big hand was on twelve; the small one on two. Ann smiled. Two o'clock in the morning. She could tell time. That was very good for a little girl. Daddy would be proud of her.

She wondered where he was. Maybe at a big meeting with the President. He was a very important man. Sometimes he stayed out all night and then he and Mother had big arguments when he came home. Mother could never understand how hard Daddy worked, but Ann understood. Hadn't he told her that she was the only one who understood him?

She tried to remember how old she was. Seven? Eight? She hoped she'd grow up soon so she could go away with Daddy. She was so proud of him. He was like a king. And she was his princess.

The night light that burned in the baseboard of her room gave off just enough illumination to let her see the framed letter on the wall. It was a letter from President

Roosevelt to her father. She remembered a man bringing it to her and explaining what it was. The strange man had read the words to her and she had understood some of them. Perhaps she could make out more of them now if she brought the letter into bed with her. Quietly she got up and took it off the wall. They must have hung it very low, she thought, it was so easy to reach.

Holding the frame tightly to her bosom, she began to make her way back to her bed. Halfway there, she changed her mind. She'd have to turn on the bedside light to read the words. Mother might see the lamp burning and come in. The bathroom, she thought. I can go in there and read Daddy's letter.

Ann opened the door to the bathroom, still hugging her most precious possession. She did not notice the small stool on which she sat when the nurse dried her after her bath. Before she could reach for the light switch, she fell over the little bench, handing heavily on the cold, tiled floor, her weight coming down hard on her cherished burden. In that split second she tightened her hold on the letter, dimly heard the harsh crunch of thick glass, felt a sharp pain as the jagged, knife-like edges cut deeply into her body. In the last instant of consciousness she was dimly aware of a warm, sticky substance on her chest, spreading over the front of her nightgown, spoiling the writing on the page. Daddy will be angry, Ann thought. But he'll forgive me.

The hospital administrator called Peter Richards at six o'clock in the morning. He was distraught as he broke the news of how a nurse had found Mrs. Richards dead on the floor of her bathroom. He tried to sound sympathetic about the tragic accident but Peter knew that the man's only concern was that the institution not be held responsible.

491

"It was you who insisted she be allowed to have the letter in her room, Mr. Richards," he said. "I wish now that I had not granted your request. It's against rules. The patients are never allowed to have glass or any potentially sharp objects around them. Not that you should blame yourself, sir. You wanted her to be happy. We all did." He sighed. "Who could imagine such a horrible, freak mishap? We must be thankful that death was instantaneous. She never knew what hit her. I'm deeply sorry for you and your family, Mr. Richards."

Peter wanted to shout at him to shut up. The insincere condolences were insulting. The man didn't care that a woman was horribly, violently dead. He was concerned only with the hospital's culpability.

"Don't worry," Peter said, "I'm not going to sue you for negligence."

The administrator pretended indignation. "I assure you, such a thought never crossed my mind! As I said, the object was there over our objections, at your insistence. We were very much against it, right from the start."

"I know," Peter said wearily. "I understand. You'll hear from me in a few hours about arrangements for my wife's body."

The official hesitated. "I had to report it to the authorities. The county medical examiner is on the way. In cases like these, there has to be a routine report filed with the police. They may insist on an autopsy, Mr. Richards. I'll do my best, but I'm not sure . . ."

"You'd damned well better do your best!" Peter shouted. "I won't have my wife carted off to the county morgue to be pawed over like some stranger found dead on the road! You say it's obvious what happened. Well, you just make sure you convince the local authorities of that!"

"I'll try. The police out here know us well. I'm sure a

formal investigation won't be necessary when they see for themselves, but perhaps you'd better come right away, Mr. Richards."

"I'll be there in two hours. I don't want her moved before then."

He put down the phone and sat staring at it. Ann was dead. Poor, sad, angry Ann, who lived and died alone. He could not pretend deep, rending sorrow. He'd loved her once, but that was another woman he loved. Not the one he'd come to know in all the married years. Not the cold, ambitious woman. Not the hostile, vindictive one. And certainly not the mad creature who thought she was a child and who died searching for her father. What irony that the thing she loved best, the only tangible reminder of the one man she adored, should have killed her. But the letter had not really been the cause of her death. It was merely the final instrument. Ann had not lived for a long time except as a physical body. She had been his wife, the mother of his children. He grieved for what they'd had in the beginning, but there was precious little happiness to remember, pitifully few good memories for him or for those people to whom she'd given birth.

His orderly mind began to function. There was so much to do. Alan and Joanne had both been in Haiti for a week. He'd have to try to get through to them by telephone. At least young Peter was in town. He'd be composed and helpful in these next few days but, strangely enough, despite his lack of warmth, Ann's eldest child would be the one most deeply affected. Ditto was closer to his mother than the other two. Not that Jo and Alan did not have ingrained filial loyalty, nor would they be untouched by Ann's tragic death. But they saw her more clearly than their brother, who had never felt the sting of a mother's accusations or suffered from the back-lash of her selfish determination. Young Pete had instinc-

493

tively behaved as Ann had felt people should behave—properly, unrebelliously, dully. She approved of him as she approved of none of the others in her family.

The thought brought Charlene to his mind. She and Toni were also part of Ann's family, by far the most disapproved part. Ann had come to hate her sister and her sister's child and yet Charlene, though she felt human resentment, had been unable to summon up real hatred for Ann. In the week that Charlene had been in New York looking after Elieth, she and Peter had dined together every night. There was nothing illicit about these meetings. They enjoyed each other's company and they carefully avoided anything that touched on a deeper relationship than that of in-laws.

They had even driven up to the sanitarium the previous Sunday to see Ann. It had been Charlene's idea, tentatively suggested to Peter. He was scheduled, as usual, to visit the child-woman who did not know him.

"I'd like to go with you, Peter," Charlene had said the evening before. "I'd like to see Ann after all these years."

He'd been surprised and at first unwilling. "Why?" he'd asked. "Charley, it won't mean anything to Ann. She doesn't know anyone. She thinks she's a little girl. And it will be painful for you to see her this way."

"I know. I wouldn't go if she recognized me. I wouldn't distress her that way. And I know it will be terrible to see. But she's my sister, Peter. I'm haunted by the idea that Mother would want me to go, and *I* want to, as well. Don't ask me why. I can't really explain it. It's one of those crazy feelings I get now and then. Like it's important that I make contact with Ann, even if she doesn't know who I am."

He'd still held back. "I don't see why you should put yourself through this. I don't think Elizabeth would want you to."

494

"I told you I can't explain it," Charlene said, "but something is drawing me there."

He thought about that visit now. It had gone just as he'd expected. Ann looked at both of them with no sign of recognition when they came into the room. She'd been docile, uninterested in these strangers except to tell them about her Daddy, who was coming soon to take her away. The pain in Charlene's eyes was devastating, especially when Ann took her hand like a child and led her to the wall to see the framed letter from FDR to her father.

"The President depends on my father," Ann had said proudly. "See? It says so right there."

"Yes," Charlene had answered. "That's wonderful. It must make you very happy to have such a fine father."

"He loves me more than anybody. Much more than he loves Mother."

Impulsively, Charlene had said, "Doesn't he love your brothers . . . or sisters?"

"Oh, I don't have any. I'm an only child. I'm so glad. I wouldn't share him with anyone."

They'd stayed only a few heartbreaking moments. On the way home, Charlene said, "It was ghastly but I'm glad I went. At least I've seen her happy. I'll never go back, Peter. I'll never see her again."

"You shouldn't," he'd said. "There's no point."

He shivered as he thought about it. Had Charlene had some second sense of impending tragedy? Not consciously, Peter was sure. Not in the way of feeling she should go to see a sister who soon would die. But there'd been something inexplicable, almost mystical, in her sudden decision to visit Ann. He, too, was glad she had, now. Slowly he dialed Toni's apartment. Charlene answered.

"Ann's dead," he said baldly. "The hospital just called. I'm on my way there."

He heard her gasp, and then she said very quietly, "How?"

He explained, experiencing a strange feeling of disbelief as he told the story for the first time.

"Oh, God," Charlene said. "Oh, my God!" There was a brief pause and then, "What can I do, Peter? How can I help you?"

"I'm not sure. I'm going to call Pete now. Then I'll try to get Joanne and Alan at the Oloffson. I have to leave as soon as I can for the hospital, but I'll talk with you later. The best thing you can do is stand by."

"Do you want me to come with you?"

He hesitated. The steady presence beside him was something he selfishly would have liked, but this chore he had to do alone. It would not be pretty. He wouldn't subject Charlene to the callousness of official inquiry or even the possibility that the newspapers might get interested. So he said, "Thank you, dear, no. I'll be okay. Will you?"

"Yes. I'm glad I saw her again."

"I had that same thought," Peter said.

As Peter had, Charlene sat quietly, not moving for a few minutes after the phone call, trying to realize that all her family was gone. Not that she'd felt Ann was family, in any true sense. And yet a little piece of her died with her sister. Just as big pieces died with Elizabeth and Jim. Thank God for Toni, she thought. She's all I have left. Toni and Elieth. All my flesh and blood.

Only then did it occur to her that Peter had mentioned Alan being in Haiti. Charlene hadn't known that. Curious that Toni hadn't mentioned it before she left. Perhaps, Charlene guessed correctly, she didn't know he was there. And they had spoken so briefly a few days ago, Toni'd had no chance to mention it. But Peter knew and hadn't told her. That was odd. She wondered if it had any special significance. It certainly was more than coincidence that Alan should be in Haiti at the same time as Toni. Charlene smiled. They were probably all hoping—Alan, Joanne and Peter—that the way would be cleared for Toni and Alan. Perhaps, Charlene thought, Peter was afraid that I might not approve of Alan "moving in" so quickly, that I might urge Toni to be cautious about another involvement, especially one rekindled in the seductive atmosphere of the tropics. If so, he doesn't know me very well. I'd like nothing better than to see those two together. If ever people deserved happiness, they do. They've tried to do the right thing, each in his own way. They've borne their separation without whining and never stopped loving each other since the day they met. I hope with all my heart that they've found each other for keeps; their life together will be all the sweeter for having had to work so hard for it.

A wave of bittersweet sadness swept over her as she also realized that Toni and Alan's greatest obstacle was now gone forever. She could not weep for her sister, that cruelly righteous woman who had become a stranger, but she could ache with pity for the life that Ann had thrown away long before her madness overtook her. She condemned me for my marriage, Charlene thought, but mine was rich and full, where hers was poor and empty for all its outward signs of success. Hatred and fear had consumed Ann until, mercifully, she had returned in her mind to the only truly happy period of her life—the time when she was Daddy's little girl.

Poor Ann. Charlene was glad that she'd never know about Alan and Toni. Even in the end, she never really got her way.

The pool at the Oloffson seemed the least likely setting for news of tragedy. Late in the morning, Toni and Alan lay sunning themselves in comfortable chaises, talking with calm assurance of the days that lay ahead, unaware that at that moment in New York the woman who most resisted their happiness lay dead.

"Only two more days left," Alan said, "before our triumphant return to the big city. I wish we didn't have to go back at all, darling. I wish we could call Charlene, have her bring Elieth here and all live happily ever after."

Toni turned her head to smile at him. "And you were the one who thought I was crazy to want to settle in Haiti. Now you don't want to leave even temporarily."

"Don't misquote me. I never thought you were crazy. You just took me by surprise." He grinned. "The house is terrific, isn't it? We couldn't have found a more perfect one if we'd had it built to order."

Yesterday they'd signed a five-year lease with an option to buy the most wonderful house they'd ever seen. From the beginning, Haitian architecture had fascinated them. The Victorian gingerbread houses built between 1880 and 1913 were like deliciously demented decorations on a flower-filled landscape. Some of the earliest had iron balconies and columns imported from France. These fixtures had served as ballast for the ships that returned with coffee, cacao and campeche wood. The mulatto aristocracy of Haiti grew from the wealth of these exports and they put much of their money back into homes that were rampant with tall doors and windows, turrets, cornices, peaked roofs and shingled sides.

There was a dream quality about these houses that Toni and Alan found irresistible. Many of them, they found sadly, were in danger of extinction, like the termite-ridden, rotting old building that had once been as graceful as an Indian wicker bird cage but which was now no more than a sad slum, its four master bedrooms rented to twenty families who paid ten dollars a month to sleep on dilapidated mattresses. To compound the insult, a hideous concrete bungalow had been built directly in front of the mansion which had once housed a Haitian president.

But still standing, elegant, haughty and yet somehow whimsical, were many poetic, fantastic houses, and Alan and Toni were fortunate enough to find one of the best. High on a hillside, it had spacious, sundrenched rooms and wide verandas, stained mahogany floors and wainscoting. The balconied main house, almost hidden by the lush growth of bougainvillea, was made to order for them Not too large, not too small, it had a beautiful, newly added pool and pool house, and, a small distance away, a tiny guest house, complete in miniature, that they instantly recognized as "Charlene's place."

Its owner, the recent widow of an American manufacturer, was amenable to their terms. They could take possession in January, she confirmed, and, as an added bonus, she was sure the staff would be happy to stay on. The wages were ludicrously low. "My God," Toni said later, "I couldn't hire a cleaning woman for a week for what we'll pay a cook, housekeeper and gardener for a month!" She looked troubled. "They're being terribly exploited."

Alan had patted her hand. "By our standards, yes. But these *are* the standards, darling. These are the very things you want to help change. You'll throw the island into an uproar if you move here and start paying New York prices. We're 'in Rome,' Toni, and if we don't 'do as the Romans do,' we'll all be miserable. It will all change in time, love. But not overnight."

It was very like what Jim had said long ago about the plight of blacks everywhere. Realism, Toni, she reminded herself. All you can offer is a slow, unrelenting determination to make the future better.

The future was all she thought about these days. Hers

499

with Alan; Charlene's, one day, perhaps, with a man she could love; Elieth's, which, she prayed, would lack the traumas of her own childhood. She closed her eyes, lying there at the pool, enjoying visions of a rich new life.

The voice of the young man who worked in Al Seitz's office interrupted her daydreams.

"Telephone, Mr. Richards," he said. "New York. A Mrs. Jenkins calling you."

Toni and Alan sat bolt upright.

"Calling *me?*" Alan said. "Are you sure the call isn't for Mrs. Sumner?"

"No, sir. She wants to speak to you."

Cold fear enveloped Toni. There could be only one reason Charlene would call Alan. Something had happened to Elieth. Charlene would want to tell Alan first, to spare Toni the shock. No! Toni screamed silently. Not that! Please don't let anything have happened to my baby!

She heard the quiver in Alan's voice as he told the messenger he'd be right there, knew the first thought that had come into her mind had also entered his.

"I'll be right back, darling. Charlene probably wants to know what time we're getting in." He tried to sound convincing, reassuring.

"She wouldn't call you for that. She'd call me. Alan, it's bad news. I feel it."

"Easy," he said soothingly. "I'll be back in a minute."

She jumped to her feet. "Don't leave me."

He held out his hand. "All right. We'll go together."

She stood beside him, scarcely breathing, as he took the call, watching the dreaded shadow of sadness come over his face as he listened to the voice on the other end. And then, hating herself for her relief, she realized from his responses that it was not Elieth. Something had happened to Ann.

"We'll leave this afternoon," Alan had said. "Tell Dad

to hang on. It's for the best, Charlene. We all know that. I'll tell Joanne and Toni. We'll be there tonight."

He hung up and looked at Toni. "Mother's dead. An accident. Dad's been trying to get through but he couldn't, so he asked Charlene to reach Jo and me." His voice tremelbed. "Let's get out of here."

She took him up to her suite, away from the sympathetic but curious eyes of the young man at the desk. Alone, he told her what he knew. "I've got to find Jo," he said. "We've all got to get on the afternoon plane." Suddenly, unexpectedly, he began to cry. It was wrenching to see him try to hold back his tears, to watch him turn from her as though he was afraid she'd think him unmanly. Toni put her arms around him and cradled him as she would comfort a child.

"Don't ever be ashamed of tears, darling. They have no gender. Cry for your mother, Alan. For all the sadness in her life, for all the things she might have had. I'm crying with you, love. Not just for Ann. For all the lost, lonely, frustrated people in the world."

She put her tear-stained face next to his.

He clung to her like a bereaved little boy.

Chapter 35

Snow fell softly but richly, covering the sidewalks as quickly as the doormen shoveled them clear. It was like a game, Charlene thought, standing at the living-room window of her daughter's apartment. A game in which, as always, the odds were in nature's favor. Perhaps it was one of God's minor amusements, sprinkling handfuls of snowflakes, watching the antlike mortals sweep them away and then dropping another giant fistful to make their effort futile. Neither man nor the Almighty gave up. They were engaged in an endless struggle, a one-sided battle in which man, eternally optimistic and ego-ridden, thought he could outmaneuver fate, whether he was fighting the path of the snow or the course of his life. People who didn't believe in destiny were fools. Perhaps every second of one's time on earth wasn't literally written in a giant book like a battle strategy in which each step was mapped in advance. God surely was too busy to bother with such trivia. But there was a Master Plan. There had to be. It was the only way one could accept the strange, sometimes sad, sometimes wonderful, always unaccountable progression of events.

She turned back to look into the room. There was nothing quite so depressing as the sight of packing cases and barrels and wisps of excelsior, all of it transforming the most personal possession into burdensome things that had to be boxed and crated and moved from one place to another. Beloved objects became merely Things, mute reminders of other days when their owners lived other lives.

Not that she was sorry to see Toni's household packed and waiting to leave for Haiti. It was simply hard to realize how suddenly everything had changed.

Ann's children and her own child had come swiftly home only two weeks before, stunned, as they all were, by the unexpected. There had been the methodical mechanics of arranging Ann's burial, the third I've been part of in as many years, Charlene thought. But this one was different from the others. There had been no memorial, no heart-felt words spoken, no gathering of friends who deeply, truly mourned. Ann went to her rest as she would have wanted it: in the Richards family plot in Westchester, expensively gowned and perfectly coiffed, immaculately intact like a costly doll in a vulgarly expensive mahogany box. They'd all hated this pretension. All but young Peter, who had almost angrily demanded that his father go through the motions of a conventional, "decent" funeral.

"Mother would have wanted it this way," he'd said.

"Yes," Peter said, "I suppose she would."

Charlene and Toni had felt strange about going to the church, which was so heavily laden with flowers from Peter's business associates and so sparsely filled with people who cared. But Peter had asked them to be there. "I need you both," he'd said. "Don't feel hypocritical about coming as part of Ann's family. No matter what your differences were, you *are* part of it."

It had been ritualistic, doleful and distasteful. The impersonal funeral oration. The long, dreary, silent ride to the cemetery. Only Ann's eldest child found it "suitable." Just as he found "unsuitable" Alan's plans to marry so soon after his mother's death.

Listening to his brother, Alan felt he was hearing Ann.

"You can't consider getting married a week after Mother's passing!" he'd said, outraged. "My God, Alan, have you no sense of decency, no feeling of respect?"

"I don't think six days or six months makes any difference to her now, Pete," Alan had said. "Why should it to you?"

"Because it simply isn't done! Even if you hated her, you could observe a decent period of mourning for the sake of the family!"

Alan hadn't been angry. He'd simply stared at his brother. "Would you feel the same if I were marrying someone other than Toni?"

Pete flushed. "Of course! I don't approve of Toni. You know that. Mother was right. You don't marry mixed blood. And you don't marry within your family. But that's not why I'm objecting. It's the way it *looks*. Like you don't give a damn for her or the rest of us!"

"Then," Alan said, "you won't mind not coming to the wedding, will you? It's nothing much to miss. Just a quiet ceremony in Dad's apartment."

Peter turned away angrily. "In *Mother's* apartment, you mean! Jesus, you are incredible!"

"I'm being married in my home. In my father's house. The place where we grew up, Pete. There are no ghosts there for me and none for Toni. She had every reason to hate Mother, but she doesn't hate. She feels sorry, as I do, that Ann Richards was a blind, pathetic shell of a woman."

He didn't recount the conversation to Peter, Sr., or to Toni, but he did discuss it with Charlene. "Do *you* think

t's bad taste?" Alan asked. "Not getting married so soon:
I have no qualms about that. But is there something
offensive about having the ceremony in Dad's
apartment?"

"I suppose your brother would see it that way,"
Charlene said. "I suppose a lot of people might. But you
and your father and Joanne don't. Neither do Toni and I.
We think as you do. That was your home. If it weren't for
the difficulties of transporting everybody to California, I'd
like you to be married in Toni's home. But this is more
practical and much warmer than the anonymity of a New
York hotel suite." She did not say that Toni certainly
didn't want to be married in the half-packed apartment
she'd shared with Bryce or in the impersonal ugliness of
City Hall, where they'd gone, almost furtively, a little
more than two years before. "Places are like possessions,"
she'd said to Alan. "They represent what you see in them.
It's not whether they're 'correct' but rather how you feel
about them."

Charlene looked out again at the snow. The wedding
service had been simple and brief, but beautiful because
everyone in the room was bound together by love. She
could feel it in the way Alan and Toni stood together, in
the misty expression on Joanne's face, in the tentative
touch of Peter Richards' hand as he took her own when
their children repeated their vows.

They'd gone now, Toni and Alan and Elieth, to Haiti,
to stay at the hotel until the furniture arrived and they
could move into the beautiful house they described so
glowingly. Martha Cabot had promised to help Toni open
a nursery school and had even miraculously produced a
young French woman to care for Elieth. Martha had been
amusing about that on the telephone.

"It seems disloyal of me not to grab the job for one of
my own children," she'd said, "but poor Elieth can't grow

505

up speaking this peculiar, bastardized French! There's a lovely young girl from Paris living here. A painter. She'd be glad to care for the baby in return for room and board."

There had been only one disappointment for Toni. Charlene had been touched by their offer of the little house near their own, but she gently rejected the idea.

"I'll come often for long visits," she'd promised. "You can put a sign on the front door of that guest cottage saying 'Granny's House,' if you like. But become a permanent part of the Richards family? No, darlings. You have your own lives. And believe it or not, I have mine. I'll stay here long enough to see your furniture on the way and then I'll go home to Pasadena for a while." She patted Toni's cheek lightly and smiled at Alan. "Don't look so bereft, for heaven's sake! It's very flattering to be wanted. I'm glad to know I'm welcome. I just wouldn't want to wear it out."

She wondered where the movers were. They should have arrived an hour ago. The apartment seemed very gloomy and lifeless on this cold, white winter morning. She was glad she'd be back in California tomorrow, back to her own little house, her beloved garden. And back, Charlene thought ruefully, to the solitude, the feeling of emptiness. That she'd *not* be glad to return to. But that also was fate moving her like a pawn in its own cosmic chess game.

Her introspection was broken by the shrill ringing of the doorbell. She moved quickly to admit the movers. But it was not a burly crew that stood outside when she opened the door; it was an unannounced Peter Richards, covered with snow, smiling crookedly, appealingly at her. Charlene smiled back.

"Come in," she said. "I think I'm glad to see you."

"Think?"

"Well, I might like you even better if you were four brawny guys. Meanwhile, I'm glad to have company. It's spooky being in this place all alone."

"It's always spooky being alone."

Charlene didn't answer. Instead, she led the way to the kitchen. "Coffee?" she asked. "Or something stronger to ward off pneumonia?"

"Coffee, please."

Peter took off his coat and perched on a packing box, watching her. She moved so easily, so gracefully, with such a young air. Toni was like her, all beautiful coordination and unselfconscious dignity. Without turning around, Charlene said softly, "You're staring."

"Yes. I'm envying my son."

With a forthrightness like Toni's, she turned to look directly at him.

"And perhaps I'm envying my daughter."

Hope came into Peter Richards' eyes. "Charley, I know it's too soon to talk about things like this, but I must. You're going home tomorrow. I don't want you to leave. I love you. I've loved you since you were thirteen. Do you think, I mean, after a while, you might . . ."

"Change my mind about what I said to Toni? That I wouldn't become part of the Richards family?"

He nodded.

"Yes," Charlene said, "I think I very well might."

He started toward her but she stopped him. "No, Peter. Not now. You're right. It *is* too soon. Too much has happened too fast. I need to go home and think, about us, about everything. I've been alone for quite a while. I want to feel sure that I can share, that I won't only be taking love but that I can give it again as well. There's so much inside of me still to be given, but there's a lot I need from the one I love."

"That's all I wanted to hear," Peter said.

507

She woke slowly, not knowing for a moment where she was. Overhead the sky was bright blue and cloudless, the sun dappled on the blue-green water of the pool, flirted with the seductive red hibiscus blossoms, danced playfully over her slim, firm body.

It was so quiet. Not deathly still but peacefully hushed, a rare, golden moment between the fading memory of her dreams and the lovely recognition that she was safe and happy.

Toni lay motionless, unwilling to disturb this serenity by so much as a gesture. She'd relived her life in her dreams, compacting twenty-three years into an hour's siesta. How tidy. She'd heard that dreams took only seconds, but to the dreamer they were hours, days, years—a straggly parade of memories that marched through the mind, keeping time with the beat of her heart.

From the veranda of her dream house, all filigree and spun sugar, she heard the businesslike sound of a typewriter being tapped in spasms as Alan's long, sensitive hands hovered over it, searching for a perfect phrase, a cliché-free sentence. For more than a year she'd heard that wonderful sound, incongruous, somehow, in the indolent Haitian air. It reassured her, as surely as the words her husband spoke to her in the depths of passion reassured her that she was loved and wanted.

Voices reached her now. The sweet treble of a two-year-old and the melodious tones of her companion in reply.

"Non, non, ma petite Elieth! C'est pas bell!"

A little smile played around Toni's mouth. The French had a delicate, almost poetic way of teaching children the difference between right and wrong. Americans corrected them differently. She herself might have frowned, hardened her voice and said sternly, "No, Elieth! That's bad!" Mademoiselle's reprimand went far beyond, to

508

breed awareness, not guilt. Her way was to say, "No, no, my little Elieth. That is not beautiful!"

Toni silently mouthed the words. Perhaps that was the ridiculously simple secret of everything. Nothing is bad. Some things are just not beautiful.

How lucky she was, how blessed. The sad moments of her past had been nearly forgotten in this new-found happiness. But I must not forget, Toni thought. To forget is to lose the yardstick of despair against which to measure the length of joy.

I must always remember how bad some of it was.

She corrected herself.

Not how bad. How much less beautiful.

ALL TIME BESTSELLERS
FROM POPULAR LIBRARY

☐	AFTERNOON MEN—Powell	04268-0	1.95
☑	MARINA TOWER—Beardsley	04198-6	1.95
☐	SKIN DEEP—Hufford	04258-3	1.95
☐	MY HEART TURNS BACK—Patton	04241-9	2.25
☐	EARTHLY POSSESSIONS—Tyler	04214-1	1.95
☐	THE BERLIN CONNECTION—Simmel	08607-6	1.95
☐	THE BEST PEOPLE—Van Slyke	08456-1	1.95
☐	A BRIDGE TOO FAR—Ryan	08373-5	2.50
☐	THE CAESAR CODE—Simmel	08413-8	1.95
☐	DO BLACK PATENT LEATHER SHOES REALLY REFLECT UP?—Powers	08490-1	1.75
☐	THE FURY—Farris	08620-3	2.25
☐	THE HEART LISTENS—Van Slyke	08520-7	1.95
☐	TO KILL A MOCKINGBIRD—Lee	08376-X	1.75
☐	THE LAST BATTLE—Ryan	08381-6	2.25
☐	THE LAST CATHOLIC IN AMERICA—Powers	08523-2	1.50
☐	THE LONGEST DAY—Ryan	08380-8	1.95
☐	LOVE'S WILD DESIRE—Blake	08616-5	1.95
☐	THE MIXED BLESSING—Van Slyke	08491-X	1.95

Buy them at your local bookstores or use this handy coupon for ordering:

POPULAR LIBRARY
P.O. Box C730, 524 Myrtle Ave., Pratt Station, Brooklyn, N.Y. 11205

Please send me the books I have checked above. Orders for less than 5 books must include 75¢ for the first book and 25¢ for each additional book to cover mailing and handling. I enclose $_____ in check or money order.

Name_____

Address_____

City_____State/Zip_____

Please allow 4 to 5 weeks for delivery.

FREE
Fawcett Books Listing

There is Romance, Mystery, Suspense, and Adventure waiting for you inside the Fawcett Books Order Form. And it's yours to browse through and use to get all the books you've been wanting... but possibly couldn't find in your bookstore.

This easy-to-use order form is divided into categories and contains over 1500 titles by your favorite authors.

So don't delay—take advantage of this special opportunity to increase your reading pleasure.

Just send us your name and address and 25¢ (to help defray postage and handling costs).

FAWCETT BOOKS GROUP
P.O. Box C730, 524 Myrtle Ave., Pratt Station, Brooklyn, N.Y. 11205

Name _____
(please print)

Address _____
City _____ State _____ Zip _____

Do you know someone who enjoys books? Just give us their names and addresses and we'll send them an order form too!

Name _____
Address _____
City _____ State _____ Zip _____

Name _____
Address _____
City _____ State _____ Zip _____